A Deadly
Deception

Books by Tessa Harris

Dr. Thomas Silkstone Mysteries
THE ANATOMIST'S APPRENTICE
THE DEAD SHALL NOT REST
THE DEVIL'S BREATH
THE LAZARUS CURSE
SHADOW OF THE RAVEN
SECRETS IN THE STONES

Constance Piper Mysteries
THE SIXTH VICTIM
THE ANGEL MAKERS
A DEADLY DECEPTION

Published by Kensington Publishing Corporation

A DEADLY DECEPTION

TESSA HARRIS

KENSINGTON BOOKS
www.kensingtonbooks.com

KENSINGTON BOOKS are published by

Kensington Publishing Corp.
119 West 40th Street
New York, NY 10018

Library of Congress Card Catalogue Number: 2019940160

Kensington and the K logo Reg. U.S. Pat. & TM Off.

ISBN-13: 978-1-4967-0660-7
ISBN-10: 1-4967-0660-9
First Kensington Hardcover Edition: September 2019

ISBN-13: 978-1-4967-0662-1 (ebook)
ISBN-10: 1-4967-0662-5 (ebook)

10 9 8 7 6 5 4 3 2 1

Printed in the United States of America

For my husband, Simon, with love and thanks

Oh, what a tangled web we weave . . . when first we practice to deceive.

—Sir Walter Scott, "Marmion," 1808

ACKNOWLEDGMENTS

This, the third novel in the Constance Piper mystery series, is once again set against the backdrop of the so-called Jack the Ripper murders in Whitechapel, London, between the years 1888 through 1891.

In my research for this book, I am indebted to so many historians who have spent endless hours trawling through archives and original source material in order that I could put my own interpretation on events and weave even more mysteries into this already-fascinating period of British history. My imagination has been fueled and sustained by Christy Campbell and his groundbreaking book, *Fenian Fire* (HarperCollins, 2002). The *Observer* newspaper described the work as "one of the most remarkable examples of a 'black operation'" ever revealed, and I am most grateful to Mr. Campbell for his meticulous research, which was the trigger for this novel.

For background reading I would recommend Paul Begg and John Bennett's *Jack the Ripper: The Forgotten Victims*, which concentrates on murders contemporary with the canonical five attributed to the Ripper. I have endeavored to source my factual information from articles and accounts as they were reported in contemporaneous newspapers, and for these I am indebted to the seminal website on matters pertaining to Jack the Ripper, https://www.casebook.org.

Conspiracy theories are nothing new and swirled around in Victorian London at this time, too. For more about these theories—most of which I view as completely implausible—I would recommend *The Terrible Quiet* by Peter Wilson and *Jack the Ripper and Black Magic: Victorian Conspiracy Theories, Secret*

Societies and the Supernatural Mystique of the Whitechapel Murders by Spiro Dimolianis.

As ever, my thanks also go to my editor, John Scognamiglio, and my agent, Melissa Jeglinski, and to my husband, Simon, and our children, Charlie and Sophie, for their support.

A DEADLY
DECEPTION

CHAPTER 1

London, Wednesday, July 17, 1889

CONSTANCE

It was the footsteps that woke me. From the cradle of my deep sleep, I supposed the noise to be rain splattering the window, or maybe even a trotting horse. Opening my gritty eyes, I looked up at the square of light on our moldy ceiling and thought perhaps I'd dreamed the sound. But then I heard the cry—the cry that we all know round here too well. That's when I knew it was real. "Murder! Murder!"

Scrambling out of bed, I rushed over to pull up the sash and there he was, in our street, a little nipper, shouting at the top of his voice. "Murder! Murder!" Cupping his hands round his mouth, he called out once and then he cried again. He hollered words that turned my blood even colder, and everyone else's, too. "Jack's back!" he bellowed, and a chill ran down my spine quicker than a rat along a drainpipe.

For a moment I was numb. I couldn't believe it. Still can't.

Just as we were all feeling safe in our beds, just when we dared leave our windows ajar at night on account of the warmer weather, just when we could walk out at twilight again, we hear there's been another killing. Of course, the cry made us all sit up and take notice. If Jack is back, none of us is safe.

Flo was quick off the mark. Pushing me out of the way, she shoved her head through the window.

"Where?" she yelled. "Where's the murder?"

The lad turned and, still running backward, gulped and yelled up, "Castle Alley, by Goulston Street Wash'ouse."

Ma shuffled in with her shawl drawn round her shoulders and a frown on her brow. "What's amiss?" she wheezed, all blurry-eyed.

Flo and me swapped glances. We knew she wouldn't take it well.

"There's been another killing," I said as soft as I could, but it still didn't stop her from gasping for air, like a fish out of water. I feared the shock would bring on another attack, and it did. I rushed over to her and sat her down beside me on the bed.

"I'll go and see what's what," Flo told her, pulling on her skirt. She tried to act all cocky, as if she could make things right, but, of course, she couldn't. We both knew that if Jack was back to work, then no amount of brave words would help soothe the terror that'd return. There's been nothing since November; not since Mary Jane Kelly was found on the day of the Lord Mayor's Parade. She was Jack's fifth—or, some say, sixth victim. After her, of course, came poor Rose Mylett. At first, we all thought she was one of *his*, too. With the help of my friend Acting Inspector Thaddeus Hawkins, I proved Rose's murder weren't Jack's handiwork, after all. So that's why, eight months on from the foulest murder of all, it's come as the most terrible shock to everyone to think the fiend stalks among us again.

Emily

Yes, eight long months have passed since Jack last struck. Eight months in which the people of Whitechapel and beyond have tried to rebuild their lives. Yet, the brutal killings still cast their shadow. I well remember the morning they found the body of what everyone prayed would be the Ripper's last victim: Mary Jane Kelly. In a squalid room in Miller's Court, it was. I was there when the rent collector first put his eye to the broken pane, but couldn't quite comprehend the scene at first. He'd been banging on the flimsy door for the past few seconds, fearing it might splinter under his fist. He'd even called the tenant's name. "Mary Kelly! Mary Jane!" He was used to her scams— the way she'd pretend she didn't know what day of the month it was, or how she'd sometimes just flutter those long lashes of hers and beg a favor. Her wiles were enough to make a grown man weak at the knees. Or how she'd call him "dear Tommy" in that singsongy voice of hers, which reminded him of a skylark on a spring morning. But six weeks is a long time in any landlord's book, and Mr. McCarthy wasn't having any more of her shilly-shallying, so on this occasion Thomas Bowyer was under instructions to return with the rent, or not at all.

His knocking having met with silence, Bowyer went around the corner of the premises to where he knew the windowpane was broken. Carefully he reached through the jagged glass and drew back the curtain so that he could see inside. It was a sight that would come to haunt him for the rest of his days. He withdrew his hand so quickly from the broken pane that his skin was caught and torn by the glass as he staggered back. Yet, he did not make a sound, save for a violent retch in the gutter nearby. Despite his dizziness and nausea, he managed to alert his boss to what he had just seen—to the two pieces of cut flesh on the table and to the blood on the floor and to the fact that the body of

Mary Jane Kelly, the prettiest and sweetest of the street girls he knew, lay mutilated beyond all recognition.

That was last November. On the ninth day of the month, to be precise. Not that time means anything to me. It is but a ticking of a clock. I am no longer of this earth, you see. I am a revenant. I died, or, more accurately, was murdered, because I tried to expose a secret society of powerful men that preyed on my young pupils. I was handed over to a cruel bully, who I now know went by the name of the Butcher, and paid the ultimate price for my discovery when he cracked my skull against a wall. Now, however, I have returned to right the wrongs committed against me and so many others who cannot defend themselves against the powers that control their lives.

London's East End, where this shocking crime against Mary Jane Kelly was perpetrated, is where I usually roam. Unseen by nearly all, I am to be found underfoot in the cobbles of Whitechapel, on the panes of grimy glass, in the fabric of people's clothes, on wood and on brick, even floating on the air you breathe. There are traces of me all around—of what was, what is, and what will come—but only the chosen few can sense them. Constance Piper is one of them and I am able to live on through her.

CONSTANCE

This time the killing's even closer to home, just a couple of streets away from us. The washhouse is where Ma, Flo, and me go for a bath now and again. 'Course we have to go second class: a cold bath and a towel for your penny. Someday I'll treat myself to first class: that's two towels and warm water. Someday.

"Let's get the kettle on," I say, guiding Ma downstairs. I sit her in our one good, horsehair armchair by the empty hearth just as Flo steps over the threshold to find out what's what.

"I won't be long," she calls back to Ma, trying to reassure her; only, she's wheezing that much, I'm not sure she's heard. So we sit and we wait.

Already there's a dreadful brouhaha outside. People are coming round our way to get to Castle Alley. You wouldn't ever catch me down that dingy rat hole. Never gets any sun, even when there's some to be had. In shadow all day, it is. It's where some of the local costermongers park up their barrows for the night. You get all sorts coming and going and all manner of diseases lurking there, so they say. Some ragamuffins and unfortunates even kip down under the carts. If you can put up with the stink, I suppose it's out of the rain. But I needs hold my breath just when I'm passing, the stench is that bad.

At least half an hour goes by before Flo's back. She takes off her shawl as she blusters through the front door. "It's Bedlam out there," she tells us, like she's the one who's having it hard. "There's crowds all round the mortuary, as well as where she was found."

It's been raining in the night and there's mud on her boots. She's all flushed as she sits down to ease them off. I'm watching her and I'm waiting for her to say something more. It's like she's trying to think of how to get something off her chest. But she just gives me the eye and bites her lip.

"Oh, God!" I mutter, watching her stand up real slow, like she's trying to put off what she knows she must do. "It's someone we know, ain't it?" I keep my voice low, but Ma, still in the chair, senses something's amiss.

"Well, Flo?" she puffs.

Dread flies up like a black crow from somewhere deep inside me. My whole body tenses as I watch my big sister stand in front of Ma, take a deep breath, and say, "Word is it's Alice Mackenzie."

EMILY

Florence is correct. Indeed, it is Alice Mackenzie who has been slain, and it was her imminent murder that brought me back to Whitechapel last night, shortly before the attack hap-

pened. Like all the other barbarous murders I have witnessed, I recall the event vividly.

It may be mid-July, but last night was unseasonably chilly. Earlier in the evening, skies had threatened rain, and building up to midnight they began to deliver in heavy intermittent bursts. The potholes and muddy ruts quickly filled with rainwater. It was not a good night to be abroad and Police Constable Joseph Allen was not relishing pounding the beat. Such was the reputation of Castle Alley that, up until last month, there'd been extra police patrols in the area. A filthy cut-through that harbored the twin evils of disease and vice, it is no place for God-fearing souls. The patrols had, however, been stood down, even though the police were still vigilant in the vicinity.

Shortly after the midnight bell sounded at St. Jude's, during a dry spell, PC Allen decided to stop for a snack in an archway that leads off Whitechapel High Street. Standing under the glare of a lamppost, he took from under his rain cape a paper parcel containing a sausage roll. As he munched away contentedly, he looked around him. He neither saw nor heard anything suspicious. Making light work of the pastry, he proceeded to walk on in the direction of Wentworth Street, passing the Three Crowns public house. The landlord, he noticed, was shutting up for the night. Shortly after, he met a fellow constable, PC Walter Andrews, heading toward Goulston Street. The two men exchanged greetings; then they proceeded to go their separate ways. Five minutes later, PC Andrews was plodding down Castle Alley when the beam from his bull lantern picked up the figure of a woman slumped on the footpath between two wagons. At first, he thought she was just sleeping off the drink, like so many of her sort do. It was only when he raised his lamp that he could see her sightless eyes gazing back at him. Her throat was slit from ear to ear. But perhaps, most telling of all, her skirt had been pulled up to expose the lower half of her body. It was covered in blood.

Two blasts were sounded on his police whistle and within seconds more officers arrived at the scene. Yet, in their haste to give assistance, not one of them noticed what I saw quite clearly in the nearby darkness. As the constables stared wide-eyed at Whitechapel's latest murder victim, my own gaze was firmly fixed on a shadowy figure creeping quietly away with all the stealth of a professional assassin.

CONSTANCE

I'm glad that Ma is sitting when she hears the news; else I'm sure she'd have keeled over. Her lips fly apart in a gasp. She holds her hankie to her mouth and I see her horrified eyes fill with tears.

"Oh no! Oh no!" she blurts. I put an arm around her and feel a shudder building up in her chest, like an Underground train, until it breaks out into a full-blown sob.

"They're not sure," insists Flo, trying to put on a brave face. "Her old man and Betsy Ryder from the lodgings have still to see her."

But the thought of her friend lying cold on a slab is enough to set Ma off. "Oh, Alice! Alice," she wails until, a moment later, it strikes her. She darts up at Flo, a look of terror twisting her face. "Was it . . . ?"

It's like she can't bring herself to say *his* name. Flo doesn't have to. I can tell by the fear on that pretty face of hers that it's what we all dreaded as soon as we heard. Jack's wielded his knife and left poor Alice bloody as a butcher's shambles.

"I need to go!" coughs Ma, all of a sudden. She's heaving herself up from her chair.

"Go where?" says I with a frown.

"I can tell them if it's Alice or not."

Flo's scowling, too. "You want to go to the dead house?"

Ma looks put out and seems suddenly stronger, like she's had a slug of hard liquor. "Well, I ain't just going to stay here and twiddle my thumbs, and that's a fact," she counters, reaching for her bonnet.

We watch helplessly as she ties the ribbons under her chin.

"Well, are ya coming with me, or not?" she asks, stomping toward the door, huffing and puffing. She's got the wind in her sails, and that's for sure.

All three of us make our way through Fashion Street to Old Montague Street, where they've taken the body. The mortuary is where Polly Nichols and Annie Chapman have lain, too, but mortuary's a grand name for a place that's little more than a brick shed. I know some of the medical men have complained about having to do their business in there, so cramped and dirty and dark, is it.

In ten minutes we've reached the gates at Eagle Place. There are two or three coppers trying to keep order, but the crowd's growing by the minute. There's a lot of jostling and a fight breaks out a few yards away from us. I spot a couple of the usual suspects from down our way: nosey Mrs. Puddiphatt and Widow Gipps. Keen as mustard they are, to find out who's copped it this time. But there's another familiar face that I'm happy to see. Gilbert Johns towers above most people. Flo sees him, too, and by jabbing both her fingers into each corner of her mouth, she whistles as loud as any docker can. It does the trick and Gilbert whips round. His face cracks into a grin when he clocks us and he plows toward us through the crowd.

"Can you get us to the front?" yells Flo above the din.

He bobs down and cups his ear as he looks to me for an explanation.

"Ma wants to know for sure if it's her friend," I tell him.

"I'll do my best," says he, straightening himself; then taking Ma by the hand, he shoves some blokes out of the road and leads her toward the gates.

"Clear the way. Coming through!" Gilbert booms in a voice deep as a mine shaft.

The crowd parts like the Red Sea for Moses, and me and Flo follow, marching straight to the mortuary gates. I don't recognize the coppers on duty, but I tell Flo to keep her trap shut and leave the talking to me.

"Excuse me," says I, all polite. "My mother thinks she may know the victim." I cock my head toward the mortuary.

The older copper narrows his eyes. "Does she now?" says he, looking me up and down with a snarl on his lips. But before he can answer, a man wearing a stained apron appears from the shed. He's young, with thick, dark hair that's wavy as seaweed. Leaning in toward the copper, he asks: "Any news on the inquest jury, yet, Officer?"

I feel Flo nudge me in the ribs. "He's a looker," I hear her whisper in my ear. "And a Yank by his voice, I'll wager," she adds. As if he can feel we're giving him a good old butcher's hook, I mean look, he turns and throws us a glance with a pair of brown eyes bright as garnets.

"Any time now," replies the copper to the man in the apron.

Barely has the news been delivered, when I see the crowd part again and a man and a woman are coming through the press of people with two blues on either side. The bloke looks dazed; the woman seems scared and pale.

"Mind your backs. Mind your backs!" cry the coppers. The pair can't be some of the jury—it's only men allowed, see—but it suddenly dawns on me who they are.

"John!" Ma calls, her voice cracking. John McCormack is Alice's other half. They've been living together as man and wife at Mr. Tenpenny's lodging house for the last few months. With him must be Betsy Ryder, the landlady there. We all know the reason they've come, to identify the body. It makes it real again. But neither of them can hear Ma's plea over the din and she starts to weep once more as we watch the two of them go through the gates.

The man in the bloody apron fixes them with a stare, nods solemnly, and then lets them pass before shutting the gates behind them. For a few minutes the crowd, while not silent, is quieter. We're all waiting expectantly for news, but we're respectful at the same time. Gilbert stays with us and for that we're glad. He tells us what we already know—that the body was found in Castle Alley by a policeman in the early hours.

"You all right?" he asks me, all caring. He's looking into my eyes like a lovesick puppy and then suddenly I feel his big hand press on my shoulder and give me a squeeze, but it don't feel right to me and I shrug it off. Thankfully, we're not kept long before John McCormack and Betsy Ryder are back out. She's got an arm around him as he fights back the tears. It's his Alice, all right, and the sight of his grief sets Ma off again, too.

Clay Pipe Alice, we called her. She was partial to her pipe. People said she was a surly old crone because she didn't smile much. Once I even heard a bloke order her to perk up. "Put a roof tile on your boat race, love!" he'd called. But anyone who knew her would tell you it was because the 'baccy had left her with a head full of rotting teeth. The few pearlies she had were stained yellow. Hers wasn't what you'd call a girly grin.

Ma met her when she was cleaning at St. Jude's. That's the church that me and Ma go to, just on Commercial Street. A few extra pennies never go amiss and Alice was always short for her doss. A while back, she took up with John. He worked for a Jewish tailor in Hanbury Street, but between them they still never seemed to have two brass farthings to rub together. Jack certainly wasn't after her money, and that's for sure.

Back home in White's Row, I don't bother putting on the kettle. I reach, instead, for the bottle in the brown paper bag on the top shelf in the kitchen. At times like these, tea's not strong enough. It's gin that consoles when the shock's so great. So we sit there, in the front room, cradling our mugs of mother's ruin, thinking on what's happened. For the next few minutes we say very little, when suddenly there's a knock at the door that makes us all jump out of our skins. Before I can scramble up to answer, there's a face leering in at the window that damn near frightens the life out of me. Then I realize it's Flo's best pal, Sally Richardson.

Next thing we know, she's sticking her head inside the door. "You 'eard?"

Flo rushes up to her. " 'Bout Old Alice? Yes."

"Opening the inquest this afternoon they are, at the Working Lad's Institute on the High Street, if you're up for it." There's a grin on her face and a gleam in her eye, like she's just told us Dan Leno's going to be playing the Cambridge Music Hall. It's entertainment to her, but not to me.

"I'm up for it." Flo jumps in. She looks at me. "Con?"

"Yes," I say, but it's not for the fun of it that I'll take my seat. I hold no truck with the appetite for ghoulish stories and bloody tidbits that are filling people's bellies these days. I'll not lick my lips when I read about women's wombs being ripped out and their kidneys being eaten. The newspapers love Saucy Jack and they're whipping up all of London into a frenzy of fear. They'll be rubbing their hands in Fleet Street, hoping that this latest killing bears his usual trademarks. But there's some of us who won't be forced to bolt our doors and stay off the streets. There's some of us who'll fight tooth and nail to get to the bottom of this cesspit of evil.

I'm hoping I can count on Miss Tindall to stand by me, even though I've not seen nor felt her near me for a while. She was my best friend and my mentor. She showed me that there's a way out of Whitechapel if you make up your mind to better yourself, learn your lessons, read lots of books, and talk proper.

A shining light, that's what she was—and still is—to me. But to everyone else she is dead.

Miss Emily Tindall was a teacher at the ragged school and St. Jude's Sunday School. Dead she may be, but there's no fancy way to dress up the fact that she was murdered—cut up by a brute and buried on the banks of the Thames. Her murderer's still not been brought to justice and that's why she's chosen to speak through me. I'm her spirit guide and she visits me in times of strife and turmoil. Through me she lives on; she guides me and helps me do the right thing from beyond the grave. She comes to me when life becomes a trial. But there's someone else now, too. Someone I've come to know and trust. Someone who's still flesh and blood. More important, he trusts and believes in me, too. I'm hoping he'll be at the inquest, and I'm hoping he'll call on my special gifts to help solve this latest ghastly murder.

The Working Lad's Institute is so crowded I have to stand at the back. Our old friend Mr. Wynne Baxter, him that's done Polly Nichols, Annie Chapman, and the other inquests before, is in charge, so I know Alice will be in good hands. There's some bigwigs come to watch on behalf of the Old Bill's Criminal Investigation Department, too. Sounds grand, don't it? Or *doesn't it,* as Miss Tindall would have corrected me. Truth be told, I was half hoping Acting Inspector Hawkins would be here. Last time I saw him, when we had tea together at Euston Station, he said I could call him Thaddeus and I said: "I'm Constance," and he repeated it. The way he said my name, like he was sipping French wine, made me sound so special, like a real lady. But I can't spot him here this evening.

We settle down and the jury's sworn in. They've all seen the body. First up is John McCormack, Alice's old man, and he's asked all about her: where she lived, what she did the time before she was killed, all the usual. The coppers who were on the scene come after and then it's the turn of Sarah Smith, who takes the money at the bathhouse. Her bedroom backs onto the alley and she was awake and reading, the time they say Alice was attacked, but she didn't hear nothing above her old man's snoring. Nothing at all. Same ol'. Same ol'. It's like the killer's a ghost or a specter. He leaves nothing behind but death. Yes, it certainly seems that Jack's back, all right.

At the end of the first session, I'm filing out of the hall with everyone else, when I suddenly see a familiar face, standing near the door.

Flo nudges me. "There's that fancy detective of yours. You ain't seen 'im in a while, have ya?"

I shift uncomfortably. It's true. I haven't seen Thaddeus for a few weeks, since April, in fact. Truth be told, I'm gutted he hasn't been in touch again, but I know that now he's taken charge of Commercial Street Police Station—even though it's only for a short while until his boss returns—he's got no time to be sociable with the likes of me. Even so, as soon as I set eyes on him, my heart gives a little leap. I don't think he's seen me, so I sidestep and hope I can wheedle my way into his view. I pretend to be going about my business, closing in on him with every step I take, until we're only a few feet apart. It's then that I look up, all casual like, and it does the trick. His gaze latches onto mine and there's a flicker of a smile. I smile back, but I just can't help myself; mine's more of a big, wide grin. I'm that happy to see him.

"Miss Piper." He doffs his hat at me, passing his hand over his slicked-back hair. I understand he can't call me Constance when he's on duty. But the trace of the smile I detected before swiftly disappears. He looks worried, strained. Those bags are back under his lovely brown eyes. Nevertheless, he asks me how I fare and I tell him I'd be better if Jack hadn't returned.

Instead of agreeing, he counters with a frown. "We should

leave such matters to the coroner, Miss Piper," says he, with a shake of his head. "The same man may not be responsible."

I'm just about to quiz him, to see what reason he offers for saying such a thing, when a gent I recognize as Inspector Reid, from the Leman Street police headquarters, comes up behind me.

"Ah, there you are, Hawkins," says he, and with that, Thaddeus gives an apologetic shrug and turns to follow his new master. I watch him go, sensing that behind those hard-to-fathom eyes of his is a knowledge, something not known to the public. It sets me thinking what manner of circumstances the police are keeping to themselves.

CHAPTER 2

Thursday, July 18, 1889

EMILY

*A*s *Acting Inspector Thaddeus Hawkins walks up Commercial Street toward the police station, he carries the weight of the world on his shoulders. His normally quick step is slowed by thought, and his invariably pleasant, yet serious, demeanor has been severely compromised.*

It's nine o'clock in the morning. He managed to grab just a few hours' sleep in the section house last night. This latest murder has put everyone back on their mettle. All his men had finally returned to their normal beats after the terror that the depraved killings of the previous year had wrought. Petty theft, drunkenness, and the usual abhorrent abuse to which women are continually subjected by their menfolk were all habitual crimes starting to occupy his constables' time once more. Most of the men were relieved to return to the basic business of policing;

the policy of "prevention rather than the cure" is what the new police commissioner, James Monro, is so keen to pursue. But Alice Mackenzie's murder has certainly set the cat among the proverbial pigeons again.

Nevertheless, despite this latest killing, life continues as normal on Commercial Street.

"Parnell Commission latest. Read all about it!" shouts a young newspaper vendor. Hawkins stops to buy a copy of the Telegraph. *He will peruse it later. These days the goings-on at the Parnell Commission appear to have replaced talk of Jack the Ripper in the fashionable clubs and drawing rooms of the West End. It seems the Establishment has put the Irish nationalist leader Charles Stewart Parnell "on trial" for allegedly supporting violence to further the cause of Irish Home Rule. The* Times *newspaper, Hawkins knew, had published some articles that showed him to condone outrages committed by the Fenian Brotherhood, and these were subsequently proved to be forgeries. Politics is a messy business, the detective knows, but he'll read about it later.*

Folding the newspaper under his arm, Hawkins continues down the road, passing deliveries of fruit and vegetables to the greengrocer and crates of fish to the nearby fishmonger.

"'Morning, Inspector," greets Mr. Bardolph as he guts a herring on a marble slab outside his shop. His sharp knife slits the fish's gullet with a ruthless efficiency that is all too familiar to the detective. The sight of the blade triggers an old and unwelcome feeling in him. Although he tries to conceal his unease, the shock comes again, the stab in his abdomen. He'd thought he'd be able to consign that terrible, sickly reaction, which he used to suffer during these awful cases, to the recesses of his memory. But in the past two days those old presentiments of dread and the rising nausea have returned. He knows he must inure himself to them. He touches his hat and manages a smile.

"*Good morning, Mr. Bardolph.*"

Thaddeus Hawkins is a familiar face to most of the shopkeepers and costermongers round here. He's made it his business to get to know the local community, to share their concerns and fears. Up until two days ago he'd been convinced that the world had heard the last of this Jack the Ripper. He'd seen for himself the conviction held by Commissioner Monro that Montague Druitt was the fiend behind the killings and that his suicide last December had put paid to his nefarious deeds once and for all. Rumor had it, however, that any public announcement on the subject had been barred by the suspect's brother. William Druitt, it was said, had threatened that if his brother was exposed, he would reveal that there were homosexuals in high positions in the army, in Parliament, at the bar, and in the Church.

Now, however, with this latest unfortunate's murder, that whole hypothesis had been thrown into the air. It has come as a huge blow and, Hawkins is convinced, will resurrect the terror felt by so many East End residents last autumn. Of course, it is not yet proven that Alice Mackenzie was felled by the same killer. Indeed, within the force itself, there are conflicting opinions—some say Jack the Ripper is returned; others that this murder is unrelated. Whatever the veracity of either claim, the press is already sharpening its metaphorical knives and pointing them at H Division once more.

Events, however, are about to take an even more challenging twist. Sergeant Halfhide, with his unfeasibly large whiskers and bluff manner, is behind the duty desk as Hawkins walks into the police station.

"*'Morning, Inspector,*" *he greets the young detective, but his eyes, shaded by bushy brows, are brighter than usual. There is something conspiratorial in his look that makes Hawkins linger. And then it comes. A white envelope slides across the counter.* "*I'm to personally see you get this,*" *says Halfhide, his tongue suddenly bulging against the inside of his mouth in a show of self-confidence. "Came not an hour ago."*

Hawkins picks up the envelope, looks at the back, and as soon as he registers the crest of the Metropolitan Police, his head jerks up again in shock. "From the commissioner!"

Sergeant Halfhide nods, raising his brows simultaneously. "From the very top, sir."

Wide-eyed, the young detective also nods and, letter in hand, marches into his office, shutting the door firmly behind him. Such is his curiosity he can't even wait to sit down. Standing over his desk, he takes a paper knife and slices into the top of the envelope with surgical precision. Extracting the contents, he unfolds the single sheet of paper. The handwritten letter reads thus:

> Dear Acting Inspector Hawkins,
> It is with great concern that I learned of the latest killing in Whitechapel. I would therefore be most grateful if you could meet with me in my office at your earliest convenience to discuss the case.
> I am sure you will understand the confidential nature of my request.
> Yours,
> James Monro (CB)
> Commissioner of Police of the Metropolis

Hawkins leans on his desk and considers this rather unorthodox summons from his superior. He wonders why he, an acting inspector, not even a full-fledged one to boot, should be singled out for such a confidential briefing. His former boss, Inspector Angus McCullen, has been on leave since earlier in the year, citing stress due to the exertions of the Ripper investigations. Yet, there are others far more senior than him: Fred Abberline and

Edmund Reid, to name but two, whose knowledge of the Whitechapel murders is just as detailed as his own. Nevertheless, who is he, he asks himself, to turn down such a request? An urgent one at that. Whatever the commissioner has up his sleeve, he clearly doesn't want to involve any senior officers.

CHAPTER 3

Friday, July 19, 1889

CONSTANCE

I'm on my way to Mr. Tenpenny's in George Yard. It's where Alice used to lodge. Business is slow at the moment. No one is keen to buy my blooms. Or maybe it's just me. My heart's not in selling flowers after this latest killing.

On the other side of the street, I spot two girls, sellers like me, squabbling over territory. Truth is, I'm hardly ever in one place long enough to fight over a patch. Flo's line of work, relieving ladies and gents of their handkerchiefs, pocket watches, and, if she's lucky, banknotes, means that we're always on the move.

Coming or going, my head's in a mess at the moment. Earlier on, I shifted a few blooms at the corner of the High Street and Commercial Street and made a shilling or two, but as the bell of St. Jude's struck ten, I decided to call it quits and do some digging. Old Bill is making inquiries, as they always do, but just like before, there don't seem to be any strong clues to follow. That's why I'm wanting to know what Alice did in her last hours before she was killed. Like I said, the police have been ferreting and taking witness statements, but they can't read people as I can. Faces are like books to me in this neighborhood. Miss Tindall used to say it was my "intuition." I can sense when a person's lying, or keeping something back, just like I knew Thaddeus was holding his cards close to his chest. I need an excuse to visit him, so I'll do some poking myself on Alice's old stomping ground and tell him what I've gleaned. Seeing him yesterday with that haggard look on his face makes me think he can do with all the help he can get.

Mr. Tenpenny's is a big building, spreading over about four houses. A lot of people lay their weary heads there of a night. I knew Alice and her man, John, had dossed there on and off for the past year. I've come under the archway that leads from the High Street to George Yard and I'm just by the lodging-house gates when I recognize the large woman carrying a pail of water up the front steps.

"Mrs. Ryder?" I call out. Her hair's the color of baked bread and she wears it in a bun. Reminds me of a cottage loaf, it does.

She stops and turns to take a look at me. "Yes, my dear?" she says, giving me a good shufti, but her face is friendly enough.

I summon up my courage and start with a smile. "It's about Alice," I tell her. "Alice Mackenzie."

Mrs. Ryder puts down her pail. She squints at me, but she's still seeming decent. "You're Patience Piper's girl, ain't ya?" she says.

"Yes. Yes, I am," I reply.

She nods her head. "I thought so. Knew Alice, did ya?"

"My ma did," I answer. "They were friends."

She tilts her head in a nod. "Bad business," she replies. But just when I think she might start loosening her tongue, she tells me, "Anyway, I said all I had to at the inquest." She's turning, and I think I'm losing her, when, all of a sudden, a little lad appears at the top of the steps in front of her. He can't be more than six. There's snot running down his face and his curly ginger hair is all awry. He's dressed in rags and his feet are bare and grimy.

"I'm hungry," he groans.

"I'll give you hungry, Timmy Kelly," she chides, picking up her pail once more. "You'll eat me out o' house and home, you will."

Timmy Kelly. The name echoes in my head and bounces about in my skull. It can't be, can it? Mary Jane had a son. Six or seven, he was. Like so many women forced onto the streets round here, she was married and respectable once. The boy's father was a miner who died before Mary Jane came to London. They say little Timmy was out the night Jack came for his mum. Thank the Lord he didn't see what the fiend did to her. With that thought planted in my brain, I jump in before the door's slammed in my face.

"That's not Mary Jane's boy, is it?" I ask.

Mrs. Ryder stops suddenly at the top of the steps and the pail swings round. "What if it is?" She's suddenly all defensive now.

"I knew his mum," I say, thinking on my feet. "Poor little tyke."

Mrs. Ryder looks at me and nods, as if I've just reminded her of the boy's terrible circumstances, as if she feels less inclined to be angry with him on account of them.

"In yer go. I'll get you something in a minute," she tells him before switching back to me. Her lips flatten. "I mind 'im now and again. As a favor for Lizzie."

"Lizzie Albrook?" I ask. "Weren't she Mary Jane's friend?"

I remember the name from the newspapers. It was Lizzie Albrook who was one of the last to see her in Miller's Court that night.

"That's right. Mary Jane asked her to take care of him, if anything should happen to her, but she's got to earn her crust and . . ."

She shakes her head again, and closes her eyes, as if trying not to think about what became of poor Mary Jane. For a second I think of her, too, and before I know it, Mrs. Ryder is turning again to go inside.

"I'd best be off," she mumbles, and she's shutting the door on me before I've a chance to ask her any more.

"Wait up!" I call after her, but it's too late. She leaves me standing there in front of the lodgings, thinking on what she's just said. *"If anything should happen to her."* Does that mean Mary Jane knew someone wanted her dead? That she feared someone was out to get her?

I'm just contemplating the notion as I about-face and begin to walk back toward the High Street. I'm thinking of having a word with Lizzie Albrook next, to hear her version of events, when someone catches my eye. I suddenly see a woman, dressed in black from head to toe, stepping out of the shadows of the nearby archway. I've a strange feeling that she's been watching me, or, at least, the lodging house.

"Miss Tindall," I mutter under my breath. I feel my heart beat faster in my chest as I think of my teacher. Is it her? Could she be back? It's been so long since I felt her comforting presence. When she's near, I get a warm glow inside me. She shines light into my darkness. Time seems to slow when she guides me, but right now, I don't have that feeling. I am numb. I turn back to see if Mrs. Ryder and the boy are still there, but they're long gone and the door's shut. I turn again and a carriage, drawn by two horses, rattles along in front of me. It only takes a second or two to pass, but by the time it has, the woman has vanished. There's no sign of her. She's just disappeared.

EMILY

Acting Inspector Hawkins has spent a decidedly uncomfortable half hour in the back of a hansom cab. The driver's propensity to weave in and out of the London traffic has done nothing to calm his nerves. In fact, it has only added to his anxiety at being summoned to a personal meeting by no less a person than the commissioner of the Metropolitan Police himself. Hawkins knows James Monro only by reputation. A deeply religious man, Monro had resigned his post as assistant commissioner just before the murder of Polly Nichols in August last year. He was subsequently appointed to head up Special Branch, but promoted three months later following Mary Jane Kelly's murder. His sudden rise has made him unpopular with certain of his ex-colleagues.

Scotland Yard stands among buildings designed as bastions of the British Empire, bulwarks of security and stability. The grandiose architecture only adds to the sense of duty felt by Acting Inspector Hawkins. As he follows a secretary along one of the many corridors of power in this august institution, his anxiety is almost overwhelming. The secretary knocks. A voice booms. The secretary enters. Voices are heard until finally comes admission.

"Hawkins." James Monro stands to greet his nervous guest. His handshake is firm, confident. With his skin bronzed from his days as a missionary in India, and his eyes dimmed by years of dazzling sunshine, he cuts an imposing figure. Yet, he possesses an understated authority that warrants the deference paid to a favorite armchair; the commissioner is both sturdy and dependable. Hawkins also knows him to be hugely popular among the rank and file of the police force. Monro, it's said, places his faith in the ability of officers to reassure law-abiding citizens by their visible presence on the streets; in other words, he's an advocate of so-called bobbies on the beat. Not for him the cloak-and-dagger approach to policing eschewed by some in the Home Office and in the Special Branch in particular. That is most definitely not his style; so why, wonders Hawkins, has he been summoned for this confidential and highly unorthodox meeting?

"Sit down, won't you? Tea. Coffee?" The commissioner would never offer any alcohol.

The young detective is too nervous for either. "No, thank you, sir." He has just spotted the nest of tubes, like indolent snakes, at the side of the commissioner's desk. Monro is clearly in speaking connection with the home secretary on matters of urgency. It's not just the radical press but also the queen herself who continues to lambast both the police and the Home Office for failing to catch the perpetrator of the Whitechapel murders.

They both sit. Monro begins. "Very well. Let's get down to business, shall we?"

Hawkins appreciates a man who doesn't beat about the proverbial bush. "Yes, sir." But the commissioner's first question is not one for which he is prepared.

"Tell me what you know about the Fenians."

"Sir?" Hawkins frowns. Straightaway the question knocks him off guard.

"You heard me. The Fenians." Monro leans back in his chair, trying to appear less intense. Like Inspector Angus McCullen, he is a Scot, but unlike McCullen, Monro comes from the Lowlands. His character has been shaped by the softer curves of the hills, rather than the craggy peaks of the Highlands. He tents his fingers.

"They're Irish nationalists, sir," comes the reply. Hawkins thinks of the commissioner's background as the former director of the Special Branch. Until very recently James Monro was at the vanguard of the fight against Fenian terrorists.

"Go on."

"They seek an independent Ireland and are prepared to use violence to achieve their aims."

"Good. Go on." Monro twiddles his thumbs.

"They are well-funded by American sympathizers who supply not only money, but also weapons and, in particular, dynamite." Hawkins wracks his brain. "In 1882, a breakaway group *calling themselves the Invincibles murdered Lord Frederick Cavendish, the chief secretary for Ireland, and Thomas Henry Burke, the permanent undersecretary, in Phoenix Park, Dublin."*

"Very good, and . . ." Monro's hand gestures in a circular motion, as if cranking a wheel.

Hawkins's brain whirls into action. *"And a few years later, they proceeded to wage a dynamite campaign on the United Kingdom mainland."* His delivery speeds up with each sentence, like a schoolboy reeling off facts he has learned for an examination. *"Several targets were blown up, including the London Underground, the House of Commons, and the Tower of London. Then two years ago they devised a plot to blow up Westminster Abbey during the Jubilee celebrations, with the aim of killing Her Majesty and half the cabinet. Two men were jailed and, I believe, are still serving sentences."*

Monro gives a satisfied nod. *"Ah, yes. The Jubilee Plot."* There is a faraway look in his eye, as if he is reminiscing, although there is no fondness in his memory. *"Eighteen eighty-seven was a most stressful year. It was a dreadfully anxious time, trying to bring about those arrests. Up until two days ago I thought we had succeeded in wiping out the benighted Irish terrorists."* His tone suddenly changes and he switches back to the detective. *"Now, however, I cannot be so sure."*

"Sir?" Hawkins leans forward on the edge of his seat, eager to hear what the commissioner has to say next.

"I fear, Inspector, this latest Whitechapel atrocity is not the work of a lone psychopath, this so-called Jack the Ripper, but of a Fenian."

"A Fenian!" the detective exclaims, a little too loudly than he knows he should.

Monro nods. *"Perhaps one of those who plotted to kill Her Majesty, but who escaped arrest."*

Hawkins feels the breath that he has unknowingly been holding for the last few seconds escape from his chest. For a mo-

ment he remains speechless. "With respect, sir, this sheds a very different light on matters."

"Indeed, it does, Hawkins," the commissioner agrees, leaning forward. "The Phoenix Park murders, to which you referred—"

"Yes, sir."

Monro knuckles his desk and heaves himself up to walk over to a safe, which stands in the corner of the room. He turns the combination dial once, twice, three times and the lock gives a satisfying click. The door is opened and from inside the safe comes a long, thin box. He strides back to his desk and places the wooden case in front of Hawkins.

"In there is our evidence that links two of the most notorious murders of the decade," says the commissioner, grimacing as he taps the box with his forefinger.

"Sir?" Hawkins is not following.

"Open it." The commissioner stares at the case. "Go on."

The young detective leans toward the plain wooden box and slowly lifts the plain metal clasp to open the lid. The contents shock him. His head lurches up.

"Sir?"

Monro's shoulders heave in a sigh and he interlaces his fingers as he eyes the contents. A long surgical knife lies on a blue cushion. Beside it is an empty depression, presumably where another once lay. "One of the twelve knives purchased by an American surgeon and used to carry out the dastardly Phoenix Park operation," he explains.

Hawkins searches his memory once more. He remembers that the murder weapons were surgical knives.

"So this was found at Phoenix Park, sir?" he asks quite reasonably.

The commissioner shakes his head. "Oh, no, Hawkins. And here's the rub. This knife"—he points to the box—"this murderous blade was found at Number 13 Miller's Court."

"Miller's Court!" Hawkins is suddenly dumbfounded. "Where Mary Jane Kelly . . ." His jaw drops.

Monro nods as he pushes the box away from him, as if he cannot bear to look at the object, knowing where it has been. "Your expression is an absolute picture, if I may say, Hawkins."

Yet Hawkins barely registers the remark. From the back of his mind, the young detective seizes upon the memory of a report into Mary Jane Kelly's death. He recalls that the head of the Ulster Constabulary visited the ghastly scene shortly after the murder. He did not understand the connection at the time. Now its significance is becoming clearer.

"So the knife used to butcher Mary Jane Kelly was similar to the ones used in the Phoenix Park murders?" He stares at the blade in the box once more.

Monro raises his brows and nods. "I confess when I was shown the knife, I, too, was, flabbergasted," he admits.

"So this could mean that both these violent killings were perpetrated by the same associates?" Hawkins speaks slowly, as if the shock has temporarily paralyzed his facial muscles. He feels his body brace against any more revelations that he believes might follow. If the commissioner thinks, as it seems he has grounds to, that this latest Whitechapel murder of an unfortunate is the work of a Fenian, then it is tantamount to an assassination, a murder carried out for political purposes. What good can the Fenians possibly think they'll achieve for their cause by killing a fallen woman, such as Mary Jane Kelly, and drink-addled Alice Mackenzie—desperate, penniless nobodies, both? *Hawkins asks himself. As if reading his mind, Monro comes back at him with the answer.*

"By perpetuating the terror seemingly wrought by this Jack, the terrorists are making the police look helpless," he explains. "In the meantime they are regrouping in order to commit more mainland atrocities."

The notion jolts Hawkins back into the moment and he takes up the thread. "You crushed their network before, but now they are planning to make a comeback. The Whitechapel murders are decoys."

Monro *jabs a finger at the air. "And there you have it," he replies with an emphatic nod of his head. "But to draw attention to such perpetrators would only give them oxygen."*

"So no one must know of the possible Irish-American connection," suggests the detective.

Another nod from the commissioner. "You understand me, Hawkins. As I'm sure you are aware, I have no time for the amateur sleuths favored by the so-called Special Branch." He picks up a pencil from his desk and brandishes it at the detective, as if it were a sword. "Bernard Royston and his ilk I regard as below my contempt."

The name is unfamiliar to Hawkins. "Royston, sir?" he queries.

"Let's just say my deputy and I did not part on the best of terms when I left Special Branch. His spies called themselves policemen, but they were of no more assistance than novelists in solving crime. Such secrecy may be favored in Russia, but we are not a police state and, as long as I have breath in my body, will never be."

"No, sir. Of course not, sir," agrees Hawkins.

Then, as if his rousing speech has drained his energy, the commissioner's voice dips confidentially. "You must work only with your most trusted men. Word of this must not reach the press and you must communicate with me directly, in person. There are those who make it their work to know other officers' business," Monro tells him cryptically, although it is clear to Hawkins that he is talking about Royston. "They will only damage our mission. You follow me?"

"Absolutely, sir."

"Good man." Reaching into the top drawer of his desk, Monro next brings out a thick folder. He lays it in front of Hawkins. The young detective regards it suspiciously.

"A dossier of suspects with possible Fenian connections," the

*commissioner explains. "They will all need following up. I shall
leave it to you to establish priorities."*

*Hawkins draws the folder close and opens it. Leafing through
quickly, he needs only a moment to realize that he has been
handed a chaotic collection of typed reports, handwritten mem-
orandums, newspaper cuttings, and several lists.*

*"This is what we have to go on," says the commissioner, his
tone registering an apology. Hawkins is unsure if this refers to
the state of the paperwork or the quality of the information it
contains.*

*"I'll do my very best, sir," he tells Monro as he rises from his
seat.*

*"You have my full confidence, Hawkins," replies the commis-
sioner, also rising. The two men shake hands, and with his commanding officer's words still ringing in his ears, Acting Inspector
Hawkins returns to his station. The weight he now bears is even
more onerous than before. Not only is he tasked with tracking
down the fiend or fiends behind the Whitechapel murders, he
has also become, to all intents and purposes, a secret agent.*

CONSTANCE

I'm lying in my bed, my mind raking over events, and my
grim thoughts stray to poor little Timmy Kelly and the day
they found his mother's body. Ma, Mr. Bartleby, her beau, and
Flo, my big sister, and me were watching the Lord Mayor's Parade by Ludgate Hill. Everyone was dressed in their Sunday
best, and you couldn't hear yourself think for the cheering. It
didn't matter that it was cold and rainy. Not to me, at any rate,
although I'm sure Mr. B would rather have been in the snug
room at the Britannia, downing his whisky.

Anyway, all eyes were on the procession that was bringing
the new Lord Mayor back to the Guildhall in his coach. He'd
just met our dear queen and the judges of the High Court in the
Strand. Up front were the guards, looking so fine in their blue

and gold. Then there was this pompous old duffer—the city chamberlain, someone said—all done out like a Christmas tree in his cocked hat with tassels at his shoulders. Sat astride a big white horse, he was. Thought he was God's gift. 'Course we poked fun at him. A few even jeered. We Londoners are hard to impress when there's a murderer on the loose. Jack the Ripper had been putting the fear into every woman's heart around these parts for many a long month, but no one had been caught. And for that, we blamed Old Bill and the top brass in the government. Even Her Majesty was losing patience with the police. Wrote to them, she did, wanting the fiend caught and quick about it. By this time most reckoned there were already four dead by his knife: Polly Nichols, Annie Chapman, Liz Stride, and Catherine Eddowes, even before Mary Jane.

Soon as we caught sight of the procession, there were loud cheers and we'd all raised our flags and banners.

"Here he comes!" Mr. B had cried. Even Flo took her eyes off the sailor she'd been sizing up to look at the procession. We all surged forward, but the coppers on horseback kept us back. There was such a palaver that at first I didn't notice what was happening. Somehow two young lads had managed to break through the crowd and fight their way toward the front, sandwich boards around their necks. They'd scampered out in front of the procession and begun to dance and lark about, just ahead of the prig on his pony.

I recall Flo crying out: "What the hell are they playing at?" and Mr. B saying that they needed "a damn good hiding." I remember, too, that the horse took fright at the boys' shenanigans. The crowd took fright, too. The last thing they wanted was for the beast to run wild. For an instant everyone was relieved when the old duffer brought the poor creature under control, but our attention was soon diverted again.

Flo, a full two inches taller than me, nudged me. "What do them boards say?" she asked, looking at the two nippers.

I stood on tiptoe to have a butcher's, but as I did, I remember a hush falling on the crowd. The rain had started again and was slanting into my eyes, so I had to squint to see proper. Blinking the drops away, I could read what was written clear as day.

"Oh, my God!" I'd muttered as, all around me, the crowd fell silent.

"What is it? What do they say?" Flo'd urged.

I'd turned to her, a terrible feeling in my stomach. There was no other way to break the news, so I told her straight. "They say, 'Another Whitechapel Murder.'"

It's a little over eight months since that day and for most people life has moved on. Ma says they've pushed the bad memories to the back of the cupboard to gather dust. For many, the horror of last autumn seems to be fading. For some of us, though, especially us girls and women who need to be about our business, Jack still casts his eerie shadow over our neighborhood.

I knew Mary Jane, see. Whenever she had a spare penny, which in truth wasn't often, she'd buy a bloom from me and wear it in her hair. A cheerful soul, she was, always singing. So when, all those months ago, I dreamed that something terrible had happened to her, I took myself to her lodgings. Only, I never made it to her door. I saw Mrs. Maxwell, a friend of hers. She told me she'd just seen her, looking the worse for wear, but alive at least, and that I wasn't to fret. So I didn't. I went home and even joined the crowds to watch the Lord Mayor's Show without a care in the world—well, hardly. Little did I know that all the while Mary Jane was lying there, all sliced and cut like a piece of meat on a butcher's block.

These dreams of mine: I think I ought to tell you about them. They all began after I saw a showman at the Egyptian Hall who put some of the audience into a trance. He managed to work his magic on me, and all, and I've not been the same since. Some say they're not dreams I have, but visions, or, to give them an even fancier name, premonitions. I think I'm what they call a spirit medium. That means I can see things that most people are blind to, and sometimes I can foretell the future. For such a gift I have my spirit guide, Miss Tindall, to thank.

So, like I said, Whitechapel seemed to have settled back all comfy into squalor, like a pig in its own filth. It doesn't matter that brawls and scrimmages break out every minute outside pubs, or that so many babes die before they reach five. Who cares if a wife is bludgeoned to death by her drunken husband on a Friday night, or that children are sold to wicked men to pay the rent? It's Whitechapel. It happens. Only, when it comes to Jack, it's a different matter.

CHAPTER 4

Saturday, July 20, 1889

CONSTANCE

I don't mind telling you that what I learned yesterday at Mr. Tenpenny's—that Timmy is staying there awhile—came as quite a shock. I'm not one to put two and two together often, because I know it can sometimes make five, but it set me wondering. Was it just a coincidence that Clay Pipe Alice was lodging there as well?

I've just poured Ma another cup of tea when I say, all casual, "I didn't know Mary Jane's little 'un stayed at Tenpenny's on the regular."

Flo, chewing a hunk of bread, looks up sharpish. "Get away," she says. But Ma's not surprised at all. She nods and cradles her cup in her hands.

"Betsy Ryder knew Mary Jane from way back when. She often helped out with the lad." She stares into her cup, then adds, "Alice helped out with him, too. Loved him, she did. He used to call her Nan."

I've a mouthful of tea that's suddenly hard to swallow. "*What?*" I splutter, spraying hot liquid on the table. "Alice knew Mary Jane's boy?"

"What's the fuss?" asks Flo.

I shake my head. "Could be something. Could be nothing," I say.

"You been reading too many of them penny dreadfuls, you have." Flo shakes her head. "Fancy yourself as a proper detective." She looks at the tea stain on my dress and smiles at Ma. Two left feet has my sister at times.

While Flo's busy tittering over her own joke, I'm reminded of the woman in black—the one I saw over the road who seemed to be watching me, or Betsy Ryder, or little Timmy, I can't be sure who. Nor can I be sure if she was real, or, like Miss Tindall, someone who's passed over. Could I have been the only one to notice her? The lines between what's real and what's in my brain are all smudged these days. As I said, ever since that showman at the Egyptian Hall put me into a trance, I've felt queer.

Ma's in no mood for silliness from Flo. She's still thinking about Timmy Kelly and seems suddenly teary. "Poor little fella," she says, then pauses for a moment before she adds, "But at least he weren't there when his mum were killed."

I remembered a newspaper report mentioning the lad. It said that evening it was lucky he'd been taken out, so he wasn't around when the killer struck, thank the Lord.

"No, he weren't," I reply, reaching across the table to pat Ma's hand. At the same time I'm thinking, *But what if he was?*

EMILY

Acting Inspector Hawkins has had to wait until the day shift has left the police station before he can begin his highly sensitive inquiries. It's approaching eight o'clock, but for the detective, the night is yet young. Yesterday's meeting with Commissioner

Monro has fired his investigative zeal. Above him a gas jet hisses, while in front of him a lamp provides extra illumination for the close work he is undertaking. At his side is a welcome third mug of tea, courtesy of PC Tanner. Tanner is the only officer he has trusted, as yet, to be privy to the nature of his mission.

His task is Herculean by any measure, but it is rendered considerably easier by his trusty card index system. It has made him the butt of many a joke from his colleagues, but he has become used to their mocking. The system was taught to him by his late father, a librarian at the grammar school he attended. He is most gratified that he undertook to document each of the Whitechapel murder victims in this way. While his work has been painstaking, it is making this new challenge infinitely easier.

Arranged alphabetically on his desk are several oblong boxes, each bearing letters: A–D, E–G, and so on. Once grasped, the system's intricacies, its cross-references and orderings, are quite simple to the organized mind. Each victim is assigned a card detailing basic facts, which feature keywords. These keywords then spawn other cards, which can be compared and coordinated. The cards are then divided into subsections under various generic headings, such as Addresses *(past and at time of death),* Known Family, Known Associates, Coroner's Key Findings, *and so on. Each is written neatly on a piece of thick card, measuring three inches by five, and placed in a catalog box, which a carpenter fashioned from wood to specific measurements.*

What he is now endeavoring to do is find any references to Ireland and the Fenians amid all of these cards. Such activity will probably continue to engage him for many evenings to come. His travails are, however, already producing several interesting leads. It transpires that three of the murdered women had lived with Irishmen. One John Kelly was the common-law husband of Catherine Eddowes, for example. Joseph Barnett, the common-law husband of Mary Jane Kelly, was of Irish parentage, while the couple's landlord, one John McCarthy, was also an Irishman. As for Alice Mackenzie, her partner of several years, John McCormack, was an Irish porter who had been doing casual work for Jewish traders in Hanbury Street. Yet, while Hawkins knows these discoveries are grist to the investigatory mill, they do not prove, in themselves, that any of these men had links with the terrorist Fenians. To establish that will require a much more systematic line of inquiry. Each of them will have to be subjected to further investigation, which may take a different tack. Their backgrounds, political affiliations, and movements will all have to be thoroughly investigated to ascertain whether they might be linked to the Irish nationalist movement in any way.

Hawkins rubs his eyes and reaches for a clean sheet of paper. Dipping the nib of his pen into his ink pot, he writes across it, according to surname alphabetical order, the name of the first Irishman he plans to question further. It is Joseph Barnett.

CONSTANCE

I'm in Dorset Street. It's just over there, through that archway, that Mary Jane was cut to shreds. The thought of it sends a shiver down my spine. I've not been back since it happened, and I wouldn't be here now, if it weren't for Alice's murder. I know she's not the only one who looked after little Timmy, see. Mary Jane's friend Lizzie Albrook takes her turn with the lad, too. They share him out. But when Betsy told me Mary Jane had asked her to mind him "should anything happen" to her, well, that set me thinking. It may be something and it may be nothing, but I know Lizzie told one of them newspaper hacks something like it, too. That's why I'm off to meet her at the Britannia pub. It's known round here as Ma Ringer's, on account of its landlady, Mrs. Ringer. Lizzie works in one of the lodging houses nearby. The coroner never called her to give evidence at Mary Jane's inquest, so I reckon she might have a fair few things to say that she hasn't told no one before.

It's dusk and I'm not keen about being out after dark on my

own these days, but five minutes should see me to the pub if I take the shortcut. The evening's a little chilly, so I twitch my shawl around my shoulders and set off at a good pace. There's a few people around, scurrying about their business. Not many stop to talk these days. We'd all sooner be safe at home. Anyhow, I'm slipping along Tenter Ground, where the lanes all crowd in on each other and alleys crisscross it like veins, when I spot a man leaning against a lamppost, paring his nails with a penknife. He's wearing a flat cap, and I can't see his face proper, but there's something about him that gives me the chills. All of a sudden I'm feeling unsettled. I keep my eyes to the ground and walk on. A cart rumbles past and the clatter on the cobbles bounces off the walls of the nearby warehouses. It's then that I think I hear them. Footsteps. Behind me. The skin on my neck starts to prickle. *This was a mistake*, I think. I should never have left the din of Commercial Street. I'm realizing I should make my way back there, when suddenly, just as I'm under a gaslight, I see a shadow loom behind me. I let out a muted cry, but before I can turn, I feel an arm clamped round my neck. There's a horrible stink in my nostrils and then there's a voice in my ear.

"Leave well alone, will ya?" comes a harsh whisper. "Don't go messin'. She's dead, ya hear?"

I'm too shocked to reply. But the grip tightens until I answer. "Ya hear?"

"Yes," I bleat. I feel the hold loosen and my attacker steps away from me and back into the shadows. I don't dare look round. I just start toward the main road, slow at first; then I break out into a run.

My heart's still pumping nineteen to the dozen when I arrive at the tavern. It's a seedy old place—a spit-and-sawdust on the corner of Commercial Street and Dorset Street. Flo came here a few times with Danny Dawson when they were betrothed, but it's busy and stuffy, too, and the pipe smoke stings your eyes.

I've a mind to order a gin to calm my nerves, but I quash the urge and fork out for a lemonade, instead. I need my wits about me, even though my neck's giving me grief where I was grabbed from behind. I find a spot in the corner, away from the noisy cartmen at the bar. And now I see Lizzie coming over with a pint.

"You all right?" she asks above the din. She sits herself down and peers at my neck. "Nasty bruise you've got coming there," she remarks.

"Took a tumble on the way here, I did" is my line.

She nods sympathetically. She's the sort of gal who recognizes—what's the word Miss Tindall taught me?—a *euphemism* when she sees one. Women round these parts "take tumbles" and "bump into doors" more than any in the West End. She arranges her lips into a smile, even though I don't think she's looking at ease as she sits herself down beside me.

"You doing all right?" I ask.

"I'm getting by" is all she says at first.

"It's all we can do," I reply, noticing that my own hands are shaking. "But now with Alice . . ." I know I don't need to say any more.

She nods. "Poor Alice. She wouldn't hurt a fly," she says.

There's a respectful pause as we both think on another life lost, before she says, "So you said you wanted to talk about little Timmy." Suddenly she's urgent. "It'll hit him hard. First his own mum and now Alice."

"Fond of her, weren't he?" I remark.

She smiles, but her look is a faraway one, as if she's remembering something. "Like his nan, she was."

I pry deeper. "I saw him the other day with Betsy Ryder. She told me Mary Jane has asked her to take care of him if anything happened to her."

Lizzie switches her face up to mine. "That's just what she says to me, an' all."

"Get away," I cry. "Why would she say that?"

She takes a gulp of her beer. The foam sticks to her top lip and she wipes it away with the back of her hand. "She was always talking so. Telling me I shouldn't go on the streets. Warning me, like."

"Warning?" The word makes my ears prick up even more.

She shrugs. "Like a mother to her daughter, you know. About the last thing she says to me was 'Whatever you do, don't you do no wrong and turn out as I have.' She often spoke to me like that and warned me against going on the streets."

Regrets are like rats in this neck o' the woods. They gnaw away at you. We've all got them, but none more than what most call the unfortunates. I nod to show I understand, but then I think Lizzie's got more to say, the way she's looking troubled, her face all screwed up.

"What is it?" I ask.

She comes closer. "There was this bloke. A Yank, he was."

"American?"

"Important. Swanky. Big 'tache. Used to be a soldier, I think."

"What of him?"

"Joe introduced her to him."

"Joseph Barnett?" I ask, picturing Mary Jane's man, dry-eyed at the inquest and his expression hard as the knocker of Newgate. They lived together until a few days before she was murdered. No wonder he was a suspect, even though it was for less than a day, before Old Bill let him off the hook. I didn't like the look of him one bit with his piggy eyes. In my book a man with such small peepers can never be trusted. Fancied himself, he did, with his loud manner and his plaid jacket. Someone ought to tell him that he stank of fish guts and all.

She nods. "That's 'im," she says. "So this Yankee gent took a shine to her. Asked for her a few times. Went to fancy hotels, they did. I think he might have turned her head."

"What d'ya mean?" If I'm reading this right, it's sounding to me like Joe Barnett pimped out his own woman to a rich American.

She shrugs. "She and Joe started to fight a lot."

"You reckon that's the real reason he left? 'Cos she'd fallen for this Yank?" I remember at the inquest Joe swore he'd walked out because Mary Jane let her girlfriends use the place at Miller's Court like a brothel.

"Could be," Lizzie replies, cradling her beer mug. She stares deep into the froth. "She told me that she was sick of the life she was leading." I see her eyes start to mist.

"Oh?"

"Yes," she replies with a nod. "And that she wished she had money enough to go back to Ireland to be with her sister. She only earned her living as she did to feed little Timmy. He was everything to her."

I nod, but hold my tongue. I can tell from her look that she's remembering Mary Jane, and I think she wants to keep talking.

"The last I heard through the window was her trilling to her little man. 'A Violet from Mother's Grave.' That was his favorite. Used to sing it to him before bed."

I watch her take another gulp of beer as I think on what she's just said, but something snags in my brain. "So you heard her singing to the boy the night she was killed?"

Lizzie nods. "I'll never forget the sound."

My eyes widen "But don't that mean that little Timmy was sleeping in the room when . . . ?"

Lizzie frowns. "Surely not? No," she replies, like the notion's just risen up and hit her in the head. "If he'd seen something, he would've said. He would've told someone. Wouldn't he?"

Her words drop from her lips and echo all around us. I know the police never interviewed the lad, but a hack spoke with him and reported the nipper never saw anything. So someone must've been looking after him while his mother was being cut to shreds. But who?

"Could he have been with Betsy Ryder?" I ask.

Lizzie shakes her head. "No. He weren't."

"Joe Barnett, then?" I think of the Billingsgate porter, stinking of fish and knocking poor Mary Jane about when he'd had a few too many.

"No." She shakes her head. "I saw him visit that afternoon, but I saw him leave, too. It weren't him. I'm sure of that. Although . . ."

"Yes?"

"Nothing." She shuts up like a cockleshell.

"There was someone else around that time, wasn't there?"

She nods. "I can't be sure, but I think I saw a fella go into the room that night. On the sly, like. I don't know who."

I think for a moment. "So Timmy might've seen this person?"

"You'll have to ask him yourself," she tells me with a shrug, then empties her glass.

I nod. "You're right," I agree. "I will. He's got a tongue in his head. He'll be able to tell me." Although, I think, if the lad did see someone in his ma's room that night, I'll wager the man who attacked me earlier on this evening won't be too happy, neither. Both Timmy and me could be in deep trouble. Hold up! The more I think on it, the more I fear both of us could be Jack's next target.

EMILY

At the Montague Street Mortuary, Dr. George Bagster Phillips is hard at work on a mutilated corpse. In his large white apron, and with a pair of spectacles perched on his nose, he is examining the latest Whitechapel unfortunate to fall victim to a knife-wielding maniac. This particular postmortem on one Alice Mackenzie is, however, presenting him with something of a conundrum.

The vulgar press would have it that this Saucy Jack, or Jack the Ripper, has struck again. It would also appear that his fellow surgeon, the esteemed Dr. Thomas Bond, is of the same opinion. Yet, on this occasion he finds himself at odds with his colleague. Bond's vast knowledge and experience have already been brought to bear on several of these unfortunates' murders. Like Phillips, Bond has examined the majority of the women post-mortem, but neither man can agree on the perpetrator of this latest crime. True, the latter examined the body the day after Phillips, when it was already starting to decompose, but the state of the corpse has no real bearing on the disparate conclusions drawn by each surgeon.

While Bond is convinced that the murder was performed by the same person who committed the former series of Whitechapel murders, Phillips begs to disagree. That's why he has asked for more time to conduct further investigations, necessitating a postponement of the interment. Forced to eschew the comforts of family life yet again in the name of duty, he has ventured into the mortuary on a Saturday evening. On his way, he has enlisted the help of a mortician from the London Hospital to assist him. He is the same young man whom Florence remarked when she and Constance waited for news outside the mortuary the other day.

Accustomed as both Phillips and his assistant are to the reek of death, it does not grow sweeter with the passing of time. Poor Alice Mackenzie is turning fast. She lies, under a stained sheet, on the slab before them. On the doctor's signal, the assistant rolls back the covering to reveal the face of a plain, slightly plump woman, almost matronly in her mien. Her curly hair is swept back to reveal a large expanse of forehead and her nose is slightly bulbous, with a sprinkling of freckles over the bridge.

As the young man readies the surgeon's implements, Phillips takes out his notes and lays them on a small table to his right. A slight mishap during an earlier procedure has left a reddish-brown stain on one corner. The name on the top of the covering sheet reads: Annie Chapman. *He refers to them, turning the pages quickly. He has either conducted or been present at autopsies into four of this so-called Jack the Ripper's victims: Elizabeth Stride, Catherine Eddowes, and Mary Jane Kelly, as well as Chapman. The viciousness and depravity of the attacker's blade has astounded him each time, but this poor woman is slightly different. He finds a particular paragraph in his notes and rereads it, just to satisfy himself of something, then nods. Returning to Alice's file, he nods once more.* "Left to right," *he says out loud.*

The assistant looks up from washing his hands at the sink. His thick, dark hair has flopped forward and he uses the back of a wet hand to push it off his face.

"Sir?"

"I said, Flood, the cut was made from left to right," *reiterates the doctor.*

It is at this moment that they both look toward the door as they hear footsteps approaching along the stone-paved corridor outside. A knock. The assistant goes to answer it. On the threshold stands Inspector Hawkins. He is another man whose duty and natural curiosity cannot be rested on cue.

The detective did not anticipate seeing Dr. Phillips today, intending simply to inspect the cadaver himself, but he is glad he has.

"Sir!" *He looks beyond the young mortician to greet the surgeon.*

Peering over his spectacles, Phillips recognizes the smart young policeman with the bright expression from Commercial Street Station.

"Ah, Inspector Hawkins."

"Acting Inspector Hawkins, sir," *comes the awkward reply.*

Phillips shrugs before returning to the body. "What brings you here, Hawkins? You've not seen the body already?"

The detective moves closer toward the table and the corpse. "I read your interim report, sir, and heard that you have asked for a further examination. I feel fortunate to find you here."

Phillips, an unfashionable sort, who still sports clothes that were in vogue at least forty years ago, smiles once more. "Well, here I am, as you see. And in need of assistance. The good fortune is mutual!"

The young detective smiles weakly and throws an anxious look at the mortician. He is always queasy around corpses, but Phillips, intercepting the glance, merely chuckles.

"You'll be relieved to learn that your assistance will be of an administrative nature, while this fellow here takes care of the rest," *says the surgeon with a smile.* "If you could be so good as to help me cross-reference and compare my notes," *Phillips says, handing Hawkins a sheaf of papers. He turns to bend over the head on the table.* "The cut was made from left to right. Yes?" *His finger points to the lacerated throat.*

Hawkins flips a page. "Yes, sir," *he concurs.*

"Now let us compare this with the other four women. Chapman, right to left."

Pages are turned. "Yes, sir."

"Stride, right to left."

More pages flicked. "Yes, sir."

Finally Eddowes and Kelly are similarly checked, although the latter's injuries were so extensive it was impossible to say.

"Read me what I've written regarding this one, will you, Inspector?" *asks Phillips, nodding at Alice Mackenzie's corpse.*

Hawkins clears his throat. "Left carotid artery severed. Consistent with previous murders, although the injuries inflicted on the other were deeper and longer, cutting down to the spinal column. Only two jagged wounds were inflicted on Mackenzie's left side—no longer than four inches a piece. Air passages remain untouched."

Phillips nods. "So, what can we deduce from this?"

Hawkins finds the surgeon's tone a little patronizing, but is in no doubt. "That the murderer of the other women was right-handed, sir, cutting from right to left, while Miss Mackenzie was cut the opposite way, suggesting her killer was left-handed."

"*Very good, Hawkins,*" *says Phillips with a nod. "I couldn't have put it better myself. Now let us turn our attention to the abdominal wounds, shall we?*" *He motions to the sheet covering Alice's torso, expecting the officer to fold it down for him. Hawkins swallows hard and steels himself to grasp the covering and pull it as far as the pelvis. He looks away as he does so and steps back to allow Phillips to approach once more, this time with a magnifying glass in hand. After a moment's deliberation, he speaks.*

"*These mutilations are mostly of a superficial manner,*" *he pronounces, pointing with the scalpel. "Even the deepest of them hasn't opened the cavity.*"

"*Really, sir?*" *Hawkins forces himself to look.*

"*And these finger marks also suggest that our killer is left-handed.*" *Phillips draws attention to a number of bruises on the corpse's left side, then glances up at Hawkins. "Looks to me like an imprint of the killer's right hand.*"

"*So he must've made the cuts with his left?*"

"*Precisely, Hawkins.*" *He nods. "Find me my notes on Eddowes, will you?*"

So this is what the detective does, and once again Dr. Phillips's memory has served him well. The same goes for Kelly and Chapman. In each instance the abdominal wounds inflicted were much more severe than Alice Mackenzie's. They also indicated the killer was right-handed.

"*So you disagree with Dr. Bond?*" *ventures Hawkins as Dr. Phillips walks over to the basin to wash his hands. The assistant offers the surgeon a small brush and soap.*

"*Yet again, we must agree to differ on this one, I fear,*" *says the surgeon, scrubbing the blood from under his fingernails. He throws a glance back at poor Alice. "I don't believe she was one of Jack's.*"

Hawkins takes the news with the reserved fatalism that he has been forced to cultivate since his secondment to H Division.

What Dr. Phillips has just unwittingly declared is that there is yet another depraved fiend roaming the streets of Whitechapel. Jack the Ripper may have drowned with Montague Druitt in the Thames, but it seems that another equally deranged monster has risen from the depths to take his place. Whereas before, the general consensus was that the killer had a hatred of prostitutes, or some sexual depravities, this time the motive may be of a different nature. Thanks to Commissioner Monro's startling intervention, he is now beginning to think that this latest death could be connected to the Fenian cause of Irish Home Rule. What's more, he's hoping this new assassin may yet prove far less elusive than Saucy Jack.

CONSTANCE

That night Mr. Bartleby pops round. He's been courting Ma for nigh on two years now. Calls himself a businessman, he does. Ma met him when she was off-loading a few of Flo's so-called trinkets in Limehouse. Now he fancies he's one of the family. He'll stop for supper. It's pigs' cheeks tonight.

As usual he blusters in, whips off his bowler, and addresses us all, like he's just stepped onto a stage. "I'm sorry I couldn't get here sooner, my dears," he tells us, without bothering to wipe his muddy boots. "Business," he mumbles; only, we all know his business revolves around handling goods under the counter, so to speak. "Patience," he says when he sees Ma, and marches over to where she's sitting. Standing behind her, he grips her shoulder as she stays in the armchair. She cups her hand over his. "Don't fret so. I'm here now," he tells her, like he's just jumped off his white charger.

I catch Flo rolling her eyes. We both know that Mr. B sees himself as a knight in shining armor, riding to the aid of all us damsels in distress in Whitechapel. Full of his own self-importance, he is, but Ma loves him, that's for sure, and he her. He's brought her new life after our pa died, and for that, Flo and me are grateful, but he still rubs us up the wrong way some of the time, like when he teases me about my gift. He sits himself down on the broken chair opposite Ma.

"We'll call the committee together again," he declares with a nod of his black head. He's a member of the Whitechapel Vigilance Committee, see. They're a bunch of businessmen and worthies who put up a reward for information leading to Jack's arrest. Fat lot of good that's done. "We'll start patrolling again," he tells us. That'll mean Gilbert Johns and his ragtag ilk will be wandering round the streets, looking for trouble once more. None of us is impressed by his fancy words. It's actions we want. The fiend needs to be caught.

"And you, Con," he says, suddenly turning his black button eyes on me. I hate it when anyone calls me Con. My name is Constance.

"Yes," says I with a sullen face.

"How about you get on to that detective of yours? What's his name?" I think he's baiting me.

"Acting Inspector Hawkins," I reply.

Mr. B hooks his thumbs under his braces and winks at me. "Now we've got friends in high places, we'll be able to catch the fiend all the quicker," he tells us.

Try as they might to solve these crimes, it seems the police are just a bunch of bungling idiots, outwitted at every turn. No one in Whitechapel has any faith in them. What's worse, I've got a feeling that there's a lot more to this latest murder than meets the eye. Let's hope that having Thaddeus on our side will make a difference.

EMILY

Farther to the west of London, a dinner of infinitely more substance and quality than pigs' cheeks has been served at the

Richmond—a rather splendid neo-Gothic gentlemen's club on the Embankment. Here talk among the members centers not on the depravities of a crazed killer, but on the dramatic developments at the Parnell Commission. The Commission is in progress at Probate Court Number One at the Royal Courts of Justice. The club's normally sedate atmosphere is alight with the latest revelations exposed at the hearing. For those not au fait with one of the most important judicial inquiries so far this century, allow me to elucidate.

The Parnell Commission was formed as a direct response to the reaction of certain Irish politicians to, among other acts of violence and notable plots, the notorious murders of two leading members of the British government in Phoenix Park, Dublin. In 1882, the British peer Lord Frederick Cavendish and the head of the civil service, Thomas Burke, were cut down with surgical knives in a horrific attack that had shocked the world, almost as much as Mary Jane Kelly's murder six years later.

At the heart of this commission lies the eponymous politician Charles Stewart Parnell. He is what many Establishment figures regard as a traitorous Irishman who has dared to question the status quo. In other words, the Conservative government, led by Lord Salisbury, sees him as an enemy. Mr. Parnell does, however, have cause to feel aggrieved. The calamitous famine in his homeland, two decades previous, was, according to him and many others, greatly compounded by the unspeakably callous behavior of the English landlords. Yet, his credibility as a politician has been challenged by accusations that he condoned previous acts of Fenian violence—namely, the terrible double murder in Phoenix Park.

So, amid the fug of Havana cigars and the clinking of port glasses, the proceedings have disturbed a hornet's nest of intrigue involving not just mainland Britain and Ireland, but America, too. Gossip is rife and slander almost mandatory among members. Yet, despite the odds being stacked against him, Mr. Par-

nell, it seems, is emerging as a man of good character, contrary to the well-laid plans of the government. So much so that the Old Testament battle between David and Goliath springs to mind.

Away from this general hubbub, however, two senior intelligence officers are about to engage in a deep conversation in one of the members' lounges. One of them, Bernard Royston, is the head of the Special Branch, a department recently formed to investigate Irish revolutionary activity. He and his large network of spies have been obliged to work behind the scenes, monitoring suspects, collating information, and making arrests. There have even been a couple of inconvenient accidents—inconvenient for the wanted men, that is. These days, however, Royston's services are no longer in as much demand, since James Monro has stepped into the post of commissioner. As the saying goes, the devil makes work for idle hands, so thus officially restrained, Royston finds himself unofficially engaged in his most sinister plot to date.

He and the other officer have just enjoyed two excellent filets mignons and are settling down to port, cigars, and a very important conversation.

"Parnell is smelling of roses at the moment," opines Royston. "Perhaps it's time we caused a stink," he suggests. His delivery is somber, even though he's rewarded with a smile from his companion opposite him.

The spymaster's guest is none other than Inspector Angus Mc-Cullen, formerly of Special Branch and currently of H Division, Commercial Street Police Station. You may remember the fiery Scot. The officer has ostensibly taken sick leave following his onerous investigations into the Whitechapel murders, although he has certainly not been idle, either. Quite the opposite. You see, he has never lost touch with his old boss from Special Branch. Having worked under Royston for three years, McCullen knows the department is a law unto itself and that its head does not play by conventional rules.

Royston inspects the butt of his cigar, then casually sniffs the length of it. "I am happy to report that all seems to have settled down across the Atlantic," he begins.

McCullen cuts the head off his own cigar. "So . . . the American's death has been put down to natural causes?"

His host nods and shows his yellowing teeth. "Yes, it seems our cousins across the Atlantic are a fairly gullible lot. A key witness in one of the most sensational commissions of the century is found slumped in his study and no one cries foul." He crosses his legs, as if to draw a line under the death of General Frank Millen. Millen was an Irish-American mercenary in the pay of Her Majesty's government; he was found dead at his New York home earlier in the year. "Besides," Royston resumes more cheerfully, "it suits the government's purpose and means we can get back to our Whitechapel business, eh?" He pulls his mouth into a tight smile. "And that's where you come in, Mc-Cullen."

"I'm assuming that's why you called the meeting, sir." The Scot appears intrigued as he takes a sip of his port.

"With Millen out of the way, we need someone else to infiltrate."

McCullen suddenly leans back in his chair, as if to distance himself from Royston's suggestion. The prospect of stepping into a dead man's shoes—a murdered man's shoes—is not something to be taken lightly. "I . . . It's . . ." He throws a wary look at the master spy.

Royston laughs. "Don't worry. I'm not asking you to put your head on the block, and, as you know, I've already got a thug to do all the messy stuff."

Messy stuff? *thinks the Scot, reflecting on the murder at Number 13 Miller's Court.* "That's an understatement," *he mumbles under his breath. He feels that now is as good a time as any to air his apprehension.* "With respect, sir, he appears more of a deranged psychopath than a thug. I'll ne'er forget the *lassie . . ."* The Scot's voice dips as he suddenly recalls the orgy of blood and body parts he witnessed in the squalid room; then it rises an octave when he says: *"He sent me her . . ."* He looks away as if trying to dispel the image. The delivery of the victim's heart in a box had come as a terrible shock, even to a hardened detective such as himself. He still suffers nightmares.

Royston's muted laugh is tinged with disgust. *"And that's why you were given time off from your post."* For once, Royston appears a mite sheepish. *"I'll admit he was a little"*—he casts round for a word—*". . . excessive. His is an acquired skill."* He gives a little nod and adds as an aside, *"Apparently learned in the butchery trade, but your hands will never be sullied. The brute just needs a handler, a middleman, someone who can assess his information and report to me."*

A sheen of sweat has broken out on McCullen's brow. *"I'm not sure . . ."*

"It was all rather unfortunate," admits Royston.

McCullen balks at the recollection. *"Indeed. All that effort and he got the wrong woman."* He takes a handkerchief from his pocket and starts to dab his forehead.

"Yes, but at least leaving the knife there has given Monro something to go on," counters Royston. He had personally seen to it that a surgical knife, almost identical with the ones used in the Phoenix Park murders, was left at the crime scene.

"A stroke of genius, if I may say," ventures McCullen, adding, *"And this Mackenzie."*

Royston nods. *"Related, yes."*

The Scot's gaze drops as he pauses to consider the recent East End murder to be laid at Jack the Ripper's door.

Royston strikes a match. *"I'm pleased our man went a little easier on the old woman."*

The inspector's brows lift. *"Quite."*

Royston puffs on his cigar, sending clouds billowing toward the Scot. *"So this latest exercise,"* he begins. *"Has it borne fruit?"*

The inspector glances about him. There are at least two dozen other men in the room, but all seem to be engaged in conversation. He leans forward as Royston holds the flame to the cigar and screws up his eyes as the first puff of smoke drifts upward. "It's a little too early to say, sir."

Royston relaxes in his chair. "Give it a few days. I'll wager our prey will be at the funeral. You have a date and venue?"

"Not yet."

He nods. "But when you do, I'll be sure to have one of my spies there. This time there can be no mistake."

CHAPTER 5

Sunday, July 21, 1889

CONSTANCE

I'm woken by the bells. That's how I know it's a Sunday. For me and Ma, it means a service at St. Jude's. For Flo, it's a lie-in. I sit up and cast an envious eye down to the bottom of the bed, where I know she'll still be in the Land of Nod, but no. I pull myself up. She's not there. It's then that I see her over by the broken mirror on the wall, brushing those lustrous locks of hers.

"What you doing up at this hour?" I ask.

She doesn't bother to turn round, although I see her full lips twitch a smile in the mirror. I can tell by her look she's up to something. She's already in her stays and petticoat. Scrambling out of bed, I pad over to her. Just as I near her, I catch a whiff of something: a flowery scent and my eyes widen.

"You've got a new man!" I exclaim.

"Shush!" She puts a finger to her lips. "I don't want Ma knowing. Not yet, anyroad."

The thought settles in my mind. I'm pleased for her, I think. She had a tough time of it earlier this year when she found she was with Danny Dawson's child. Typical man, he didn't want anything to do with a babe, so he broke off their betrothal. Then came the terrible attack up in Poplar and Flo lost the little one she was carrying. That was in January and she's not walked out with anyone since.

I perch myself on the bed and watch her reflection in the mirror. "Who is he?" I ask, unable to bridle my curiosity.

Flo tuts, puts down the brush, and starts to pin up her tresses. She's fobbing me off. "It's early days."

"Why won't you tell me?"

"'Cos . . ."

"'Cos what? I won't tell Ma, promise."

"Mind your own business, will ya?" she says in a voice that's becoming quite scratchy.

She sees my reflection in the mirror and gleans I'm a little hurt. Nevertheless, she flattens her mouth as if to say her lips are sealed. Leaving the looking glass, she slides into her Sunday-best dress and presents her back to me. Silently I fasten her little buttons. She nods by way of thanks when I'm done, then picks up her hat—a new red feather stuck in it, I see—and goes downstairs. There's no two ways about it. I can't help thinking there's something fishy about this new man of hers.

EMILY

In another church not so far away, but this time of the Roman Catholic persuasion, the tabernacle flame on the altar burns as brightly as ever, reminding the faithful that the Lord is present. Father Keegan genuflects before it, prayer book in hand, and opens the door to the confessional. Every morning and evening he, or one of his fellow priests, takes confessions. There is a large Irish community in Whitechapel. It's rare that he hears any penitent confess in anything other than a breathy brogue. True, there is the occasional Italian or French immigrant, but it's the Irish mammies and the thick-necked laborers, by and large, who come to unburden themselves of their sins. Very often the men admit to drinking too much and indulging in fisticuffs later. If they beat their wives and children, they're always sorry for it afterward. They rarely intend to be violent, but when Satan calls them to the pub, usually on payday, hard liquor is difficult to resist after twelve hours of backbreaking work. The women, of course, are by nature less raucous. Naturally, there is the odd spat, usually over a man; otherwise, Father Keegan is told of petty pilfering, white lies, a covetous thought, and, very occasionally, an adulterous affair. He absolves them all, of course. Only once has a man ever admitted to murder and then he managed to persuade him to turn himself over to the authorities. The sacred bond between penitent and confessor is sacrosanct. It can never be broken. A secret is always safe with a Catholic priest, so that is why on this particular evening, Father Keegan receives a visit from a deeply troubled young woman. He's just heard his fourth or fifth confessor bemoaning they coveted a rich woman's hat or used curse words toward their husband, when he receives an altogether different class of sinner into the confessional box.

"Bless me, Father, for I have sinned," comes a sweet voice. She is young by the sound of it. There is a lyrical lilt. Irish, he thinks, but many years off the boat.

"How long is it since your last confession, my child?" he asks. There's a pause. "I can't remember, Father. It's been that long."

"So, what brings you to the Lord to ask forgiveness now?"

Another pause. "I am guilty of deception, Father. I have deceived those I love and those who love me."

This is a bright one, thinks the priest. She's not your usual fishwife. "So you are living a lie?" he asks.

"That I am," comes the whispered reply. The young woman

sighs heavily. "*It is not what I wish, and I hope to put it right soon, but for now I need to know I am absolved on my sin.*" *Her breath snags on a sob.* "*I beg God's forgiveness for causing such pain.*"

CONSTANCE

It's a good service, even though my throbbing neck makes it hard to concentrate. Canon Marriott himself delivers the sermon. Naturally, it's about poor Alice. He tells us that it's at times like this that we must all stand together and look out for each other: rich for poor, strong for weak. He quotes us what Jesus said on the Sermon on the Mount about the meek being blessed. He tells us, too, that we mustn't blame the Jews nor the Irish nor any newcomers to our parish. We're all looking at each other with different eyes again, you see. Every time there's a killing, it's the foreigners that get it in the neck. The reverend has us eating out of the palm of his hand. We all nod and look pious when he speaks; he's that good a preacher. But, of course, as soon as we're out of the church, we all go back to our old ways and regard every stranger with suspicion. It's only natural.

It's a fair morning, and as we file out of the church, the sunlight that's been fighting against the gray haze above us breaks through. People are lingering on the steps to talk and I spot Isaac Parker, the bowlegged landlord from the Tower. He and Mr. Tempany from the lodging house are paying for old Alice's funeral. Mr. Parker is waddling from person to person. He seems agitated. Whatever he's saying, it's putting frowns on faces. He's coming up the steps now.

"'Morning, Mr. Parker," says I as he passes. "Something amiss?"

"Ah, Constance. Mrs. Piper," he greets Ma and me, whipping off his hat. "The police've just called round to say we have to postpone the funeral till Wednesday. I need to tell the canon. Can you spread the word?"

I nod. "I certainly will," I say, even though I'm surprised by the news. I look at Ma. She's not happy, neither.

"Why would they want to do that?" she asks me when Mr. Parker is out of earshot.

I shrug in reply. The only reason I can think of is that the police surgeon needs more time to examine Alice's body. He must be onto something.

"I don't know" is all I say. But the news sets me wondering.

CHAPTER 6

Monday, July 22, 1889

EMILY

Luncheon is being served at the Richmond Club. The grand dining room is busy with peers up from their country estates, who've swapped tweeds for formal frock coats, and the occasional self-made businessman from Manchester or the Midlands. The latter always spends more freely and talks louder than those born into the upper classes. It is in Bernard Royston's interests, however, to remain discreet. Yet again he is entertaining Inspector McCullen, this time over braised pigeon breast. The Scot has been summoned at short notice.

"This Hawkins chap seems to be doing a good job in your absence," remarks Royston as he slices into the meat. It is a little pink, just how he likes it.

McCullen narrows his eyes. Ever since they met, about half an hour ago, he's been on edge, knowing that he'd have to tell his superior about the latest developments. Now, he fears, is the time to divulge them. "A little too good, I fear. He's got the scent of Fenian in his nostrils."

"So I hear." Royston's knife and fork are rested. Is there nothing that escapes his notice? thinks the inspector. "That's why we needed to talk. I have it on good authority that Commissioner Monro summoned Hawkins a couple of days ago. So you know he's got him working on the Irish angle. Strictly secret, of course." He waits for a reaction.

McCullen flinches. "Och! He's a bright lad. And like a dog with a bone when he knows he's onto something."

"So I gather. He'll be on the trail of every Paddy in Whitechapel ere long. That's why you'll be pleased to hear that help is at hand." Royston picks up his knife and fork and resumes eating.

"Oh?" The inspector's braised oxtail remains untouched.

"I think it's time you returned to your duties at Commercial Street, McCullen."

The Scot leans in suspiciously. "Something has happened?"

Royston's lips switch a smile. "Something will happen if you so choose."

McCullen scowls. "I'm a Scottish Protestant and proud. You know I'll do anything to nail these Irish Catholic bastards."

Royston sweeps the room for possible eavesdroppers, then lowers his voice. "My spies tell me that a seaman and convicted larcenist by the name of William Wallace Brodie is obliging us, for a small fee."

"Go on."

"Last month he went on a 'spree,' as he told it, in Cape Town."

"South Africa?"

"The very same," replies Royston, taking a sip of claret. "In a drunken delirium he confessed to the Ripper murders, but was discharged by magistrates. As luck would have it, he arrived back in London two days before this Mackenzie woman was murdered."

Wide-eyed, McCullen nods. "So he needs to be arrested and charged?"

"Already taken care of by my good friends at Leman Street HQ." Royston dabs the corner of his mouth with a napkin. "That's why I believe it's time you returned to your post, don't you agree, Inspector? Just to make sure that justice is at least seen to be done, so that some of us can get on with managing the really serious issues of the day unfettered by political sensitivities."

McCullen allows himself a rare smile. "Mrs. McCullen will certainly be glad to have me out from under her feet," he replies, lifting his glass. "So I'll drink to that!"

Royston raises his glass, too. "To William Wallace Brodie, alias Jack the Ripper. May he remain in custody for as long as possible."

CONSTANCE

It's late and Flo and me are readying ourselves for bed. I stand in the mirror and see that the bruise on my neck has bloomed all purple. It's sore to the touch and I wince as I press lightly on my mottled skin. I haven't told Flo that I was attacked and warned off trying to find out any more about Alice's murder. She'll worry for me, and as for Ma, well, she'd literally have a fit. I keep my counsel and button up my nightdress so that my neck is all covered. My bruise may be out of sight, but I can't help thinking about the man who damn near throttled me. It means I'm on the right path. I've relived the moment a hundred times in my head: the feel of his hands, the stink of his breath, and the sound of his voice. Rough as sandpaper it was, and although it was couched in a whisper, I could tell he was from round these parts.

Flo's sitting on the bed. She seems quite contented these days. This new man in her life is filling her thoughts most of the time. She's brushing her locks and humming a tune in time with each stroke. It's only when she starts singing the words that I recognize the song. That's when my blood turns icy.

"What you singing that for?" I snap.

She stops brushing and looks at me with a frown. " 'A Violet from Mother's Grave'?" she replies, quite put out.

"Yes. Why are you singing that song?" I ask, trying to rein in my tetchiness.

"I don't know." She shrugs. "It just came into my head. You got a problem with it?"

"No," I say slowly; only, in truth, I have. Flo starts her brushing again—and her singing. Suddenly I sense Miss Tindall's hand in this.

CHAPTER 7

EMILY

The Royal Courts of Justice are housed in a grandiose building on the Strand, one of London's most prestigious thoroughfares. In this large gray stone, Gothic-style edifice, the most important political cases in the land are heard. For the past few months it is also where a most controversial royal commission has been in session. It is to Number One Probate Court that Acting Inspector Hawkins now makes his way. Although he has followed the controversial proceedings of the Parnell Commission in the newspapers when his time has allowed, he has never attended the court in person, his attention being rather occupied with other, equally pressing matters of late. It pleased him to be able to demonstrate a rudimentary knowledge of the inquiry's dealings to Commissioner Monro the other day, but in light of his current assignment, he feels it his duty to attend at least one session in person.

In the wake of the shocking killings at Phoenix Park in Dublin, the Times *newspaper had published a series of articles accusing Charles Stewart Parnell, the leader of the Home Rule movement, of excusing and condoning the murders in a series of letters to associates. Over the course of the last few months, the inquiry has discovered, however, that these letters were, in fact, forgeries. It seems Mr. Parnell has been, at least in part, vindicated.*

The Commission has been in session for almost one hundred days, yet public interest in it shows no sign of abating. Quite the contrary. This morning, even before the court is opened, a large crowd awaits outside the doors. Admission is by ticket only and members of the public speedily secure seats when officials allow them to enter. The gangways are blocked by an excited throng of politicians, and Hawkins is forced to jostle with other spectators to find a place. Large numbers of ladies and gentlemen are even accommodated in the jury box. After several minutes of searching, the acting inspector is finally able to squeeze himself into a small space a few paces from the front. Satisfied he's managed to secure an excellent view of the proceedings, he settles himself to await the opening of the session.

The hushed audience watches enthralled as, one by one, two members of Parliament and a representative of an obscure Irish organization give their evidence. All of them seem to vindicate the Irish leader and clear him of supporting violence.

As Hawkins listens, it becomes clear to him that the British government, which believes Parnell to be guilty, is being shown in a less than favorable light. In view of what Commissioner Monro has ordered him to do, the tenor of the proceedings leaves him with a very bad taste in his mouth.

When the session adjourns for luncheon and he slowly files out of the courtroom, Hawkins feels as if he is treading on treacherous ground. He's been tasked to investigate a possible Irish link with the Whitechapel murders, but could it really be, he wonders, that these barbarous killings of unfortunate women were politically motivated, designed to make Her Majesty's Constabulary of Police look like fools?

Are the Fenians so hell-bent on Home Rule that they're willing to sacrifice innocent lives to further their cause? The dynamite explosions of a few years ago demonstrated that they are. But then again . . .

He is just musing on the dilemma when he feels a shoulder clip his own. His gaze darts up to see a young man with long, dark, wavy hair vying for the doorway. "I beg your pardon," he reacts with involuntary politeness.

The young man whose shoulder he brushed is equally apologetic. "Forgive me, sir," he says sheepishly, his pale complexion coloring a little. He gestures to the detective to go first.

As Hawkins passes in front of the young man, he thinks there is something familiar about him. He has seen him before, but where? It is not until he is outside again that he remembers. He is the mortician who attended at Alice Mackenzie's postmortem.

CHAPTER 8

Wednesday, July 24, 1889

CONSTANCE

We're at Plaistow Cemetery, just east of Whitechapel, paying our last respects to Alice. She was older than the other victims, although just how old I don't think even she could say. I'd put her around the same age as Ma, although her years on the street had left their mark on her face just as surely as the scars men gave her.

There was a good turnout for the funeral. Hundreds of mourners lined the pavements in Whitechapel. Even hanging out the top windows, they were. Like a river of black, it was, running down Artillery Street, where we set off from the Tower at half past one. Messrs. Parker and Tempany certainly did her proud. Along with the hearse there were two mourning carriages, pulled by big glossy-black horses. Behind the hearse walked a handful of women, Lizzie Albrook among them, and three gents, including Alice's man. They were led by the undertaker in his claw-hammer coat. Betsy Ryder, from the doss house, was there, too. Homely as a pair of slippers, she is. Walking by her side was little Timmy Kelly. This time there were shoes on his feet. Done up all smart, he was, with a dapper cap that he took off to walk in the cortege. Looked a proper picture. Poor, lost lamb.

I followed the hearse with Ma and Flo, passing in slow procession some of the other places where Jack had been about his fiendish work. Along Commercial Street we filed, past Dorset Street and the archway leading to Miller's Court, where they found Mary Jane. Through into Hanbury Street next we went, where Annie Chapman met her grisly fate at Number 29, then on into Baker's Row and the western end of Buck's Row, where Polly Nichols felt Jack's blade.

As we turned onto Whitechapel High Street and onto Commercial Road, the crowds started to thin and everyone went back to their own business, leaving our little band to proceed here, to Plaistow. Yes, they all did Alice proud. Even Joseph Barnett put in an appearance, although I think he's got some nerve showing up, now we all know he roughed up Mary Jane. He accompanied the hearse to the cemetery, too, but stood back when they lowered the coffin into the ground and only nodded at little Timmy when he came face-to-face with him afterward.

There was barely a dry eye at the graveside. All in all, it's been a good show. Everyone's made a fuss of poor Timmy. He was that well behaved. When he saw everyone else all teary-eyed, he shed a few of his own for dear old Alice, but I don't think he understands death. I hope not, anyway. I'm not sure he can get his head around the ending of everything on earth—not the going away of it all and the emptiness that's left behind. That's not easy for anyone to get to grips with, let alone a nipper like him. What that little 'un's been through and he's not yet seven years of age!

Now that Alice has been lowered into the ground, I grab a

clod. The earth feels cold and sticky in my hand and I throw it into the open grave. It makes a dull thudding sound on the coffin. The little party of mourners is breaking up, and I leave Ma and Flo to talk to Betsy Ryder and the others. I slip away, quiet like, to pay my respects to someone else who's remembered in the graveyard. I don't think they've noticed me.

Walking along the headstones, a few rows back, I come to Miss Tindall's memorial stone. It's quite plain: no angels or urns for her. Just a round-topped granite slab with a simple inscription: *Emily Frances Grace Tindall, 1862–1888, a beloved daughter who died in the service of others.* I think she would approve, although, perhaps, she would prefer *passed over* to *died.*

All visitors to this place have their own sad story to tell, but surely none as strange as mine. It's been almost eight months since they buried Emily Tindall, or rather what remained of her, and I still miss her most terribly. Sometimes when I'm alone or at night, I get this terrible ache in my chest and I just want to reach out and touch her. But I can't. Of course, I'm luckier than most bereaved people because I have seen her since she passed. It may only have been a fleeting glimpse now and again, in a crowd or even in the mirror, but I know she's been there. As strange as it may sound, I'm almost expecting to catch sight of her here, in this resting place.

I've saved a flower from the bunch I put on Alice's grave. It's a single rose. Bobbing down, I lay it by the stone and say a few words. Only, just as I'm straightening myself up again, I suddenly see, a few yards beyond, a woman step out from behind a nearby tree. She's all in black, with a veil over her head, and for a second I think it's her.

"Miss Tindall," I mutter, only not so loud as the others can hear me. For a moment she is still. Her head turns and I think she's staring at me, even though I can't see her face beneath the mesh. Then she turns back and starts walking. But I won't let her leave. Not like that. I hurry after her. "Miss Tindall!" I call, only louder, but she ups her pace. There's something not right. Something different. She's not walking like Miss Tindall walked, not like a lady. Her shoulders are rounded and she's not wearing a hat, like Miss Tindall always did. This woman's taller, too. She's soon at the cemetery gates, but before she goes through them, she stops and glances back once more. Only, she's not looking at me. She's gazing beyond to Alice's grave and to the party of mourners that's making slow progress toward the gates, too. By the time I reach the railings and look down the street, the woman's gone; she's melted into thin air. Vanished. She weren't no Miss Tindall, and that's for sure. But who was she? *Or what?* The thought has already bloomed in my head. We are in the place of the dead, surrounded by them. Perhaps she was a ghost. Perhaps she'd crossed over. Perhaps she wanted to welcome old Alice to heaven.

"You all right?" asks Flo, coming up to me, with Ma on her arm.

"Yes," I say, looking about. I'm all distracted and flustered and she knows it. I've got that feeling again, like someone's been inside my head and rummaged around in my brain. Am I seeing things? I'm not sure.

"Been paying your respects to Miss Tindall?" asks Ma, her sad eyes rimmed red.

"That's right," I reply with a nod. I hope she doesn't notice I'm all atremble.

Just behind Ma comes Betsy with little Timmy. She's holding his hand.

"You're a brave boy," says Ma, patting the top of his ginger head as he draws alongside.

"That he is," agrees Betsy. "That he is. His ma would have been proud of him today."

That's when I get this feeling. I look at little Timmy and I see in his face his mother's good looks: the pert nose and the clever eyes. I wonder if it was her I saw just now, even though her features were hidden by the veil. The woman I saw was watching the boy as he bowed his little head by Alice's grave. It was the same woman I saw by the doss house the other day. I'm sure of it. Maybe Mary Jane's come back to see her son. That's it! Just like Miss Tindall, she's still walking the earth, even though her body's in the ground. What was the name Miss Tindall gave herself? A revenant. Yes. Could it be that Mary Jane Kelly, whose body they found locked in that bloody chamber, slashed and cut, has returned to her home turf? When they found her, there was talk that no human thing could have wrought such evil on a body, that she was the victim of a demented creature. Some even said it was a golem from Jewish folklore that did it: a thing of clay that's given life, only to take it from others. The demon may have mutilated her body, but it didn't destroy her spirit and it couldn't break the bonds of a mother's love. That's it. The thought suddenly seizes me: Mary Jane's returned to watch over her little Timmy, to see that no harm comes to her boy. I hold the idea tight in my head to stop it from slipping away. It's a fanciful notion, but I think it could be true. I think I may have just seen the ghost of Mary Jane Kelly.

EMILY

It's evening in St. James's, in a very fashionable district of London, not a stone's throw away from the Richmond Club. This time they've agreed to meet in a side street, so that to passersby it appears a casual encounter between acquaintances.

"McCullen," greets Royston, raising his hat. "I hear the funeral this afternoon was most touching, a fine turnout."

The Scot lifts his bowler. "Indeed so," comes the reply.

"And I trust a particular mourner came to pay her respects."

McCullen nods. "There was a sighting," he says nonchalantly; for all the world it seems as if he is inquiring after his friend's family.

Under the glow of the streetlamp, a smile spreads across Royston's face. "Don't tell me." He flattens his palm in front of him. "The graveside!"

"Yes."

Royston nods. "I knew she'd be back for him sooner or later. A man should never underestimate a mother's love," he muses.

But what McCullen has next to relate quickly wipes the smile off his co-conspirator's face. The Scot shakes his head and leans forward. "The bad news is we lost her." Royston drops his smile and his jaw begins to work angrily. He is trying to hold back his temper. "Sir?" McCullen is unsure about his master's silence, but needs a response. "How should we proceed?"

The master darts the Scot a wry look. "Do you fish, Inspector?" he asks, fixing him with a curious stare.

McCullen is confused. "I've been known to bag a salmon or two from the Tay."

"Then you'll know how important it is to have good bait."

"Indeed, sir."

"And we have the perfect sort. Our colorful fly will make our fish move soon enough. But when she does, we need to be able to reel her in as quickly as possible. Do I make myself clear, Inspector."

"Yes, sir."

"Then find her, and find her quickly. Or there'll be hell to pay."

CONSTANCE

Death is never far away from my thoughts these days. Tonight, as I lie in bed, in the darkness, my mind wanders back to Miss Tindall. It's been so long since I've felt her presence—four months now, or maybe more. I was thinking that perhaps when the killings stopped, she might cease her visits to me, too. It certainly seems that way. She comes to me when there's trouble and fear all around. So, if I'm right, she's due to visit any time soon. She'll show me what I must do to help make things right. I must not resist. My door must always be open to her, even though it unsettles me and makes me fretful, I know I need her help. I pray I will hear from her erelong.

Just then, Flo stirs and pulls the cover off me. I yank it back. She grunts. I seize my chance.

"Flo," says I.

"I'm asleep," she replies.

I carry on regardless. "Did you see a woman in a black veil at the cemetery today?"

There's another scornful grunt. "What you on about? There were lots of 'em," she replies unhelpfully.

"No, there wasn't," I insist. "Everyone in our party had hats on, not just veils."

There's a short silence, followed by: "How should I know?" I see her shoulder work a shrug under the sheet.

"Never mind," says I, after a moment. Only, I do mind. It matters to me whether the woman in the black veil I saw was flesh and blood or a spirit. Was she a revenant like Miss Tindall, or, as I'm starting to think, was she real? The way she walked, the way she stared. The way she was just, well, there. Whenever Miss Tindall has come to me since she died, it's been strange. I've seen her reflection in a mirror, or there've been flashes before my eyes and I've swooned. But this woman was different. She was solid and unyielding. Perhaps she was real, after all?

I close my eyes. *Miss Tindall, will you tell me?* I pray.

EMILY

Yes, dear Constance. The woman you saw in the cemetery this morning is as real as you are. You have begun well, but next you need to find out her identity. Tonight, in your dreams, you will revisit Alice Mackenzie's graveside. You will study the faces of the mourners: There is your own mother, supported by your sister, Florence. There are women from Mr. Tenpenny's, too: Among them is henna-haired Margaret Cheeks, who, but for the grace of God, was to have accompanied Alice out that night. At first, it was feared she might have fallen victim to an attack, too, until she reappeared the following day telling the police she had spent the night with her sister. There is George Dixon, the blind boy in his dark glasses, who swears he accompanied Alice to a public house the night she died. Despite extensive inquiries the investigation has not been able to corroborate his story. There is Alice's common-law husband, John McCormack. He cries copious tears, but are they real? Finally you will see Betsy Ryder, both her plump hands placed protectively on young Timmy Kelly's shoulders, as both of them watch the coffin lowered into the soil. Let your eyes settle on the child for a moment, then lift them slightly so that you gaze directly beyond him. There, in the distance, you will see the woman in the black veil who is so occupying your waking thoughts. I cannot reveal her identity to you. Only you can discover who she is. All that I can tell you at the moment is that her sights are still set on little Timmy. Until she has him within her power, she will not rest.

CHAPTER 9

Thursday, July 25, 1889

EMILY

Acting Inspector Hawkins arrives at work this morning to find an unusually reserved Sergeant Halfhide behind the desk at the station. The veteran officer's greeting seems a little muted and Hawkins puts it down to Mrs. Halfhide's rheumatism. He knows it's flaring up again; although a glance toward his office door tells him there may be something else troubling the hirsute policeman. To his surprise he sees Constables Semple and Tanner shuffling out of it under the weight of several large files, together with his precious boxes of card indexes.

"What the devil . . . ?" Hawkins stops short.

"Orders, sir," says Semple, his embarrassed gaze dropping to the floor.

"Whose orders?"

Constable Tanner pulls his mouth into a grimace and lets his eyes slide to his right, from where a voice suddenly booms.

"*On mine, Hawkins.*" *Standing at the doorway, arms spread wide and hands gripping the posts on either side, is Inspector McCullen. The fiery Scot, who appointed Hawkins to take charge in his absence, has, it seems, neglected to inform the junior officer of his intention to return to work quite so soon.*

The younger man's jaw gapes. "*Sir, I did not know . . . I . . .*"

"*Och, spare me the drama, laddie.*" *He stands back a little from the threshold.* "*Come in,*" *he orders, hooking his arm and gesturing Hawkins inside.* "*We've work to do.*"

McCullen shuts the door behind him. "*So, Detective Sergeant,*" *he begins, making sure Hawkins understands he's been instantly demoted to his former rank, now that his boss is back.* "*Let's get down to business.*"

Hawkins, very much in shock, and not a little annoyed at his sudden eviction—not to mention his immediate relegation—nevertheless obeys. He remains speechless as he takes a seat in front of the desk that less than twelve hours before he regarded as his.

Without prior notice it seems Inspector McCullen has returned from his "rest" with an air of confidence and renewed vigor that makes Hawkins feel that a spell of extended leave might be just the tonic he needs at the moment.

In front of the inspector is an open file. "*This latest killing,*" *he says, his hand swiping across the pages of the report that he's just been reading.* "*You've been at the inquest, yes?*" *McCullen remains as forthright as ever. Circumlocution is not his style.*

Hawkins nods. "*Yes, sir. Both days so far.*"

"*And what do you make of it?*"

"*You mean, do I think this latest murder the work of the Whitechapel fiend, sir?*"

"*Of course, that's my meaning, laddie,*" *barks McCullen.*

Hawkins clears his throat. "*There are two schools of thought, sir. One . . .*"

"*Damn it, laddie.*" *The Scot's palm slaps the desk.* "*I'm per-*

fectly aware of other opinions. I want to know what you think."

The younger man tilts his head for a moment. What his superior does not know is that he has seen Alice Mackenzie's body for himself. As with the other victims, her corpse was not a pretty sight, but at least her face had escaped the knife this time, if not her body. There were other, more subtle differences, too, although without Dr. Phillips's authority, Hawkins does not feel himself at liberty, as yet, to disclose more. He therefore settles on saying: "I am not convinced that we are dealing with the same killer, sir."

Another slap on the desk is accompanied this time by a heavenward rolling of the eyes. "Not another of your wretched theories," replies McCullen. "The top brass was clearly wrong about Montague Druitt being Jack, I'll give you that, but you seem to delight in complicating matters." The Scot does nothing to hide his irritation with his junior's circumspection.

Hawkins is a little put out. His feathers are ruffled, but he remains calm, as ever, on the surface. "I believe Dr. Phillips wants to reserve various points for a later date, sir," he counters.

McCullen flares his nostrils and blows through his nose, like an angry bull. "And why might that be, in your opinion?"

Hawkins states the obvious. "Because he is unsure, sir."

"Unsure of what?" McCullen leans forward and elbows the desk.

"Unsure as to whether the modus operandi of the murderer matches the earlier cases?" Hawkins delivers his answer as a question, with an inflection at the end, which only serves to further irritate his superior.

"Nonsense! Balderdash! Piffle!" cries the Scot, slapping the desk once more. "I'm not alone in thinking that this latest killing is by the same hand." He narrows his eyes under his rusty red brows as he reaches for a report in front of him.

"Sir?" The younger detective is eager to know what his superior is driving at. Thankfully, he doesn't have to wait long.

McCullen picks up the letter and waves it in front of him. "Fortunately, Bond has come to the rescue again."

Hawkins recalls the difference of opinion between the two medical examiners, although he had no idea that Dr. Bond had already made his conclusions known to the police.

"This is a copy of a letter the good doctor sent to Sir Robert," McCullen begins. *Sir Robert Anderson is the assistant commissioner of the Metropolitan Police, you understand. The inspector hands the missive over to Hawkins so that he can read it for himself:* I see in this murder evidence of similar design to the former Whitechapel murders. A sudden onslaught on the prostrate woman, the throat skilfully and resolutely cut with subsequent mutilation, each mutilation indicating sexual thoughts and a desire to mutilate the abdomen and sexual organs. I am of the opinion that this murder was performed by the same person who committed the former series of Whitechapel murders.

McCullen leans back triumphantly as soon as Hawkins looks up. He sniffs and loosens the catarrh caught in his throat. "So we don't have to wait until the coroner's verdict to go about our business. As I've told you before, Hawkins, Bond's opinion carries more weight than your Bagster Phillips's. And not only that."

"Sir?"

"Monro backs him, too. He also thinks Jack's our man. We must carry on looking for him. Do I make myself plain?"

Hawkins nods, even though duplicity does not come easily to him. So the commissioner is also outwardly throwing his weight behind the theory that the killer is a lone psychopath, while secretly backing the idea of a Fenian plot. "Yes, sir."

In a way such differences of opinion suit his purpose. They muddy the waters, as it were. If Inspector McCullen is thus diverted and distracted from the Fenian loop, then the Irish connection to this latest murder will not be compromised. It simply means that the detective sergeant's workload will double and that he will have to be even more careful in the pursuit of any further leads. If only he had someone to assist him—someone in whom he could place his trust; someone who is not a member of the police force; someone on whose good sense and intuition he could rely.

CONSTANCE

All day long I've waited for my moment. It's been hovering in the air like one of them flies that looks like a little bee; only, when I've come to pin it down, the moment's flown off again. And, of course, as soon as Mr. B walks in to sup with us, I think I can wave good-bye any notion I might have had of bringing Ma round to my way of thinking.

She's been in the dumps all day. I put it down to her mourning the loss of Alice. Said very little, she has, since they lowered the poor old dear into the ground. It's like she's caught up in a web of her own thoughts. But it's not long before I find out that she's not been thinking of herself or Alice at all.

Mr. B blusters in all full of himself, as usual, a parcel under his arm.

"What ya got for us today, then?" asks Flo, cheekily.

"Nice Victoria sponge," says he, then adds with a wink at Ma, "I know how you like a bit of raspberry jam, Patience."

Normally, Ma would blush and say something like: "Oh, Harold! What are you like?" But today, as he hands her a small box with the cake in it, she don't—sorry, *doesn't*—even raise a smile. She just turns and walks into the kitchen to put it on a plate.

"Who's rubbed her up the wrong way?" complains Mr. B in a hoarse whisper.

Flo shrugs. "Must've been something you said," she chides, never one to take his part in a barney.

He throws me a questioning look and I don't see any point beating about the bush. "They buried one of her best friends yesterday," I tell him straight. "She's got a right to feel low."

Instantly I see his big moustache droop. Clams up for a minute or two, he does, and sits himself down without a word while I go and fetch the supper. We eat in silence, apart from Mr. B's lips clapping. The mutton's tough as old boots, but that don't put us off. Mr. B wolfs his down quick, but Ma's not eating much, and the mood is as miserable as a wet Monday. After we've cleaned our plates, Mr. B tries to lift our spirits. He pokes fun at his neighbors in Limehouse and tells us how his business is booming, and just when I think it's time his tongue took a rest, he puts his foot in it.

"So, the ol' girl had a good send-off yesterday?"

Ma sends him a sour look. I worry such thoughtlessness might bring on another of her attacks.

"Ain't you got no feelin's?" asks Flo, even though she's a fine one to talk.

Mr. B lifts both hands up and shows his palms, like he's surrendering. "Begging my pardon, ladies. No offense meant."

But Ma shakes her head and pushes herself away from the table. "Apology accepted, Harold," she tells him. "I'm not myself. I know it. None of us is." She looks at Flo and then at me. "Truth is, with all these killings, it's the ones that are left behind that suffer most, and seeing Mary Kelly's little boy at Alice's do, well, it just upset me."

Mr. B looks duly humbled. "Of course, Patience," he replies. He wipes his bushy 'tache with his napkin.

"Timmy was a credit to his mother, God rest her soul," says Flo, patting Ma's hand.

"That he was," I agree, thinking of the little lad, meek as a lamb by Alice's graveside.

Ma nods, too; then she lobs a grenade. "Such a pity it's the workhouse for him."

"*What?*" shrieks Flo.

"No!" I snap in disbelief.

I reckon you could hear our cries down the end of our road. Ma nods as the dust settles and I see her lips tremble. "Betsy

Ryder says she can't keep him no more and that he'll have to go to the workhouse."

I think of the ragged nippers I've seen from there. All skin and bone they are, with a haunted look in their eyes. "That's not right," I protest. It can't be, I tell myself, but then the worry that's been swimming around in my head, ever since I first saw the woman in black, springs to the surface. It's like she's got Timmy in her sights: first at the cemetery and then outside the lodging house. If the child's sent to the workhouse, where nobody cares for him, then I'll worry even more for his safety. Tom, Dick, or Harry will be able to whip him away. He'll be easy prey for any monster that wants a piece of him.

CHAPTER 10

Friday, July 26, 1889

EMILY

Reluctantly for many, and happily for a few, the London season is drawing to an end. In less than four weeks' time the glorious twelfth—that is the twelfth of August for the uninitiated—will herald the start of the shooting season. Grouse will be "fair game," we are told. This is when families of noble birth will move out of their London homes in Belgravia, Mayfair, and Knightsbridge and partake of the fresher air and bucolic vistas offered by their country estates.

Lady Theresa Burke-Mellor, the third Countess of Kildane, is one such. This morning we find her writing letters in the conservatory of the house in Ennismore Gardens that she and her husband, Anthony, have taken for the summer so that they can attend the various balls, concerts, and social gatherings the season has had on offer.

The conservatory has rather splendid views over the small

park and for that she is thankful. Even though the family seat in Ireland is drafty and damp, she does so miss the wide-open spaces and the verdant lusciousness of her native land.

Just six years ago, at the tender age of seventeen, she married Lord Anthony Kildane, one of the very few Catholic peers in the country. To date, she has not borne him any children, but until the heavenly Father sees fit to bestow upon her such blessings, she busies herself furthering her husband's political career and chaperoning young Catholic ladies. She also has every sympathy with the new suffragists and has entered into very lively correspondence with radical women from all over the British Isles. Since her sojourn in London, she has even attended a meeting where the speaker, a Mrs. Millicent Fawcett, proposed a formation of a large, national women's society.

Anthony has no objection to his wife exercising her intellect in this direction. She is, after all, a stunningly good-looking young woman, and her mind, he thinks, is surely better occupied with such matters than with her many male admirers. He smiles at the sight of her as she sits writing at the table. The summer sunlight shines through the glass panes, illuminating her auburn hair and making it shimmer like copper. He is dressed to go out. As soon as she sees his shadow thrown over her letter, she looks up.

"Off to the Commission again, Anthony?" she asks.

"Yes, my dear." He is not a very sociable individual, and rather dull, too, but all the entertainment he could ever really want is to be found at the Parnell Commission at the Royal Courts at the moment. His fellow Irishman and his legal team are proving as witty and surprising as any parliamentary debate. "You cannot be persuaded?"

"No, thank you," she assures him with a nod, even though she has more of a direct interest in the Commission than almost anyone else. That's because one of the victims of the Phoenix Park slaughter, which became the precursor to the ghastly Fenian bombing campaign, was none other than her dear uncle.

Thomas Henry Burke, the senior civil servant, who was felled alongside Lord Frederick Cavendish, was her father's brother. A more dedicated and dutiful gentleman would be hard to find. His murder has left a hole in her life, and even though the incident happened seven years ago, the countess still bears the scars. She fears if she attends the Commission in person, old wounds will be reopened.

"Of course," Anthony replies, touching her lightly on the shoulder. He appreciates her attendance might resurrect painful memories.

Her suffering is also one of the reasons she feels these ghastly Whitechapel murders even more keenly than some of her London-dwelling peers. She has been deeply troubled to read about the nature and extent of the victims' numerous injuries, so reminiscent of her own dear uncle's. The barbaric use of surgeons' knives, it seems, is something that the grisly episodes have in common.

A copy of the Times, held in her husband's hand, only compounds her disquiet. "Today's newspaper," he tells her, laying it down in front of her. On the bottom right-hand corner of the front page is an account of Alice Mackenzie's funeral.

"Thank you," she calls after him as he exits the room, even though she'd have preferred it if she hadn't seen a copy. It only reawakens thoughts that would be best left undisturbed, and in particular the ghastly slaughter of Mary Jane Kelly. The Irish newspapers had reveled in every disgusting anatomical detail, sensationalizing the murder of an Irish compatriot for days afterward. What few knew, however, was that the dead woman was also the sister of one of her housemaids at her Irish residence.

Last autumn, when Lady Kildane was about to leave for a short sojourn in London, the maid Patricia, known as Patsy, had prevailed upon her mistress to take a letter to her errant sister from whom she had not heard for several weeks. The countess had agreed and even tasked herself to deliver the missive in per-

son. When she'd acted on her promise, however, she was assured by the supervisor of the lodgings at Mary Jane's last known address that Kelly had not resided there for at least two months.

The news was received with consternation by the maid, and she subsequently begged leave from her mistress to journey to London herself to search for her sister. So desperate were her entreaties that Lady Kildane had not only consented, but had also paid the girl's fare and given her money for food and accommodations. When she did not return to Ireland on the appointed boat, nor on subsequent vessels, the countess felt let down, to say the least. To date, it's been almost eight months since she's heard from Patricia, and she doubts that she ever will again. London's pleasures obviously proved far too tempting for her.

"Never trust the servants," Anthony had upbraided her. "Give them an inch and they'll take a mile," he'd reminded her in a self-righteous tone when the girl hadn't returned.

A few days later, however, when news of Mary Jane's murder made headlines around the world, Lady Kildane no longer felt betrayed by her maid, but fearful for her. She could only imagine how devastated she must have been at her sister's horrific death. Perhaps that was why she had not returned home to Ireland. Her shock had confused her, and her grief sent her mad, she'd supposed.

The countess had felt her grief, too. She'd made inquiries about the girl's whereabouts via English friends, but to no avail. That was why she was still intent on making inquiries about Patricia. Now that yet another unfortunate has been slaughtered—once again struck down in the same barbaric way that her uncle had been cut down, too—her anxiety has returned. Once again the knife had been employed; it was chosen because it's a swift and silent weapon, able to carry out executions with ruthless efficiency.

The very thought of it makes her shiver. She reaches for her writing case. Nestled in one of the compartments is a letter from me. *The countess and I had been corresponding for many months about the rights of women and social reforms. Naturally, I had read the harrowing reports of the terrible murders at Phoenix Park, so when she mentioned her loss in one of her letters, I offered my deepest sympathies. She found my letter of condolence so comforting that, thereafter, the tone of her missives changed and became even more intimate. From then on, our friendship blossomed. We corresponded regularly on several topics. The last letter I sent her made mention of the first of the ghastly murders in Whitechapel. She had replied a few days later, but it was not until several weeks afterward that her letter was returned to Ireland with the words* Gone away *scrawled across the envelope in an uneducated hand.*

At the time she'd thought it strange. She had hoped to meet up with a fellow campaigner with whom she'd enjoyed such intimacies, and she had vowed that on her next trip to London, she would seek me out. Her letter was, of course, addressed to me at my former lodgings in Whitechapel. It is almost a year since she last heard from me. My erstwhile landlady, the benign Mrs. Appleton, must simply have returned the missive to the countess without volunteering an explanation for my absence.

Although we never met in our earthly lives, I feel I know Lady Kildane well. I believe her to be a dynamic and determined woman. She will want to find out what has happened to me. She will not be fobbed off. I'll wager that very shortly she will be making the journey to Whitechapel, to my old lodging house, and she will ask Mrs. Appleton in person if she knows my whereabouts. Only then will the truth out.

CONSTANCE

Come the end of the day, Betsy Ryder brings little Timmy round to ours. Mr. B may rub Flo and me up the wrong way some of the time, but, Gawd love him, he's wangled it so that the Vigilance Committee will stump up two shillings a week for the boy's keep. I can hardly believe it, but little Timmy Kelly is to live with us for the time being and he'll be starting at the ragged school on Monday. I think his coming is just what we all need; it's like a ray of sunshine breaking through our gloom. My dear old pa used to say there's nothing like a nipper to cheer a place up, although at supper we did see for ourselves why Lizzie and Betsy Ryder found it hard to keep him. We swore that the little fella has hollow legs—the food he can shovel away! Before bed he downed two bowls of porridge and a doorstep of bread with dripping on.

Flo and me have stuffed an old sack with rags. I've even persuaded her to give up some of her filched handkerchiefs for Timmy's bedding. So he lays down in his makeshift cot on the floor near my side of the bed. I kneel down by him.

"You'll be all right, won't you?" I say, looking into his big blue eyes. There's that sadness in them I'd seen before, a sort of longing that tugs at your heartstrings. "Let's say a prayer, shall we?" I palm my hands together. He looks at me, all curious, but after a moment does the same. I bow my head. "Dear God, please bless Timmy's mum and our friend Alice Mackenzie. Let them find peace in your love and please watch over Timmy and deliver him from any harm. Through Jesus Christ, our Lord. Amen."

When I open my eyes, I see that the boy is just staring at me with a slightly bewildered look on his gaunt face. He doesn't know his age. He's the height of a four-year-old; only, we reckon he's at least six. I think he must have been taught how to pray because I know Mary was a left-footer—beg pardon, I mean a Catholic—although I can't be certain. His hands are still together and gently I uncouple them.

"Sleep well," I tell him, and brush his cheek. It's still soft to the touch and I suddenly worry he might think my chapped hands all rough. I snuff out the candle, but it's not yet fully dark outside, so there's a little light in the room and I'm hoping there's enough to stop him being afraid.

"Is the mite off?" asks Ma after I've tiptoed back downstairs. She's sitting by the candle, straining her eyes to mend one of Mr. B's socks.

"Yes. Good as gold," I reply, settling myself on the hearth rug, a book in my hand.

She beams at me. "You'll make a good mother one day," she says all proud, before she spoils it all by adding, "And Gilbert would make a fine father."

Flo looks up from her own sewing to catch me shaking my head. "Or maybe that fancy detective fella. Your little 'uns would never have to go hungry, then," she sniggers.

EMILY

In a room not far away, a young woman lies listless in bed. Her heart aches so much that rest eludes her. When she'd agreed to flee that night in fear of her life, she'd no idea how much it would hurt to leave her son behind. She'd escaped to the coast, to the marshes, and tried to settle there, but her heart remained in London. That's why, after seven months away, she'd returned.

The night sounds of Whitechapel have not changed in that time. The babies' cries, the persistent fights, and the banging of doors are the lullabies of the city, but now she must add her voice to them.

The slow, steady breathing of her lover tells her he is asleep, so she slides off the covers carefully and crosses the floor to where her clothes are folded on the chair. Without making a sound, she dresses swiftly, then creeps out of the door and into the night.

CONSTANCE

Flo and me both peek at Timmy just before we turn in. He's lying on his side, his hands folded under his cheek, eyes shut. We climb into bed as quietly as we can, fearful that the creaking springs might wake him, but they don't. We're both lulled to sleep by the gentle sound of his breathing.

That's why at first, when I see him standing at the window, I think I must be dreaming. It's the singing that's woken me: a sweet, high voice, like an angel's. I'd sat up in bed to find Timmy wasn't lying on the sack as we'd left him. Following the sound, I'd found him peering between the ragged drapes and out of the casement.

Carefully I move toward him. I think he must be sleepwalking. I know you shouldn't wake a person in such a state, lest they take fright and their heart stops dead. But as I pad nearer, I suddenly realize the tune that he's singing is familiar to me.

"'Only a violet I plucked when but a boy, and oft' times when I'm sad at heart, this flow'r has given me joy . . .'" come the sweet lyrics, and I suddenly feel as if I must join in.

"'But while life does remain, in memoriam I'll retain, this small violet I plucked from mother's grave.'" I mouth the words as I draw level with the window. Timmy seems transfixed, like he's looking into Mr. Winckle's pastry shop, so I, too, peer out between the curtains and follow his gaze through the open sash and onto the deserted street below. It's then that I think I spot someone in the shadows, flitting from under the gas lamp.

Timmy sees someone, too. "Mamma!" he cries. He balls his fists and slams them against the pane. "Mamma!"

"What the . . ." Flo stirs and sits up in bed.

I'm quick to explain. "He's had a nightmare, bless him," I tell her, putting an arm round the little 'un and trying to guide him back to bed, but he doesn't oblige me.

"I want my mamma," he cries as his face screws up. He bolts back toward the window. "Mamma!" This time it's a scream. I catch hold of his nightshirt and bring him toward me, gentle-like. The tears are flowing and he's stamping his feet on the floorboards.

Flo's getting angry, too. "It's enough to wake the dead!" she hollers before crashing back down onto the mattress and burrowing her head into her pillow.

"Calm down. Shush," I soothe. I stroke Timmy's hair. "You had a bad dream," I tell him, but he'll have none of it.

"Why can't I go with Mamma? I want to go with Mamma!" he sobs in shaky breaths. "She was there. I saw her. She was singing to me."

My own heart is breaking for the little lad as I try and hug him, but he just pushes me away and runs toward the door. Luckily, Ma's there to block his path. Candle aloft, she's come to see what all the fuss is about.

"Now, now, young man," she tells him gently, bending low and patting his curly ginger head. "Calm down now. Calm down, and if you do, you can have a cup of milk."

I stand beside him and I see his scowl melt as he looks up at Ma's kindly face. Her offer seems to do the trick and the lad quiets down. I lead the way downstairs and fetch the jug. Taking the cup in both hands, he gulps the milk down, then lets out a big breath.

"Will ya look at that 'tache," chuckles Ma, tracing the white line above Timmy's top lip with her finger. He almost manages a smile.

"He dreamed he saw Mary Jane," I whisper as we watch him devour a stale biscuit I found in the cupboard.

"Poor lamb." Ma touches her heart and her eyes go watery.

Ten minutes later, I'm tucking him up under his blanket on the sack again and he seems to settle down. I wish I could. The whole episode's set me thinking. What, or who, did I see in the shadows? Could the little lad really have been singing to his dead mother? Is there a chance Mary Jane's spirit might have returned to visit the people she cares about, just as Miss Tindall does? The thought of it makes me shiver, even though I know I shouldn't be afraid of a life beyond the grave. I close my eyes, but see only endless darkness stretching out in front of me. I finally drift off into a dreamless sleep.

CHAPTER 11

Saturday, July 27, 1889

EMILY

It is a fine morning and there is a gap in her busy diary, so Lady Kildane decides it would be a good day to call on a particular house in Richard Street. She orders her driver to take her there at noon.

The journey is actually much farther than she remembered. London is such a sprawling and, indeed, diverse city. Her carriage trundles along the elegant, yet teeming, streets of the West End to the Strand and from there down along Fleet Street toward St. Paul's Cathedral. The East End is, however, another country to her, a place of the utmost squalor and depravity, where poverty and disease proliferate.

She is herself no stranger to human despair. She has witnessed enough of it in her native Ireland. Her father has told her stories of Gorta Mór, or the Great Famine, when the potato crop failed and thousands died. He recalled the smell in the air that foretold the blight, and sometimes when he stood looking at the land without seeing it, he would lift his head, sniffing for a warning, for fear it might come again. In its wake, she'd seen with her own eyes children dropping by the roadside. Yet to her it seemed the population bore their poverty with complete resignation. They were deeply religious, and believed that a better life awaited them in heaven, but famine was different. It was a more malevolent, more insidious beast that gnawed away in silence from within, until the bones were bare. Famine was intolerable.

As her carriage passes the Tower of London and the Roman wall marking the old city boundary, Lady Kildane notes the streets begin to narrow and the houses appear more decayed. They lean drunkenly on each other. The painted shop signs are blistered, tiles are missing from roofs, and weeds grow through cracks in cobbles. The piles of horse dung that lie steaming in the street are twice as high as the ones in the West End, and the people who weave their way between them wear sludge-colored, ragged clothes. This is clearly a poor area.

She glances down at the address she holds in her hand. It can't be far now, she thinks. Sure enough, five minutes later, her carriage starts to slow and turns down an unprepossessing street that's barely wide enough to accommodate it. It comes to a halt and the driver jumps down from his perch and opens the door.

"Thank you, Mallet. I am looking for Number 24," she tells him.

Mallet points to the ramshackle row on the left as he helps the countess down the steps. "Just there, I believe, Your Ladyship," he tells her.

She is rather surprised at the nature of the dwelling, a boardinghouse it seems. It is tall and narrow, sandwiched between two equally tall and narrow redbrick houses. There is flaking paint on the door and the windowsills are rotting. A handwritten sign advertises a vacancy. From my letters she gleaned that I was an *educated personage who studied at Oxford. Such a humble abode does not seem fitting for an academic and a lively mind like mine, she thinks. Nevertheless, she knocks at the door.*

Mrs. Appleton opens it. It is more than a year since I saw my former landlady. It was she who was so generous to me in my hour of need after I lost my employ at the ragged school. She had been most attentive to me in my subsequent illness. These past twelve months have not been kind to her, however. She has more lines, is further stooped, and there is a sadness in her eyes when Lady Kildane tells her she seeks me and asks if I left a forwarding address.

"Did you write this?" asks the countess, waving the envelope upon which is scrawled Gone away, *in front of Mrs. Appleton's troubled face.*

She owns up. "That I did. Miss Tindall, well . . ." She shakes her head. "I fear that the good Lord saw fit to take her," she says, bunching up her shawl as if to protect her from further unwelcome onslaught.

Lady Kildane shakes her head. "Take her," she repeats. "You mean she is deceased?"

Slowly Mrs. Appleton nods her head. It's best to come clean, she tells herself. "Sad to relate she was killed. I didn't like to say. I . . ." Her voice trails off. This lady's inquiry has reminded her of something that she'd really rather forget.

"How very terrible," says Lady Kildane, genuinely shocked. "Do you know what happened?"

Mrs. Appleton sticks her head into the street and glances from left to right. She'd rather not talk about murder where everyone can hear.

"Wait there, if you'd be so kind," she bids her unexpected visitor. Lady Kildane begins to feel uncomfortable as she's kept loitering on the doorstep. She is glad that her driver is within plain sight. In a moment Mrs. Appleton returns with a scrap of paper that had been kept in an old biscuit tin for the past few months.

A flower seller had given it to her at the memorial service, telling her that if anyone were to inquire about Miss Tindall, she should redirect them to her at the address below.

The landlady hands the note to the countess. "This is all I've been given. I fear I can say no more." And with that, the door that has seen much better days is shut firmly in Lady Kildane's face, leaving her on the front step, wondering how on earth I met my fate.

CHAPTER 12

Sunday, July 28, 1889

CONSTANCE

I awake with thoughts of Timmy filling my head. Through bleary eyes I see him, still asleep, in his little bed, despite the racket from the bells of St. Jude's. He slept better last night. He whimpered and called out a couple of times, but he didn't get up like before, and for that, I'm most grateful. I'm planning to take him to the Sunday service with Ma, but when I come downstairs, I find her hunched over the table, all wheezy again.

"Why don't you stay here and look after Timmy today, Ma?" I suggest over tea. "It would be a shame to disturb his sleep, and you ain't feeling your best."

At first, I think she'll protest, but she just nods. "The Lord'll understand," she offers by way of an excuse, but she doesn't need one. I know the incense in the church will only irritate those poor lungs of hers, and Timmy's not used to sitting still and will only fidget. I'll wager Flo will be off to see her new man again, and won't be of any help, so it's agreed. I'll go to church on my own.

EMILY

In St. Jude's this morning, among the upright businessmen and their wives, among the black-clad widows and the righteous stalwarts, there is another celebrant who hasn't set foot in a church for a while. Detective Sergeant Thaddeus Hawkins sits on the back row, his hymnal open. While no sound emanates from his lips—by his own admission he has a terrible singing voice—he valiantly mouths the words to Psalm 23. For the past few days he has been thinking of the most discreet way to contact Constance once more. He is no longer at liberty to summon her to the police station. With Inspector McCullen now back in charge, he is being watched closely. Any false move will mean a reprimand at best and a demotion back to Whitehall at worst. Nor does he want to visit Constance at home. Idle tongues would soon spread the word that the Pipers were in trouble with the law again and her good character would be further besmirched. So he has settled on what he believes is the most sensible course: a Sunday-morning communion at St. Jude's.

At the end of the service, when the congregation starts to file out, he positions himself strategically by the main door, so there is little chance of Constance leaving unremarked. And there she is, looking most pleasing in her Sunday best, which is a blue skirt, linen jacket, and her button boots. He will make his move as soon as she walks past the last pew.

CONSTANCE

Gawd, forgive me, I was so distracted during the service that I couldn't tell you what the sermon was about. There's this dread that I'm carrying round with me. It's like a heavy weight that's dragging me down. I keep thinking on little Timmy standing by the window. He was so sure he'd seen his ma. I know little 'uns imagine things—fairies and goblins and the like—but I'm certain there was someone there under that streetlamp. I saw her myself. And the more I think about it, the more I'm convinced it was the woman in black again—the one I saw in the street outside Tenpenny's and at the cemetery.

I join the queue to leave my pew and move slowly down the aisle toward the main doors. I'm a little light-headed. It must be the incense clouding the air that makes me feel as if my mind is leaving my body. Stars suddenly dance in front of my eyes and the ground feels uneven. Putting my arm out to steady myself, I suddenly see a row of women I don't recognize. Some are tall, some short, some fat, some thin, but they're all dressed in black, and all have veils over their faces, as if they're in mourning. A shiver courses down my spine as, one by one, they start to lift their veils to reveal their faces to me. My mouth goes dry and I think I will fall as I see, quite clearly, that these women all have the same features: the pert nose, the clever eyes fringed by long lashes, the same face. They are all one. They are all Mary Jane Kelly.

"Miss Piper." A voice breaks through my terror and the spirits, for that is what they surely are, suddenly disappear. In their place are a few old women, Widow Gipps among them. I clamp my hand on my breast to still my thumping heart.

"Miss Piper," comes the voice again. "Are you unwell?"

I manage to lift my head, but my vision is blurry at first. I fear I must've fainted. I blink once or twice until the mist clears and I see a welcome face before me. "Thaddeus," I mutter, and manage a weak smile.

I catch his look and think he seems concerned for me. Finding me so unsteady, he offers me his arm and together we head for the side door, managing to avoid the vicar and the other church worthies who line up to greet the parishioners. As soon as we're outside in the light, I take in a lungful of air. Even the filthy grime of Whitechapel is welcome to me as I try and clear my head of the vision I've just endured.

"Forgive me, Miss Piper," says Thaddeus. He thinks he's the one to blame for unsettling me and he's gone all formal again. It's back to "Miss Piper," and that makes me sad. He leads me out of the gates and along the street as the rest of the congregation pours out of church. "It was not my intention to startle you."

I shake my head and carry on walking, my arm still in his. "Will you come with me to White's Row?" I ask him. What I saw in church has disturbed me. The creeping fear of something I don't understand has returned. I'm afraid for Timmy, too. I need to get back to check on him. Of course, I want to tell Thaddeus about what I saw; yet I don't. I hold my tongue for now, sensing he's the one who needs to unburden himself; otherwise, why would he seek me out at St. Jude's? I think he may need my help.

As we start to walk, he leans in a little, like he's checking we're not overheard. "I did not mean to alarm you, but I must speak with you on a matter of the utmost secrecy." His eyes bore into me and he's all serious. I've seen him po-faced before, but this time I sense he's in trouble.

I put my hand on my heart. "You have my word I'll not tell a living soul," I say, mindful, of course, to exclude Miss Tindall from my oath. What she made me witness in church will have to be consigned to a later time.

Thaddeus sighs and I feel his warm breath brush my cheek as we walk. "Inspector McCullen is back," he tells me.

I think of the crusty Scot who talks like he's got a biscuit in his mouth. I can tell he's not happy about it.

"What does that mean for you?" I ask.

"It means I'm a sergeant again," he says, but adds, "That's the least of my worries." He shakes his head, then stops dead to look at me straight. "I know I can trust you, Constance," he murmurs. It's strange hearing him call me by my Christian

name again, but the sound of it sends a little thrill right through
me. Suddenly I'm not just a lowly flower seller, but his equal. I
think of the times he has sought my help in the past, in the case
of the Whitehall torso, which turned out to be my own dear
Miss Tindall, and with the dead mites who were killed by that
evil baby farmer. He's placed his trust in me—and Miss Tindall,
of course—before, and now he's wanting to do it again. He
needs to get something off his chest.

"Of course, you can," I say. "What is it?" He believes in me
and in my special powers. How can I refuse? Then comes the
sledgehammer blow. "I know you have contacts," he tells me.
"Good contacts. People who do not feel comfortable talking to
the police."

Suddenly I feel all cheap—not his equal at all. I know he
don't—sorry, *doesn't*—mean anything by it, but I'd hoped
there'd be more to my help than nosing around in grubby tav-
erns or backstreets talking to crooks who might have heard
something on the sly. He wants me to grass on people, to be an
informer.

I'm silent for a moment. My heart's just dropped down to
the pavement.

"Well, Constance?" he presses. "Will you help me?"

I force out a reply, as if nothing's wrong. "If I can."

"You're sure?" he asks. Perhaps I wasn't very convincing,
after all.

"Yes, I am," I try to sound as if I mean it.

"I need you to ascertain if either Mary Jane or Alice had any
Irish friends or connections," he tells me.

So he wants me to do his spadework for him, like a proper
copper, I think. Because I'm a woman and an East End girl, he
supposes Whitechapel folk will be more likely to open up to a
pretty face. I'm only half listening to him as he asks me to talk
to this person and that, because I feel my steps are weighted
down by my fears.

"There's something I think you should know," I tell him quite sudden, breaking him off midflow. "Something strange."

"Oh?" My brisk manner surprises him.

"I've seen a woman. A woman in a black veil. Twice she's been lurking near Timmy, Mary Kelly's boy. Then last night . . ." I stop, fearing I'm sounding foolish.

"Yes?"

"Last night I think she might have been standing outside our house."

"Have you any idea who this woman may be?" Thaddeus asks with a frown.

I shake my head. "I don't," say I, not daring to mention I'm not even sure if she's real, "but it makes me think Timmy may be in danger. He's staying with us at the moment."

He nods. "I'd heard you've taken the child into your care. Is this why? Because you are concerned for his safety?"

"It is," I reply, relieved that we understand each other.

He looks at me straight. "Do you fear he may have seen his mother's killer?"

I nod, glad that our thoughts are running side by side. "And that he might have told Alice," I add. Remembering how I was warned off the other night, I touch my throat and his eyes travel to my neck.

"You were attacked?" His eyes are charged with shock as he inspects my bruise.

"I didn't see his face," I reply. "But he told me not to meddle."

"Your gift," he begins. He's regarding me differently; it's like he's looking inside me, as it seems only he can. "You've had an-other"—he casts around for the word—"another vision?"

I return his gaze, fearful that he will dismiss me. "I have," I mumble.

Yet, instead of a skeptical smirk, I see an understanding in his expression. "And will you tell me what you saw?"

So I do. And he listens intently as carts clatter past us and people walk by, many gabbling in foreign languages. All around is noise, but we don't hear it because we only have ears for what matters to us. We're surrounded by bustle and traffic, but we don't see it because we only have eyes for each other.

"And do you know what this vision means?" he asks me earnestly as we arrive back at White's Row. The sky has clouded over, but it feels quite warm. We are just about to turn a corner when I see, plastered on the side of a wall, in among the many torn old posters, a large bill. It's not jagged at the edges, like all the others, and must have been plastered newly, otherwise it would have escaped my notice. Thaddeus and me both stand stock-still as we read the six-inch-high letters: MARY JANE KELLY. Underneath are the words: *Madame Morelli, the famous medium, will summon her spirit.*

I look at Thaddeus, and he at me. I'm recalling the other time the old Italian charlatan held a séance at the Frying Pan pub. Got caught out she did when one of Jack's "victims" suddenly appeared to the audience, snagged her white sheet and scarpered, screaming off the stage. If she's a medium, then I'm the queen of England, but her shenanigans draw in the paying punters and earn her a pretty penny.

Thaddeus shakes his head disapprovingly. "Making capital out of such a heinous crime," he growls. He should know how heinous it was, and all. His gaffer summoned him to Miller's Court to see the carnage for himself. He still can't speak about what he witnessed in that room, and I notice the shadow of a frown settling on his brow, like a terrible memory has been dug up from the grave of his recent past. Something has stirred in his mind, but he's not the only one who's been pulled up short by the poster. As I stare at it, the letters loom large in front of my eyes. As we've walked back from St. Jude's, the thoughts that have been whirring away at the back of my mind, buzzing like bees in my brain, suddenly make sense. My vision of Mary Jane in church was Miss Tindall's way of telling me that the figure in black *isn't* her ghost. She's not a revenant come back to haunt us mourners or, for that matter, little Timmy. Underneath that veil of hers, there's a living, breathing woman. She's real, all right. The words crowd onto my tongue, even though I'm not the one who's putting them there. I know Miss Tindall is with me. I feel her presence and it's not me talking when I deliver the message that, after all that's passed, I never thought to hear. I look at Thaddeus, my gaze sure as an arrow, and I tell him what no one else would believe—what everyone else would think impossible. Mustering all my strength and conviction, I tell him straight, "Mary Jane Kelly is alive and she is among us."

EMILY

The die is now cast. Constance speaks the truth. Had she but known it, Mary Jane Kelly's secret has been hovering around her for some time, ever since that first sighting outside the ragged school. It has taken her a while to realize it, but now she has shared it with Detective Sergeant Hawkins, I cannot tell her what action to next take. She has to decide for herself which path to choose. She is aware that if whoever wanted Mary Jane dead knows that she still lives, then she remains in mortal danger. So, too, does her son. Constance's first priority must be to make sure the boy is safe. You see, as long as she lives, Mary Jane Kelly is a wanted woman, and her child can be used as a lure. Constance has to protect him.

CONSTANCE

Does Thaddeus believe me? I thought I saw a flicker of doubt, like a speck of dust in his eye. As soon as I told him, he was no longer what Miss Tindall might call a *confidant,* but a detective again. His face had hardened, his brow had shot up, his eyes had widened, and he'd said the words I knew he would say.

"You have proof that she is alive?"

I had to shake my head. Of course, I couldn't *prove* that the woman in the black veil who's been stalking Timmy was his mother, but because Miss Tindall had shown me that she was, I had a new resolve, and a new conviction that I wanted to share with him.

"Not at the moment," I'd replied to his question. "But I'll get it for you," I'd told him. And I'd meant it.

So that's how we'd parted, at the end of my street. Instead of bringing us closer, my revelation has pulled us further apart. The onus is now on me. I am to prove that the flailed corpse found at Number 13 Miller's Court wasn't Mary Jane's; that it was some other poor woman's, with neither friends nor family to remark her absence. Yet, as I'm trying to digest the thought, another one rises up from my gut. There's something even more urgent that needs my attention. As Detective Hawkins disappears out of sight, another panic seizes hold of me. It's the one I'd felt in St. Jude's and it starts rising again as I think Timmy might be in danger. As I approach our front door, the feeling grows by the second. So that when I walk in and find the house is empty, my nerves are pulled tight.

"Ma! Timmy!" I call out, but no one replies. I dart into the kitchen and back to the front room. Something's not right. A chair's upturned and there's a tablecloth in a crumpled heap just by it. Someone who shouldn't have been here was here. Fear grips my throat. "Ma!" I cry out again. My hands clamp onto my face as I think what to do next. "Miss Tindall! Miss Tindall!" I mouth as I stand in the center of the room, trying to understand what's just happened.

Suddenly I hear a noise, footsteps from the yard. Rushing to the back door, I fling it open to find . . .

"Hello, Con love," Ma greets me. Timmy is by her side, fastening his trousers.

I let out a long sigh. "Thank God you're safe," I say, looking at the little nipper.

"Just needed a Jimmy riddle, didn't ya, love?" Ma says with a grin on her face.

The lad nods and then holds his nose, making Ma laugh out loud. I can't help but smile, neither.

"But the chair and the cloth," I protest, suddenly remembering my earlier fears. For a terrible moment I'd thought the boy might have been kidnapped, but I keep my worries to myself.

"We was having a game, wasn't we?" replies Ma, ruffling Timmy's curls. "In yer go now," she tells him as he scampers off into the room. When he's out of the way, she fixes me with a frown. "What's up? You're all on edge." She leans in. "You 'eard something at church?"

"No," I say quickly. Even if I told her about my vision, and that I knew Mary Jane to be alive, she'd never believe me in a month of Sundays. "I just think we need to keep an eye on the little 'un until he settles in, that's all, and when I saw—" I'm about to point to the overturned chair, but Ma cuts me off and lays a hand on my arm.

"Don't you worry about Timmy. He's as safe here as anywhere," she tries to assure me. I only wish I could believe her, just as I only wish I knew what his mother thinks she's playing at.

CHAPTER 13

Monday, July 29, 1889

EMILY

*O*n the corner of Whitechapel High Street, the newsboy's proclamation is the first Sergeant Hawkins hears of it.

"Ripper arrested! Read all about it!"

The youth is surrounded by clamoring people, pennies at the ready, eager to read the latest revelations. The detective is one of them. He grabs his copy and scans the front page quickly as he hurries toward the police station. He's barely had time to digest the facts before he arrives at work.

"What's this?" he cries. He brandishes the broadsheet before Sergeant Halfhide's bewhiskered face as he strides past the station desk. He does not wait for a reply, but instead plows on to Inspector McCullen's office. He raps loudly on the door.

"Come." The inspector sits at his desk, a mug of tea and a plate of toast at his side. "Ah, laddie!" he greets him cheerfully as he clocks the newspaper in the young detective's hand.

Hawkins does not stand on ceremony. His recent demotion does not sit easily with him and he forgets his place. "What is the meaning of this, sir?"

McCullen, who has been enjoying a relaxed breakfast, sits forward and wipes his buttery fingers on a nearby napkin. Taking the reprimand in his stride, he remains placid.

"Dunne fache yourself, laddie," he says, reverting to a native colloquialism to urge his junior to stay calm. "I thought you'd be pleased. A man confessing to nine murders in one fell swoop! Now, that's got to be good news!" He dabs his chin with the napkin.

The newspaper article confirmed what Hawkins heard a few days ago from his colleagues at the divisional headquarters: The man who has been arrested, seaman William Wallace Brodie, walked into Leman Street Station the day after Alice Mackenzie's murder and confessed to having committed eight or nine of the Whitechapel killings. When, however, his story was investigated, it transpired he was in South Africa during the "autumn terror," although his return to London came just two days before Alice Mackenzie's murder.

Hawkins waves the folded newspaper in the air in front of his inspector. "But, sir, the man's a drunken fantasist. He wasn't even in this country when most of the killings were done! And as for this latest . . ."

"Enough!" McCullen suddenly leaps up and snatches the newspaper from the young detective, slapping it down onto the desk. "Let the judge decide that, shall we? Brodie appears in court today. So we shall see, eh, laddie?"

For a moment the two men stand and regard each other in a silent battle of wills. Although McCullen has tried to control his temper, his throat has turned red with anger. Hawkins's face registers sullen resistance. He understands his superior's game. McCullen wants Whitechapel, and his masters in Whitehall, to know that now he is back in charge, no stone will be left un-

turned until Jack is caught. By giving Brodie's arrest credence, he is merely playing for time—stalling—but to what end? So that he can claim any subsequent credit? Hawkins thinks.

The young officer is puzzled and frustrated, but he also accepts he is relatively impotent. The one true weapon he has on his side is Constance Piper. He appreciates he will need the assistance of her extraordinary powers if he is to make any progress at all in this quagmire of deception and intrigue.

"Yes, sir," replies Hawkins finally, giving his green silk waistcoat an emphatic tug. "We shall see."

CONSTANCE

Timmy's holding my hand like he never wants to let it go. I feel his palm all clammy in mine, but at least it's clean. He's scrubbed up nice again and I'm glad he's got shoes on his feet, not like some of the other poor nippers. We're on our way to the ragged school in George Yard for his first day of lessons. He may be the one who's starting school, but I'm all jittery, too. I keep looking about me to see if—and I can hardly bring myself to say it—to see if Mary Jane is watching us, skulking round the corner. I'm not sure what she's up to, although I'm convinced she must be in some sort of trouble. What's more, if it wasn't her body they found cut to pieces in Miller's Court, then whose was it? No other gal's been reported missing to Old Bill. Thaddeus would have told me. If only I could speak to her, maybe I could help in some way.

We're close to the black courts and alleys where no one worth their salt dares venture, even during the day. The school is like a lifeboat bobbing on a sea of dirt and squalor. Grab hold of the rope it throws out and it can lift you up from the poverty and despair that's all round. Miss it and you'll drown in the murky depths. Leastways that's what Miss Tindall told me.

As we arrive, a band of scrawny scallywags give us the eye.

Their grubby cheeks are all caved in and their eyes are missing their childhood innocence. They've seen things, all right—things that no one should ever see, let alone a six-year-old. I look down at little Timmy by my side and wonder what his wide eyes have witnessed.

Miss Fanshaw greets us at the gate. She'll be Timmy's teacher. Knows me from St. Jude's, she does. A bit prim and proper, but she can belt out a hymn better than any of the other ladies, and her heart's in the right place. She's savvy about the little lad's background, too; like most others, she thinks he's lost his mum to Jack. I'm hoping she'll go easy on him after all he's been through.

"Well, good morning, Timmy," she greets him with a nod.

I thank her for taking him on such short notice, but she tells me to think nothing of it, and the smile she throws me when I say good-bye to Timmy tells me she'll take him under her wing.

As I leave him in the playground, I try to satisfy myself he'll be safe enough in school until I come to collect him later on. I glance about me. A few of the mothers gossip by the school gates, and a couple of men, too. I don't like to peer too close, but there's something about one of them that looks familiar. My main concern is with the woman in the black veil and there's no sign of her; so as happy as I can be that Timmy's taken care of, I set off toward Miller's Court. If Sergeant Hawkins wants proof that Mary Jane Kelly is still alive, I'm going to have to work very hard to get it for him. But the good thing is, I know just the place to start.

EMILY

For the second day in a row, Lady Kildane is out and about in a less than salubrious part of London. In fact, this vicinity, around Spitalfields, is markedly worse than the district she vis-

*ited yesterday. There are certainly more beggars on the streets
and the buildings are even more dilapidated. It is, however, a
relatively prosperous area compared with the squalor she has
encountered in Ireland. She has to keep reminding herself not to
lose sight of the fact.*

*Spurred on by a compulsion to find out how, and even why,
her erstwhile correspondent Emily Tindall met her untimely
end, she has ordered her driver to bring her to White's Row, the
address on the scrap of paper that the landlady thrust into her
hand. It is an unprepossessing street, quite narrow, and home to
a number of down-at-heel dwellings where, no doubt, many
dubious practices occur. There is also a rough-looking tavern on
the corner. Urchins play hopscotch on a patch of flat ground.
The dwelling she seeks is not even numbered. She has left it up
to Mallet to make inquiries of the women who sit open-
mouthed on their doorsteps, pondering who might be visiting
them in such a fine carriage. Once the information is obtained,
Lady Kildane asks her driver to accompany her to the door, such
is the nature of the street. At her request he knocks, for fear that
she might snag her gloves on the peeling paintwork. As she waits
for an answer, she sees a curtain opposite twitch. The neighbors
are obviously curious to see a lady in their midst, but the countess is clearly slightly uneasy about being in theirs. She glances
down at the torn scrap of paper, just to reassure herself that she
has the correct address. Mallet stands back to await a reply.
There is none, so he knocks again, slightly louder. This time,
however, his concerted rap engenders a sharp response.*

*"All right. Keep your 'air on!" comes the admonition from in-
side. After a moment or two, Patience Piper shambles to the
door. Her breathing is bad again and walking takes unwelcome
effort. She frowns when she sees such a well-dressed visitor on
her doorstep, although she's sure she must be one of Constance's
acquaintances.*

"Good day to you," greets the countess. She's a handsome

young woman, and underneath her fine hat, her bright eyes twinkle with a keen intelligence. "I'm looking for a Miss Piper. Miss Constance Piper. Do I have the right abode?"

Of course, Constance is not at home, because she is pursuing a line of inquiry that I planted in her head last night as she slept fitfully. I am glad to say it has taken root. She is retracing a journey she made early on that fateful misty morning in autumn last year, on the day of the Lord Mayor's Parade. She has replayed the encounter she had in her mind many times before. In a dream I had shown her Mary Jane Kelly's bloody chamber and she had heeded my warning and made straight for the lodgings in Miller's Court. She had drawn almost level with the entrance on the opposite side of the street, when she'd seen a figure appear from the archway, not ten yards ahead of her. A tall woman, wearing a brown linsey skirt and a red knitted shawl over her head, was walking away from her, not seeming to notice Constance's remonstrations.

"Mary!" she'd called, waving madly.

At first, there had been no response. At the second call, however, the figure turned and paused for a second to see who was hailing her, then waved back. Yet she did not stop. She simply hurried on toward Commercial Street. This behavior did not overly concern Constance at the time. She was simply relieved to confirm that her nightmare was clearly just that: a nightmare, not a premonition, as she'd feared. Afterward, she had turned to head toward home, when she'd spotted Caroline Maxwell, the wife of one of the lodging-house keepers. She had crossed the street to speak with her.

"Well, if it ain't Connie Piper," Mrs. Maxwell had greeted her, a basket of firewood on her arm. "What you doin' here at this time o' the mornin'?" she'd asked.

Constance had made up an excuse about retrieving a bonnet from Mary Jane so that she could wear it for the impending Lord Mayor's Show.

Mrs. Maxwell had chuckled and shifted her heavy basket to her other arm. "Oh, bless you, you needn't bother going down there. Mary's already up and out. I saw her not a minute ago," she'd reassured her, before adding, "Looking the worse for wear she was, an' all. She told me she'd 'ad a right night of it!"

Constance was glad to hear confirmed what she'd already thought she'd seen with her own eyes. She thanked Mrs. Maxwell for sparing her the journey into Miller's Court. Had she bent low through the archway that leads from Dorset Street, she would have been the first to see, through the broken windowpane, the horribly mutilated corpse on the bed. So for Mrs. Maxwell's intervention, Constance will be forever thankful. But last night when I visited her as she slept, I made her recall the subsequent inquest into Mary Jane's murder and Mrs. Maxwell's testimony.

I took her back to the time when, in the witness stand, the lodging-house keeper's wife had related how she had spoken to Mary Jane hours after she was supposedly murdered; how she'd remarked on the young woman looking the worse for wear, and how she recommended she take herself to the nearest bar for a drink. In reply Mary Jane had pointed to the pool of vomit on the ground and told her that she already had, but it had clearly not agreed with her. Mrs. Maxwell swore that encounter had taken place at least two hours after Dr. Bond estimated the time of death and subsequent mutilation had occurred.

So, who, you may ask, is correct?

CONSTANCE

I'm glad to find Mrs. Maxwell in. She's skinning a rabbit at her kitchen table. I call to her through the open window, and when she looks up, she smiles.

"Well, if it ain't Connie Piper! Come on in," she cries, standing and wiping her bloody hands on her apron. "How are you doing, my dear? And how's your mother? And what of that sister of yours? Up to no good again, I'll be bound!" she asks with a chuckle, thinking of Flo. "What a rum do she had earlier in the year." She pulls out another chair from the table. "Sit yourself down, won't ya?"

Her words come out in a flood, but when I tell her why I'm visiting, the deluge suddenly stops. For a moment her tongue turns to stone. She picks up her knife again and starts cutting the rabbit's feet. I know it's not been easy for her since the inquest. Her good name has suffered at the hands of those who sneer and say she must be going round the bend. When they talk of her in these parts, they touch their temples and roll their eyes. They say she's lost her marbles, and I have to admit that I doubted her myself.

Of course, I'd gone to the police and told them that I thought that I, too, had seen Mary Jane after the murder had supposedly taken place. That Scottish inspector, though, the one who's Thaddeus's boss, convinced me I was mistaken. The person I'd spoken with on that terrible morning couldn't possibly have been Mary Jane Kelly, I'd been told time after time. Against the might of the police and the surgeons, it was easy to question my own judgment.

Mrs. Maxwell, however, has stuck to her guns throughout and has paid the price for her pluck. I have to say I admire her for it. What's more, now I'm thinking she could be right. After what I've seen these past few days, it's dawned on me that it could've been Mary Jane Kelly I saw that morning and that Mrs. M saw her, too. We both saw her, even though Old Bill would have everyone think she'd been lying dead in that squalid room for a good few hours while Saucy Jack got down to his dastardly business.

"You see, I believe you," I say to her. "I thought I must've been mistaken before. The coppers told me I must've been, and all. But then I remembered you said how she was sick on the ground in front of you."

"As a dog she were," agrees Mrs. Maxwell.

"What if it weren't the drink that made her so, but what she'd just seen?"

Mrs. Maxwell looks at me odd, like she's back in Miller's Court. "The body, you mean?" Her face is full of surprise.

"Yes. Yes, I do," I say. "I . . ." My tongue suddenly cleaves to the roof of my mouth. Even now, I can barely believe it myself.

"Yes?" she wills me on.

"I think I've seen her again." My revelation comes out in a rush, and when I dare to look at her, Mrs. M's all flushed. She bites her lip and lets the knife clatter on the table before grabbing hold of my hand.

"Where, my gal? Where?" She's gasping like she's just run a mile down the Old Kent Road.

So I tell her about the woman in the black veil near Tenpenny's, then at the funeral, and finally outside our house the other night. "She's back, and I reckon it's Timmy she's after," I say.

Mrs. M's shaking her head, trying to take it all in. "I knew it. I just knew it," she mumbles over and over. "I knew she was in trouble."

"*Trouble?*" I repeat with a frown. "What sort of trouble?"

Her eyes clamp onto mine. "The company that gal kept," she begins.

"Yes?"

"She weren't no ordinary unfortunate. There were gents." She nods her head.

"*Gents?*"

"I know the quality came calling a few times," she says, arching a brow. "An American gent, there was. Looked like a military man with a big door knocker." She touches her top lip. "Then there was a good-looking young fella, with wavy hair, who came now and again. I'm not sure that fish porter of hers knew about him."

I immediately think of Joseph Barnett at Alice's funeral. His parents were Irish, I know that much, but he was as much of a

Cockney as me. He'd been living with Mary Jane, but they'd rowed a couple of weeks before she was killed. He'd moved out before the murder, but he'd insisted they'd remained friends.

"And can you tell me why all them toffs turned up to see the body in the room?" asks Mrs. M, shaking her head.

"Toffs?" I repeat.

"Some bigwigs—police chiefs and members of Parliament to boot," she tells me, jutting out her chin.

It's true I'd heard about the visits to the bloody room by the two officials from the Royal Ulster Constabulary and the postmaster general. Why were they so interested in Mary Jane? It made no sense. In fact, nothing was making any sense anymore.

"What do you reckon happened?" I press her.

Keeping her voice low, she tells me: "If you ask me, that girl was up to her neck in something bad. Someone was after her. Why, only the day before they say there was some gal asking for 'er."

"What girl?" I dive in.

"I dunno," she replies with a shrug. "Knocking on doors, askin' for her. Mary Jane had to escape before they got to her. That's what you get when you dance with the devil, as my sainted mother used to say."

"But if the body in the room wasn't hers, then whose—"

She breaks me off. "There's dark forces at work here, Connie. Powerful people who can snap their fingers and have the likes of you and me slaughtered in a trice. Keep your head down, my dear. Best not ask questions, eh, or you'll end up like the poor soul in Number 13, whoever she was."

EMILY

Caroline Maxwell is right. There are powerful people at work behind the scenes of this bloodthirsty tale. There are puppet masters and there are puppets. General Frank Millen was a pup-

pet that decided he wanted to cut himself free of his strings. You see he is the American, the former soldier with the large moustache, who was known to Lizzie Albrook, and for a while he held center stage in the show.

Earlier this year, on April 10, I was sent to the city of New York to the home of this adventurer, mercenary, and journalist. Granted, I was a very long way from my usual haunts in London's East End, but I do not choose where I am sent. Just why I was there only became clear to me during the course of the evening's events.

The general's study was on the second floor of his Manhattan brownstone. As was his habit, he had retreated to it with a pile of newspapers and a decanter of whisky. The Russian cavalry saber, the Salvadoran musket, and the framed commission from the Mexican Army, signed by President Benito Juarez himself, that hung on his walls told me he was once a fighting man. Yet even though his body was past its prime, he believed there was still a lot of fight left in him. And the biggest fight of all, he knew, lay just ahead.

I watched the general walk over to his desk. It was strewn with old newspapers and letters and the false starts of articles that ended life as scrunched-up balls. On top of this unruly pile was a telegram that arrived two days before. A British Royal Commission had asked if he might testify in a hearing that was gripping the nation. He'd already agreed to appear, on his own terms, of course. Ten thousand pounds was this maverick's price for standing in the witness-box. But just what he would say was anyone's guess. He was a gun for hire, a mercenary, but a mercenary with a cause. He disliked the English, just about as much as he'd disliked the Catholic conservatives whose brains he'd blown out in the Mexican civil war, but such a man had to do what such a man must do. So, would he declare that he was a secret agent with a mission to blow up Her Majesty Queen Victoria no less, or that Charles Stewart Parnell, the leader of the

Irish nationalists, was a revolutionary, who was plotting to overthrow the British to establish Home Rule in Ireland? Even he hadn't quite decided that evening, although he freely admitted that, either way, his evidence would be every bit as explosive as any bomb he'd ever planted.

Millen stroked his unruly moustache, swallowed a slug of whisky, and sat back in his leather chair. Taking a long, hard drag on his firecracker cheroot, he'd already decided to cross the Atlantic again. He was awaiting the call, which he expected to come any day now. He only hoped that by the time he boarded the ship for England, he'd be in better health. For the last few days he'd been suffering from acute stomach cramps. He'd endured a strange tingling sensation in his extremities and chest pains, too. From out of the blue another stab of pain doubled him over. The spasm lasted only two or three seconds, but it left him gasping for breath. The sweat broke out across his brow.

As he recovered sufficiently to sit upright once more, his watery eyes settled on a postcard he kept on his desk, although hidden from his family. It was a painting of a London street. A girl had gifted it to him. She'd been offered to him by one of the Irish gang during his last stay in England. Over the years there'd been many loose women, of course. By and large he'd found the Americans too brash, the French too lazy, and the Mexicans too violent. This London girl, however, had suited his tastes. What's more, she'd been born in Ireland and that's where her heart clearly lay.

As well as enjoying her body, he'd found her blessed with what the Irish call the gift of the gab, too. As she lay in his arms at his hotel suite, the colleen had regaled him with her memories of the Emerald Isle. In return, he'd told her how, a decade before, he'd planned to lead a fleet of rebel ships up the Shannon to liberate the city of Limerick from the occupying English. She hadn't believed him, so, to try and impress her, he'd told her more about his exploits. The worst of it was he'd said too much.

On those few nights they'd spent together, the drink and the intimacy had loosened his tongue. Revealing information about the plot to blow up the Lord Mayor's coach had been a huge mistake. He'd thought he could trust her. How wrong he was.

The week before, she'd rowed with her minder and threatened to warn the authorities. That's why Mary Jane Kelly had to die. He'd distanced himself from it, of course. He'd only read about the killing in the New York Times *when he stepped off the passenger liner four days later. Even he, a veteran of so many uprisings and bloody battles, had been disgusted when he'd learned the lurid details that so delighted the popular press. Was that really necessary? Her murderer certainly had a vicious streak in him, he thought at the time.*

Staring bleary-eyed at the postcard once more, he'd flipped it over to read the message, scrawled in an uneven hand on the back. He'd screwed up his eyes to focus on the writing, but the words appeared blurred. He'd tried to pick up his pen, but found he could not control his hand. "Oh, Mary Jane," he'd whispered just before another stab of pain robbed him of his breath. Her name was the last word he'd issued as his body went rigid. His eyes bulged in their sockets and slowly his skin turned the color of ashes. Within two hours he was dead, still clutching the postcard in his hand. The following morning his eldest daughter, Kitty, found him slumped in a chair at his desk.

CONSTANCE

I spend the rest of the day in a trance. I've a basket of blooms to sell as I stand on the corner of Whitechapel High Street and Commercial Street, but my mind's on other things. My visit to Mrs. Maxwell's has certainly set the cat among the pigeons. If the person we saw was Mary Jane on the morning of the Lord Mayor's Parade, then what made her so on edge? She wasn't a drinker, and yet she'd taken to the booze just before she disappeared. She'd made sure that Timmy was taken care of, too. The more I think about it, the more convinced I am that she's in deep trouble. I need to see Thaddeus to tell him what I've learned; only, now that his boss is back, I can't turn up unannounced at the station, as I used to. It'll only arouse suspicion.

I'm in so much turmoil that it's only when I hear the bell of St. Jude's toll three o'clock that I remember I'm supposed to be at the ragged school to collect Timmy. It's a good job my basket's almost empty as I race along the street and under the arch into George Yard. I can't be late for him.

My breath rasps in my chest and my legs feel like lead, but I'm just in time to hear the bell ring and see the first pupils start streaming out of the doors. Miss Fanshaw appears to shepherd the younger ones into the playground. I catch sight of boys in trousers with holes in the knees, and a few without shoes on their feet. Some are tall and scrawny, others knee-high to a grasshopper, but I'm on the lookout for Timmy. There are mothers crowding in front of me, so I'm up on my tiptoes, craning my neck like a nervous hen. And then I see him, and he sees me; running up to me, he puts his arms around my legs. Bending down, I give him a big hug.

"You had a good day?" I ask him.

"He's done very well," says Miss Fanshaw, sidling up with a smile.

"That's good to know," says I, standing straight. "Thank you."

"We'll see you tomorrow," Miss Fanshaw tells her new pupil.

Timmy manages a "Yes, miss," and then I take his hand to turn toward the gate. It's then that I see him: Joseph Barnett, in his plaid jacket and billycock hat, leaning against the lamppost on the opposite side of the road, smoking a cigarette. I don't know how long he's been there, but it's clear he's been watching us with his piggy eyes. I'm grateful Timmy doesn't spot him. I steer the nipper through the school gates and in the direction of White's Row. Whatever that man is up to, it's no good.

I hurry us home, not daring to look behind, in case he's on our tail. I'm fearful it was him who damn near throttled me the other night. Every alley we pass, every court we cross, becomes a trap. I imagine Barnett stepping out of the shadows at any time. If he's trying to scare me, he's doing a good job. He must know I'm onto something, even though I'm not sure myself what I've uncovered.

Ma's in the kitchen, cutting a slice from the loaf, when we walk in. It's good to hear the kettle's on, too.

"How was your first day at school, young man?" she asks Timmy, greeting him with a hug. But before the little 'un has a chance to answer, Ma has another question for me. "You all right, Con love. You're looking a bit peaky."

I shrug. "It's nothing that a cup of char won't fix," I reply with a smile.

She returns to the kitchen and puts the bread onto a plate for Timmy. "I thought it might be somefink to do with the lady," she says, watching the nipper tuck into the doorstop like he hasn't eaten for a week.

My head whips up. "*Lady?* What lady?" says I.

Ma hooks a glance over at the mantelshelf. "She left that."

I stalk over and pick up the calling card that's propped against the wall. It's fancy, with gilt edging and curly writing. It reads: *Lady Theresa Burke-Mellor, Countess of Kildane.* My jaw drops and that odd feeling returns, like someone's walked over my grave. I turn to Ma, then back to the card. The address is in swanky Knightsbridge, but it's the name that swims in front of my eyes. *Burke-Mellor.* I'm not sure how I know it, but I'm certain it should mean something to me.

"What did she want?" I manage to say.

Ma looks straight at me with sad eyes. "She came to ask about Miss Tindall."

My heart misses a beat. "But how . . . ?"

"She'd seen her old landlady."

It's then that I remember having left my address with Mrs.

Appleton. At the memorial service I'd told her if anyone ever came asking after Miss Tindall, she was to direct them to me. I'd written down my name and address on a scrap of paper.

"She wants you to call on her as soon as you can," Ma tells me, handing Timmy his plate. " 'Important,' she said."

An Irish countess who knew Miss Tindall, I think. It's like there's suddenly light at the end of a dark tunnel. Miss Tindall has guided this lady to me. She'll surely have new information that'll help us track down Alice's killer, and maybe even Mary Jane. Her visit is no coincidence. I just know it.

CHAPTER 14

Tuesday, July 30, 1889

CONSTANCE

It's evening and I'm upstairs readying Timmy for his bed when I remember Ma bought a nightshirt for him from the market earlier. It's still downstairs, so I go to fetch it. I'm not gone two minutes, but when I return, blow me, if the nipper isn't at the window again. A sickly feeling rises from my stomach. *Could Mary Jane be outside?* I wonder. But no. As I move closer, I see Timmy's not looking down at the street, like he did the night before, but drawing in the mist on the pane. His finger is tracing a big arc, but I don't stop him. I just watch until a moment later, he takes a step back to admire his artwork. I'm not quite sure what it is, although it's some sort of creature with big wings.

"That's a fine birdie," says I, all gentle like, even though I've no idea why he's drawn such a thing. He can't have seen much but an East End pigeon in his short life, yet this creature is a great specimen, with huge outstretched wings and a big hooked beak. At the end of its legs, when I look closer, I notice it's got talons, too. "What sort is it?" I ask, not really expecting a reply.

Timmy tilts his head, studying his masterpiece, then turns to me all earnest. "It's a phoenix, Miss Connie," he tells me, straight-faced. "It's a bird that can rise from the ashes of a fire."

EMILY

Detective Sergeant Hawkins finds it easy to spot Joseph Barnett. A stout fellow with a small, light moustache, he sits with two other men. One looks so like him, save for a large scar on his cheek, they are probably brothers. The other, in a cloth cap, has his back to me, although I can see he is broad with a bullish neck.

"Mind if I join you?" asks the detective, a beer in each hand.

The two other men rise and silently part as if a leper had just come among them. Hawkins is used to such behavior. Even when he is off duty, he wears his authority like a badge.

Barnett shrugs. "Please yourself."

The detective sets down the pint glasses and watches in silence as the porter slugs back his whisky before starting on the proffered beer without so much as a pause.

"You know who I am?" asks Hawkins.

"That I do," replies Barnett. "And I know you'll be asking more questions." He stares straight ahead as he wipes the beer foam from his lip. Hawkins detects a slight Irish accent, although given that Barnett was born in London, albeit to Irish parents, it is barely discernible and only truly manifests itself in his phrasing.

The detective is at pains to tell the porter that he is off duty. Pointing to his own pint to show that he's imbibing, too, he lets out a slightly nervous laugh. "Just a friendly chat, you understand."

What Hawkins does not let on, of course, is that in his metic-
ulous combing of his precious index cards—for obvious reasons
now stored in his room at the section house—he has discovered
something rather perplexing. His records show that despite
Joseph Barnett's history of violence toward Mary Jane Kelly, he
was only detained for a mere four hours after her murder. Nor
does it appear, from his statement, that his questioning was rig-
orous. In fact, Hawkins would go as far as to say it was down-
right shoddy. Indeed, there had only been four days from one of
London's—if not England's—most barbarous murders to the
close of the inquest. There remained several inconsistencies in
Barnett's statement. Incompetence or conspiracy? *Hawkins*
cannot be sure, but since his meeting with Commissioner Monro,
he is certainly erring toward the latter. It is his mission to pick
apart this tangled web of duplicity and concealment to expose a
possible connection to the Fenians, but he knows it will not be
easy.

The detective takes a gulp of beer. "I believe Mary Jane knew
the lately dead woman Alice Mackenzie."

"Why would you be thinking that?" *asks Barnett, his eyes*
suddenly narrowing.

"Because she tasked her to take care of her son should anything happen to her," *replies Hawkins, casually sipping his beer.*

"Did she now?" *The porter is a little ruffled.*

"What do you suppose she thought might happen to her? Why
might she have been nervous?" *Hawkins is starting to apply a*
little pressure.

Barnett pushes his hat even farther to the back of his head
with his thumb and clicks his tongue. "All her sort is nervous
with Jack about."

Hawkins acknowledges the truth of this with a nod, then
starts to pry once more. "Do you know if Mary Jane kept up her
Irish connections? Did she mix with any of her fellows, apart
from yourself, of course?"

Barnett seems put out by this last remark. "I'm born-and-bred London," he replies, jutting out his chin in a show of mock pride.

Hawkins smiles and counters, "But your parents fled from Ireland during the famine."

The porter clicks his tongue again. "You know an awful lot about me, Sergeant." He picks up his beer once more and takes a gulp, not meeting the detective's gaze.

"I make it my business to know, Mr. Barnett," Hawkins tells him, just the hint of a threat in his voice. His pint barely touched, he stands and tugs on his waistcoat. "If you think of anything that may be helpful to our murder investigation," he says, "you know where to find me."

CHAPTER 15

Wednesday, July 31, 1889

CONSTANCE

I pulled out my best togs this morning: the jacket with velvet lapels that Miss Beaufroy bought me and the button-sided boots that Ma and Flo so admire. I'm off to swanky Knightsbridge on the omnibus to meet this mysterious Lady Kildane. Last night, as I lay awake in my bed, I tried to reach Miss Tindall. As Flo drifted off into a deep sleep, I shut my eyes and pictured my dear teacher at St. Jude's and I started to talk to her, in a whisper, mind. I asked her who this countess was and what she wanted. I reckon she's an old friend of hers who's in need of help. After all, that's why the quality have sought her out before; Miss Beaufroy trying to find her lost sister, and Miss Fortune frantic about her baby, Bertie. It seems that fate can deal that sort, the higher sort, just as bad a hand as us from the lower classes, except they don't have to cope with the cold and the hunger at the same time. Facing up to problems with a full belly is a lot easier than on an empty one, I can tell you.

In my head I talked to Miss Tindall; only, she never heard me, or if she did, she never replied. So I remain in the dark as I climb aboard the bus. Smoothing my skirts and sitting with my back straight and my ankles crossed, I try and slip into the skin of a lady so that this countess won't regard me as a lowly flower seller, but more of an equal. The trouble is, I may be dressed in my Sunday finery as I head for the cleaner air and the grander houses of the West End, but there's still a black cloud hanging over me. I very much doubt that this Irish countess will do anything to lift it.

It's a short walk down a tree-lined avenue to Ennismore Gardens. The houses here are all very grand, with pillars on either side of their fine doors. I stand at the foot of the front steps. I need to put on my "hairs and graces," as Flo calls them. Not for me the tradesman's entrance. I was humiliated before when I tried to enter Brown's Hotel in Mayfair through the main door and was turned away by the doorman, but I'll not be put down again.

Taking a deep breath, I make ready to climb the steps, when I sense someone standing by me, close to my right shoulder. I turn, but there's no one there. There's a warm glow that spreads inside me, as if someone who cares for me is holding my hand. That's when I know I won't be alone when I meet Lady Kildane. Miss Tindall will be at my side, guiding my manners and my tongue. I stride up the steps and tug confidently on the doorbell.

When the maid answers, she doesn't look me up and down, like I'm something on the sole of her shoe. She smiles politely, showing her bucked teeth.

"How can I help, miss?"

I smile back, not a wide smile, mind. "Good morning," says I. "I believe the countess is expecting me. My name is Miss Piper. Miss Constance Piper," I tell her, my tongue suddenly smooth as velvet.

It's as if my clothes and my voice hold the key. The door is opened wide and I'm invited into a huge hall with a black-and-white floor, tiled like a checkerboard, with a grand staircase in the middle. It's hard for me to hide my wonderment.

"I'll tell Her Ladyship you're here, Miss Piper," says the toothy maid, dipping me a curtsy. I confess I have to fight the urge to curtsy back, but I do; and a moment later, I'm being shown into a beautiful, light-filled room, with velvet drapes at the long casements and more blooms in the vases than I've ever sold in a week. And right at the center of this heavenly vision is Lady Kildane. She rises effortlessly from the sofa to greet me, with the grace of a ballerina, and I see, to my surprise, that she's not much older than me. I was picturing a crusty old matron with a pince-nez and a walking stick, but I'd put her at about the same age as our Flo. She's a beauty, too, with lush auburn hair and eyes that twinkle, like one of Mr. Sickert's paintings of ladies I've seen in gallery windows. Her dress is made of cream silk, with an embroidered bodice, and at her throat she's wearing a blue velvet choker.

She quite throws me off kilter when she smiles and holds out her hand. Her arm peeps out from a three-quarter sleeve trimmed in lace, and it's white as alabaster. For a moment I just want to look at it; it's so long and clean and perfect. I was about to curtsy, but she is being generous with her greeting, so I reach out and we shake hands.

"Miss Piper," she says, pressing her other palm onto the top of the hand she holds so delicately. "Thank you for coming so promptly. Please." She speaks softly, but breathily, like she's talking through fluffy clouds. There's a smaller chair next to the sofa. She's gesturing toward it.

"Bring us tea, Kathleen," she orders the maid. "And some barmbrack, will you." She directs her look at me. "It's a traditional Irish tea bread," she explains, settling herself on the sofa opposite. Next there's a pause, more reverent than awkward before she tells me: "I was so very sorry to hear about Miss Tindall's"—she flounders for the word—"demise," and adds, "I must say I had quite a shock the other day when I learned of it from her landlady."

"It was a shock to us all," I reply, knowing that Miss Tindall is with me in the room and aware that her murder is a subject she wants avoiding.

"Did they . . . ?" the countess begins, playing with a jade bracelet on her wrist. "Did they apprehend—"

"No. No, they did not." I am abrupt because I'm told to be. I can tell Miss Tindall does not wish her death to be discussed in this way. She also gives me an inkling that even more pressing matters are afoot.

"I believe you know Miss Tindall through correspondence," I say suddenly, the words just filling my head and spilling out from my tongue.

Lady Kildane frowns. "Did she mention me to you?"

I smile. "Oh yes! Miss Tindall spoke very fondly of you. I know she admired your strength of character," I reply.

She tilts her head in thought. "She was a fine woman. I know I could've counted on her help."

"*Help?*" I repeat.

The countess shifts in her seat, as if she is sitting on something slightly uncomfortable. "I was looking for someone, you see."

"Oh?"

"A housemaid of ours, to be precise."

A clatter outside the door stops the countess midflow and alerts us to the return of the maid with a tray of tea and some sort of fruitcake. The countess clams up as tea is poured and served and cake offered. I take a piece, even though I'll have to force it down, for I'm so anxious to hear what this high-born lady has to say.

As soon as the door is shut, I prompt her to continue. "You were saying about the maid, Your Ladyship . . ."

"Ah, yes. Patricia had a sister, you see, who had moved away to live in London. As she was her only surviving relative, and was used to receiving weekly correspondence from her, you can imagine that she became anxious when she did not hear anything from her for almost two months. I had done my best on her behalf, making inquiries when I was here, but last November she asked me if she might travel to London to seek out her sister for herself." She lifts the teacup to her lips and takes a sip.

Suddenly cold creeps through my veins, as I recall Mrs. Maxwell's words about a girl asking after Mary Jane. "And you allowed her to come?" I ask.

"Yes," she says with nod. "I could tell she was so concerned for her sister's welfare, I even paid for her board and lodging."

"That was most generous," I hear myself say.

The countess shrugs. "Perhaps, although . . ."

I return my cup to my saucer to listen, just how Miss Tindall taught me. "Yes?"

"The girl never returned."

"I see," I reply. Normally, I'd feel almost ashamed for the fickle nature of some of my class who choose freedom over loyalty, but Miss Tindall has planted a question in my mind, and I know I have to pry deeper. "So that was the last you heard from Patricia?"

The countess shakes her head. "I fear so."

I frown. "You *fear so*?"

Breathing nervously, out of pursed lips, she tells me, "I worry that something may have happened to her."

"Why is that?" I press her, wanting to find out how much she really knows.

Her gaze is fixed on her cup and saucer as she places them onto a nearby table, looking at them very deliberately. I think perhaps she is playing for time, composing her thoughts, or maybe it's because she fears her hands may tremble at what she is about to say. Then she looks up at me. I see dread in her eyes.

"Because, Miss Piper," she tells me, "Patricia's sister was Mary Jane Kelly."

I try to swallow down my shock, but it's not easy. "Really?" There were no relatives at Mary Jane's funeral, except for poor Timmy, and no one has come forward since to claim her as their own. "But surely your maid was aware of her murder last autumn?" I can't hide my surprise.

The countess shakes her head and screws her handkerchief into a ball. "I have heard nothing from her since the murder. Of course, I have made inquiries, but to no avail. All these months I have heard nothing, but now, with this latest killing—"

I break her off. "Of Alice Mackenzie?"

She looks at me straight. "Yes. What if something has happened to Patricia, too?"

I think of the young girls, fresh up from the country, who couldn't tell a moll from a maiden aunt. They're easy prey for madams and pimps. Poor Patricia could've fallen into one of their traps while she was seeking out her sister. She's just as likely to be in a brothel as in a pauper's grave.

"I thought perhaps Miss Tindall might help me find Patricia. I know she worked with unfortunates."

Suddenly it's like she's shone a light in my head and my purpose becomes clear. This is why Miss Tindall wanted us to meet and she guides my tongue in reply, putting the words into my mouth.

"I can safely say she would have been sympathetic to your task," I respond. The countess smiles with relief. It's then Miss Tindall adds a phrase that I don't like the sound of one bit: "If Patricia is alive, we will find her."

The omnibus on the way home is so crowded that men are forced to stand. One thug treads on my foot as we take a sharp corner, but I'm so distracted I don't even feel the pain. I am numb to all around me, thinking about what Lady Kildane has just told me. Mary Jane's sister, Patricia, has been missing since she came to London last November. If, as I believe, the flayed body found at Miller's Court wasn't Mary Jane's, maybe, just maybe, it could've been her poor sister's.

My mind's still in a whirl as I traipse back down our row and suddenly see Ma's screwed-up face at the window. That rouses me from my listlessness, I can tell you. She's biting her lip and her look tells me something's happened—something bad. My stomach knots, but before I can open our front door, she beats me to it. Her head shakes from side to side, as if she were possessed.

"Connie. Oh, Connie love!"

"What's wrong?" I shut the door behind me, whip off my hat, and rush toward her just as her legs buckle beneath her.

"He's gone!" she cries as I drag her to the armchair.

My heart stops. "Timmy? Oh, God! What happened?"

She's gasping for breath through her words. "I went . . . I went to school, but . . . but they said he'd gone." She lifts her apron to dab her teary eyes.

"*Gone?* Gone where?" I fear I seem angry, but I'm just afraid.

"A man came. Said he was from an orphans' charity. He . . . he took Timmy with him." Her voice dissolves into sobs.

"Flo! Where's Flo?" I say, casting forlornly about the room.

Ma lifts her glassy eyes to mine as I bend over her. "She's out looking. Harold too. He's got the lads of the Vigilance Committee helping."

I think of Mr. Bartley's motley crew of cartmen and barrow boys combing the alleys and courtyards willy-nilly. They're well-meaning, but they've no clue where to look, and most of them have no idea what Timmy even looks like. "They're wasting their time," I snap.

Ma's head bobs up. "What . . . what do you mean?" she asks through sobs.

I remember Joseph Barnett's brooding figure outside the school yesterday. Up to no good, he was. "I know who's taken Timmy," I tell her as I stand up straight. "And I'm going to get him back."

I march to the door, grab my hat, and leave the house with Ma's stricken pleas ringing in my ears. "Be careful, love. Please be careful."

Down our row I march and onto Commercial Street. By now, it's early evening. The claxon's just sounded and the workers from the starch factory are pouring out of the gates. They're joined by hundreds from the brewery. I know where I'm likely to find that bastard Barnett. He'll be slaking his thirst in the Britannia already. I head straight for the pub, but just as I'm only a few yards away, I see a familiar figure up ahead. It's Flo and she's about to go inside the tavern.

"Flo!" I call, waving to her, but my voice is drowned out by the din of the workers and the carts and horses. She doesn't notice me, just disappears into the pub. I'm thinking she'll be asking the locals if they've seen Timmy. It was the place, after all, where Mary Jane used to drink now and again. I follow her inside.

The saloon is busy, packed to the gills with working men who've just finished their labors for the day, but amid the chaos I spy the red feather in Flo's hat. I trail her as she barges her way to the snug. I barge after her and straight into the path of some bloke.

"Mind 'ow ya go!" he growls, screwing up his ugly face.

"Sorry," I bleat, keen to keep latched onto Flo. I push forward into the snug, where it's a little quieter. My eyes soon catch up with her, but as soon as they do, I feel them widen in shock. I can hardly believe what I'm seeing. She's just found a fella who's snogging her like he hasn't eaten for a week. She doesn't seem to mind as he dives for her neck. Just closes her eyes, she does, and giggles, like she's enjoying it. Mind you, when she opens them again, the sight of me soon wipes the smile off her face. And when I see who's been slobbering all over her as she pulls away from him, I damn near think I'll hit the roof.

"What the . . . ?" I exclaim as Flo breaks free from the clutches of none other than Joseph Barnett.

At first, she's lost for words. Her mouth works like a fish, but there's no sound. Then, as I draw closer, she comes out with, "I was going to tell you, Con. Honest." She's all sheepish with me, but it's that no-good porter that needs to feel ashamed. I hook him with a glare. Yet there's no sign of humility on that piggish face of his as he greets me all snide. "Miss Connie," he says.

I try and swallow down my contempt. A stiff "Joseph" is all I manage before I turn instead to my wayward sister. "Ma said you were looking for Timmy," I say, unable to hide the scorn I feel.

"I was," she protests, then quickly corrects herself. "I am. I was just asking Joe here to help me." She tugs at his sleeve.

There's anger in my hard stare. I can't hold back my feelings any longer, so I come out with it. "I'm sure he can help you, all right. In fact, I'm sure he could take you to the boy straightaway."

Flo frowns. "What you on about?"

Joseph shifts on his stool and tugs at his jacket. "Hold up. You accusing me of kidnap?" he barks, pointing the finger at himself, like butter wouldn't melt in his mouth.

"I most certainly am, Joseph Barnett," I snap back. "I saw you watching us yesterday."

His mouth droops. "Ain't a man allowed to see his kid on his first day at school?" he whines, all innocent.

I think he's got some neck. "He's not your kid!" I protest. I know Mary Jane had Timmy when she was a respectable married woman.

Joe fights back. "I loved him as my own!"

But I'm a good match for him. "You've a funny way of showing it—leaving him in the care of others after Mary Jane was killed!"

Flo suddenly decides to come between us and break up our shouting match. "Stop it, you two," she tells us, flattening her palm against my chest and pushing me back. "We won't find Timmy in 'ere, and that's for sure."

For once, I agree with her. She's being the sensible one. I've let my anger blind me. It's clear Joe's not taken the boy. He couldn't have. I nod. "I'll report him missing to the police."

She nods, too, but all her reason vanishes in a flash as she gives me a wink. "Get that detective of yours on the case, eh? He'll soon find the nipper."

I feel like stamping on her foot, but I just nod and turn tail, knowing that, in Miss Tindall's absence, if anyone can find Timmy Kelly, it's not Flo or Mr. B's bungling boys, but Detective Sergeant Thaddeus Hawkins.

Sergeant Halfhide—Whiskers, I call him—is behind the desk at Commercial Street Police Station when I arrive; I'm all flushed and out of breath. I'm hoping I'll be able to cut through any explaining to him, but he's not a soft touch.

"Here to see Sergeant Hawkins, are we, Miss Piper?" he asks. There's disapproval in his voice. He's stroking his whiskers and giving me that haughty glare of his from under those bushy brows.

"There's been a kidnapping," I tell him, just to show him I'm not wasting anyone's time.

His look suddenly shifts from suspicious to earnest. "A kidnapping, eh?" He opens his big book and picks up his pencil. I fear he's not going to let me see Thaddeus, when all of a sudden a door opens and the man himself comes striding toward me.

"Miss Piper, I thought I heard . . ." He's eyeing Whiskers. "I'll deal with Miss Piper, Sergeant," he tells old Halfhide.

I'm that relieved as he leads the way into the interview room and, shutting the door, bids me sit. I know we agreed not to meet at the station anymore, and I think he seems a little put out.

"I understood we—" he starts, but I jump in straightaway.

"This is different," I tell him sharpish. "Mary Jane's boy's been kidnapped."

His eyes widen as he takes his seat opposite me. "*Kidnapped!*" he repeats.

"Taken from school by a stranger."

He thinks for a second. "Joseph Barnett?"

I shake my head. "No," I snap back. "I found him drinking in the Britannia. He'd been there all afternoon, according to the regulars." I don't mention it was with my sister. "It's not him."

Thaddeus looks grave. "Then who?"

I shake my head. "The man told Timmy's teacher that he was from a charity. He took the boy, no questions asked."

Thaddeus is up on his feet again. "Then we'd better get to the school immediately," he tells me. I rise, too, and when I follow him, he doesn't order me to stay away, like he has before. He knows as well as me that the boy could be in danger and that I may be able to help. The longer Timmy is missing, the more our fears will mount.

Mr. Antrobus, the headmaster, is still at the school. When we tell the secretary the purpose of our visit, we're shown into his study to find Miss Fanshaw there already. She's sitting, dabbing her eyes. She seems all in a blather. Mr. Antrobus rises so quick that those big jam-jar glasses he wears slip down his nose.

"I'm glad you've come, Sergeant," says he, pushing his glasses back up the bridge. When he catches sight of me through those thick lenses of his, he understands how we know about what's happened. He's all stuffy when he speaks, like he knows he and his teacher are to blame for letting Timmy go off with a stranger. Nevertheless, panic *isn't* in his vocabulary. He keeps his calm as he tries to talk his way out of the mess.

"Miss Fanshaw here tells me that it seems one of our pupils has been collected by an unauthorized guardian," he says, tossing a glance at the flustered teacher.

That's one way of putting kidnap, I think, but Thaddeus is all official. He checks his tongue and speaks with authority.

"I fear, sir, it appears so, and I wonder if Miss Fanshaw might be able to offer a description of the gentleman who took the boy."

The sniveling teacher looks up. Her cheeks are all blotchy and she seems smaller and more vulnerable than I remember. Her scrunched-up eyes widen with terror when she sees Thaddeus take out his notebook and hold his pencil at the ready.

"Can you describe him to me, miss?" he asks her direct.

She shoots a look at the headmaster, who nods, and when she speaks, her voice quavers in her throat. "I'm so sorry. I didn't . . . I mean, I never imag—"

"His description, please, miss," Thaddeus cuts her blubbering short. "His age, how was he dressed?"

She shoots a look at Mr. Antrobus, then clears her throat and starts again. "He was quite young. Late twenties, perhaps. He was dressed smartly. A brown jacket, a bowler hat, and his hair . . ."

"Yes?"

"His hair was dark and wavy. And quite long." She brings her hand to her collar to signify the length.

Thaddeus continues to write. "Any distinguishing features?" he asks.

She shakes her head. "I cannot recall."

"What did he say?"

She straightens her back, realizing this is the one area where her testimony might be of some help. "Yes. He told me he was from some charity."

A Cruelty Man, I think, remembering my previous dealings with babies. "The National Society for the Prevention of Cruelty to Children?" I suggest.

"Yes, that's right," she tells me. "I confess I'd never heard of it before, but he told me the boy was now in his care and that all had been arranged." She looks up at me. "He even mentioned you by name, Miss Piper."

"Me?" I blurt. I'm shocked.

"What exactly did he say?" asks Thaddeus.

Miss Fanshaw thinks for a moment as she looks at me. "I told him that I would have to check if he could take Timmy, but he said, 'Miss Piper is aware of the arrangement.' That is the reason I was convinced he was genuine." Her voice begins to go reedy again. "That is why I allowed the child to leave with him." I almost feel sorry for her as her shoulders heave and she dissolves into tears.

"Apparently, he headed off down the road in the direction of Whitechapel High Street, if that is of any use, Sergeant," adds Mr. Antrobus. "And now perhaps"—he rises, like he's had enough of us—"I think Miss Fanshaw here has been taxed enough, don't you?"

He asks the question in such a way that makes it difficult for Thaddeus to refuse him, and before we know it, he's walking us both to the study door. "I do hope you find the child," he says. "He has been through so much, what with his mother's murder, then this latest killing of the older woman."

"Indeed, he has," agrees Thaddeus. "But, rest assured, we shall make every effort to find him and reunite him with Miss Piper's family." He bows his head toward me as he speaks, and his look tries to reassure. I know he and his men will do their damnedest, but it still doesn't make me any less fearful for the little lad's fate. I can't help thinking Timmy knows something about the murders of both his ma and old Alice, and this knowledge is putting him in harm's way.

With good-byes said, we are marching out of the study, when suddenly I see Thaddeus's expression change, like he's remembered something. He pivots.

"There is one more thing, Miss Fanshaw, if I may?" he says, lifting a finger high in the air.

"Yes, Sergeant?" She looks up.

"Did this gentleman have any sort of accent?"

The teacher considers the question for a moment, biting her lip as she does so. "If I come to think of it, yes, Sergeant, he may well have spoken with an accent that indicated he did not come from London. From where, I'm afraid I cannot say, but possibly American or, then again, Irish."

I can see he makes a mental note of this. "Thank you, Miss Fanshaw. You've been most helpful," he says.

Side by side we make our way down George Yard toward the High Street. We're both so lost in our own thoughts that neither of us says a word for a while. I'm itching to tell Thaddeus what I learned from Lady Kildane, about Mary Jane's sister, but I daren't. Not yet. Not when, in his heart, I know he didn't believe me when I told him that Mary Jane is alive. When we do speak, our words collide.

"What will . . . ?" I begin.

"We have little to . . . ," he starts over me.

We both stop dead on the pavement and look at each other.

"I shall organize a search party, Constance."

I nod. "The Vigilance Committee is already looking," I tell him, knowing Mr. B is on the case.

Thaddeus manages a tight smile just before we part. "Please be assured that we will leave no stone unturned."

I try and smile back. I know he's sharp as a trouser crease, but even he has to admit that the Metropolitan Police don't have a very good record when it comes to solving crimes of late. It seems they need divine intervention to make any headway. As I walk back down our street without any positive news about Timmy, my feet turn to lead. It's going to be hard to face Ma again, knowing how bad she'll take it. I let myself in, to find Flo trying to comfort her. As I feared, her lungs are working like bellows.

"Anything?" asks my sister. I give her a dirty look, suddenly remembering the sight of her with Joseph Barnett in the pub. I can tell I wound her with my glare, but the shake of my head hurts both of them even more.

"Where is he?" sobs Ma. "Where's little Tim?"

"The police are on it, Ma," I cry, hurrying over to put a comforting arm around her. "Sergeant Hawkins is sorting out a search party."

Flo turns to me. "Your Gilbert Johns is looking, too," she says all smug. *"He's not mine,"* I want to scream. If she's trying to suck up to me after her show with Joe Barnett, she's just failed. She's only made me even angrier with her. I'm ashamed to say I can't even reply. I just nod to acknowledge that she's trying to be helpful.

"I'll make us a brew," she says, standing and striding into the kitchen. She needs to act useful. We all do at a time like this.

"Connie," wheezes Ma, reaching for my hand.

"Yes," says I, feeling so helpless. I hate to see her suffer so.

She lifts her gaze and her rheumy eyes focus on mine. "Connie, will you do something for me, love?"

My heart leaps. Right now, I'd fly to the moon and back for her. "Yes, Ma. Of course," I reply.

She licks her lips and wrestles with a breath. "Your gift," she says.

I frown, not sure what she means. "My *gift*?"

"You know, love. The way you see things. Feel things."

And then the penny drops. She wants me to channel Miss Tindall's spirit to see if we can find out what has happened to Timmy. I suddenly feel uncomfortable. My powers are not like that. They can't be summoned in the blink of an eye. I know she no longer believes in the likes of Madame Morelli and her cheap tricks. The old Italian's a charlatan, right enough, and Ma knows it, but she believes in me. She'd trust me with her life. How can I let her down? "You want me to hold a séance?"

Her hand tightens around mine and her eyes suddenly twinkle. "Would you, Connie? Would you for me?"

I would for her. Of course, I would. So I do, even though the notion grates on my nerves. I'm waiting for Flo to chip in with a sarky comment, but no. She seems to be up for it as well, like sitting down and trying to contact the dead is as natural as having a cup of tea. She closes the drapes and I draw up the chairs so that the three of us are seated round the table.

We all shut our eyes and I tell Ma and Flo to think of nothing but little Timmy. In my mind I'm also asking Miss Tindall to forgive me for what I'm about to do. I'm not supposed to contact her like this. She's the one who calls on me, but I'm hoping she'll understand. I go through the motions.

Flo's a bit fidgety at first, like her nerves are getting the better of her. We're holding hands, but I can feel her feet moving impatiently under the table now and again. As for Ma, she's trying to steady her breathing, but it's still as raspy as a blade on a whetstone.

"We are listening and waiting for any message about Timmy Kelly. We need to know if he is safe, or if"—my voice breaks at the thought—"if he has passed over. Miss Tindall, if you are there, if you can hear me, please make yourself known to us."

I hate myself for sounding so fake, like a magician that conjures up doves from thin air, when they're really up his sleeve. I'm not an illusionist. Everything I hear and feel from the other side is real, to me at least.

I take a deep breath and repeat, "Miss Tindall, if you are there—"

A sudden knocking smashes into my words. Flo screams. Ma jumps with fright. My racing heart leaps into my mouth before I hear the immortal words "It's me, ladies!" coming from the other side of the door.

I stand and stride angrily toward the sound. Mr. Bartleby's on the doorstep. "Never fear," he cries, barging past me like a cock o' the walk, not bothering to wipe the dirt from his boots.

"Oh, Harold!" chides Ma. She's annoyed by the interruption, but I have to admit that for once I'm grateful for Mr. B's arrival.

"No news yet," says he, striding over to her. "My boys are still out. We'll find the nipper, don't you fret." He pats Ma on the shoulder and she grabs his hand and starts to tear up again.

The rest of the evening is all comings and goings by the committee lads. We can hear people talking on the lane outside our house. Gilbert Johns drops by, but he's nothing to report. Flo and me go out for a bit, but it's no use. I'm boiling that many kettles for tea that by nine o'clock we've run out of coal for the stove. It's midnight before Flo suggests we all turn in, even though we know none of us is likely to get any shut-eye. I snuff out our candle and we lie there in the darkness, our frantic thoughts keeping us from sleep.

"So, when were you going to tell me?" I ask Flo as we lie, top to toe, in our beds.

Of course, I'm worried about Timmy, but my question to Flo has been simmering on my tongue since earlier in the day when I saw her with that worthless fool, Joe Barnett. She certainly can pick them, can my sister, but how she can even stomach the touch of a man who we know to have beaten up Mary Jane is beyond me.

There's silence for a moment; then she turns onto her back. "I suppose it's 'cos he makes me laugh," she replies.

"It's the port and lemon that makes you laugh, not him."

She props herself up on her elbows and looks down the bed at me. "Joe's had a hard time of it, and no mistake, he deserves a bit of understanding," she whines.

We've all had a hard time of it, I think, but I say, "Ma'll be none too pleased when she finds out." I picture the first meeting between the brash fish porter and our poor mother. I'll vouch she's bound to have an attack as soon as she sets eyes on the scoundrel.

Flo slumps back down again. "We'll see soon enough, won't we?" she counters, a smug note creeping into her tone.

"What do you mean?" I ask.

She coughs out an irritating laugh, like she knows she's got me beaten on this one, then she says, "He's coming for dinner on Sunday."

EMILY

Detective Sergeant Hawkins is true to his word. Overnight teams of officers scour the streets and alleys of Whitechapel and visit any addresses suspected of housing children for nefarious purposes. His constables nudge rough sleepers under barrows and peer into storm drains. They make inquiries down by the Thames, where the miserables huddle under bridges, and they call at the infirmaries and workhouses in the district. All to no avail. A small boy is missing? There are dozens who vanish into thin air every day. People may shake their heads and look worried when asked if they've seen Timmy Kelly, but they'll all have forgotten about him tomorrow.

Poor Constance is obviously beside herself. She and her mother are suffering cruelly with the boy's disappearance. But they need not fear. His seeming "abduction" was nothing of the sort. The truth is, Mary Jane Kelly's young son is not lost at all. Nor has he fallen prey to the criminal gangs that comb the city of London looking for new members. He is safe and with someone who loves him very much. In a cramped and damp room a stone's throw from the London Hospital, off Whitechapel High Street, and not a mile away from the Britannia public house, Timmy Kelly is sleeping soundly next to his recently resurrected mother.

The reunion, a few hours ago, was a scene so touching that it would have moistened even the most arid of eyes. Amid a torrent of joyful tears, Mary Jane's arms were clamped around her son in a passionate embrace. She vowed that she would never let him go again; she would always be there for him.

"My darlin'. My darlin' boy," she'd cried, over and over, running her fingers through his hair and kissing his cheeks.

The little boy cried, too, overwhelmed by the occasion. Happy tears streamed down his face. "Mamma! Mamma!" he'd sobbed.

Watching this heart-wrenching tableau was the man who facilitated the emotional reunion. The moment of unfettered joy and tenderness between mother and child affected him, too. He was also forced to wipe away tears.

After what seemed like an age, Mary Jane had looked up to acknowledge his presence and to offer her gratitude. The man she'd met through Joseph Barnett and his Fenian friends had come to her rescue yet again. "Thank you so much, Sam," she'd said, reaching out to touch his arm, the arm tattooed with an image of a phoenix. "How can I ever repay you?"

CHAPTER 16

Thursday, August 1, 1889

CONSTANCE

The bells of St. Jude's cough out the hour as I push open the heavy church door. Overnight there's been no news of Timmy, so I've told Ma and Flo that I'm off, out and about searching for him once more. It was only a little lie. In truth, my head's spinning like a top and I've no hope of finding the boy until I arrange my thoughts after everything that's happened of late. Above all, I have to speak to Miss Tindall, and this is the place I'm most likely to find her.

I take a seat at a small side altar. It's quite dark. The sun's hardly ever strong enough to shine through the stained-glass windows, and the flickering candles dip and dance, casting eerie shadows along the walls and over the pews. On the altar is a big statue of the Virgin, holding baby Jesus in her arms. There's some of the congregation want her removed. They say she's too Roman, but I like her. She's got a kind face. She's smiling as she cradles her infant son.

It's here that Thaddeus and me agreed to meet when we parted yesterday. The police station is no longer a safe place for us to talk. But in the church we're far away from prying eyes and gossiping tongues, and, moreover, you won't catch Inspector McCullen stepping over the threshold. He's kept that William Brodie, the one who said he'd killed Alice, in jail on some trumped-up charge, even though it's been proved he's nothing but a barmy old drunk. The inspector's got something up his sleeve—I know it and so does Thaddeus.

I still haven't been able to prove that Mary Jane is alive. I find it hard to believe myself, despite my vision. But it's not just me that thinks it wasn't her they found in Miller's Court. Mrs. Maxwell, her old friend, is of the same mind. Of course, I've yet to convince Thaddeus that I'm right, but I'm sure my meeting with Lady Kildane wasn't an accident. It might go some way to proving my theory, too. If God works in mysterious ways, then Miss Tindall's methods are even more curious. I'm sure she'll be able to cast her light on the whole sorry show if I can only reach her. That's why, while I'm waiting for Thaddeus to arrive, I start to pray.

I settle down on the kneeler, clasp my hands, and fix my gaze on the statue of the Virgin Mary. Clearing my mind of all worldly troubles, I put my thoughts to Timmy. With my eyes closed, I picture him sitting in a chair by the stove at our home, warming his little feet, and I ask Miss Tindall to intercede with the Holy Mother to protect him wherever he is and to help us find him.

I'm not sure how long my eyes are closed, but when I open them and look up to the Virgin Mary's statue once more, something strange has happened. Her face has changed. It's not the pale plaster mask with the blue veil and the serene smile anymore. For a moment I can't quite believe it. It's Mary Jane. Her head's tilted toward the baby she's cradling; only, it's not the infant Jesus, but little Timmy. He's looking up at her, his bare feet nestling in the folds of her blue gown. Suddenly there's this feeling of love and joy that wraps around me. I'm no longer afraid for him. That's when I know he's safe, too. He's out of harm's way. For a moment I'm so happy, I think my heart will burst, until I remember my other woes. Timmy may not come to any harm, but does that mean Mary Jane is safe, too? I'm still in the dark when it comes to her. If she did escape the killer's knife on that fateful night, then could it be Patricia's bloody corpse that was found at Miller's Court? Did the same fiend butcher Clay Pipe Alice? My thoughts are still all jumbled and I find I'm as confused as ever.

"Constance," comes a soft voice behind me. In my prayerful state I didn't hear footsteps coming up the aisle. Looking round, I see Thaddeus and I'm so relieved he's come. I ease myself up onto the pew and he sits himself down beside me. His eyes flit to the statue of the Virgin and I follow his gaze. Only, now it's just as it was before; it's a plaster image of Jesus' mother cradling her baby son again.

"A dozen men are out searching for the boy," he tells me urgently. "I have—"

"Wait," I say in a loud whisper, lifting my hand.

He shoots me a curious look and reads the signs on my face. "Something's happened? You've had one of your . . .

I nod, saving him having to say the word "vision," which I know he still struggles with. "Timmy is safe," I tell him. "I believe he is with his mother, although I do not know where."

Thaddeus blinks and starts to shake his head. "First you say Mary Jane is alive, and now the boy is with her. You really believe . . . ?" He mistrusts me. My news, he thinks, is too far-fetched to be true. It belongs in the pages of one of the novels I read. "I very much hope that you are right, Constance," he says, his words couched in a long sigh. "Really, I do, but, as I've told you before, until I have proof, we detectives must pursue our own line of inquiry." There is a note of—what's the word?—*skepticism* in his tone. For all his seeming sympathy he's still a doubting Thomas. He'd be the first in line to put his hand in the risen Lord's side if he had the chance.

I nod. "I understand," says I. "I'm working as hard as I can to help you, Thaddeus."

A nub of unease fills the space between us, as if even though our bodies aren't touching, we're chafing against each other. That's when, in the awkward silence, my thoughts stray to the Irish countess. I think it's time I told Thaddeus that Mary Jane's sister has also gone missing.

"Does the name Lady Kildane mean anything to you?" I ask.

Thaddeus frowns as his memory spirals. "Yes," he says after a moment. "Her uncle was Thomas Burke, the Irish civil servant who was murdered alongside Lord Cavendish in Dublin." I can see his mind at work.

"*Murdered?*" I repeat. "Who? Who murdered them?" I ask, noticing his eyes have come out on stalks.

"A Fenian gang, back in 1882," he replies. "A group of Irish nationalists, who'd stop at nothing to get Home Rule for Ireland."

"And were they all caught?"

His face is suddenly urgent. "Most were. Five went to the gallows and eight to jail for a very long time, but the masterminds escaped." He searches my eyes. "Why? You have met the countess?"

Slowly I nod. Unknowingly, Thaddeus has just confirmed that my meeting with Lady Kildane must have been arranged by Miss Tindall.

"Yes," I reply. "Yes, I have, and she told me something I think you ought to know." That's when I relate to him the tale of Patricia and how she came to London to look for Mary Jane, but hasn't been seen or heard from since.

Thaddeus has been listening intently and I've barely finished my story when he suddenly rises to his feet.

"You're going?" I ask, perplexed.

He picks up his bowler and slides out of the pew. "Yes," he replies, all earnest. "Thank you, Constance," he says with a shallow bow.

I'm confused. "For what?"

He bends down again and leans toward my ear. "Your theory puts a whole different complexion on matters. Mary Kelly was Irish by birth. Alice Mackenzie was her friend and was living with an Irishman, too."

He's ahead of me in his theory, and that's for sure. I'm still not certain what he's driving at. My blank look floats up to his face and he shakes his head at me. "I am sworn to secrecy on the matter," he whispers. "All I can tell you is that what you have uncovered means that . . . ," he says, but then pauses.

"Means what?" I press.

"It means it's possible that Jack the Ripper is a Fenian."

CHAPTER 17

Friday, August 2, 1889

EMILY

*I*n the smoke-filled surroundings of the Richmond Club, Bernard Royston and Angus McCullen are deep in conversation once more. Their meeting has been arranged rather hastily in light of certain information the former has received. The men are sitting, side by side, in the book-lined reading room; each pretending to peruse a copy of a newspaper: Royston, the Times, and McCullen, the Police News. The smell of leather and tobacco hangs heavy in the stuffy air. Despite the heat, the windows remain closed so as to keep out the noise of the traffic from nearby Piccadilly.

There are only two other members about, seated sufficiently far away from them that they may speak in whispers and not be overheard.

Without bothering to lift his gaze from his reading matter, Royston leans over and says, "You need to take Hawkins off the Ripper case."

With an adept flick of his wrist, McCullen manages to fold a corner of his newspaper so that Royston is in his sights. "You think he may be getting too close?"

"Better safe than sorry," suggests Royston.

The Scot concurs. "If you think—"

Royston reaches closer. "I most certainly do." This time the newspaper is consigned to his lap as he moves in: "And there's that flower seller."

"The Piper girl?" McCullen raises a brow.

"I believe that's her name. She's in on it, too. She called on the countess." Royston harrumphs. "No doubt Her Ladyship enlightened her about Kelly's sister." He rustles his paper in a fit of pique.

"I see," McCullen agrees, loosening some phlegm at the back of his throat.

"And that'll go to Hawkins," muses Royston.

Another nod from McCullen.

"He's getting too close, and now that you've had to release Brodie, he'll become even more"—Royston searches for the word—"problematic." He peers over the obituary column to face the Scot. "Best put him on something that'll keep him occupied, but as far away from the murders as possible." He gives a self-satisfied nod. "There's certainly no shortage of crimes that need solving in your parish, what?" He lets out a chuckle that is rather too loud. One of the other members looks up from his newspaper and tuts.

McCullen shrinks back into his winged chair. He shrugs and purses his lips in a disgruntled show of annoyance, which is hidden by his broadsheet. "If you think it'll help . . ."

Dispensing with his newspaper shield, Royston makes sure he is not being watched. His yellowing teeth are suddenly clenched. "Kelly's close by," he tells him, suppressing his undoubted frustration. "You know it as well as I. Once we've disposed of her, then we can focus on getting Parnell behind bars."

*   *   *

Mary Jane Kelly is, indeed, close by, at least geographically speaking. She is to be found in a shabby rented room, in Whitechapel, although it is a world away from St. James. It is where she is hiding and where she has been expressing her gratitude to her son's rescuer in deeds, as well as words. Exhausted, Mary Jane lies in the arms of her hero in a bed in his down-at-heel lodgings. Together they have been through a great ordeal. She believes the worst is now over.

The man beside her is naked. His long, wavy hair is damp with sweat. The large tattoo of the bird that covers his right forearm glistens in the candlelight. The room is stuffy. There is little air, and the couple have not dared open the windows, for fear of being heard and discovered. Now that Timmy is back, Mary Jane will have to be doubly careful. Her son sleeps soundly, a few feet away on the floor, lying on an old mattress and draped in a blanket.

"It's going to be all right. Tell me it is, Sam," she purrs as her lover strokes her head.

The man—an American—wishes he could share her optimism, but he nevertheless makes an effort.

"We'll be away from here soon, my love," he assures her. "Just a few more days, then we'll have enough for our passage."

She lifts her head to gaze into his eyes and puckers her lips for a kiss. Entwining her fingers through his long hair, she pulls down his head so that his face meets hers. She finds his lips and they gently caress before she nestles against his shoulders and starts to trace the deep blue lines of the tattoo on his arm. "Like a phoenix, we'll rise from the ashes, eh?" she says before her tongue appears from between her full lips to lick the bird's head.

"Yes, we'll rise," he repeats, even though he knows there are so many obstacles in their way.

CHAPTER 18

Saturday, August 3, 1889

CONSTANCE

Timmy's been gone for four days now. There's been no word. Not even any reassurance from Miss Tindall. Despite my vision in church, even I am beginning to doubt that he's safe. We've had well-meaning people telling us this and that: They saw a young lad looking like him working as a pipe boy, or Mr. So-and-so has a new apprentice. However, they're all fanciful. Nosey Mrs. Puddiphatt's having a field day, of course. Rumors are running amok, sightings are ten a penny, and Ma's nerves are as tight as fiddle strings. There's still no sign of the poor little lad, and try as I might to reassure Ma that he's safe, I'm not convinced she believes me. Truth be told, we're all losing faith.

I'm glad Thaddeus seemed to think the information I passed on to him in St. Jude's was helpful, although I'm not really sure why. It was when I mentioned Lady Kildane and her missing maid that his eyes lit up. I'll wager there's something he's not telling me. But there's a thought that's been gnawing away at my brain since we went to the ragged school together to look for Timmy. It's something Miss Fanshaw remarked. As I recall, she told us the man who collected Timmy weren't from round these parts, the way he spoke. That he might have been American or maybe he spoke with an Irish accent. That's what gave me the idea.

I've heard it said that when you lose one of your senses, the others are sharpened to make up for it; deaf people notice more things going on around them, and then, of course, blind people, well, they see things with their ears. That's what got me to thinking about old Alice again.

The night she died, she was in the company of young Georgie Dixon, the blind boy who was at her funeral. I was there at the inquest when he took the stand to tell us all how Alice had called for him and taken him by the hand to a pub. He said it was next door to the Cambridge Music Hall on Commercial Street, although when Old Bill made inquiries, they drew a blank. They can't—what's the fancy word?—*verify* what he's said is true.

I know Georgie dwells in George Yard, so that's where I go. Lives with his mother, he does, although she works all day, so I find him sitting on his doorstep, a begging bowl by his side. It's not a bad morning and the sun's trying to break through the cloud. He's lifting his face toward the sky, hoping to catch the first rays, if they come, but he's wearing his dark glasses to spare us the sight of his eyes swiveling in their sockets.

" 'Morning, Georgie," I greet him.

I'm just about to tell him it's me, when he pipes up, " 'Morning, Miss Constance."

I'm impressed that he's recognized me after I've just said two words.

"How are you doing?" I ask.

"Not so bad," he replies cheerfully. He grabs hold of the door jamb to heave himself up, but I tell him there's no need to budge.

"Just passing, I am," I tell him casually, "and wondered if you'd heard any more about poor old Alice."

He shakes his head, all miserable. "Nah," he says, face like a flat fish. "No one will say they saw us that night. I'm not sure anyone even believes me."

"I do," I jump in, even though I know the coppers can't find out which pub it was where she's supposed to have taken the poor lad. "You remembered any more about the man who stood Alice a drink?"

"Nah." He shrugs. "I told them he sounded like he wasn't from round here, that's all. She asked him to buy her a drink and he did."

"Do you think she knew him?" I ask.

"That I can't say."

I'm just about to give up hope when, from his expression, I can see he's suddenly perking up. His nostrils flare as he cranes his neck.

"Roses," he declares. "They don't half-smell sweet."

He's following the scent from my basket, so I pick a bud without thorns, and fold his fingers around it. "Here you go," says I.

He holds it to his nose and breathes in the perfume. "That's real kind," he tells me.

"Think nothing of it," I reply. "You take care now, and if you remember anything . . ."

"I'll be sure to let you know," he says.

I turn to walk back down the road, when suddenly I hear Georgie's voice again. "Miss Constance!"

I turn back. "Yes?"

"There was something, miss."

"Yes?" My heart's suddenly in my mouth.

"The bloke in the pub. I just remembered, he didn't half-whiff."

"*Whiff,*" I repeat. "What of?"

"Of blood."

"*Blood?*" I wasn't expecting that.

"Yes. Dry blood. Dirt and old blood. Sort of like the smell in a butcher's."

The familiar knot of fear tightens in my stomach once again as I picture poor Alice's final moments.

"Did you tell the coppers about him?" I ask, walking back toward him.

He shakes his head. "They won't believe me," he says. "They think I'm making it up, 'cos they can't find the pub where she took me, but I swear it's the honest truth."

I bend low and kiss him on the top of his head. "God love you, Georgie Dixon. I know you're not telling lies," says I, and I walk back down the street, thinking I might just have taken a step closer to tracking down Alice's killer.

EMILY

Dusk descends on Whitechapel; it's a milky glaze that coats the sky and lengthens shadows. Detective Sergeant Hawkins leaves Commercial Street Station to head for his lodgings in the section house but a few streets distant. He has endured yet another frustrating day at his office. No one is any nearer, it seems, to finding evidence that will lead to the arrest of the Whitechapel fiend, and as days since Alice Mackenzie's killing slip into weeks, it seems that her murder will also be consigned to a file with the word Unsolved *stamped across it.*

Bidding adieu to the desk sergeant, he steps out into a warm evening. He sniffs the air. The smell of dung is particularly pungent, thanks to the higher temperature. It's almost eight o'clock as he strides down Commercial Street lost in his own thoughts. There are a few people about and the ubiquitous carts and wagons ply up and down the main thoroughfare, but he pays little notice as he turns down Cloak Street for the section house and, he hopes, some of Mrs. Moody's pie, which she so often leaves to warm for him. A sudden pang of hunger reminds him he forgot to eat anything all day, when, from out of the shadows in front of him, a man steps into his path.

"Detective Sergeant Hawkins?" asks a strange, nasal voice.

Hawkins stops dead and lifts up his head to see not one man, but two—one, quite tall, in a slouch hat, the other in an odd-looking cap—barring his way. He does not care for their mien. Their stances appear aggressive.

"Who wants to know?" he asks, drawing himself up to his full height. At the same time, he's considering just how he might dodge any imminent assault.

One of the men, the taller one with a close-cropped beard that hugs a pointed chin, suddenly reaches inside his coat.

A knife! *thinks Hawkins immediately, and he is just about to take flight when he sees that what the man is doing is nothing more than showing him a silver badge pinned to the lining of his jacket.*

"Walter Hahn, from the Pinkerton National Detective Agency," he says in an accent that Hawkins suddenly finds easy to place. "And this here is Detective Lewis Kowalski." He points to the short man at his side with the odd hat, and, it appears, a hostile attitude.

Feeling somewhat relieved, although not entirely convinced that his personal safety is assured, Hawkins nods. He is familiar with these so-called Pinkertons. They come from across the Atlantic. He knows that although the organization, this "agency," is a privately owned concern, it is hired by the United States government to cover the shortfall in its law enforcement requirements.

"If that's the case, then the answer is yes. I am Detective Sergeant Hawkins, gentlemen. But to what do I owe the pleasure?" he replies, doffing his bowler.

The detective's dry humor is clearly lost on the ill-tempered man, who scowls at him.

"*You trying to be clever?*" *he growls, clenching a toothpick between his flaccid lips. But Hahn, clearly the senior officer from his manner, manages a wry smile as he, too, removes his hat and holds it to his chest.*

"*Commissioner Monro requests the pleasure of your company, Sergeant Hawkins,*" *he replies.*

For a moment the summons shocks the detective. His brows shoot up. "*The commissioner,*" *he mutters, knowing that the matter must be of the utmost urgency, given the clandestine manner in which it is delivered.* "*You're working for him?*"

"*With him, Sergeant,*" *corrects Hahn.* "*Our cab is round the corner,*" *he says, gesturing with his hat.* "*We are to escort you to his residence.*"

Hawkins digests the news as the men lead him to the waiting hansom. To be summoned to the commissioner's own home for a meeting is, indeed, most extraordinary, but then again, he tells himself as he climbs aboard, these are extraordinary times.

As the carriage jounces through the rutted thoroughfares toward the more salubrious parts of London, Hawkins naturally tries to ascertain more information from the Americans. He cannot believe that Commissioner Monro, a stalwart policeman, who surely likes to do most things by the book, has engaged these men himself. For one thing, they do not seem very professional. The sullen Pinkerton with the toothpick has an irritating habit of fiddling with a coin he has retrieved from his pocket and is flipping it intermittently.

"*So, who has employed you, Mr. Hahn?*" *Hawkins asks as the dome of St. Paul's looms over them.*

"*We've been hired by the wife of a dead man in the United States,*" *comes the reply.*

"*Oh?*" *Hawkins begs the question.*

"*Contrary to what the federal police say, his widow believes her husband was murdered and has engaged us to investigate.*"

Hawkins nods. "*And are you at liberty to disclose the name of the dead man?*" *he asks.*

His request is met with a stern riposte. "*Only Commissioner Monro can tell you that, Sergeant Hawkins, if he chooses to.*"

Kowalski has been flipping the coin again. Suddenly he pipes up from the opposite bench. "*Heads or tails, Sergeant?*" he asks.

Hawkins is a little peeved by the man's childish behavior. "*I don't see . . . ,*" he snaps.

Hahn shoots his colleague an irked look. "*Cut it out, Kowalski,*" he chides. "*There'll be no winners in this game unless we all get our acts together,*" he says, looking pointedly at his English counterpart.

The commissioner's residence is a relatively modest affair—a Georgian townhouse in Vauxhall. The cab arrives in darkness and the butler shows the three men directly into the study. The detective and the two Americans file past as the manservant holds open the door. Monro is standing at the window to receive them.

"*Hawkins!*" the commissioner greets the detective. "*Forgive all this cloak-and-dagger stuff,*" he says, gesturing to a chair in front of his desk. A very large portrait of Queen Victoria hangs above it. "*Can't be too careful at the moment,*" he says with a tight smile. He is clearly trying to put a brave face on the difficult situation currently confronting the Metropolitan Police Force.

"*Sir.*" Hawkins nods as he takes a seat. The two Americans are directed to other chairs beside him.

"*So . . .*" The commissioner sits behind his desk. "*No doubt these two gentlemen have introduced themselves.*" His eyes slide from one Pinkerton to the other. Kowalski's attention, straying as it is toward the many volumes on the commissioner's bookshelves, is swiftly brought to heel via a sharp nudge to his side from Hahn.

Hawkins does not notice the reprimand. "*They have, sir.*" A hundred questions have been rising and whirling inside his *brain ever since being accosted by the Americans, but he knows it is up to his superior to make the running.*

"Good." Monro nods. "I shall fill in the details." He clears his throat. "Does the name Frank Millen mean anything to you, Hawkins?"

The detective scours his memory. "Millen," he repeats, mentally thumbing through his card index.

"General Millen, to you," pipes up Kowalski.

Hawkins ignores the interruption. "Was he the American mercenary who was due to give evidence at the Parnell Commission earlier this year, sir?"

The commissioner nods. "The general was a double agent," he begins.

"Ah, I see," responds Hawkins, fully aware that the department's spy network is extensive and, quite frankly, a law unto itself.

"He was in the pay of both the Fenians and Special Branch," Hahn comments.

"Indeed," says the commissioner, "but conveniently found dead at his desk just before he was to be summoned to London."

Unfortunate, indeed, *thinks Hawkins,* but for whom? *"And foul play is suspected?"*

Monro shrugs. "Not by the New York authorities. They discovered that Millen suffered from a chronic stomach complaint, although his family believe it was not the cause of his demise." The commissioner looks to the left. "Perhaps you can take up the story, Hahn," he suggests, addressing the senior Pinkerton.

The smarter detective clears his throat and narrows his eyes. His long, thin face is the sort that does not easily accommodate a smile. "When we looked into Millen's death, we uncovered several interesting documents among his papers."

"Oh?" says Hawkins, his gaze darting back to Monro.

"Letters from Whitechapel, Sergeant. Written cryptically to Millen and under false names, but nonetheless interesting." He

picks up an envelope, then drops it again. "From the postmarks found on correspondence at Miller's Court, we've ascertained an active Fenian cell is probably operating from somewhere in the East End."

Hawkins is staring at the pile of documents. "And you think it's possible that the Fenians wanted Millen dead before he could testify in London. They were afraid he might betray them?"

"That's the theory we're working on," ventures Hahn.

"And has any progress been made?"

Monro raises his hand. "Your eagerness is perfectly understandable, Hawkins. We all want to get to the bottom of this damned tawdry business, but you know this particular patch of the East End better than any of us, so I have decided to entrust you with the task of tracking down this nest of Fenian vipers before they strike."

"Me, sir?" repeats Hawkins. He suddenly feels his face flush and hears his heart pumping in his ears.

"Yes, Hawkins. You have shown yourself more than capable in the past in the case of the Whitehall torso."

"I'm flattered, sir," he replies. "And honored," he adds as an afterthought, before returning to the Fenians. "You think they are planning some sort of outrage, sir?"

Monro nods and defers to Hahn, who takes the reins. "Among them we believe is a certain Samuel Doyle, son of a surgeon implicated in supplying knives for the Phoenix Park murders. Instead of bedtime tales of knights and dragons, little Sammy was weaned on starvation and injustice. When he was fifteen, his family left Ireland for New York, and his pop enrolled him at the Brooklyn Dynamite School."

"The what?" Hawkins looks askance, first at Hahn, then at his superior, as if seeking reassurance as to the veracity of the last statement.

"I fear it's true," confirms Monro. "There exists a school for

dynamitards, just outside New York. As you know, after the earlier outrages this decade, British ports have been on high alert for passengers with American-style luggage." He fixes on the senior Pinkerton. "Perhaps you'd like to tell the sergeant more."

Hahn clears his throat. "The Irish rebels were sick of being mocked in the press over their bungled bomb attempts, so their head, a man named O'Donovan Rossa, hired a Professor Mezzeroff to teach volunteers how to make bombs on the British mainland, instead of having to ship them from the United States."

Hawkins frowns. "And I'm assuming these devices can be assembled from materials that are easily amassed."

"Right," agrees Hahn. "A clock, a percussion cap, string, a metal case. Simple."

Monro looks grave. "You see, Hawkins, it's all so terrifyingly easy with the right knowledge, and we fear the Fenians are planning other terrorist attacks, similar to the ones of a few years back." The commissioner rustles some papers on his desk and brings out a sheet. "We know, for example, that they planned to detonate a bomb on the route of the Lord Mayor's Parade last November, but that the plot was, for some reason, aborted."

This attempted outrage is news to the detective sergeant, but he does not stop to question.

"So we are racing against time," ventures Hawkins. The enormity of the looming challenge is threatening to overwhelm him. "Surely, the entire force needs to be notified about this, sir?"

Hawkins notes the look of unease that passes between the senior Pinkerton and Monro. "This is a Special Branch matter, Sergeant. No one in H Division must know, especially not McCullen. You understand?" asks the commissioner in a hushed tone.

"Yes, sir."

Leaning to his left, Monro unlocks his desk drawer and a thick file lands with a thud before the detective. "All the intelligence we have," he says, passing a hand over the unruly pile of papers. "It's at your disposal."

Hawkins eyes the folder, knowing that although it contains mere paper, it, too, will possess explosive characteristics.

"I am grateful for the information, sir," he tells the commissioner. He truly is, and he appreciates the secretive nature of the task, but he suddenly finds his gaze drawn to the portrait above his superior's head. Her Majesty suddenly looms large in his vision.

"As much as I'd like to give you more manpower, I fear that owing to the sensitivity of this matter, you really are on your own, Hawkins," the commissioner tells him. "I'm depending on you to see this through."

"You have my word that I will, sir," Hawkins pledges with a shallow bow. He is about to head for the door, when Monro lifts a hand.

"One more thing."

"Sir?"

"These Fenians are dangerous men. I don't need to tell you to be very careful."

CONSTANCE

John McCormack, Alice's old man, drinks in the Frying Pan on the corner of Brick Lane most afternoons, so that's where I'm headed. My mind's not on selling blooms. How can it be when so many questions are running helter-skelter through my head? I can't rest till I've discovered what's happened to Mary Jane and Timmy and who did for poor Alice.

I find John, as I supposed I would, drowning his sorrows, all alone, in the corner of the pub. He's a whippet of a man, small and lean, who wouldn't say "boo" to a goose.

"Mind if I join you?" says I, pulling up a chair.

Not even bothering to look up from his pint, he mumbles, "I ain't got no money."

I reckon he thinks I'm a brass nail, so I pipe up, "It's Constance. Constance Piper. I was a friend of Alice's."

That makes him look up sharpish and he comes over all embarrassed. "Sorry, love," he tells me. "I figured you wa . . ."

"Don't you worry," I reply with a smile to show no offense was taken. "I just thought you look like you could do with some company."

He nods and stares into his beer again. "I miss her, to be sure."

"We all do," I agree. I've bought myself a lemonade and take a sip. There's a soft silence that hangs between us. I don't think he'll mind if my words break into his mood, so I tell him, "I was talking about her, about Alice, with Georgie Dixon only yesterday." I think mention of the blind boy who was with his old lady the night she died might loosen his tongue.

John shrugs and manages a smile. "She had a soft spot for him, she did. She liked youngsters. Missed her own family and that's no lie." He takes a gulp of beer.

I nod, thinking of the sons she had in America. "She loved Mary Jane Kelly's boy and all," I tell him.

His reaction surprises me. His head whips up and suddenly he's all wide-eyed. "Timmy! Found 'im, have they?"

I shake my head. " 'Fraid not," I reply. He slumps back down, so I try again. "I know Alice was so fond of him."

"I 'ope he's not in no trouble," says John, his voice all quavery, like he's got something stuck in his throat.

"Trouble?" I repeat.

He regards me with glazed eyes. "What with his ma and that."

I bite the bullet and ask him outright, "Was Mary Jane up to something?" I say. "Was she in danger?"

He sniffs and shakes his head again. "I warned Alice. To be sure, I did."

I dip closer. "Warned her about what?"

"About getting herself involved in Mary Kelly's affairs. But she was a good soul and she loved that boy, she did. She'd do anything for 'im."

I think I'm finally getting somewhere. I know I have to tread careful, but the question needs to be put. "Timmy was with Alice that night, weren't he?"

John fixes me with a look that's suddenly switched from sad to scared. A pulse of fear appears to beat in his neck. His face wears a silent terror as he scans all around him, searching for any eavesdroppers. Luckily, there's only two old blokes propping up the bar.

"The night she was slain? Ey, he was," he croaks in a whisper.

I bite back my own fear. It's as I hoped. I'm thankful that the child was spared the sight of his mother being butchered, if she was. Being a witness would've put him in more danger than he might already be. "Did Alice bring him back to your room that night?" I ask gently.

He grunts, but keeps staring at the table, like his memory is playing out the scene in front of him. "That, she did."

"And he'd never stayed with you before?"

A shake of the head. "Never."

I swallow hard. I'm about to ask a tricky question, but it's an important one. "Do you think Alice might have known that something was afoot? Something bad?"

For a moment he's dumb, as if he's considering all the wickedness he's ever come across in Whitechapel, until finally he nods. It's a slow up-and-down of his weary head, before, nudging closer, he tells me, all confidential, "From that night on, she were never the same. Always restless and fearful for the boy, too." He sucks the air in through his jagged teeth. "I'm only glad she was spared knowing he's been taken."

I take a sip of my lemonade, just to show him I'm in no hurry. "You think she was worried someone was after him?"

His face suddenly lifts to meet my regard. "That, she was. To be sure, she was," he replies without a shred of doubt in his voice, as if he's never been more certain of anything in his life. He swallows down the rest of his beer, slams the mug on the table, and stands. It's like he's suddenly sobered up and regrets spilling the beans.

"Don't go," I say, looking up at him from my stool. I surely don't want to lose him, just as he's started to open up. But he seems resolved.

"I've said too much already, my girl," he tells me, and with that, he slaps his flat cap on his head and walks out into the warm afternoon. And me? I'm left to ponder. Why would Alice take little Timmy away from his home that night, and that night only, unless Mary Jane knew something might happen to her? Unless Mary Jane knew someone planned to kill her?

EMILY

"You wanted to see me, sir?" Detective Sergeant Hawkins has been summoned to McCullen's office.

The inspector is looking out of his window; his hands are clasped behind his back. "Yes, laddie," he says, turning.

Hawkins is nervous. He fears he may have been caught out. Was his encounter with the Pinkertons witnessed by officers the other night? If it was, and he was trailed to the commissioner's house, then his number is up. He's aware that his mission carries with it innumerable dangers; the greatest being, he is uncovered and the London Fenians are provoked into enacting an atrocity in retaliation.

At the inspector's bidding, the sergeant sits himself opposite, rubbing his clammy palms on his trousers. McCullen sits, too, with his gaze now locked firmly onto the young detective's face.

"*My, my, you look as though you are overdoing things*" is his first, most unexpected comment.

Unsure as to how to react, Hawkins sniffs and tries to loosen his collar with two fingers. He has, of course, been working long hours, but he had no idea that his labors were visible in a physical manifestation. "*I am simply doing my job, sir,*" he replies uneasily.

"*Burning the midnight oil, so I hear.*" McCullen picks up a pen and loops it through his fingers.

Hawkins frowns. "*There is much work to be done, sir,*" he counters indignantly. The sudden thought of an eye at his keyhole flashes into his mind. He worries his master is having him spied upon.

McCullen leans back in his chair. "*You always were conscientious.*"

Hawkins notes the worrying use of the past tense. "*And will always remain so, sir, to the best of my abilities.*"

The inspector nods. "*That's good to hear, Hawkins, because I've decided to give you a new assignment.*"

"*Sir?*"

"*Something a little less challenging.*" McCullen slides a brown leather folder across the desk. "*A bit of a respite.*"

"*Sir?*" repeats a confused Hawkins, opening up the file. "*But I'm fully engaged in my case, sir,*" he protests. Then, as if his superior needs reminding, he adds, "*The Whitechapel murders, sir.*"

The inspector coughs out a laugh. "*And I know, firsthand, what they can do to a man, laddie.*" He straightens his lips as he recalls his enforced period of rest. "*You've been trying to catch Jack for what? Eleven months now, is it? The task is taking its toll. Look at you! The bags under your eyes, skin as pale as pastry—you need a change of pace.*"

Hawkins suddenly finds himself feeling terribly drained, as if the mere suggestion of ill health has had an effect on him. "*A change of pace,*" he repeats. "*I don't understand, sir.*"

"*Read what's in front of you,*" *orders McCullen, gazing at the open folder, filled with recent report sheets.* "*There's more to Whitechapel than Jack, laddie. Take your pick.*" *He nods at the pages detailing various felonies and assaults.* "*I'm sure you'll find something to keep you occupied,*" *says McCullen with a disingenuous smile, as if he is bestowing upon his junior officer an immense honor.*

"*But, sir...*" *The detective is on the verge of protesting, when McCullen flattens his palm at him.*

"*You'll thank me for this, Hawkins. No more late nights, just good, honest detective work. It'll keep you busy enough for the next few weeks, then you can return to the Ripper case with renewed energy.*" *He leans forward with a caveat.* "*If, of course, we haven't caught the fiend by then.*"

The young officer knows there is more to this demotion than meets the eye. McCullen is up to something, he is sure of it, but he also knows there is no use in challenging his orders.

"*Very good, sir,*" *he says as the inspector shuts the folder and hands it to him.*

Dismissed with a nod, Hawkins tucks the papers under his arm, rises, and is heading for the door, when McCullen suddenly calls him back.

"*Oh, and, Hawkins...*"

"*Yes, sir.*"

"*If I were you, I wouldn't see that flower-selling friend of yours anymore.*" *The inspector delivers a rather suggestive wink.* "*It does your reputation no good to be mixing with her sort.*"

McCullen's advice hits the sergeant like a blow to his abdomen. Hawkins senses the hairs bristle on the back of his neck. His cheeks flush with anger. However, he resists the temptation to answer back. If he does, he knows he will expose both himself and Constance to accusations that might impede his investiga-

tion into the London Fenians. Constance will have to wait a lit-
tle longer for her honor to be defended.

"Sir," he replies with a nod. From now on, he appreciates he
will have to be even more careful in his movements.

CONSTANCE

I'm back flogging my flowers. Someone's got to earn a crust,
even though eating's the last thing on my mind right now. I'm
at the junction of Hanbury Street and Brick Lane. Elsa, the old
dear who's usually here, has gone down with something nasty,
so I've seized my chance to take a prime pitch. It's midmorning
and the lane's choked with traffic streaming in and out of the
Eagle Brewery. There's always the clerks and boss types, who'll
pay for a bloom to brighten up someone's day. I douse a rose in
cologne to make it smell more than it really does, and waft it
under the noses of passersby. When they catch a whiff, some of
them can't resist.

I've just scored another sale when I see a bloke in a bowler
crossing the street and making a beeline for me, like he doesn't
need any persuading to buy. It's only when he's a couple of feet
away that I realize it's Thaddeus, looking dapper as ever, this
time in a yellow waistcoat. He doffs his hat, but he's all stiff,
like he doesn't want anyone to know we're already acquainted.
I cotton on to his game and play along.

"A buttonhole, if you please, miss," he says, keeping po-
faced, then all cloak-and-dagger, he adds, "We need to meet urgently."

"What's happened?" I ask, selecting a bloom.

"I've been taken off the Ripper case," he mumbles.

Just then, I catch sight of a copper—I don't recognize which
one—plodding along the pavement just a few feet away. I still
my tongue until he's passed.

"*What?*" I can't hide my shock as I stick a pin into the rose's
stem.

"McCullen's told me to investigate less taxing crimes."

"Why would he do that?"

Thaddeus looks about him before he speaks, like he's worried we're being watched. "It's time I told you, Constance," he confesses.

"Told me what?" I damn near prick myself as I fiddle with the pin.

"That I'm working directly for Commissioner Monro."

You could knock me down with a feather. "*Commissioner Monro!*" I blurt, then realize my indiscretion. "Why?" I whisper.

He looks along the road in the direction of the infirmary as he speaks. "As I said, we need to talk, in private."

"I'll say we do," I agree, handing him the rose. "This one take your fancy?" I ask.

I watch him reach into his pocket for his tuppence.

"No," says I. "It's a gift."

He smiles. "I will find a way to repay you," he tells me, sending a tingle down my spine; then, from out of nowhere, he adds, "But I fear we can no longer meet at St. Jude's."

I was returning his smile, but his words have suddenly wiped it away. "Inspector McCullen again?" I say.

He nods. "I think he's afraid of you."

"*Afraid?* Of me?"

"You have hitherto made us police look rather inept," he tells me with a shake of his head. "He's ordered me not to see you again."

All of a sudden I'm feeling almost flattered that I'm seen as a threat; then the worry kicks in again. "What shall we do?"

He shoots back, "Can I come to your home tomorrow evening?"

I frown. There's obviously something troubling him and we need to get down to the business of detecting, but he's still set me on edge. "I'll be there," I tell him, adding: "But make sure no one recognizes you. I think of nosey Mrs. Puddiphatt. If she catches Thaddeus calling round late it'll be all over the street that

I'm in jail before the day's out. "Dress in workman's clothes and I'll tell Ma I'm teaching you to read."

"But . . ." he protests, all puzzled.

"And I'll make sure Flo is out."

"If you think it's really necessary."

"I do," I cut him off.

"Very well," he says with a sigh, doffing his hat. "Until tomorrow."

EMILY

London Hospital's Pathological Museum is a veritable treasure trove of body parts, and only a short distance from Whitechapel High Street. From deformed fetuses to tumors the size of footballs, all manner of human life—and death—is to be found here, preserved in formaldehyde or surgical spirit and arranged in glass jars for the education and edification of the medical profession. To this end, the museum works very closely with the hospital's mortuary, which is also where Detective Sergeant Hawkins is hoping to find a certain Fenian dynamitard.

You see, he is here by design rather than luck. Last night, as he leafed through the files he obtained from the Pinkertons and examined the information pertinent to one Gabriel Flood, he could barely believe his eyes. The name on the file may have been different, but there was no mistaking the face in the photograph: the piercing eyes and the flowing locks. More proof, if more was needed, was found in a handbill. Dated August 1887, it read: WANTED FOR CRIMES IN ENGLAND, Samuel Doyle, the notorious dynamitard, dead or alive. Reward $200.

There, staring out at him from a wanted poster, was the face of the young mortician who had assisted Dr. Bagster Phillips with Alice Mackenzie's postmortem. There was even mention of a distinguishing mark: *a tattoo of a phoenix on his right forearm.*

With mounting alarm he'd read that Doyle's father, Padraig, was the surgeon who'd supplied the knives for the Phoenix Park murders. The thought had struck him like lightning. The commissioner had told him a similar knife was found at Miller's Court. The connection was made. There was no mistaking it; Gabriel Flood and Samuel Doyle were one and the same. But how to investigate him without arousing suspicion? Then it had come to him.

Sifting through the various crime records in need of investigation that were bestowed upon him by Inspector McCullen, he'd come across the perfect excuse to visit the hospital: a rather ancient report of petty pilfering at the infirmary's mortuary. It's an ongoing problem; so habitual, in fact, no one has ever bothered to investigate it, until now. It suits his purpose remarkably well in light of what he has learned. So it is Gabriel Flood, also known as Samuel Doyle, who now brings Hawkins to the pathology museum, which harvests specimens from the mortuary. He intends to ask questions of the doctor in charge, a Dr. James Holt.

Hawkins has heard the rumors: Holt is a man fallen from grace after an unfortunate misjudgment with a scalpel as he performed surgery on a society heiress. The incident, it is said, drove him to drink—a probability borne out by the fact that it is not yet midday when Hawkins finally tracks down the doctor to the hospital mortuary, and smells alcohol on his breath. Nor does Holt seem particularly concerned when the sergeant reveals the reason for his visit.

"Pilfering?" he reiterates. "That comes with the territory, doesn't it?"

Holt, once a good-looking man, but now clearly addicted to alcohol as evidenced by his bulbous, veined nose, stands at one of the sluices in the large room. His dark hair is disheveled and his eyes are already bloodshot. He has just finished examining the corpse of a recently deceased patient and is clearly not giving the detective his undivided attention.

"Here, Flood," he calls to his wavy-haired assistant as he shakes his wet hands over the sink.

The assistant hurries over, towel in hand, and it takes Hawkins all his self-control not to handcuff his suspect there and then. The young mortician who aided Dr. Phillips at Alice Mackenzie's postmortem the other day is most certainly Samuel Doyle. The two men's eyes meet fleetingly before the assistant turns away and scurries off to busy himself with the cadaver on the table behind. It is enough, however, to confirm to the detective that he has nailed his suspect.

He switches back to the doctor. "We are obliged to follow up reports of criminal activity, sir," Hawkins points out.

Holt shrugs. "But the theft of the pocket watch was at least two months ago," he replies.

Hawkins nods. "I fear we are hard-pressed at the moment, sir, with the recent murders."

Holt, his hands now dry, nods his understanding. He walks over to where his jacket hangs on a nearby hook. "It was a relative who made the complaint, anyway. I merely passed it on. Such pilfering is regarded as one of the perks of the job for these wretches." He glances over to the assistant. "I'm inclined to turn a blind eye if a few trifles go missing."

The detective remains silent as the young man collects some bloodied dressings and leaves the room.

"Your mortuary assistants," Hawkins says as Holt picks up his case. "Do they not normally come from the workhouse?"

Holt slips an arm into his jacket sleeve. "Yes." Then following the detective's gaze toward the door, he nods. "He's an exception," he replies in a low voice. "Something in his past, I'm told. But I don't pry, Sergeant. We all have things we'd really rather forget."

Bearing in mind the doctor's own questionable history,

Hawkins raises a brow. "Quite," he replies, then pauses before asking, "How long has that man worked here, sir?"

"Flood?" says Holt, confirming Hawkins's suspicions. "I'm afraid I've no idea. Since before I started," he replies, reaching for his case, but his curiosity is now piqued. "You didn't come here to investigate a petty theft, did you, Detective? You came for Flood. He's in trouble, isn't he?"

"What makes you say that?" asks Hawkins.

Holt forces a smile. "You're looking at a man who's seen his fair share of it." He glances over to the door through which the assistant left. "I can spot it a mile off."

CONSTANCE

Today I've come to Billingsgate. You'll remember it's Joe Barnett's old stomping ground, but I know his brothers still work at the fish market and he's a regular round these parts, too. The more I think on it, the more I reckon he was the one who warned me off asking about old Alice.

Up early, I am, to arrive just as the big gong sounds across the Thames, calling all the merchants to market. Did I say "market"? More like a palace, and that's no lie. It's a fine new building, built in the Italian style, like the ones I've seen in art gallery windows, with a bell tower. It's a sight for sore eyes, I can tell you, but it's not so easy on the nostrils. My blooms would be lost in such a place. It don't half-stink round here. That's why I brought a load of oranges to shift, instead.

At first, I just stand on the quay and marvel. Boats of all shapes and sizes, and from all around this island, are moored up and being rid of their slippery cargo. Boxes full of cod from Yarmouth and Lowestoft, and baskets and hampers of sprats, and herrings and mackerel from the southern ports, are shifted quick as you like. Some look fresh and shiny, but it's obvious which ones aren't from their pong.

Carefully I lift my skirts and pick my way over the entrails and fish heads that slick over the wharfside. I don't relish the prospect of spending the rest of the day with fish blood on my hem, I can tell you. Inside, panniers are piled up for sale: plaice, bass, and all manner of flounder. There, amid the colonnades, auctioneers shout out the prices for the goods, and costermongers and auctioneers haggle and barter over the catches. It may only be early, but the rising heat is already making the smell worse, but it's the foulness of the language that turns it blue.

The porters in their strange, flat-topped bobbin hats are the worst offenders. They dash hither and thither along the slippery avenues between stalls, carrying crates on their heads. But what really gives me the creeps is that they're skilled in the art of boning and gutting, too; in other words, they're handy with sharp knives.

Up until just a few months ago, Joe Barnett worked here among this stinking market mayhem, although his light-fingered ways led to his dismissal. So he labors, now and again, with his brothers. Georgie Dixon couldn't tell me much about the man who stood Clay Pipe Alice a drink that night, although he did say he smelled of dry blood. That's what set me thinking. That is why I'm here in Billingsgate, to do some poking.

Of course, Joe's been questioned about Mary Jane's murder before, but he's as slippery as an eel, if you'll pardon the pun, and didn't give much away. He's been a free man ever since. He may have been born in London, but I know he still mixes with Paddies. It's a long shot, I know, but I can't ask Flo anything about him. According to her, he trumps perfume, but inside I suspect he's as rotten as a year-old halibut.

I wonder where on earth I'll find Joe Barnett among this teeming mass of people. As my old pa would say, I've got a tongue in my head, so I may as well use it, and I do. I ask around: An old fish-fag tells me to "go to hell"—if you'll excuse such language—then a porter, and finally a merchant who, in exchange for one of my oranges, directs me to a shop at the end of a row. I know I'm in the right place when I spot how the men at work outside stacking the crates all look alike. Peas in a pod, they are: Joe Barnett's brothers, all three of them with the same piggy eyes and stocky build.

This is one time when I don't need Miss Tindall holding my hand. You've got to be stern with men like these; show them who's boss and see who blinks first.

"I'm looking for Joseph," I call out.

The one nearest me, the one with a scar on his cheek, puts down his crate and looks me over.

"What's he done now?" he asks with a sneer. "Got you knapped, 'as he?"

The other brothers look over our way and start to crowd round. They're curious, not threatening. Even so, most girls might have been put out, but I stand my ground and take a deep breath, knowing there's a chance that what I'm about to say may go down like a lead weight.

"I were a friend of Mary Jane Kelly's," I say. In an instant their expressions change. Their faces turn to stone. They batten down the hatches, wanting nothing to do with me, like I've got the plague. One of them takes a step back. The others follow; then comes the warning.

Scar Face gurns at me and snarls: "If you know what's good for you, my gal, you'll not breathe that name round 'ere again."

EMILY

Samuel Doyle is worried. The visit from the detective has riled him. There was something about the policeman's manner, something in his look. He's been a wanted man long enough to know when his days are numbered. Eager to leave work as soon as he can, he locks up the museum's back door as the clock strikes six; he exits the London Hospital via a side entrance.

In the absence of the sun, the evening sky grows dim relatively early. Still, the weather has been quite temperate and the air is now thick with the grit and grime that seems to tarry at the end of the day.

Looking to his left and then to his right, Doyle steps out into a filth-strewn alley and onto the main thoroughfare. He is wary, glancing sidelong every few steps to ensure no one is following him. Every water barrel is a hiding place. Every coster's cart a shelter. Every roof a sniper's perch. There are those who would kill him without a second thought, and those who would kill him, only after he has done their bidding. Once he is exposed, he may as well pull the trigger himself.

This is why he is so wary. This is why his eyes dart from side to side as he walks. The trouble is, he does not look hard enough. Unbeknownst to him, he is being followed. A figure, lurking in the shadows, tracks him across Whitechapel High Street. Once he is safely over the road, Samuel Doyle zigzags through an alley and carries on.

A blind youth calls after him. "Spare some change, please, sir!"

An old woman offers him apples, but he has no time for them. Now six streets away from the hospital, he turns down a row of redbrick terraces and stops in front of the door of a modest abode. Throwing a nervous glance behind him, he fumbles in his pocket for the key, turns it in the lock, then enters. The door swings open into a cramped, dingy room. Plaster peels from the ceiling and there is black mold on the walls. The relief he experiences from a safe arrival makes him lean his head against the shut door, but the look on his face is anything but relaxed. Mary Jane Kelly can tell something troubles her lover.

"What is it, Sam? What's wrong?" she asks, approaching him with outstretched arms.

Pushing himself away from the door, he stands upright and strides to meet her, but instead of returning her affection, he uncouples her hands from around his neck.

"*You've got to get out of here, now!*" *he replies with a scowl.*

Plowing past her, he starts gathering up her belongings: a shawl from a nearby chair and a pair of stockings drying on a line by the hearth. He shoves them into a carpetbag that lies by the table and continues to scout around for more evidence of her presence.

"*Why? What's happened?*" *Mary Jane clutches Timmy to her skirts as he starts to whimper.*

A hairbrush and a pot of ointment are next thrown into the bag. Not bothering to face her as he collects the rest of her possessions that lie scattered about the room, he tells her, "*You and the boy, out now.*" *He flicks his thumb toward the door.*

Mary Jane reaches for his arm and tries to turn him round to face her as he marches over to a chest of drawers. "*Tell me, please.*"

He whips round, his eyes on fire. "*They're onto us.*"

"*Who?*"

"*The police. A detective was asking questions at the hospital today. I've got to get you away.*"

Timmy's cries become louder.

"*Away? But where?*" *asks Mary Jane, stroking her son's head.*

Following Doyle over to the bed, she watches him reach for her nightgown and stuff it into the bag.

He twists round. "*There's a shed at the hospital. They keep some medical supplies there. It's locked and I've got the key.*" *He walks toward her and fixes her with his large brown eyes. What he does not tell her is that he keeps his own* "*supplies*" *there, too.*

She frowns and screws up her face. "*You want us to go there?*"

"*It's no palace, but beggars can't be choosers, and it won't be for long. A couple of weeks at the most.*"

"*But what about Timmy?*" *Mary Jane glances down at her*

son, her arms on his shoulders. "He can't live in a shed for that time. He needs fresh air. And food." She strokes his head again. "How will we eat?"

Doyle takes a deep breath, thinking on his feet. "I'll bring you food. I'll visit every day, I promise. Just till it's safe, believe me. You and the boy are the most important thing in the world to me." He bends low and, gathering her face in his hands, kisses her long and hard on the lips. She feels herself dissolve into his arms; then, as if suddenly remembering what he is asking her to do, she pushes him back again.

"Is this the only way?" she pleads, searching her lover's eyes.

He nods. "I swear it is," he tells her, then holds out his hand to Timmy. "Come now," he tells the child. "We're going to have a big adventure."

CONSTANCE

It's all arranged. I know Flo is down the Frying Pan this evening to meet Joe and I've told Ma I'm giving a bloke from the brewery a reading lesson. She's chuffed when I tell her. "Your dear old dad would be proud," she replies, adding: "Better make myself scarce then." She's glad to take herself upstairs for an early night just before there's a knock on the door at eight. I answer to find Thaddeus dressed in a cap and a wool sack jacket. He's supposed to look like a working man, but he can't lose his gentleman's gait. Nor his manner. He doffs his cap and I let him in quick as I can, casting a wary eye up and down the street to make sure we've not be seen.

"I'm sorry about this, Constance," he begins, all apologetic.

"Never you mind," I whisper, pointing up to the ceiling, to Ma's room.

He nods his understanding and silently we get down to business at the table.

"We shan't be disturbed until eleven at the earliest," I assure him, but really I'm all aquiver knowing that he is going to tell me something of the greatest importance. He's about to share a very big secret with me, and my hands are damp at the thought of it.

Settling beside me, he angles himself toward me, so that there's only a few inches between our faces. "What I am about to tell you is of the utmost secrecy," he begins. His eyes twinkle in the candlelight. "I must have your word that you will not breathe a word to another living soul."

I think of Miss Tindall and wonder if he understands the meaning behind his words. "You have it," I tell him, knowing that my mentor will be sharing in our secret.

He clears his throat to say, "A few days ago I was summoned to Whitehall by Commissioner Monro. He has a theory that the Fenians may be behind the Whitechapel murders."

I think of what Thaddeus confided in me in church. "And now you judge it possible that Jack might be an Irishman, too?"

He nods his head. "It is not such a far-fetched notion, as you may think, Constance. There appear to be several links to the Irish cause that have been thus far ignored in the investigations. I have been given the job of rooting them out."

I take a deep breath. "So you're saying that the Fenians might be behind all the murders."

"Not all of them," he tells me. "But it may well be that these last two victims—"

"Mary Jane and Alice?" I break in.

"Yes. Disturbing evidence from America has emerged." He points to the folder. "I am asking you to examine these documents with me to see if you can throw light on anything. With Inspector McCullen back in charge, I cannot be seen to step out of line."

"I understand," I tell him. "You can count on me."

He smiles. "I knew I could."

We hold each other's gaze for a moment, until, a little embarrassed, I let mine fall onto the folder again and tuck a wayward curl behind my ear to hide my coyness.

"The file on the Fenians," he tells me. Wordlessly he slides it over to me and gingerly I open it at the first page.

The flyleaf is printed with the words *Metropolitan Police, Criminal Investigation Department.* There is a date: *June 1882– December 1888,* and across the page in large capitals is stamped in red ink the words *STRICTLY CONFIDENTIAL.*

I shoot an uneasy look at Thaddeus. "You're sure?" I whisper. I see him swallow, but he nods to let me know that he is. I lift my hands and poise them, like a priest over a saintly relic. Taking a deep breath, I turn the first page to see a handwritten list of what looks like documents; it's some sort of index of everything that's inside the folder and it all comes underneath the heading written in capital letters: *FENIAN ACTIVITY.*

I can't hide my surprise. "This is what you told me about," I say, keeping my voice low, despite wanting to shout from the rooftops. "The connection with Ireland."

Thaddeus nods. "This is why I couldn't show it to you in a public place."

"I'll say," I whisper. "Can I?" I grasp the corner of the first page between my finger and thumb.

"Go ahead," he tells me. "It's all the information that the commissioner has provided—papers, reports, newspaper cuttings."

A quick look tells me that someone, maybe Commissioner Monro himself, has underlined any possible Fenian links in green ink. The documents seem to be divided into letters from someone called General Millen and copies of reports into the Whitechapel murders. There's scrawl and initials and all manner of doodles that make no sense to me.

Thaddeus waves a despondent hand over the papers. "They contain mainly witness statements and postmortem reports on the Whitechapel victims that I've read a hundred times over," he tells me, hanging his head and letting out a long sigh. When his weary gaze rises again, it settles on me, like he's asking for my help when all hope is lost. "I need some fresh evidence, Constance," he tells me.

I look straight back at him. "Or is it that you just need to look at old evidence with fresh eyes?" I suggest.

As the night wears on, I wade through all the information that's been gathered about the Irish terrorists at work in London. Disbelief wraps itself around me as familiar places parade in front of my eyes: Buck's Row, Mitre Square. Familiar names too: Polly Nichols, Annie Chapman—all tainted by the dark dealings of these men. It's like a shroud of terror is hanging over the district. Then I see something else that pulls me up. I turn to Thaddeus and mouth the words, "New York."

He nods. "The American police are involved as well," he tells me. "They call themselves Pinkertons and they, too, are working in secret for the commissioner." Suddenly I'm sharing his huge burden and he sees the panic in my eyes. "I know it's a lot to take in."

We're sitting so close, his hot breath brushes my cheek. But I can only feel my head shaking. Despite Miss Tindall's help and her showing me all sorts of things that most people are blind to, I never imagined such a spiderweb of lies and deceit hidden so deep from plain view. Suddenly I feel like a fly caught up in it. All unawares I've flown into it and now I can't escape. But then the thought drops into my head—perhaps Miss Tindall puts it there—and I'm reminded of my reason for becoming involved in the first place. It was for the sake of Alice and for Mary Jane and little Timmy.

"So you think Mary Jane was caught up with these Fenians?" I ask softly.

Thaddeus looks at me, all intent. "I fear so."

"You have proof?" I hear myself say, knowing that I am mimicking his line of thought.

He sucks the air in through his teeth, like he's unsure about telling me something, but it only takes a second before he opens up. "A knife was found at Miller's Court," he tells me.

"And?"

"I have reason to believe there could be a link with the Phoenix Park murders."

Thaddeus's words come as a thunderbolt. "Oh!" is all I can muster at first, then follows the sense of betrayal. "You're keeping things back from me, aren't you?" I tell him, suddenly wanting to distance myself from him. "Didn't you trust me?" I ask, rising.

I'm about to walk to the window, but in my haste to stand up, I must have disturbed some loose pages on the table, and the strangest of things happens. From between the sheets a picture postcard floats slowly to the floor. Its descent is so gradual that I think it's being slowed down by an invisible hand. Mesmerized, I follow the card until it settles on the hearth rug. That's how I know I've been sent a sign. That's how I'm sure Miss Tindall is nearby. I sense her in the room. *She's here. I know she is.*

Thaddeus pays little attention to it, but I bend down, knowing it is important, although just how I cannot say. It must've been sandwiched between the larger sheets of paper and not properly clipped in place. The picture on the front is familiar. I've seen it before. "That's Wentworth Street in Whitechapel," I say.

Thaddeus leans over and he's hooked. "By Gustave Doré, a French artist," he tells me. "He painted a series of pictures of the East End to publicize the squalid living conditions of residents."

I flip the card over. The message on the back, written in a poor hand that is familiar to me, reads thus: *My Dear, Remember me when you are far away. These Irish eyes will always be smiling for you. MJK.*

Suddenly I feel the hairs on the back of my neck bristle. "It's her writing," I say, shaking my head. "It's from Mary Jane."

Thaddeus swivels back round on his chair and frantically scans the documents, trying to trace where the card came from. Halfway through the sheaves of paper, he finds an empty folder marked *Millen*. The card must've escaped from it, but it's where it was filed that's most shocking for us both.

"Do you know what this means?" he asks me, taking the card from my hand. "The Pinkertons found it in General Millen's office in New York."

Suddenly I remember my meeting with Lizzie Albrook in the Britannia. She spoke of Mary Jane having another man. *"Important. Swanky. Big 'tache. Used to be a soldier, I think."* I recall her exact words.

"Millen?" I repeat.

Thaddeus nods and rakes his hand through his hair. "Yes, the American due to testify before the Parnell Commission!"

It's only then that I truly realize how important the discovery of the card is. The obvious conclusion shocks me to the core. Could it really be that this Millen, this agent in the service of both the British government and the Fenian Brotherhood, was one of Mary Jane Kelly's clients?

It's a question I ask silently as I look into Thaddeus's eyes. It's normally me who knows just what he's thinking, but this time it's him who reads my mind.

"You're right. It seems theirs was more than a fleeting relationship."

"But it's not proof of it." I'm starting to understand how the law works.

"No." He brings me down to earth. "Although it's a start."

"And a motive?" I suggest.

"As I said," he tells me with a faint smile, "we'll make a good detective of you yet." His smile drops and he pauses, and I know there's something more on the tip of his tongue. "Constance," he carries on. "I need you to do something very important for me."

"What might that be?" I ask, knowing from his look that he's not asking me to go for a walk in the park.

"I would never normally ask, but . . ."

". . . But you don't have the men and you don't want Inspector McCullen to find out you're working for Commissioner Monro," I finish his sentence for him.

I think my words knock him back a bit, but he plows on, regardless. Even though I'm not quite sure what he wants me to do, I can glean from his earnest expression that it won't be without risk.

CHAPTER 19

Sunday, August 4, 1889

CONSTANCE

While Ma and me have paid our Sunday visit to St. Jude's, Flo's been preening herself at home. In between peeling spuds and setting the table, she's been in front of the mirror, adjusting her hairpins and touching up her rouge.

A few minutes after we arrive back from church, there's a knock at the door and my sister rushes to answer it. Side by side we line up, like a welcoming committee; only, I'm not sure how welcome Ma'll be inclined to make Joseph Barnett feel in our home.

So there he stands, all scrubbed up in his plaid jacket, and instead of fish guts he whiffs of some cheap cologne. As soon as he's over the threshold, Flo grabs him by the hand and drags him inside.

"Ma, this is Joe," she says.

Ma prefers to be a bit more formal, on first meetings at least, but this time there's no ceremony.

"Joe Barnett, well, I'll be!" It's hard to know if she's angry or happy, but she's surprised, and that's for sure.

For once, there's no cockiness in Flo's manner. She's nervous—I can tell—as well she might be, introducing our dear mother to a man who's known to be a woman beater and an all-round good-for-nothing. There's a pause as Ma considers Flo's new beau. Joe Barnett's reputation as Mary Jane's man goes before him; it's awkward. No mistake. Sensing that he's a hot potato we really don't want anything to do with, he nevertheless steps forward.

"Mrs. Piper," he greets her, thrusting under her nose a bunch of wallflowers he's obviously filched from some toff's garden. His piggy eyes slide everywhere, but on her face.

Ma nods, shoots a glance at Flo, then returns the greeting. "Thank you, Joseph, I'm sure," she says, sniffing the flowers politely. She's acting all wary. It's looking like I've been left out of the introductions, so I clear my throat noisily and Flo glares at me in return.

"And, of course, you already know my sister, Con," she says, stony-faced.

"Constance," I correct her; then I switch my look to Joe. "Yes, we've already met," I say with a barb in my voice.

Ma's gone to a lot of trouble for our guest. Before church she steamed a pudding, and Flo took a nice bit of beef to the bakehouse for roasting.

"Flo and me will see to everything," say I, taking the lead. "You sit down, Ma." So she settles herself at the table and invites Joe to join her.

"Bring us some stout, there's a love," she tells Flo, and within a minute or two, she's supping with Joe Barnett like they were old friends. I watch them as I mash the spuds, taking out my anger on them as I pound them extra hard. Makes my blood boil to see it, it does. I'm not sure if Ma's heard the gossip, but she's willing to give him the benefit of the doubt.

When we're in the kitchen, dishing up the dinner, I can't contain myself any longer. Joe's chatting to Ma as if butter wouldn't melt in his mouth. Flo catches them chuckling together.

"There's a sight for sore eyes," she says with a sickly smile as she ladles the gravy into the jug. But me? I'd rather stick pins in my peepers than watch the show Joe Barnett's putting on.

I just want to spew into it, if you pardon my French. Knowing how he treated Mary Jane takes away my appetite and makes my simmering anger spill over. "You can't have any self-respect," I say to Flo all of a sudden.

My words are so unexpected that she pours gravy onto the kitchen table. "Why you . . . ," she tells me through clenched teeth. "You're only jealous 'cos that . . ."

"Everything all right in there, my dears?" calls Ma.

"Yes," I reply quickly. "Flo's just had a bit of a mishap with the gravy."

I plonk the beef joint down into the dish. "You know he's no good," I mutter as I lift the meat from the stove and carry it through.

Flo follows behind me with the carrots in one hand and the mash in the other.

Joe leans forward and rubs his hands together gleefully, like he hasn't eaten all week. "My word, what fine fare," he declares; then looking at Ma, he asks, "Would you like me to do the honors, Mrs. Piper?"

Ma nods. "Most kind," she says, and we all watch as Joe takes up the carving knife and steel to sharpen the edge. The swishing sound begins as he starts to hone the blade. My eyes are locked onto the knife in his left hand; the way it strokes the steel, smoothing down the rough jags. Then I watch, mesmerized, as Joe stands and starts to slice the beef. The bloody juices ooze from the joint, and as much as I want to look away, I can't. I can't because I'm seeing the knife that he's holding rip through Alice Mackenzie's flesh in a dark alley, not half a mile from here. Flo's watching him, too, not with horror like me, but with admiration. "Ain't he skilled with a knife, Ma?" she gushes.

Ma says nought, so Joe jumps in. "Learned my craft at Billingsgate, I did," he says proudly. "Surgeon's hands, I've got."

His words crash into my head and set me off balance, but it's Ma's voice that breaks into my thoughts. "You look a bit peaky, Connie love. You all right?"

Suddenly I'm released from my waking nightmare. My head snaps up. "N-no," I stutter. "I'm not feeling too good." I push myself up from the table and sense the ground sway underneath me. "I need to lie down," I tell them, and I stagger up the stairs to fling myself, facedown, on the bed.

EMILY

It's a rare day in Whitechapel; the sun is strong enough to break through the habitual murk that blankets the district, and the good burghers of the parish are taking full advantage of the Sabbath day. As there are few public spaces in the vicinity, the churchyards offer the only patches of green grass and the occasional tree for shade.

It is in one such churchyard that we find George Dixon, the blind youth. He is alone, having tapped his way from his home with the aid of a cane. He is wearing his dark glasses to ensure that no one can see his eyes. His disability has engendered pity in some, scorn in others, and indifference in most. One of his pastimes is to gauge the reaction on people's faces when they look at him. It amuses him when a sweet old lady regards him with a look of disgust and gladdens him when the most seemingly arrogant of gentlemen can find a few pennies for his bowl.

You see, George Dixon is not really blind at all. Nor does he need to beg or live off charity. He earns his shillings from his spying, and after a few pleasant moments in the sun, watching families and friends promenade, he is joined by one of his masters.

Inspector McCullen sidles silently onto the other end of the bench. His mood does not match the weather. There's a sullen expression on his face, which takes effort to conceal. As a young woman pushing a perambulator walks by, he forces a cheery "Good day, madam." Today, you see, he is an ordinary citizen, supposedly enjoying the clement August weather. Taking out a small brown paper bag from his jacket pocket, he proceeds to throw crumbs to the sparrows and pigeons that frequent the churchyard.

"What news?" he mumbles between scatterings. It's almost as if he's talking to the birds.

"Doyle has been working at the London Hospital. In the mortuary," comes the reply, delivered in a low voice. "Goes by the name of Gabriel Flood."

McCullen nods before dispensing another handful of crumbs. "And Kelly?"

"I can't be sure. She may have been with him."

"And the boy?"

"The boy too."

"You have an address?"

"He's lodging off Hanbury Street," the youth tells him, handing the inspector a slip of paper.

McCullen reaches into another pocket and brings out a linen bag. This one is full of sixpences. "You've done well," he tells George, dropping the bag into the youth's lap.

Tracking down this wayward Fenian has occupied him for the past few months. Doyle's been missing ever since Mary Jane Kelly's flight from Miller's Court. Royston suspects the Ameri-

can somehow got wind that her murder was planned and has been sheltering the intended victim for quite a while, but his duplicity will come at a price. The conditions imposed on him after his co-conspirators were jailed for the Jubilee Plot meant he was supposed to be an informer. Of course, McCullen had told Royston at the time he should never trust a Fenian. And he'd been proved right. That is why when Royston asked his former colleague to assist him in finding Mary Jane Kelly, he'd willingly relinquished his H Division job to work for the Secret Branch. The pretext that he needed a break after the Ripper in-quiry was the perfect excuse. What Kelly knew could be the end of Special Branch and—most alarmingly of all—the fall of the prime minister.

McCullen shakes out the remaining crumbs from his paper bag onto the grass. Crumpling it in his fist, he returns it to his pocket and stands. The quicker Kelly is disposed of, the better, *he thinks.*

"Good day," he says to George Dixon as he goes. His mood has been undoubtedly lifted. He is surely one step closer to find-ing Mary Jane. The net is closing in.

CONSTANCE

I don't know how long I've been lying here on my bed. I must've fallen asleep, but I'm woken by the sound of raised voices and the click of the door latch. I look toward the win-dow. The light's begun to fade and the sky's glowing pink. Heaving myself up off the bed, I walk unsteadily to the case-ment to see Joseph Barnett walking with Flo, side by side, down our street.

I'm glad he's gone. Having him under our roof was almost unbearable. I don't know how, with that stink of his, Flo can stomach him touching her. No matter how much cologne he splashes on, it'll stay on his skin forever, like the memory of it sticks in my nostrils the night I was attacked. It was him. I'm sure of it now.

As my gaze follows them reaching the end of our row, something strange happens. Just before they turn, Joe puts his arm round our Flo. It's then that she seems to shrink before my eyes. In an instant she's lost six inches in height, but broadened out. Suddenly the sky darkens and from out of nowhere it starts to rain. A squall blows up and bowls a tin can along the street. I look back at Flo, but her hat, the one with the red feather in, has disappeared and her beautiful brown hair is all gray and wiry. My eyes widen with terror as I realize it's not my sister I'm seeing. It's not Flo who's at the end of our street with Joseph Barnett's arm around her, but Alice. Old Clay Pipe Alice. I see him stop, and turn to her, and . . . Oh, my God! A knife looms in his raised hand and I feel a strangled scream escaping from my throat. Then, just as quickly as she appeared, Alice is gone and in her place it's Flo again. She and Joe aren't fighting. She's not wrestling a blade away. She's kissing him in the middle of the street.

Suddenly, I sense there's someone close to me, coming up behind. There's a shadow on the wall. I turn.

"Ma!" I gasp.

She's standing there, and from the look on her face, I can tell she's been peering over my shoulder and down the street.

"Poor man. Been through hell, 'e has," she mutters, watching Flo and Joe Barnett necking.

"You happy for them?" I ask, surprised that she's so accepting.

"Long as he don't treat her bad, like he did Mary Jane," she replies.

My ma's the forgiving sort. I wish I could be. Sometimes it's a curse being able to delve into the darkest souls. Something is wrong. Very wrong. I've just had another vision. I had my doubts about Joe Barnett before, but now I know for sure. If I've read it right, Miss Tindall's just confirmed to me what I've suspected for a while. She's shown me who killed Alice Mackenzie.

EMILY

True to his word, Samuel Doyle brings food to the miserable shed, where Mary Jane and her son are in hiding. They eat a sparse, but welcome, meal of cold sausage and bread buns together. Before long, it is time to settle Timmy for the night. Mary Jane starts singing him his favorite lullaby. Her voice is so soft and soothing Doyle almost forgets his own troubles. He may not be behind bars like his Fenian co-conspirators, but Doyle is certainly not free. He should've fled back to America as soon as the Jubilee plotters had been arrested, but he'd stayed in London out of a sense of loyalty to them. Outside Bow Street Magistrates Court, Doyle thought he'd be safe among the huge crowds that had gathered to see justice done. Yet, among the flag-wavers and the fervent patriots, there had been a certain inspector, an Angus McCullen of the Special Branch, who'd been surveilling him since the foiled plot. He'd felt a hand slip through his arm. At first, he thought he was being robbed, but then another hand looped through the crook of his other arm and a low voice had said, "Come quietly or you're dead."

So Samuel Doyle was given little choice: help the British authorities in their undercover war against the Irish Fenians, or forfeit the lives of his father and other members of his family. In other words, he was coerced into becoming a double agent.

"Lie with me," Mary Jane whispers across the room as Timmy sleeps.

Her voice breaks into his thoughts and he stands and walks over to her. Taking her hand, he offers no resistance when she pulls him down toward her so that their lips collide and explode in a frenzy of kissing. Lying on the filthy mattress on the floor, he slides his hands under her skirts and up her thighs. She reaches up and unhooks his braces from his shoulders. For the next few hours he forgets what he has been trained to do. His forgets the Brotherhood's pledge he has taken to kill as many Englishmen and their women as he can. For the next few hours he is lost in Mary Kelly's body.

CHAPTER 20

Monday, August 5, 1889

CONSTANCE

Mr. Bartleby is round at ours for supper and can tell something's up. We girls haven't touched the shepherd's pie Ma's made, even though it's our favorite. Flo and me have barely spoken since Joe Barnett came to dinner. She's icy toward me, and I want to explain why he troubles me so, but I think it'll only push her even more away from me.

"You two had a row?" asks Mr. B, digging into the mince and potato on his plate. There's gravy on his 'tache, and normally, the sight of it would make Flo snigger, but not today. She keeps her eyes down.

Mr. B bends toward me. "Over a fella, is it?" he smirks.

"Harold," chides Ma, tapping him lightly on his arm. "Leave 'em alone."

He shrugs and tucks into his food again. "Heard any more about poor old Alice, Con?" he asks me cheerfully through a mouthful of mash.

My head jerks up and so does Flo's. Our eyes meet, then slide apart.

"No," I lie with a shake of my head, hoping I've done enough to hide my untruth. Thaddeus has assured me that he takes seriously my fear that Joseph Barnett murdered Alice, but he can't arrest him until he's been investigated properly, and that will take a while. He's asked me to keep tabs on him in the meantime to make sure he doesn't do a runner. I've got my hands full right now, what with Joe and this Sam Doyle, too. Something's afoot, and no mistake. Somehow I've got to slope off later to keep watch outside Doyle's lodgings. The plan is for Thaddeus to join me as soon as he's free from the station.

"You off?" asks Mr. B a little later. Flo and me washed and dried up the supper dishes in silence and now she's gone upstairs. He's caught me by the door, just as I've donned my hat and shawl and was hoping to make a quick getaway.

"Me and some of the girls will be out looking again," I tell him. This lying is getting a habit with me.

He nods and gives me the eye. "Ah, yes, the boy. You'll be bumping into some of the lads from the Vigilance Committee, no doubt," he says all jokey, touching the side of his nose with his forefinger. "Nudge, nudge, wink, wink. Your secret's safe with me, my gal."

I think Ma must've said something about Gilbert Johns being sweet on me, but I'll take none of his nonsense. "When a nipper's gone missing, it's no laughing matter, Mr. B," I tell him straight, polishing that smirk off his face. All I want to do is kick him in the shins. "Good night" is what I say.

Turns out I don't really need my shawl, after all. The evening's quite balmy. I'd even say it might thunder later on. The streets of Whitechapel are far from deserted. Outside the pubs there's lads with pints in hand, supping on the pavement.

Mothers stand on doorsteps and watch their children play hop-scotch on the street.

I know I'll be lucky if I spot this Sam Doyle, but I promised Thaddeus I'd keep watch for a while. This is what he asked me to do the other night. He'd already followed the bloke back from the mortuary. That's how he knows he's lodging off Hanbury Street.

I don't like to loiter. No decent girl does round here. It's not safe for a woman to hang around these parts. I'm risking being propositioned just by standing here, even now in daylight. I tell myself I'll spend no more than an hour to see what I can see; then I'll call it a night. Only, I hardly have to wait at all. Ten minutes into my surveillance—that's how Thaddeus describes it—I spot this Doyle stepping out. He has his head down, hands in pockets, and that wavy hair trailing behind him. He looks for all the world like one of them Romantic poets, like Shelley or Keats; only, it's murder, not poetry, he's got on his mind, I'm sure of it. So I track him as he turns left out of the row and crosses over Whitechapel High Street. Despite the pace he sets, I manage to keep up and soon realize he's heading back toward the hospital where he works.

Still latched onto him, I see him ignore the main entrance and walk down the side of the building. Next he's along a narrow alley, heading toward the morgue, and, to my surprise, he goes beyond the door marked MORTUARY. He carries on a bit farther before turning left into a small courtyard. He stops in front of a ramshackle wooden shed, then glances round. I flatten myself against the wall for a second and watch him bring out a key from his pocket and unlock the door.

Sam Doyle is leading me a merry dance, and there's no lie. All round the houses he's taken me, ending up at this rickety lean-to. I wonder what's inside. Of course, I could leave it to Thaddeus to find out, but then again . . .

I skirt round the side. The shed's base is built of brick, but it's wood from the knee height up. Looking to the roof, I spy a window high in the planking. There's a water barrel under the guttering and a ledge halfway up, where a window's been boarded. I decide to take a chance. Hitching up my skirts, I heave myself onto the barrel's rim; then clutching the window ledge, I raise myself up on my toes to peer inside. The pane is broken, but putting my eye to it, I see a space below, lit by the soft glow of a single oil lamp.

Squinting into the gloom, I reckon it's a sort of storeroom. There's crates and barrels stacked up against the walls, and standing in the center are two figures; one is Sam Doyle and the other . . . It's not quite dark and, for a fleeting second, I can see in the lamplight the face of the woman he's talking to. I blink the sight away, then look again.

"It's true," I mouth. A storm suddenly rises in my head, raging round my mind. A wind buffets my brain, lightning forks before my eyes. I can hardly believe what I'm seeing, and yet I've thought for so long that she's still alive. Standing close to Doyle, her frame slight and her hair in a high bun, is Mary Jane Kelly.

The shock makes my body shudder and causes me to lose my footing for a moment. Forgetting I am perched on a thin ledge, I step back and slip, but my hands fly up and I clutch hold of the window frame. For a moment I freeze; then my breath returns in short pants and I clamber down quickly. The ground rarely felt so good under my feet as I try to still my pounding heart.

What to do? I ask myself. *Miss Tindall,* I silently mutter. *Miss Tindall, are you there?* But there's no answer in the twilight. I'm alone with a terrible secret that I want to share with the world. But I have to still my tongue. Questions flutter about my head like moths. What is Mary Jane doing there? Is Sam Doyle her captor, holding her against her will? Did he fake her murder? If that's so, was it Patricia's body in Miller's Court?

For a moment I stand in stunned silence. Only a rat stirs and scuttles across my boots. Followed by another. Rats are the only company I keep as I cower against the wall in the gloom trying to decide what I should do. *What would Miss Tindall do?*

I stay for as long as I dare, before the darkness makes my fear too much to bear. It's hard to think straight when you're in the coils of a snake that's sucking the breath out of you. I need to be—what's the word?—*logical,* like Miss Tindall, all calm and reasoned. After a while I can feel my heart slow and suddenly see a way out of my panic. I'm thinking that Sam might return to his lodgings for the night. So I wait. And I wait . . . until, just as the shadows disappear and darkness cloaks the alley, I hear a handle twist. A figure steps out. It's him, all right. I catch the key click in the lock once more. Mary Jane's locked in. That Fenian traitor is holding her against her will. She's his prisoner.

Waiting a few moments until I'm sure the American has gone, I scramble back up on top of the water barrel and look through the window again. The glow from the oil lamp allows me to see that Mary Jane's back is now against the wall. She's huddled on a mattress on the floor—only, she's not alone. I gasp with joy as I spy Timmy, too. She's cradling him in her arms and singing in her low, sweet voice. I can barely contain my joy. This is the scene that Miss Tindall showed me in St. Jude's and I almost doubted her. It's hard to stem my tears of relief, but I know I have to control my emotions.

Taking a deep breath, I tap on the window frame. I see Mary Jane start below, then crane her neck up toward the jagged glass.

"Mary Jane!" I call softly through the hole in the pane. "It's me. It's Constance Piper."

Her head jerks up. "Oh, God!" I hear her exclaim.

There's a rustle in the murk and she stands. I clamber down, and a moment later, to my surprise, a key clatters in the lock and I see the door come ajar. She wasn't locked in, after all. I'm confused. There she is in the doorway, Timmy at her skirts. For a second we just stand and stare at each other; then suddenly I feel her hand round my wrist as she grabs me and pulls me inside.

"It's you. It's you. I knew you were alive! I just knew it!" I cry, unable to contain myself.

I fling my arms around her. "I knew it was you," I say again. I can't stop my tears flowing as I hold her tight. She cries, too, and Timmy's clutching at my skirts. For a moment it's like my Christmases and birthdays have all been rolled into one, I'm so full of mirth. Then suddenly my merriment stops as soon as it started when Mary Jane pulls back from me. I realize the joy at her discovery is one-sided.

"What you doin' here, Con?" she asks, her voice drawn so tight I think it might snap. "How did you find us?" Looking into her eyes, I see there's fear in them. "No one knows you're here? No one followed you?"

I shake my head. "No one," I assure her. I can tell from her shaking hands that beneath her happiness at seeing me, there's a greater terror.

"How did you find us?" she asks again.

I bend low and pick up Timmy, balancing him on my hip. "Sam Doyle," I say.

"*Sam?*" she repeats.

"I followed him. He ain't hurt you? Has he . . . ?" I look at Timmy, thinking it must have been Samuel Doyle who took him from school. I hold his little hand tight in mine. "Timmy's not hurt?"

Mary Jane sings out a half laugh, the way she used to when I knew her in happier times. "No, he's none the worse." She reaches for her son and hugs him to her. "And I'm fine, too. Sam's a good man. He's helping us."

"*Helping* you?" I repeat, ignoring her last question. "Helping you to do what?"

She shakes her head and lets out a deep sigh; so deep, it sounds as though it's been pent up since last November. "I've got some explaining to do, ain't I?" she admits.

"I'll say you have."

"Let's sit," says Mary Jane, perching on an old crate, Timmy at her feet. "I'll tell you all about it."

So she does, as best she can. She tells me how she met Sam Doyle through Joe and his Irish friends. "He were always kind to me. Different from the rest." She smiles wanly and there's a flicker in her eyes. It was Doyle who warned her that she was marked, because General Millen told her of the plot to blow up the Lord Mayor's Parade, and how she needed to escape, for fear that her life was in danger.

"What did he say?" I'd asked.

"He said he knew Joe was worried I'd rumbled their plans for the bombing and that I'd grass to the coppers." She takes another deep breath. "He said me and Timmy should get away—for good."

I frown. "So the murder at Miller's Court? The body? Whose was it? I don't understand."

Mary Jane shakes her head, and her eyes start to brim with tears. "That's the thing," she sobs. "That's the most terrible thing."

EMILY

Constance's questions are forcing her to face the most shocking secret of all; so, gulping back her tears, Mary Jane Kelly decides to unburden herself. For the first time she will relate what exactly happened on the fateful night of the eighth of November, the eve of the Lord Mayor's Parade, to Constance.

Twisting her apron in her hands, she begins: "I'd been fearful for a while—fearful because I knew Joe and his brothers wanted to plant a bomb at the parade, so I'd got to thinking. I went to Sam and told him about the plot a few days before and he said he already knew what Joe was up to, but that I wasn't to worry because he'd see to it."

"See to it?" queries Constance.

"He said he could make it safe."

"How?"

"All I know is, he said he'd not let the bomb explode, and as soon as the parade was over, he'd help me and Timmy leave London." She continues: "We had it all planned. That night I sang Timmy his favorite lullaby and he soon went off to sleep. That's when Alice came to take him. She laid him in an old cart she'd borrowed, and pushed him back to her place, then I left to stay at Sam's." She wipes away a tear with the back of her hand.

Listening to her friend's sorry tale, Constance has suddenly realized the truth. "So you'd no idea that your sister was in London looking for you," she whispers.

Mary Jane's face screws into a grimace. "If only I had. Sam told me later that she'd been searching for me."

"So Patsy tracked you down and was waiting for you in Miller's Court," she mutters, horrified.

I can only shine a light on the thoughts that Constance already holds. Piecing together the information from Lady Kildane, and now from Mary Jane, she is now certain that the poor woman found dead was none other than Mary Jane's sister, Patricia. The unfortunate Irish girl had already been in Whitechapel for three days, in search of her wayward sibling, but when Patricia finally found where Mary Jane was living, her sister had already fled in fear for her life. Patricia had merely let herself into the dwelling to await her sister's return. Of course, she waited in vain, and the fiend who did visit that night butchered her beyond recognition.

"Oh, God," wails Mary Jane. "Sometimes I wish I'd stayed. She didn't deserve to die like that!"

Constance puts her arm around her. "And nor did you," she

comforts. "No one did. You mustn't blame yourself. You're the innocent victim in all of this." She pauses for a moment before she asks the question that everyone wants answering: "Do you have any . . . ?"

"No," comes the quick response. "All I know is it wasn't Joe. He'd have realized it wasn't me. He was a bully, yes, and a Fenian, but I know he wouldn't have done that."

Constance isn't so sure, even though she knows that whoever killed Mary Jane's sister wanted it laid at Jack the Ripper's door. She recalls the vision I showed her at the end of her street and begins to doubt herself. Could it be that she was mistaken? In the gloomy street she was so sure she saw Joe Barnett raise the knife to kill Alice, but perhaps . . . After all, it was dark and she hadn't managed to get a proper view. "So, who do you think then?"

Mary Jane shrugs. "A demon, and that's for sure, but I've no idea who, and that's the God's honest truth, I swear."

"So . . . after the body was found, Joe called the bombing off?" Constance tries to remain calm and collect her thoughts in a logical manner.

Mary Jane nods. "That's right. Sam said Joe was as shocked as anyone at the murder." Her voice is tinged with an odd sadness. "But Joe called the whole thing off because he was worried I'd grassed."

"So the bomb was never planted?"

"No."

"But Joe believed it was you in Miller's Court?" Constance asks.

Mary Jane shakes her head. "Only up until the time he had to see the body. That's when he knew it weren't me."

"So he lied to the police?" Constance is shocked.

Mary Jane shrugs. "Patsy's eyes were green. Mine are blue. He'd have known it wasn't me, all right."

"So he's been looking for you all that time?" asks Constance.

"Yes. I did get away from London for a while."

"But you came back because of Timmy and Sam."

"That, I did," she tells me, a weak smile suddenly spreading across her face. *"And we'll be gone real soon. When Sam's got the money for our tickets, we'll be out of here."*

Constance smiles back at her, only more out of sympathy than conviction. She fears what lies ahead for her friend and her son. As well she might.

CONSTANCE

I'm sucked into Mary Jane's sorrow, and I can't see any way out for her. She thinks I'll keep things on the quiet, but I know I can't. She needs more than a sympathetic ear. She and her son need protection.

"Let's get you out of here," I say, holding out my hand to her. She pauses for a second, then shakes her head.

"I'm not leaving," she says softly, eyes to the ground. Then she looks up at me and sticks out her chin. "I'm not leaving without Sam."

"But you can't stay here," I plead.

"It's as safe as anywhere." She dips her voice. "As long as *you* don't betray us."

A worm of guilt wriggles inside me. A chasm has opened up between us. Mary Jane stands on the other side. I need to reach out to her.

"You know we must tell the police."

"No!" she cries with a shake of her head. She clamps her hands on Timmy's shoulder. In the lamplight I see her eyes fill with tears. "This is our only chance. Don't take it away from us, Con." She reaches out her hand to me. "They'll jail Sam. I beg of you, please. No police."

I pause for a moment. *What would Miss Tindall do?* Timmy's face is all screwed up and he's starting to whimper. He's clearly afraid.

"Think of him," I say suddenly. "It's not safe here." My gaze falls on Timmy. "For his sake. Please."

Just as I reach out toward the lad, she bends low and scoops him up into her arms; then, to my surprise, she bares her teeth and growls at me like a lioness. "You take him and I'll kill myself. I swear." Her eyes are suddenly on fire and I know she means her threat.

Her desperate tears force me to think on my feet. "I know someone who'll help," I tell her, thinking of Thaddeus. "He's a friend and he's kind. He'll know what to do."

Making toward the door, I'm about to reach for the handle, but she sidesteps in front of me, blocking my way. In the lamp's glow I see desperation in her eyes.

"You understand they'll kill me if you go to the police," she cries.

I glare at her. "Who? Who'll kill you, Mary Jane?" I press.

She draws in a ragged breath and pins me with a fearful stare. "The gents that failed the first time."

I think my heart will break, but I can't lie to her, so I lunge for the door. She lurches after me, grabbing at my sleeve, but I manage to unlock the door before she can get a proper hold and I slam it behind me just in time. I hear Timmy's cries suddenly mix with her own sobs, but I'm certain I'm being cruel to be kind. I know it's the only way to save them both. She'll not follow me, and that's for sure. I hear the key click in the lock behind me. I know it's late, but the section house in Cloak Street will be my next port of call.

EMILY

Samuel Doyle arrived back at his room off Hanbury Street not ten minutes ago. He's thrown down his jacket and shucked off his boots. By now, it is dark, although by the light of the streetlamp outside, he can see to pour himself a large whisky from a bottle he keeps at his bedside. He slugs it back in one as he sits perched on the edge of the bed, then bends double. Grabbing between the bedsprings and the mattress, he brings out a small metal box. Placing it on the covers, he opens it reverently. Inside, there are bank notes and a few coins. He reaches for a candle and lights it so that he can see to count his savings. Flicking through the notes, he tots up the cash. There's almost enough. Almost.

Shutting the lid, he conceals the box under his mattress once more, then lies back on his bed. With his hands clasped under his long, wavy hair, he dares to imagine his future. He's just drifted off to sleep, dreaming about Mary Jane, when he's woken by the sound of a gun being cocked in his left ear. At first, he thinks his dream has turned into a nightmare, but when he clocks the familiar raw voice that he's not heard for nigh on nine months, he realizes he is awake.

Blinking away the sleep, he knows he dare not move a muscle.

"How did you find me?" he asks, still prone on the bed.

Joseph Barnett gives a flat smile and blows through his nose. Doyle did not see him in the shadows, standing, arms crossed, in the alley opposite the shed. He'd been following Constance and had seen her loitering by the London Hospital. The secret is out.

"My brothers and me have your number," he says, standing by the bed. "You know what we do with spies, with traitors. You're in the pocket of the English, aren't ya? Did they order you to kill my Mary Jane, too?" He jabs the barrel of the gun deeper into Doyle's ear. "Only, you killed her sister instead, didn't ya?" Suddenly his voice softens a little. "Met Patsy, I did. She came to stay with Mary Jane where she lodged a while back." He shoves down the barrel once more. "It was Patsy all right. I knew it soon as I saw them eyes."

"No!" yelps Doyle.

"And that's why you went on the run. Ain't it?" Barnett jabs again.

"No. No, you got it wrong."

"Did they give you extra for the good job you did on Patsy, eh?" Barnett withdraws the gun from Doyle's ear and thrusts it to his temple.

"It wasn't like that. I swear." Beads of sweat have broken out on the American's forehead, but Barnett persists.

"My brothers are on their way to get Mary Jane now, and she'd better be alive. Timmy too."

Doyle licks his dry lips. "She is. I wouldn't hurt her."

Barnett smirks and withdraws the gun from the American's temple. "Shall we let her watch you die, you traitor?" He whips Doyle's cheek with the pistol.

Doyle cries out and clutches his face. "No," he moans, his eyes scrunched up. "You got it all wrong."

Barnett draws up a chair and watches his victim writhe in pain. "I know they got to you, see. Outside the court that day."

"Who told you?" asks Doyle, anxious to know who had betrayed him.

"Never you mind that, but he was there, in the crowd all right. With his own eyes he saw them feel your collar and nab you." Barnett leans over the bed. "Threaten your family, did they? That's what they usually do."

Doyle brings his hands down from his face to reveal a large purple bruise blooming across his cheek. "It's true, they did force me to spy for a while, but I never hurt Mary Jane. I never," he protests.

Barnett shakes his head. "You're a good liar, I'll give you that, but before I kill you, I want you to do one more thing for me."

Doyle swallows hard. He closes his eyes and tries to suppress his rising anger. "It's been bad for me. Believe me. They've been watching my every move. I knew if I got in contact with you again, they'd round you all up. I was hiding to protect you and your brothers, Joe."

Barnett smirks. "I'm touched, to be sure. So now that I've found you again, you can show me how loyal you are to the cause." His eyes settle on Doyle's tattoo.

"I'll do anything for you and the boys, Joe. Just don't turn me over to the English."

Barnett lifts a brow. "We wouldn't do that," he says with a shake of his head. "Not while you're alive, any road," he mocks. "No. What I want you to do is make us a gift."

Doyle frowns. "A gift?"

Barnett nods. "As a mark of appreciation for sparing your miserable life, for the time being, we'd like you to make us a nice, fat bomb."

"A bomb?" This time the gun is jabbed into his rib. The American knows when he is beaten. A moment later, Doyle delivers his reluctant response. "Very well."

"You've still got the stuff?" Barnett looks around the room.

"Some." Doyle sighs. "But I thought my bombing days were over."

The gun is poked even harder into his ribs. "Your bombing days aren't over, till I say so," Barnett assures him.

CONSTANCE

As I hurry along the dark streets, I feel the blade of Mary Jane's words as keenly as if I've just been stabbed through my heart. I know I need to tell Thaddeus where she is straight-away—for her own sake, as well as her son's. Fast as I can, I hurry to where Thaddeus lodges, the section house in Cloak Street, where the single policemen live. I break out into a run when I'm sure there's no one to see me. Thaddeus once told me that if ever I needed him urgently that his window is the first one on the second floor. I grab a pebble from the ground and throw it up, but my aim is poor and it hits the brickwork. The second stone misses, too, but the third thwacks his pane. A moment later his head appears from out of the sash. As soon as he sees me, he knows something's up. In no time he's at the back door.

I'm gasping for breath, but still I manage to tell him: "Mary Jane and Timmy . . ." I double over.

"Yes," he says, resting his arm on my shoulder, looking all concerned. "Don't tell me you've found them?" His face is a picture.

I nod and straighten myself. "In a shed. Near the hospital."

"They're alive?"

I gulp down another lungful of air. "Alive, yes. But in danger."

"Then we must go at once. Lead the way," he tells me.

So I retrace my steps, back along Fenchurch Street. As we turn toward Turner Street, Thaddeus spots a copper on his beat.

"Constable," he calls, waving his identity badge at him. The copper stops and it's then that I see it's Mummy's boy Tanner.

"Sergeant Hawkins," he says, all shocked.

"Ah, Tanner. Good," replies Thaddeus. "I've a job for you."

The copper hurries with us along the side of the hospital and down the alley until it broadens out into the small courtyard.

"That's it," says I, pointing to the shed. "They're in there."

"Stay back, Miss Piper," Thaddeus tells me as he and Tanner approach the door and bang on it. "Police. Open up," he calls. I'm tense as a bowstring, knowing how terrified Mary Jane and little Timmy will be.

"It's locked!" I cry.

Ignoring me, Thaddeus wrestles with the handle and, to my shock, the door opens.

I rush forward. "Please. Let me," I ask, and taking my meaning, Thaddeus stands aside.

"Mary Jane, it's me. Constance," I call, my eyes scouring the murk. "It's all right. We're here to help you." The lamp's been snuffed out and I fear they're hiding among the crates. "Mary

Jane, please. You're not in any trouble." But still my words don't draw her out.

We file inside. It's black as the ace of spades. Tanner's lantern casts pools of light onto the mattress, where Timmy had lain, but it looks like they've fled. The blankets and the sacks are left in a pile, but of Mary Jane and her son, there's no sign.

"Over here, Tanner," orders Thaddeus. Mummy's boy raises his bull's-eye lantern and shines a light on the boxes and crates piled high around the walls. Casting around, Thaddeus sees a crowbar resting in the corner. He picks it up and wields it confidently, first opening a crate and then a nearby box. All they contain is straw for packing, but then he spots a small keg, hidden behind another crate. He's more careful with this one, using a penknife to prize it open with care. Bending over it, he sniffs; then as he reaches down into it, I sense he knows what he's looking for. He withdraws his hand and straightens himself, then sniffs his cupped fingers. I can see grains of what look like tea streaming through them, but from their smell I know it's not a caddy he's stumbled across.

"Gunpowder," he says, fixing me with a frown. From out of his pocket he produces a small paper bag and something like a flat spoon to gather a sample of the powder. Tanner steps forward to offer more light. "Keep this place under surveillance and I'll send for reinforcements," Thaddeus orders him, brushing his hands together lightly to rid them of any residue. "No one is to enter."

"What will you do now?" I ask when we're clear of the shed. I'm all anxious for Mary Jane and her boy. The state she was in! I'm hoping she's left the shed for a safer place, but I can't be sure.

"I need to go straight to the commissioner's house," Thaddeus says quick, reporting to me like he's on duty. He's all formal and proper. But just as soon as he sees the look on my face, he reads it right and softens. "And, Constance, yes," he says. "Now I really do believe that Mary Jane Kelly is alive."

EMILY

It is past midnight when a butler in his night attire answers the door at Commissioner Monro's residence. It is clear from his thunderous expression that he really is not amused at being roused at this late hour. But his mood soon changes when he realizes it is Sergeant Hawkins who is calling and pressing upon him the urgency of his visit.

The detective is ushered into the study to await the arrival of his superior.

"Hawkins!" Commissioner Monro enters and stands before him, tying the cord on his silk dressing robe. "What's afoot?" he asks.

"Sir, I would not bother you if the matter was not of the utmost importance."

"I'm aware of that. Well, out with it, fellow."

It is hard to know where to begin. Largely thanks to Constance, within the space of an hour, the detective has reason to believe that a woman officially dead still lives, a kidnapped boy is safe, and, with the discovery of the gunpowder, that a terrorist outrage could be planned. A thorough search of the shed, where Constance found Mary Jane hiding, has revealed an empty keg containing traces of explosives.

"We believe a Fenian bomb attack may be imminent, sir."

Monro frowns, but his immediate reaction is not what Hawkins expects. "We?" he repeats.

The detective, sworn to secrecy over this covert operation, has inadvertently included Constance in his discovery. "A trusted contact, sir. It was she who discovered Samuel Doyle's hideout."

"She?" Monro's brows shoot up simultaneously. Hawkins did not intend for Constance to be the focus of such attention. "How has this person come by this information?"

Hawkins pauses to frame his words. "I have worked with the young lady in question before. She assisted me in uncovering the identity of the victim in the Whitehall torso case, sir."

Monro's eyes widen. "How the deuce did she do that?"

Hawkins knows that he is risking his own credibility if he tells the truth, but there is no other way of putting it. "Miss Piper is a medium, sir."

The commissioner's puzzled expression suddenly gathers into a glare. "A medium?" he repeats. "I know the Whitechapel murders have brought many lunatics out of the woodwork, but you are telling me you've found one whose predictions have actually been proved right?"

The detective must stick to his guns. Raising his head, he recalls Constance's role in uncovering the wicked exploits of the baby farmers, too. "On more than one occasion, sir," he replies emphatically.

"Hmmm," Monro grunts, then narrows his eyes. "As long as this woman can be discreet."

"Absolutely, sir," replies Hawkins, then quickly taking advantage of his newfound resolve, he adds, "She has also tracked down Mary Jane Kelly."

"Mary Jane Kelly, but . . ." The name sticks in the commissioner's craw. "You're not telling me . . ."

Hawkins nods. "She is alive, sir."

The commissioner dips his brows. "But that is extraordinary. You're certain that this woman, this medium, can be trusted?"

"Yes, sir. I am. Kelly's son—"

"The boy who went missing?"

"Yes, sir. He is with his mother."

The commissioner thinks for a moment, as if the import of what he has learned needs to be fully digested; then he skirts round the winged chair and makes for his desk. "Perhaps you better start from the beginning, sergeant," he says as he settles himself down. He gestures to the chair by his desk and Hawkins sits opposite. "I need to be absolutely sure I know all the facts."

For the next few minutes Sergeant Hawkins remains in the commissioner's study, updating his commanding officer on the rapid developments in his covert operation.

"A potential bomb outrage, you say?" *Monro muses. He tightens the cord on his dressing gown once more as if readying himself for battle.*

"It is logical to draw that conclusion, sir, from the gunpowder found."

Monro narrows his eyes. "But this spiritualist, or medium of yours, or whatever you call her, has no idea about the intended target."

"If she had, I'm sure she would have told me, sir," *replies Hawkins with a shake of his head.*

The commissioner raises his eyes heavenward as if pleading for patience, then draws a deep breath. Clasping his hands together, he lowers his gaze to address Hawkins. "Our first priority," *he begins,* "must be to track down this Samuel Doyle. The last thing we want to do is spread even more panic among the citizens of London. You will help me direct the search?"

"Of course, sir." *The young detective's voice is urgent.*

The commissioner suddenly drums his fingers in thought and arches a brow. "This Doyle. Works at the London Hospital, you say?"

"Yes, sir."

"That figures." *Monro's eyes narrow.*

"Sir?"

"He has medical knowledge?"

"I believe so."

The commissioner slaps the desk. "Then it could be just as Phillips surmised."

Monro fixes Hawkins with an enigmatic look, as if he has just had a revelation and received some divine intelligence.

"I don't quite follow," *retorts the detective.*

The commissioner draws closer and in a low, steady voice de-

livers his shocking assertion. "Not only could we be dealing with a Fenian dynamitard, " he suggests, "but if he is familiar with anatomy, he could also be our Whitechapel killer. Don't you see, Hawkins? He could also be Jack the Ripper."

CONSTANCE

White's Row is silent as I make my way home, save for the baby crying next door to Mrs. Puddiphatt's. I arrive back and find Ma and Flo fretting. It's late and I knew they would be worried, but I had no choice.

"Where you been?" hisses Flo, her arm around Ma, all protective. "Worried sick, she were. Damn near got the Vigilance Committee on the case, we did."

She makes me feel wretched, like I'm the worst daughter in the world. "I'm sorry," I say, rushing over to Ma. I kneel down beside her and gather her hands in mine.

Ma senses something's afoot and her head jerks up to search my face. "Timmy? You found Timmy?"

The news is on the tip of my tongue. I ache to share with her that not only have I just seen the child, but his mother, too; both of them are alive. I know, though, I must keep my lips sealed. How can I tell them I was speaking with Mary Jane this evening and that she told me everything, only to lose her a few minutes later?

"No, Ma," I say with a sigh. "But we will. I know we will."

"I'm praying so hard," she tells me, the tears bubbling up.

I nod and squeeze her hand tight. "I know you are," I say, throwing a glance over at Flo, standing sullen by the hearth. "We all are."

A few minutes later, when Flo and me—sorry—when Flo and *I* are undressing for bed, I ask her outright if she's seen Joe this evening.

"What's it to you?" she snaps.

"Nothing," I reply, a bit too quick. If she was with him, then I'll feel a lot happier, knowing it couldn't have been him who found where Mary Jane was hiding and carted her off somewhere.

"You'd do well to keep your nose out of my affairs, young lady," Flo huffs. "It's clear you don't like him, but he's a good bloke, he is."

I know I should keep my counsel, but I can't have her hoodwinked like this. "So you're sure he's not taken Timmy?" I'm showing a red rag to a bull, but she's asked for it.

She's been fumbling with her buttons at the back of her dress. She's not asked me to help her, like she usually does. Now she stops dead to skewer me with a sharp look.

"Sure as eggs is eggs, Connie Piper, and no mistake," she snarls, then carries on with her buttons. Anger makes her suddenly able to work the loops and she steps out of her dress all by herself. Standing there in her petticoat, she scowls at me. "And if you so much as mention my Joe to that fancy detective of yours, I'll have your guts for garters. You 'ear?"

I hear her, all right, and so does half the neighborhood. She's got the wind up. She's afraid I'll dish any dirt I've got on her man to the police. If I know her, as I surely do, she'll be calling on Joe as soon as she can, hoping he'll put any fears she has to rest. And when she does, I'll be prepared.

CHAPTER 21

Tuesday, August 6, 1889

EMILY

*I*n Spitalfields, in the room of a Fenian sympathizer's house— *safe from the police, it's hoped—Samuel Doyle sits hunched over a table. A canister of gray powder, retrieved from a barrel in the shed just two days before, sits by his side. The idea of storing the gunpowder so close to Mary Jane and her son had sat uneasily with him. He knew it to be volatile, so he'd removed it and had planned to rid himself of it as soon as he could.*

Now, however, those plans have changed, and he finds himself toiling through the night by the light of a single oil lamp. It's safer than a candle. He cannot risk any naked flames. In one hand he holds a pair of tweezers; in the other a clock. It's delicate work, for trained hands only, although he still has to refer to the manual now and again, just to make sure he has the wiring correct. It's been a long time since he made a bomb and he'd resolved never to make another. He'd thought those days were over.

Seated in the armchair nearby, Joseph Barnett keeps watch. In one hand he holds the bottle of whisky, in the other a gun. It is a dangerous combination as Samuel Doyle is only too aware. And the more Barnett drinks, the more he talks. For the past ten minutes he has been rambling on about how he loved Mary Jane Kelly, the woman whom he continually abused. Samuel Doyle has been forced to listen to the drunken musings in silence, but there comes a point when he can take no more.

"Loved my Mary Jane, I did," proclaims Barnett for the umpteenth time, taking another slug of whisky.

Doyle, momentarily forgetting his precarious position, cannot let this last remark go unchallenged. "You've a strange way of showing it," he mutters.

"What ya say?" asks Barnett. He manages to lever himself up and stagger over to where Doyle sits. "What's she been telling ya?" The gun is left on the chair.

Aware that he is treading on dangerous ground, the American rows back. "She told me you quarreled."

Barnett narrows his eyes. "You think I killed the bitch they found in Miller's Court?"

Doyle can contain himself no longer. "Well, didn't you?"

Barnett slams his fist down on the nearby chest of drawers. "Whoever did that was a beast. I work quick and clean. Ya hear?"

Still seated and without turning to face Barnett, Doyle takes his chances: "But surely you must know who did it."

The Fenian shakes his head as a sort of drunken melancholia suddenly takes hold of him. "All I know, it wasn't my Mary Jane they found. As I say . . ." He breaks off, as if a thought has suddenly come to him that's more important than anything else. He lunges at the chair. "You!" He grabs the gun and points it at Doyle. "What about you?"

Doyle's jaw drops and this time he turns. "You can't think . . . ?" He lets out a mock laugh, even though he knows Barnett is deadly serious. "You think I butchered the woman in Miller's Court?"

Barnett shrugs. "Maybe the English made you do it!" The gun is jabbed into Doyle's chest. "Can't trust anyone these days," he says before his face cracks in a smile. "Best get on, hadn't ya?"

Doyle nods his head, smooths his hair behind his ears, and leans over the table once more. He has no choice and his work requires the utmost concentration. The light is poor and he squints hard, until, another half hour later, he finally manages to attach the watch spring to the percussion cap. The device is a step nearer to completion. He leans back in his chair and sighs with relief that at least one phase of the assembly is over. But as if to remind him that he is still in danger, he hears Barnett click the revolver once more.

"Finished, have ya?" he asks.

The American shakes his head. "Not yet."

"You'd best crack on, then. We've not much time," Barnett tells him as he heaves himself up from the chair and walks toward him.

"What do you mean?" asks Doyle.

Standing over him, he arranges his features into a mock frown. "Didn't I mention? How thoughtless of me!" he sneers, thwacking his forehead with the heel of his palm. "This bomb. It'll need planting tomorrow."

"Tomorrow?" the American repeats in a horrified echo.

Barnett laughs out his reply: "The Parnell Commission won't know what's hit it!" Reaching out, he playfully ruffles the American's hair. "Don't you worry that pretty head of yours," he chides. "You're doing just fine," he tells him. "You carry on as you were." He leans forward and whispers in his ear, "Just remember, this time I'll be watching your every move."

It's shortly before midnight and Joseph Barnett is just easing himself back into his chair, when there's tapping at the door. So soft it is that the porter thinks at first it might be a cat pawing at the wood; then, believing otherwise, he leaps up, gun at the ready. Samuel Doyle, still at work on the bomb, whips round. Barnett creeps to the window and lifts the drape. Satisfied he knows the caller, he opens the door. Denis, the eldest brother, strides in, his face like thunder.

"What's afoot?" asks Barnett.

His brother, a full three inches taller, scowls and shoots a look at Doyle. "She weren't there."

"What?" Barnett can hardly believe his ears. He needs to hear it again.

"She weren't there, I said," reiterates his brother. "The boy neither. The place was empty. They'd scarpered."

Barnett rounds on Doyle. The gun now rammed into his chest. "Where are they? What've you done with 'em, you bastard?"

The American holds his hands up in a gesture of surrender. "Nothing, I swear," he cries. "They were there when I left."

Joseph turns to his brother. "You and the lads best find them. And find them fast," he growls. "Before anyone else does."

The trouble is, of course, that someone already has.

CONSTANCE

The worry hangs over me like a cloud as I lie in bed. I fear it'll burst soon enough and the rain will fall, drowning me in a sea of troubles. I'm anxious for Mary Jane. Where has she gone? Was it that she didn't trust me? Was that why she just upped and left without leaving a trace? Perhaps she told Sam Doyle about my visit and it was he who decided I wouldn't be able to hold my tongue; he had to get mother and child to a safer place. *Or . . .* I gasp at the thought of it. *Or perhaps Joe Barnett has tracked her down? But how?*

That's when I start to shudder, thinking that maybe, just maybe, I was seen going into the shed. It was growing dark when I found the place and the shadows are always long in Whitechapel. Joe Barnett could have been lurking, like the rat that he is, spying on me, and I wouldn't have known.

I shoot a look at Flo: her eyes shut, her brown hair tumbling over the pillow, and her breasts lifting gently with each breath. The room's quite warm, almost stuffy, but the silence between Flo and me was decidedly chilly as I slid into bed beside her and said good night earlier. I only got a grunt in reply before she gave me the cold shoulder. She wouldn't be sleeping so sound if she knew the truth about Joe Barnett. But how can I tell her that Miss Tindall's shown me he's a murderer? How can I tell her that the man she loves might kill her, too, if she ever found out about what he did to Alice?

My sister, of course, will have none of it. She won't swallow that Joe Barnett is bad to the core. The notion will leave a sour taste in her mouth. After all my railings against him, I know that she'll want to hear another version from the horse's mouth, as it were: He'll try and convince her that he's innocent and that I'm making up lies because I never did like him. She'll make me out to be the villain of this piece, and no mistaking. Her old flame, Danny Dawson, may have fooled her before, but he was an angel compared with this devil.

I hold down my inclination to cry. I have to be strong. Sitting back and doing nothing has never been my way. Miss Tindall taught me to be a doer and not a watcher. I've already decided what action I'll take. I don't like spying on my own sister, but it's the only way I'll get to know where Joseph Barnett is living and, more important, what he's hiding.

If I know Flo, come first light, she'll slip out of bed when she thinks I'm asleep and go and warn her beau that she reckons I'll tell tales about him to Old Bill. That's why I'm sleeping in my petticoat and drawers. I've left my hair in a bun, too, so I can get out of the house quick to follow her as soon as I hear her stir. But first I need sleep. The bell at St. Jude's has just struck two. My lids are so heavy that I know I won't be able to keep awake. Before long, I'm dreaming of Mary Jane and her boy.

EMILY

Mary Jane did not see his face in the darkness. All she'd been aware of was someone crouching over her. At first, she'd thought it was Constance returning with help, but when she'd called out, there'd been no reply. She'd been about to scream, when she'd felt a hand press hard over her mouth. Timmy had woken then and called out to her, when he, too, was swiftly silenced. Before she knew it, she was being bundled out of the shed toward a waiting carriage with blackened windows. One of the man's arms was clamped round her waist like a vice as he dragged her along the cobblestone street; the other remained across her mouth. It was only when he reached up to open the carriage door that she took her chance. She kicked out and bounded away as fast as she could, around the corner, down an alley, and onto Whitechapel High Street. But she knew he was after her.

Now she's heading for familiar territory, back to the rookeries, where she knows she'll be harder to find. Keeping to the shadows, she reaches the familiar arch that leads into George Yard, the gateway to a malevolent world of crime and vice into which few God-fearing people venture.

Mary Jane wipes the sweat from her brow with the back of her hand. She's paused for breath in an old stairwell, but only for a moment. She knows she can't afford to rest. Joe. It has to be Joe who's after her. He thinks she'll tell the police he's a Fenian. He won't give up that easily, she knows. Gulping down a lungful of breath, she sets off, once more, along a narrow alley. It's hard for her to tell exactly where she is in the dark. One filthy courtyard looks much like another; one pinched lane overhung by dilapidated lodgings, the same as all the rest. She's

*heading for she really knows not where. She has to keep re-
minding herself that to the rest of the world she is dead, and
dead women don't have friends.*

*As she skirts a high wall, the first drops of rain, which have
been threatening all day, start to fall. Initially large and infre-
quent, they soon begin to gather momentum as the first rumble
of thunder sounds over Whitechapel like a distant cannon.*
Timmy's terrified of thunder, *she suddenly remembers.* Holy
Mother, keep Timmy safe, *she silently prays.*

*A frightened dog begins to howl. She carries on, her speed
now slowing to a stagger as the rain falls in curtains on the
greasy cobbles. Her wet hair is now a tangle of rats' tails and her
skirt is drenched. She knows she needs shelter, but danger lurks
under every overhang.*

*It's been a while since she last caught sight of her pursuer. She
thinks she lost him back near Dorset Street. She'd taken a shortcut known only to a few of her ilk that had opened onto Bishops-
gate Street Without. She'd crisscrossed through the carriages
along the road and found herself safely on the other side.*

*Another clap of thunder is followed by a streak of lightning
that illuminates the Whitechapel gloom and allows her to see, up
ahead, the railway arches of Liverpool Street Station. The rumble she hears next is not of thunder, but a locomotive, steaming
across the skyline. Lifting up her soaked skirts, she picks her way
toward the brick arches, knowing that under their wide vaults,
not only will she be sheltered and dry, but safer than in the suf-
focating rookeries, too.*

*Now believing herself to be free of her pursuer, Mary Jane
hurries along the road lined with warehouses and factories, not
straying far from the eaves of the tall buildings where she can.
Although it's still in the small hours, workers have already
started arriving for the next day's shift. Men with thick necks
and some with scars on their faces glower at her as they pass.
Two policemen stand talking by the entrance to a boot factory.*

She trains her eyes to the ground, eager to avoid their inquiring gaze. Not far now to the arches, *she thinks. She will head back toward Whitechapel tomorrow, to Timmy. She prays that Joe hasn't harmed him and that he was left in the shed. Tonight she just needs somewhere to lay her head.*

She's not gone much farther when she hears a voice behind her.

"And where do you think you're going at this hour?"

It's one of the constables she's just passed. She stops, pauses, then turns. "Me, sir?" *she asks sweetly. Playing the innocent has extricated her from so many awkward situations.*

"Yes, you." The constable, a bluff Yorkshireman, narrows his eyes. "You wouldn't be soliciting now, would you?"

"Perish the thought, sir. I'm respectable, I am."

"Who have we here, Grimshaw?" The other officer muscles in. He's senior, a sergeant by his stripes, and the moment he sets eyes upon Mary Kelly, he's wary. He recalls that face from somewhere. A recollection worms itself into his head.

Did he recognize me? *The panic takes hold.* Fight or flight? *She's outnumbered. There's no choice. She bolts down the street and turns into the nearest row; the sergeant and his constable are after her. Round a corner she darts, the sound of a police whistle blasting in her ears and bouncing off the railway arches up ahead.*

The policemen's lanterns send shafts of light into the spans. Two old men shield their eyes from the brightness and a cat jumps off a pile of rotting rubbish, but over in the far corner, they spot their quarry. The lamp light picks out, cowering against the wall, the crumpled body of Mary Jane Kelly.

"There!" cries the sergeant, pointing to the terrified woman, but she's not yet ready to surrender. Leaping up, she dives toward the far side of the arches, snagging her hair on a thorn bush growing out of the brickwork. Up ahead she sees another row of spans. Gasping for breath, and with her heart drumming

in her chest, she's almost reached them, when she thinks she can make out a man standing silhouetted in the center. She stops short of him, exhausted, knowing that she can no longer run. Joe Barnett has won the fight. He's found her and now he'll kill her.

"Well, well," comes the voice; only, it's one she does not recognize. It's not Joe Barnett's cockney twang, but a Scottish brogue.

With his eyes fixed on her, Inspector McCullen shakes his head with glee. "If it isn't Mary Jane Kelly, come back from the dead."

Once again Bernard Royston's network of spies has proved invaluable in the apprehension of a wanted person. With the arresting sergeant and constable sworn to secrecy—no one else must know that Mary Jane Kelly lives—there is only one more thing to do.

Back at Commercial Road Police Station, Mary Jane is secretly delivered into the cells via a back door. Declaring her to be alive would be akin to opening up Pandora's Box and unleashing all hell onto the Establishment and causing mayhem among the lower classes. No, for the Special Branch's purposes, Mary Jane Kelly must remain dead to the world until such time that she can be properly disposed of. No entry is made for her in the register. No charge sheet filled out. A tap on the back of the head with a truncheon was all that was needed to produce the desired unconscious state. Should any other officers come across her, she is, for all intents and purposes, merely an unfortunate who has been brought into the station to sleep off the alcohol she has consumed. There will be an interrogation to ascertain precisely what General Millen told her, but following that, an unresponsive state would also make it much easier for the assassin, who has been hired by Bernard Royston to handle her disposal, to collect her.

CHAPTER 22

Wednesday, August 7, 1889

CONSTANCE

A creak of the floorboards wakes me. My eyes spring open and the first thing I see through the ragged drapes is a pale dawn breaking over the rooftops. The next thing I hear is the click of the latch on our front door. It's Flo. Off to see Joseph Barnett, I'll wager. Leaping out of bed, I pull on my dress and boots and am out of the house in a jiffy.

Despite the early hour, I notice, there are plenty of people about. The brewery workers funnel down Commercial Street and the delivery vans are making their calls on shops. I know Flo can't be too far in front of me, and at the corner of Booth Street, I catch sight of her hat with the red feather in it. The pavement's getting busier now. In and out, Flo weaves, keeping up a quick pace, but I'm a good match for her and stay at least twenty steps behind. Over Preston Street, Flo goes, zigzagging between the wagons. Close by, a knife grinder's calls cut through the grimy air, but she doesn't even turn his way. She's so intent on arriving, she's not thinking about the journey. We're almost in Mile End now. A drooling lech rubs his thighs and calls out as she passes, but she ignores him and carries on. We must've been on the move for at least fifteen minutes when she finally slows down a little and turns along King Street. It's a poor neighborhood, even by Whitechapel standards.

Sure enough, she stops outside one of the doors and knocks. A moment later, I see a curtain twitch and the door opens. Only, it's not Joe Barnett who greets Flo, but a squat old woman without a tooth in her gums. I creep closer to listen to what she has to say, although I can tell straightaway from the shaking of her head that it's not what Flo wants to hear.

I lean in and catch an earful. "I'd like to know, too. Upped and went yesterday, 'e bleedin' did. 'Is bed's not been slept in and all 'is things are gone. Owes me a fortnight's rent and all. 'E a friend of yours, 'cos if he is, you can tell 'im . . ." The woman's words ring down the street, but Flo doesn't hear them. Shoulders slumped, she's turned away from the old landlady and starts to trudge back the way she came. Joe Barnett's done a runner. He's scarpered without paying his dues. It's not surprising, but it is worrying. What if he's taken Mary Jane and Timmy with him? I can't bear to think of what he might do to them.

Once back on home turf, I know I've got to tell Thaddeus that Joseph Barnett is on the loose and may even have taken Mary Jane and Timmy, but that means I'll have to go to Commercial Street Police Station, even though I know I'm not supposed to. Flo won't speak to me and has taken off somewhere in a lather, and Ma's out at market. So I seize my chance. I'm just shutting our front door, when I see a messenger boy approaching. It's a rare sight down White's Row and I fancy he's something for me.

"Miss Constance Piper?" asks the boy, his cap at a jaunty angle.

I nod and he hands me an envelope. I tear it open where I

stand to see that Lady Kildane is asking me to "accompany" her to the Royal Courts tomorrow. If I'm willing, she says she'll call for me at half past nine prompt.

"Any reply, miss?" asks the lad.

"Yes," say I. I know that there's a connection between her and my mentor. Any contact from the countess is as good as from Miss Tindall herself in my book. There's a reason for her request—a reason I need to be at the Royal Courts tomorrow, although I'm not sure of it. "Please tell Her Ladyship that I will be waiting at the end of White's Row," I hear myself saying, all gracious-like.

The boy touches his cap and skitters off. I'm not far behind as I make my way to the station at Commercial Street, where I find Sergeant Halfhide behind the desk. My hat has a wide brim on it, so keeping my face down, I sashay up to the counter and start to speak to him in a low voice.

"Is Detective Sergeant . . . ," I begin, but before I get any further, old Halfhide's whiskers are twitching as he shakes his head. Elbow on the counter, he tilts toward me. "He's not in today. Sent word from the section house, he did. Says he's under the weather and taken to his bed." He winks at me, like he knows something's up, then adds, "The gaffer's not happy. Not happy at all."

I thank him, but wonder where Thaddeus might be. I take my thinking outside onto the street and all of a sudden it comes to me. He'll have gone to see Commissioner Monro.

EMILY

The calm and collected atmosphere of the reading room at the Richmond Club is rather at odds with Angus McCullen's irascible mood. He is a member in his own right now, having been sponsored by Royston. It is one of the perquisites he was offered in return for his loyalty.

As he waits to be joined by his superior, the large mahogany wall clock suddenly takes on a rather chilling significance as it counts down the hours with a relentlessness that he finds slightly unnerving, yet oddly exhilarating. He has requested the meeting with the master spy at short notice. There is a development.

Royston glides silently into the room and acknowledges McCullen by directing his gaze to two chairs far away from the other nearest members. The two men sit. McCullen orders a coffee from the steward, even though he'd prefer a whisky; his superior requests a pot of tea.

"So," Royston begins, pressing tobacco into the bowl of his pipe, "is there a problem?"

The Scot takes a sip of coffee and twitches a nervous smile. "Not a problem, sir."

"Don't tell me," Royston coos. He leans forward. "You've got Kelly."

The normally tight-lipped Scot cannot help himself. There is quiet triumph in his voice. "Not only Kelly, but Doyle, too."

Royston chews on his pipe stem excitedly, even though the tobacco is not alight. "Doyle, eh? Your man has done well."

"I got word last night that Barnett has him."

Royston narrows his eyes. "The double-dealing bastard. I always thought Doyle had too much at stake to betray us." He shrugs. "No doubt he'll get his just reward at Barnett's hands, but he'll want something from him first. Am I right?"

McCullen marvels how it is that his master is so often not just one, but two steps ahead of everyone else. Royston, it seems, has the power to see through any obfuscation.

"Indeed, you are, sir," replies McCullen, a little smugly.

"Go on." Royston reaches for a match.

"It transpires that now Barnett has the bomb maker, he intends to plant a bomb."

Royston's match flares into flame. "Of course, he does." He nods thoughtfully, the cogs of his mind whirring frantically to process what he has just heard. "Might this have something to do with the climax of the Parnell Commission?"

McCullen smiles. "It may do, sir, although as yet the target is uncertain." He rubs his hands together, as if he is anxious to get on with the job. "I need your say-so to raid their hideout to stop their deadly mission."

Royston's eyes widen as he sucks his pipe into life. It seems all that whirring inside his brain has resulted in an outcome. "Not so fast."

"Sir?"

"Think of the Jubilee Plot at Westminster Abbey."

McCullen, gulping his coffee, is momentarily unable to swallow. Brown liquid suddenly sprays out of his mouth in a violent spasm as he recalls the audacious entrapment operation conducted by Special Branch just two years before.

"Obviously, you remember it," says Royston, waiting for McCullen's coughing to ease. A few seats away, two members look up and frown. They are clearly not amused by the disturbance. "It did the government a power of good," he continues. "Rallied the people and damn near destroyed the bally Fenians."

"It did damage the Home Rule cause, no doubt about it, sir," McCullen manages, trying to suppress his coughing.

"But this will be even better," declares Royston.

"Better, sir?"

"Don't you see? The evidence that convicted the Jubilee plotters was gathered from surveillance. This time we'll have an actual bomb."

McCullen nods. He doesn't like to point out that there will only be a bomb if it doesn't explode first.

Royston's eyes light up as he fixes the inspector with a glare. "This is our chance, McCullen," he hisses through clenched teeth. "Don't you see if we step up to the plate, we can turn this whole thing on its head and cover ourselves in glory to boot?"

The inspector, still dabbing the coffee from his trousers with *his handkerchief, suddenly slows at the thought of such praise. His hand rests on his knee as he listens more intently to Royston's words:* "Have our man find the target, then stop it at the last minute. Just as we did in Westminster Abbey."

"If you're sure . . ."

"Of course, I am. A handful of extra agents is all that is needed." *Royston puffs on his pipe.* "The plot will be uncovered, and for our valiant efforts, we will at worst be given a commendation and at best a knighthood." *He lets out a faint laugh.* "I can see the headlines now." *With the stem of his pipe he writes on some imaginary broadsheet in the sky:* " 'Inspector Foils Dastardly Fenian Outrage.' "

McCullen sticks out his jaw as if picturing himself on one knee at Buckingham Palace, being tapped lightly on the shoulder with a ceremonial sword by the queen herself. He needs little persuasion. "Very well," *he says with a nod.* "I'll get more agents on the case, just to be certain."

"Excellent," *says Royston, sucking on his pipe.* "Now all we need is the target and a date."

CHAPTER 23

Thursday, August 8, 1889

CONSTANCE

I've hitched a ride to Whitehall with Jim Dylan, the old joker who gave me and Flo a lift on that fateful day they found Miss Tindall's remains. I'm not feeling her presence at the moment, but I can't make things right on my own. I'm betting Thaddeus is with Commissioner Monro. I need to tell him that I fear Mary Jane and her boy have fallen into Joe Barnett's murderous hands.

The problem is, how do I get inside Scotland Yard? Surely, the coppers will take one look at me and tell me to sling my hook. Why should a humble flower girl be allowed entry into the office of the head of the Metropolitan Police? They'll chase me out of the station or, worse still, put me behind bars for wasting their time. If Miss Tindall doesn't stand with me, lending me her voice and her wisdom, then I'm sunk.

"Here we are, my gal," says Jim as he pulls up alongside the Embankment near the Houses of Parliament. "Fancy yourself as the prime minister now, do ya?" he jokes as he helps me down from the perch.

I humor him with a smile. "That's right," I say. "A woman prime minister is what we need."

The thought of it makes him double up with laughter. "A woman prime minister!" he exclaims. "There's a thing, Gawd 'elp us!" I watch him chuckling to himself as he tugs the reins and jangles down the road.

Of course, it's not the Houses of Parliament that's my destination, but nearby Scotland Yard, the headquarters of the Metropolitan Police. I know it's rich, someone like me, who's made it my business to avoid the long arm of the law, when I'm out with Flo at least. But this is so important that even if I get arrested, it'll be worth it, as long as they believe my story and act on it. That's why I'm hoping that Thaddeus is inside this great rabbit warren of a building, and that, at the very least, he's mentioned my name to the commissioner so that I'll be taken seriously.

I straighten my hat, pull down my rucked-up jacket, and pray that my voice might be heard. "Miss Tindall," I mutter under my breath. "If you can hear me, give me strength."

As I approach the entrance, it's as I feared. Two coppers are standing guard.

"And where do you think you're going, missy?" one asks me, looking down his big nose at me as if I'm something he's wiped off his boot.

I'm on my own, I know it. I don't sense Miss Tindall's presence at all. So, puffing out my chest and standing as tall as I can, I put on my best voice and say, "To see Commissioner Monro, if you please."

The other one chuckles. His ears stick out from under his helmet. Big Nose bends low, like I'm a schoolgirl. "And what might a pretty little thing like you be wanting to talk to the commissioner about?"

"I have important information" is all I say.

"Well, then, you'd be better off talking to a constable first," suggests Big Ears.

I shake my head. "No," I say firmly. "This is for the commissioner alone."

Big Nose smirks. "All high and mighty now, are we?"

I shake my head. "Not *high and mighty*, but I need to speak with him urgently. It's very important."

The other copper may have huge lugs, but they don't seem to help his hearing. He repeats, "As Constable Carter has said, you can tell an officer inside. You don't need—"

It's time to act. I know I can't hang around all day. I've got to take matters into my own hands. Lurching forward, I jink around the two coppers and dash through the main door. "It's secret!" I cry, hurtling over the threshold.

"Come back!" shouts Big Nose.

Big Ears blows his whistle.

I find myself inside a big hall with a polished floor. There's another copper on the desk and he rushes toward me. Meanwhile, Big Ears has caught up and lunges at me, grabbing both my arms and pinioning them behind my back.

"I have to see Commissioner Monro!" I scream as I'm suddenly surrounded by a sea of blue uniforms that crashes into me. My ears are buffeted by shouts and I feel someone grabbing me round the neck. The weight of it pulls me down. "Please!" I blurt. "I have to see the commissioner."

EMILY

Meanwhile, the noise carries along the corridor and into the office where Commissioner Monro is secretly at work with Detective Sergeant Hawkins. In front of them lies a map of Whitechapel.

The two men are coordinating a manhunt for Samuel Doyle, although as yet there have been no positive sightings. Hawkins has briefed Monro about Doyle's background. Fully versed in the ways of sedition, he'd arrived in England from America in 1887. For a time he was wanted in connection with the notorious Jubilee Plot, although Special Branch has no record of his movements since last November, when he seems to have disappeared. The discovery of gunpowder at his former hangout is most troubling.

"What the deuce?" asks the commissioner.

The map lying on the desk has been marked with red ink. Various locations of known Fenian haunts have been circled, while green crosses indicate Doyle's reported movements.

"Sir?" Hawkins looks up from the map. "Is something wrong?" He has been so intent on advising the commissioner of possible hideouts for the fugitive that he has not registered the melee happening just a few yards away in the hall.

Monro reaches for his telephone and calls his secretary. "Mason, what's that infernal racket?"

Mason, a previous accident confining him to desk duty, has remained at his post. Nevertheless, he has a front-row seat to the action and informs his commanding officer that a young woman demanded to see him in person, then proceeded to run amok. Thankfully, she is currently being restrained.

"A young woman?" repeats the commissioner.

Hawkins's head jerks up immediately. "Constance!" he cries. Jettisoning his red pen, he moves swiftly to the door.

"Hawkins, where do you think . . . ?" Monro begins to ask, then abandons any hope of receiving an answer. Hawkins has already disappeared from view and is on his way to rescue Constance.

"Stand back!" he calls to the grappling officers. "Stand back!"

The sea of blue serge parts as surely as the Red Sea for Moses to expose the petite figure of a young woman, crumpled up on the tiled floor below. Her hat has long since left her head, and her light brown hair is all askew, but she is nonetheless very much conscious.

"*Thaddeus,*" *she mouths, forgetting she is in company.*

"*Miss Piper!*" *he exclaims, wide-eyed in surprise. He offers her his hand and helps her to her feet.* "*Are you harmed?*"

Brushing off her jacket and smoothing her hair, Constance glowers at the officers, who remain encircling her.

"*I'll live,*" *she replies defiantly, adjusting her sleeves.*

Hawkins dismisses them with a "*That'll be all, men.*"

The constables, who were all too quick to pounce on her like dogs on a bone, start to skulk away. Shame-faced and a little bewildered, they meld into the background as Detective Sergeant Hawkins gallantly offers Constance his arm.

"*You have news?*" *he asks as together they head toward the commissioner's office.*

"*I do,*" *she replies as they enter.*

Constance is introduced with confidence. "*Sir, this is Miss Piper, the medium I told you about,*" *says the detective, shutting the door behind him.*

Monro's brow shoots up. He recalls Hawkins mentioning a clairvoyant, but he'd imagined some crusty old woman bedecked in black and reeking of fakery. He is surprised at how young and really quite pretty she is. "*Pleased to make your acquaintance,*" *he tells her after a moment's inspection. He holds out his hand.* "*Miss Piper, you say?*" *He defers to Hawkins for assurance as he shakes Constance's ungloved hand.*

"*Yes, sir.*" *Constance feels unnerved and dips an unthinking curtsy. Being described as a medium does not sit comfortably with her. She has not yet grown completely used to the notion, so I shall be with her for the next few minutes to see that she does not lose faith.*

The commissioner is about to offer Constance a seat, when he notes her attention has already been drawn to the large map on the desk. She cranes her neck to see the familiar streets and al-

leys of her home district represented as lines and squares on paper.

"*The manhunt for Doyle,*" *Hawkins explains.*

She twists round to face the detective. "*And for Joseph Barnett, too,*" *she tells him.*

"*Barnett?*" *repeats the commissioner.* "*What's Mary Kelly's common-law husband got to do with this?*"

"*We believe he is also a Fenian, sir, and that he may have a connection with Doyle,*" *ventures Hawkins.*

Constance nods. "*His landlady says he's left without warning, taking his things and owing money.*"

"*How can you be so sure, young lady?*" *asks Monro, fixing Constance with a questioning look.* "*Don't tell me you've had some sort of vision?*"

Constance parries the commissioner's patronizing remarks with a clean riposte. "*No vision, sir. Just common sense. I've been to his lodgings,*" *she explains.* "*Barnett could be out to kill Doyle, sir, for betraying the Fenian Brotherhood.*"

Monro's heavily shaded eyes widen. He is not only surprised by the news, but also by Constance's competence and the confidence with which she delivers her hypothesis. She is performing well, as I knew she would, but she leaves her most shocking intelligence until last.

"*Then we must get onto this immediately,*" *says the commissioner, reaching for his telephone.*

"*There's something else you need to know, sir,*" *Constance states. Her look and her voice convey the gravity of the news she is about to deliver.*

"*Yes?*" *Monro slowly returns the telephone to its cradle, as if preparing himself for some momentous news. His brows dip.*

Constance steels herself to say the words she still finds it hard to utter. Taking a deep breath, she blurts, "*I believe you are aware that Mary Jane Kelly is alive.*"

This time the commissioner's eyes art toward Hawkins. "So I have been told."

"I saw them both, sir," Constance continues. "Mary Jane is flesh and blood. She's with her son, and I'm sure Joe Barnett's abducted them."

"Why would he do that?" asks Monro.

"Because she knows too much," insists Constance.

"Too much about what, pray tell?"

Constance starts to explain, although I sense the pressure is mounting inside her. "Mary Jane discovered the Fenians planned to blow up the Lord Mayor's Parade last year. That's why they wanted her dead!" Then, by way of an apology for her abruptness, she adds, "Sir." In her anxiety, however, I fear she is losing her lucidity.

The commissioner's posture is rigid. "Hawkins told me about the traces of gunpowder he found."

"That's why an outrage may be imminent," she ventures.

"But do you know the target?" Monro is growing impatient with her.

"Have you any idea?" the detective jumps in. Turning Constance round to face him, he looks into her eyes as he speaks to the commissioner as if she were in another room. "Miss Piper's powers," he tells Monro. "She can channel certain"—he searches for a word that does not sound completely fanciful—"energies, which have proved most helpful." He is searching Constance's face for an answer. "Where?" he presses her.

I try and break through into Constance's mind, but my way is strewn with her anxious thoughts that choke the path with thorns. Her consciousness is so troubled that my communication is blocked.

"I . . . I can't be sure," she replies, panic rising in her voice. Alarm is charging her blood as she flails about in this sea of uncertainty. She cannot reach the answer that she knows to be swirling in the treacherous currents close by. I have tried to throw *her a lifeline, but she has not yet caught hold. "I cannot . . . !" she says breathlessly. She touches her temples and closes her eyes. The roar of her thoughts threatens to deafen her.*

She appeals to Hawkins for understanding. "There's so much, but there is nothing for sure," she tells him forlornly. "I need more time."

The commissioner is brusque. "Time, Miss Piper, is something that is in short supply."

Monro and the detective swap wary glances. It's as if Constance has suddenly become a distraction. The commissioner is losing interest.

"I think that will be all for the time being," he says, adding lamely, "Thank you, Miss Piper."

Constance has not expected to be dismissed so summarily. She is bewildered by her treatment.

"Come," Hawkins tells her softly, gesturing to the hall as he holds the door open.

Constance's shoulders slump. "I'm so sorry I cannot be of more assistance, sir," she tells the commissioner. Monro acknowledges her apology with a nod.

Escorted by Hawkins through the hall and out onto the street, she remains anxious and upset.

"I embarrassed you," she says, her look downcast.

"Not at all," the detective tells her, tilting his head to catch her eye. "I believe in you."

Constance looks up. "You do?"

Hawkins nods. "I do. I'll admit I was wary at first, but you've been proved right on so many occasions."

For a moment she feels her heart leap, until she remembers that one of her greatest challenges lies ahead. "But when it comes to where the bomb will explode . . ."

Suddenly Hawkins takes her hand in his right hand and enfolds it with his left. "It will come to you. I know it will."

With these words the weight that is bearing down on her

lightens a little. "*Thank you,*" *she replies, grateful for the trust he is placing in her. She knows there is something else, too— something unspoken, yet warm and deep. It lasts for but a moment.*

"*How did you get here?*" *Hawkins asks her, breaking away, as if suddenly realizing he has acted inappropriately.* "*Surely not on foot?*"

Jolted back to reality, she shakes her head. "*I took a ride on a cart.*"

He looks at her with caring eyes. "*That won't do. I'll hail you a cab.*"

Constance feels awkward. "*No. I'll walk,*" *she counters.*

"*I insist.*" *His arm signals to a passing hansom and he tells the driver to take his fare to Whitechapel.*

Helping Constance into the cab, Hawkins settles her onto the seat. "*If you see anything . . . ,*" *he tells her, emphasizing the word* "*see.*" *She takes it as a validation of her powers; he is telling her he has the utmost faith in her. I will keep trying to break through into her head and shine a light into the darkest recesses of her mind. If a tragedy is to be averted, she has to let me in.*

CONSTANCE

It's growing late by the time I arrive back in Whitechapel. The cabdriver drops me off on Commercial Street, so I don't set tongues wagging round here, turning up in a hansom instead of Shanks's pony.

I find Flo's been crying. Her eyes are all red and puffy. Ma's out at the pub with Mr. B, so she's had the house to herself and she's been able to let her tears flow freely. She's in the kitchen. The gin's on the table and I can tell she's had a tipple. She regards me over a bowl of spuds she's peeling. I think from the way she fixes me with a bitter look, she'd like to stick the knife into me right now.

"You been to see your detective fella?" she asks. "Told him Joe's done a runner, have ya?" Her remark is a shard of ice that freezes me in the moment.

There's no easy way of telling her the truth. I have to say it straight. I take a deep breath and she sees from my look that I'm about to deliver news that'll shock her. "You mustn't tell Ma. Not yet. Mary Jane and Timmy are alive, but I think Joe's taken them."

The potato falls from her hand into the pan and the blade of the knife is suddenly pointed at me. "What gives you the right to say that?" she cries. She rests her free knuckle on her hip, shifts her weight onto one foot, and cocks her head to mock me. "You had one of your visions? Miss Tindall told ya that Joe's kidnapped 'em, did she? *Did she?*"

I've not the strength to argue with Flo. I'm feeling drained, and all I want is to lie down, but I know I owe her an explanation at the very least.

"There's a bombing planned," I say. It's a blunt way of speaking, but it's the only language my sister understands.

The knife clatters down on the table. "*A bombing?* What you on about?"

I sit at the table and tell her, "You may want to sit down, too." She pulls out the chair with the unsteady leg, frowning. "I'm afraid Joe's a Fenian."

"*What?*" She slaps the table with her palm. "Don't be so daft."

"I think he's plotting something."

"*Plotting?*" She coughs out a laugh. "All of a sudden he's Guy Fawkes, is he?" She pushes herself up from the table and turns her back on me. "I'll not sit and listen to this."

I shake my head. Flo just can't seem to take me seriously. "Mary Jane knows too much. I'm fearful for her and Timmy," I plead.

Lifting the pan of potatoes onto the stove, she stands back

and wipes her hands on her apron. "So, where will this bomb go off? Eh?" she asks me. I think she might be softening a little.

Again I shake my head and sigh. "That's the problem. I don't know," I tell her.

She shrugs and puts a lid on the pan of potatoes. "You don't know? So you didn't see a big bang in one of your visions?"

Her mocking hurts me. I can't tell her that I fear I've been deserted by Miss Tindall, and that my head is a jumble of sounds and images that make no sense. There's no point trying to reason with her.

"I'm going to bed," I say, unable to bear her teasing tongue any longer. I rise and head for the threshold, but just as I do, I hear a terrible hissing sound behind me. Twisting round, I see the lid has lifted and scalding water is cascading down the sides of the pan of potatoes. Flo rushes toward the hob and grabbing the handle lifts the pan off the heat, and the boiling liquid retreats from the rim. She sighs heavily, then tosses me a look of relief. All I know is, I wish my task could be dealt with so easily.

Upstairs I undress and wash my face at the stand. The water is cool against my sticky skin. When I bend over the ewer, I see my own face is reflected at me. Even though I've been praying for Miss Tindall to come to me, I can't sense her at all. I loosen my hair and brush it with firm strokes, then climb into bed alone. Closing my eyes, I try to blank out all my thoughts and let Miss Tindall fill my mind with her message. Still, my head thrums like a trapped bird in an attic, ceaselessly beating its wings. Trying to rise above the storm, I tell her softly, "I am here. I am waiting for you."

Outside, I can hear the sound of fiddle music from the Frying Pan. It's a ballad that soothes my mood. My aching muscles relax and worry starts to float away as my mind drifts with the current. My head feels weightless and yet my body is anchored to the bed.

Suddenly I find myself outside a lofty building made of carved stone. I can see statues. There's Jesus, and is that Solomon? It's a church. No, wait. It's so grand it must be a cathedral. I walk up the shallow steps and enter through the huge portico. My head snaps back to look at the vaulted ceiling that rises above like a forest canopy. I'm marveling at the magnificence of this place, but then there comes the fear. It grows in my gut like a gallstone, and soon I realize why: *This is where the bomb is. This is where it'll explode. In a cathedral. It must be!*

Is it the same place where the Fenians planned to blow up the queen on her Golden Jubilee? Westminster Abbey? It's only then that I look down to see the floor is of the most beautiful mosaic. I think it odd there are no gravestones. On the walls are portraits of judges and there are stone pillars that taper into arches rising up on either side. I'm mistaken. It's not Westminster Abbey at all. I'm in the Royal Courts of Justice.

CHAPTER 24

Friday, August 9, 1889

EMILY

*T*he sound of the chimes from the Black Eagle Brewery a few yards away prompts Joseph Barnett to consult his own pocket watch.

"Six o'clock," he announces, as if Samuel Doyle needed reminding. The fish porter strides over to the table strewn with cogs and springs and canisters and peers over the American's shoulder.

Doyle has worked through the night on the bomb and now it's nearing completion. "You've got another ten minutes before we leave," Barnett snaps. The bile rises in Doyle's stomach once more at the thought of the destruction the device that is being wrought by his own hands will wreak. He inhales deeply, something he often forgets to do during the process of bomb making, and allows his thoughts to wander to his lover and her son.

"Mary Jane and the boy . . . Where . . . ?"

Barnett, standing by his shoulder, ruffles Doyle's hair again. "The Lord knows where she is, but she'll not be putting a spoke in the wheels this time," he tells him.

Doyle unthinkingly raises his arm to swat away Barnett's hand, but the porter grabs it and his eyes fall on the tattoo of the phoenix. Clenching Doyle's forearm tightly, he glares at him. "Remember, we're doing this for the cause. For Ireland," he growls.

The American meets his gaze. "For the cause," he agrees.

Barnett lets the arm fall and, bending low, thrusts his face to Doyle's. "The court will be packed with the people who are forcing families out of their homes in the winter and who turn their backs on starving children," he snarls. He straightens himself again. "They deserve to die, and no mistake, so don't go soft on me. Ya hear?"

Doyle wipes a speck of spittle from his cheek. He stares at his captor in sullen silence for a moment, then smiles stiffly. "Sure, I hear," he says.

"Now let's get on," counters Barnett with a nod. "One of the lads is waiting with the wagon."

At the back entrance of the Royal Courts of Justice, in Carey Street, a small army of cleaners moves in before the sessions begin, to ensure the courtrooms and corridors are spick-and-span. Many of these men and women are Irish, grateful to find work at all. Among their ranks are two new recruits—one with dark, wavy hair, and the other with a fair moustache and small eyes.

Doyle leads the way past two policemen on duty. He is aware that Barnett is close behind. A gun is concealed in the fish porter's pocket, but it is easily accessible should the younger man prove uncooperative. False moves are out of the question. Doyle is armed with a mop and a bucket; inside the bucket is a heavy metal box. Together the men make their way to the probate *court. It is where the penultimate session of the Parnell Commission will be held in just over three hours' time. It will be filled then with the best legal minds in the land, alongside many worthies and government officials, all come to hear Mr. Parnell himself speak.*

Just as Doyle is about to enter the courtroom, however, he hears Barnett say, "Not that one." He turns to find him shaking his head and pointing to the floor. "Below."

The American frowns.

"The coppers'll be searching the court, but they won't look in the room underneath," he mumbles in a low voice.

They peel off from the rest of the cleaners to take the back stairs and reach the vaulted corridor below, unseen. A number of doors lead into offices and storerooms on either side. Barnett enters the third door on the left. It's a relatively small room, lined with shelves used for storing court rolls, by the looks of it. Once inside, they hastily make their way to the farthest corner.

Barnett points to the ceiling. "The beaks' bench," he says with a gleeful smile, as if picturing the three judges being blown to smithereens in the planned explosion.

Doyle does not react, but merely sets down his bucket with extreme care. Delving into the pail, he retrieves the box with both hands. Slowly he opens the lid to rest it on a nearby chair while Barnett keeps one eye on him and one on the door. The American feels his mouth go dry and licks his lips as he surveys the tangle of wires, a metal canister, and a clock. It is the latter that demands his attention. Cautiously he opens the glass over the face and sets the hands—one to eleven, the other to twelve—then presses the alarm button. His next intention is to slide the box containing its unpredictable contents under one of the shelves. Before he can do so, however, Barnett grabs hold of his wrist.

Doyle's eyes widen in horror. "Careful!" he chides.

Barnett delivers a scowl and proceeds to put his ear to the casing.

"Quiet," he growls, listening for a tick. You see Joseph Barnett does not trust the American, who has shown himself disloyal before. The metallic noise marks the seconds, and once satisfied he can hear a clock ticking inside, he signals Doyle to continue. The timer has been set and the box is secreted below one of the shelves directly below the probate court, just underneath where the three learned judges will be seated. The bomb will explode in four hours, at precisely eleven o'clock this morning.

CONSTANCE

"The Royal Courts!" I cry, jerking up from my mattress.

"What you on about?" Flo's voice brings me back down to reality. I'm sitting up in bed as the daylight streams into the room.

Shaking the sleep from my head, I leap out of bed and struggle into my best clothes, mindful of my appointment with Lady Kildane.

"What's the rush?" asks Flo, an arm crooked over her tousled head.

Of course, I can't say that I've just seen where a Fenian bomb will explode. I try and dismiss her as I struggle into my skirt. "I have to see someone," I say.

The truth is, I need to tell Thaddeus about my dream straightaway. Although I've no notion when the bomb might explode, at least he will be warned of the possibility and can send extra men to patrol the courts.

Flo turns over and trains one eye on me from under the blanket. I can tell she's still bitter. "Off to see your copper, are ya?" she mocks as I pin up my hair. I ignore her, and as soon as I'm done, I head off, but she's like a dog with a bone.

"'Ad another of your dreams, 'ave ya?" she shouts after me as I rush down the stairs. "Shame you can't tell me where Timmy is!"

EMILY

The butler interrupts Bernard Royston's breakfast porridge at his home with an urgent message.

"*Inspector McCullen is here to see you, sir.*"

The spy handler rests his spoon in his bowl. He is eating alone. His wife has gone to stay with her mother for a few days.

"*Show him in,*" *he orders, dabbing his mouth with a napkin. The detective is ushered into his morning room.*

"*What is it that couldn't wait until I've taken my daily constitutional, McCullen?*" *He does not invite the inspector to sit.* "*Surely, Kelly hasn't escaped again?*"

The inspector's mouth relaxes into a faint smile. "*No. She is safely behind bars, sir.*"

"*Good. Then what is it?*"

"*One of my spies spotted Barnett and Doyle at the Royal Courts, sir.*"

"*Did he indeed? Well, well. They've wasted no time, these Fenians, and nor must we. As I suspected, they'll be gunning for the Commission. Parnell is due to appear today.*" *He sucks air through his yellow teeth.* "*Let's make sure he's seen to change his plans, shall we?*"

"*Sir?*"

"*Come, come, McCullen. That way, when the plot is foiled, the finger of suspicion will point firmly at the Irishman.*"

McCullen's brows lift in admiration. He nods. "*I've also ordered a thorough search of the probate court, sir.*"

"*Excellent,*" *declares Royston, looking beyond McCullen and out of the window.* "*Just think of it. As I said, this'll be even better than Westminster Abbey.*"

"*Sir?*"

He switches back to the slightly baffled inspector. "*In all likelihood this time we'll be able to produce an actual bomb. Hard evidence, McCullen. The Metropolitan Police will be redeemed in the eyes of the public and that knighthood of yours will be assured."*

CONSTANCE

My breath comes in short, sharp pants as I race to the police station. All the while I'm reliving my dream, seeing the Gothic arches and the holy statues. The more I think on it, the more I'm convinced that the Royal Courts are the target. The plotters were foiled at Westminster Abbey then—even though no bomb was found—and they can be foiled again, as long as Old Bill keeps his wits about him. The trouble is, I've no idea when the dynamitards will strike. Miss Tindall has given me no clue about their timing.

Tired out, I arrive to find Sergeant Halfhide behind the desk. There's surprise on his face as he surveys my fancy jacket and skirt. I can tell he's puzzled by my appearance, but after his confusion comes a scowl. He senses I'll be heaping more trouble on the station.

"You know you're not supposed to be here, miss," he tells me all serious, then leans over the counter. "Lucky for you, the guvnor's out." He winks and nods toward the big office. Thaddeus, hearing my voice, appears at the doorway.

"Constance!" He looks all alarmed as I rush toward him.

"I know I shouldn't be here, but please listen to what I have to say."

He ushers me into the interview room, but I'm too agitated to sit down.

"The Royal Courts. They're the target," I say, panting.

Thaddeus can't hide his shock. "A premonition?"

"Yes," I tell him. "Will you warn them so they can cancel the session?"

He rakes his fingers through his hair. "I will try," he replies, but he's not very sure of himself. After all, why should they close down a Royal Commission on the say-so of a humble flower girl? "But if they don't heed me . . ."

I'm struggling for words. "There must be something you can do," I protest.

He shakes his head. "Do you know when the bomb will explode?"

I shake my head. If only I did. "Today, tomorrow. I'm not sure." My bleating must sound pathetic to him.

"I'll have to go and tell Commissioner Monro in person at Scotland Yard, but no one else must know. The threat must not be made public," he warns me, heading for the door.

"What about Mr. Parnell?" I ask suddenly.

Thaddeus, reaching for his jacket and hat from the coat stand, stops to face me. "We got word first thing this morning. His appearance is postponed."

I look at him askance. "What? Did he give a reason?" Foul play's afoot. I just know it.

Thaddeus looks at me all wary, like it's not something he'd given any thought to before. "You believe it suspicious?"

"I most certainly do. It's the day they sum up the case, isn't it?"

"How do you know?" he asks, as if my sort shouldn't understand these things.

"Because Lady Kildane has asked me to go with her," I tell him straight.

"I see," replies Thaddeus, pulling down his waistcoat, like he's annoyed with me. "You do realize you are putting yourself in great danger if you attend today?"

"I know you and your men will do your best to keep everyone safe," I say, even though I think sometimes I know their best isn't good enough.

His hand on the door handle, he fixes me with a stern regard. "You must not utter a word of this, Constance," he tells me.

"Not a word," I agree.

"And rest assured, we will find the bombers and if there is one—the bomb."

As arranged, Lady Kildane's grand carriage pulls up at the end of our row. I see her mouth my name as I draw close. A lady such as her would never raise her voice in public.

"Your Ladyship," say I with a curtsy.

She tilts her head. "Good morning, Miss Piper. I'm so glad you can accompany me."

"The feeling is mutual, Your Ladyship," I reply. I try to appear all calm, but inside I'm jumping around like a box of frogs.

The driver dismounts to help me into the carriage and I slide on the bench opposite Her Ladyship. She's looking most elegant, with a fine hat and a parasol. Her silk dress is lilac, the color of half-mourning, and I wonder if she's wearing it in memory of her murdered uncle. Her expression and her bearing say she's ready to take on the world, but I know that underneath all that finery, she's still feeling vulnerable.

"I have you to thank for persuading me to make this visit to the Royal Courts, to the Commission," she tells me. She flattens her cherry lips to await my reaction.

"*Me?*" I say, surprised.

"Yes. It was something you said at our first meeting. You told me Miss Tindall admired my strength of character. I felt that I needed to live up to that reputation."

It'll have taken courage to make such a decision, I know. Seeing how she's been affected by her uncle's murder, I think she's very brave. I smile at her and she lifts her parasol and taps with the handle on the carriage roof. The driver jerks the reins and we move off.

"I'm told they are expecting a good turnout today," she tells me. "Mr. Parnell is appearing." I don't let on that I know he won't be.

There's another tilt of her head. "My husband warned me I

might find the whole thing just too distressing, but I assured him I was ready." She pauses, fixing me with a smile. "And, of course, now I have you."

The responsibility suddenly feels like a thick shawl lying heavily on my shoulders. "You have, Your Ladyship," I reply, although I worry her thoughts will soon turn dark. And they do.

"I don't suppose . . ." She fiddles with her gloves. "My maid Patricia," she says suddenly. "You have no word." It is, as I feared; I dreaded mention of the missing girl. I cannot tell her the truth. Not yet.

"No, Your Ladyship," I tell her sharpish, nipping any conversation in the bud.

She nods thoughtfully and turns to the carriage window. I follow her look and see that we're bouncing along the Strand. We're almost at the Royal Courts and I feel my stomach tighten. I don't want to be here. I shouldn't be here. I ask Miss Tindall to be with me, to give me the strength to support the countess as we pull up outside the great court building.

The driver takes my hand and helps me down from the carriage, and as I wait for Lady Kildane to join me on the pavement, I look up and suddenly freeze. This is the place I saw in my vision, all right. A fear thrills through my body as the huge Gothic arch in my dream looms before me. I tip back my head to see a central spire and atop of it is the statue of Christ, its outline sharp against the blue August sky. Arms outstretched, He seems to shake before my very eyes. The ground beneath me feels like it's trembling, too, and my arms jerk up to protect my head from falling stones.

"Miss Piper." The countess's voice is muffled, like she's speaking through a blanket. "Miss Piper, are you quite well?"

I put out my hand to steady myself against the carriage and feel the driver's arm around me.

"Quite well, thank you," I reply. "The heat," I say by way of an excuse.

"You must take care," says the countess as we walk slowly, side by side, up the shallow steps and into the building. I know I must take care, and so must she and everyone else who enters into this hallowed great hall, because I know we are all in grave danger. Miss Tindall has warned me. *Something is wrong.* I can sense it. *The explosion is imminent.*

EMILY

Constance has finally received my message and now I must guide her. The huge vaulted space of the interior of the Royal Courts is the stage upon which this drama must be played out. A specialist squad of six officers from Special Branch has already searched Court Number One, but have found no trace of a bomb. The information is relayed to Inspector McCullen, who is directing the clandestine proceedings from one of the clerk's offices on the ground floor. He is rather disturbed by the news.

"Search again!" he orders the feckless agent who is leading the team.

The man's face falls. "Yes, sir," he replies.

Back in the main hall there are many comings and goings; officious clerks, robed barristers carrying papers under their black wings, and members of the public. Dozens of them. It is busy, but not so busy that Constance will fail to catch a glimpse of me as I join the queue to enter Probate Court Number One. I want her to know that I am here.

Uniformed police officers are stationed at various points throughout the hall, as they have been throughout the proceedings. There are two on either side of the entrance, and now that I am inside, I see two by the reception desk as well. Their presence is designed to reassure rather than alarm.

On Inspector McCullen's orders, the search not only covers Probate Court Number One, but members of the public, too. Everyone who holds a ticket for the proceedings is being asked to line up in two parallel rows. Their bags are being examined and the gentlemen are being patted down by two more officers, who are no doubt looking for weapons—or, worse still, explosives.

"A precaution, sir," explains an apologetic policeman patiently. He is dealing with a man with limp sideburns who complains the search is an intrusion on his privacy. After a symbolic tut, the man reluctantly complies, huffing and shrugging at his cooperative companion, who offers an embarrassed smile to the officer.

On the opposite side of the hall, the ladies line up to wait for admittance to Court Number One. Many are dressed in their finery, as if about to attend a Sunday afternoon picnic. Constance's garb does not match the countess's couture, but her deportment is good and she is passable as her companion.

"Ladies, this way, please," calls a policeman. "Gentlemen, over there." He points to the growing queue of men, many of whom clearly find the whole process of a search an insult to their class. Some bray out their complaints like donkeys. Others tap their canes and shake their heads as they wait to be searched.

What everyone inside the Royal Courts is unaware of, however, is that a large wagon has just drawn up outside, on the opposite side of the road. As well as the driver, the man with the thick neck and the skewed nose, two men are seated inside the cart. One has a gun held to his ribs.

The ornate clock outside the Royal Courts says half past ten.

"Not long now," mutters Joseph Barnett.

They have only thirty minutes to wait before the bomb goes off.

CONSTANCE

A stone of fear hardens inside me as I walk through the vast hall at Lady Kildane's flank. On either side are the familiar stone arches and the paintings I saw in my dream. And with each step I take, I know I'm walking farther into a nightmare. Thaddeus felt he was reassuring me, but his words have only made me worry more.

"Where are you, Miss Tindall?" I mouth in a prayer. "Where are you?" I repeat, and just as we draw level with the line of ladies waiting to go upstairs to the court, I see her: her wide-brimmed hat, the green brolly, the curve of her cheek. *It's her.* I know it and the stone of fear shatters inside me; suddenly I know that she will be with me, guiding me. Whatever happens in the next few minutes, I will face the situation with a logic and a courage that come from somewhere beyond me, yet through me.

Lady Kildane turns toward me. "A queue. How tedious," she mutters to herself, as much as to me. I fall in line behind her. I stay quiet. And alert. I look around me. Men and women come and go, moving around each other like a dance from olden times. There's a low hum of conversation, like bees all about their business, that turns to girlish chatter in our queue.

I clock the policemen stationed around the hall and pray that Thaddeus is not far away. By now, I'm hoping he is with Commissioner Monro, who'll naturally want proof that there will be an explosion in this very place and soon, but I can't give him any. All I can do is be vigilant and watch for anyone behaving oddly or anything that might be considered strange.

From the top of the shallow stairs a clerk lifts his hand to the officers dealing with the ladies' queue. "All right now, ladies," says the policeman, gesturing with a sweep of his arm.

The chattering line moves forward, and lifting our hems, we all process slowly up the staircase, through another set of doors, then turn left up a narrow stairway toward a swell of sound. Already there are people in the hall outside the court. Bewigged officials are keeping order. I glance over at the high double doors that lead to Court Number One. They are shut and guarded by two more police officers.

A moment later, more men appear in the vestibule. Some of

them make straight for their wives; others drop back, not wishing to crowd in on the women. I scan the faces, looking for anyone suspicious, or, more important, for Samuel Doyle or Joseph Barnett. As more men join us on the landing, the atmosphere starts to hold a threat. I feel a heel stamp on my foot; an elbow in my ribs; stale, hot breath sullies my cheek. The smell of sweat and dirt, no stranger to us from Whitechapel, starts to linger on the heavy air. There's a mounting sense that something is going to happen and panic begins to fill the spaces left by my waning fear.

The clock strikes a quarter to eleven. All of a sudden the sound of a bolt being shot ricochets across the landing and the double doors are thrown open. The bodies begin to move, edging across the vestibule. My gaze settles on Lady Kildane. She is looking poised, ready to go. I force a smile to try and reassure her—only, I'm the one who needs reassuring right now. Taking two steps forward, she nods at me to tell me she is about to join the throng.

EMILY

Back in the wagon parked outside the Royal Courts on Carey Street, Samuel Doyle decides it is time. At the stroke of quarter to eleven, he makes his move. In one fell blow he knocks the gun out of Joseph Barnett's hand and hurls himself out of the back of the cart. Barnett grabs the firearm and takes aim, but Doyle is already dodging traffic as he jinks over the road that's crammed with carts and omnibuses. Barnett fires. The bullet tears through a passing dray cart, but the loud report is lost in the noise of the general mayhem of the street. Not even the horses react to it.

The driver, also in pursuit, makes a show of trying to catch up with Doyle, but his attempt is only halfhearted. As Barnett tries to cross the road, a coach blocks his view and in a trice Doyle seems to have disappeared.

Once over the road, the American knows he must not be too conspicuous. A glance over his shoulder tells him he's shaken off Barnett and his brute of a driver. He walks up the shallow steps and calmly through the double doors at the back, managing to avoid the guards at the entrance. Their attention is being diverted elsewhere in the busy vestibule where members of the public are funneling into the courtroom. Lady Kildane has come across an acquaintance in the crowd and is engaged in conversation, leaving Constance free to be vigilant.

The American knows exactly where he needs to go. Keeping his eyes down, he begins to push through the crowd toward the stairs, to the offices below. There is a policeman at the top of the stairs, but he seems more interested in those arriving rather than those leaving. An elderly gentleman is in his way. Doyle skirts around him, but accidentally catches his shoulder, much to the gentleman's annoyance.

"I say!" he barks.

Nearby, Constance turns round to see the disturbance. Above the crowd she spots Doyle's head and senses that the moment is upon her. She watches him bob toward the stairs and knows she must follow. Once at the bottom, she sees him disappear through another set of doors up ahead and out of her view.

CONSTANCE

Suddenly I'm on my own in a vaulted passage with doors on either side. I know Sam Doyle's up ahead of me, but I'm not sure where. In the murky glow I creep along the passage, careful to be as quiet as I can. A little way ahead I see a faint lance of light across the floor. The door's ajar. I edge toward it, but just as I'm about to push on it, it's flung open and Sam Doyle appears, clutching a box. My eyes latch onto it in horror as I realize what he holds in his hands.

"No!" I scream, and he pushes me backward so that I lose my balance and hit the floor.

"Keep away," I hear his voice through the darkness.

By the time I'm back up on my feet, he's run round the corner. Lifting up the hem of my skirts, I scramble after him along the low, ill-lit passageway, until up ahead of me I see a heavy wooden door with a barred window. It's the entrance to the cells, but I can also make out someone hunched on the floor in front of it. Drawing closer, I see it's a copper. He's been punched in the guts. He's groaning, but I carry on until where the passage forks.

"Which way?" I ask Miss Tindall. I'm pulled to the left. The place is like a maze, but suddenly I see grilles on either side of the passage. I'm in the cells and the sound of echoing footsteps up ahead of me tells me there's no turning back for Sam Doyle. I round the corner and see him. He's standing in an empty cell, holding the metal box. His breath is raw, and sweat plasters his dark curls to his brow.

"Come no farther," he tells me, shaking his head. "There's a bomb in here. Please. Keep away."

Suddenly I'm confused. He wants to kill me and all those other people upstairs, but he just keeps shaking his head.

"No. No. Please." A sheen of sweat on his face glistens in the low light. "It's a bomb. It's timed to explode at any moment. Just let me make it safe. For God's sake, please."

"*Make it safe?*" I repeat. I don't understand. *Should I trust him?* I find myself asking silently. Miss Tindall is with me. I know she is. "What should I do?" I say out loud this time.

But the next voice I hear isn't hers, but Doyle's. "It's what the government wants. It would suit them if the bomb went off so they could blame Mr. Parnell and set back Home Rule. Just like they wanted to kill the queen."

"*What?*"

"The Jubilee Plot. It was all a trick by Special Branch and sanctioned by the prime minister, Lord Salisbury himself. They're the traitors. Not me!"

Just as I'm trying to make sense of what I've just heard, Miss Tindall's voice comes to me in a distant whisper. *"Trust him,"* she says.

I search Sam Doyle's face and suddenly see there's truth in it; a goodness is shining through. With Miss Tindall's words the tension between us slackens and I start to back away. "Do what you must," I say, slowly putting a distance between us.

With my eyes still pinned on him to make sure he keeps to his word, I watch him as he moves toward one of the cells, clutching the box to his body. I hear the pent-up breath escape from his mouth as he reaches the threshold. Just as he does, I also hear the sound of footsteps echoing along the passage. Suddenly a police officer appears behind me. He is armed. Sam whips round, and seeing him, with the box clutched to his body, the officer takes his aim.

"Stop!" shouts the policeman, but he doesn't wait for a reply.

"No!" I scream as I lunge toward the constable, trying to grab the gun, but I'm too late. There's a spark and a shot rings out. Another scream escapes from my throat; then it's like everything slows down. It's like someone stops the clock and I see the bullet leave the barrel and slice through the air before smashing into the case that Sam Doyle is holding to his chest. There's a sudden flash, a light brighter than the sun. For a moment I think Miss Tindall is appearing to me again. For a moment my heart leaps like it always does when I see her. Then, just as suddenly, my world goes black.

EMILY

The bomb has exploded, right here in the Royal Courts of Justice. The blast has torn a huge hole in the ceiling of one of the cells in the basement, just below Probate Court Number One. The explosion rocked the building, plaster showered down, and shock was swiftly followed by pandemonium. Ladies were shrieking, men were barking, and there was a mad scramble for the door. The usually dignified court officials and barristers were the worst. Abandoning all decorum, and their goat's-hair wigs, they plowed through the panic-stricken public and headed straight for the exit.

The police officers tried in vain to keep order, but they could not hold back the tide of people trying to descend the staircase. Within seconds of the alarm being raised, the great hall had filled with panicking people.

"Calm down! Keep calm!" boomed a constable between blasting his whistle. His overtures had no effect. In the ensuing maelstrom friends and colleagues were separated, hats knocked off, and shoes were lost as everyone made for the main doors in fear of their lives. And well they might have been. One man has been killed in the blast and two others slightly injured. It will come to be regarded as a miracle that no more are wounded.

Indeed, in tomorrow's newspapers the popular press will hail quick-thinking officials for foiling what was surely designed to be an explosion on a par with that at Praed Street Station, six years before, that left seventy injured. Had the bomb detonated closer to its target, it may have killed or maimed dozens of the people crowded in the courtroom, among them prominent members of society, including ladies, along with several politicians, barristers, and lawyers. Yet, the damage inflicted on Probate Court Number One was perfunctory and the Commission will simply move to another room within the Royal Courts. It is the basement and, in particular, the police cells that have borne the brunt of the blast, but that was more by Samuel Doyle's design than good fortune.

CONSTANCE

"Keep away. Don't come near. It's not safe here"—although I'm not sure why. There's this strange fog scarfing my eyes, and

the buzz of a thousand bees is filling my ears. Danger's all around. I can sense it, even though I can't remember where I am. All I do recall is a terrible flash, brighter than the sun. Then came the bang. It exploded in my head. The sound crashed against my eardrums like giant waves and the breath was sucked out of my lungs. Everything went black, then quiet as the deep ocean. There was neither time nor space; a great void seemed to entomb me.

That was the moment I fancied I'd died. Yes, I thought I was dead. Only, I hadn't gone to heaven. I was suspended, weightless, somewhere between, somewhere in the middle, somewhere else. Silence was my soothing balm. Darkness was my release. But then suddenly the bright light returned, flooding my brain, and all around me there was this glow. Then I saw, silhouetted against the light, two figures. Coming toward me, they were, and I realized they were familiar to me.

"Pa!" I called out. I thought I could see my own, dear father, even though he passed four years ago now. When he moved closer, I beheld his sweet face, clear as day. Smiling at me, he were. Next to him stood Miss Tindall, my teacher and my best friend, who was cruelly taken a few months back. Looked beautiful and calm, she did. Serene as a summer sunset, but she weren't smiling. Then I realize why. She's reliving her last moments here on earth and she wanted me to share them with her.

We were in a room; it was very small and dark and she was fighting for her breath through violent coughs—coughs that splattered blood on the floor. As she gasped for breath, she cried out for water. The door opened and a brute of a man appeared, but instead of helping her, he stooped down and grabbed her by the throat. "Shut it, you stupid bitch!" he cried, tightening his grip around her neck. Then, as if he had lost all patience with her, he'd flung her head against the wall. I heard her skull hit it with a tremendous crack. Her eyes closed. Her body slumped and I screamed. She was dead, murdered. Her killer stood over her for a moment; then he turned to face me. That's when the memory came back, searing itself on my brain. The man who murdered Miss Tindall was the man I'd set eyes on only recently; the one paring his nails in the street, just before I was attacked; the one I bumped into in the pub while looking for Joe Barnett.

I'd sensed I'd seen what I was meant to see. The thought has taken root in my head. The man who murdered Miss Tindall is still among us in Whitechapel, and, what's more, it looks like he's in league with Joe Barnett.

As I pondered on what I'd just been shown, Miss Tindall filled my gaze once more. This time she was calm and radiant, until she'd started shaking her head at me. Her lovely voice suddenly came to me again: *"Go back, dear Constance. Your time has not yet come. Go back."*

I didn't want to return. I wanted to stay with her and with Pa. Holding out my arms, I tried to touch them, but this force began pulling me back, pulling me away. My brain started sparking again. My ears cracked and fizzed, and my eyes opened to slits.

So here I am, trying to blink away this strange light. This time I find myself not in the sea, but on land, a harsh and wild place. I think perhaps it's snowing. Flakes are cascading in front of my vision, silently whirling all around. *Only, wait. That's not snow. It's dust and it's plaster from the ceiling and the walls.* And those jagged peaks I see ahead of me aren't mountains, as I first supposed, but blackened beams, splintered by some gigantic force. I cough. I imagine my lungs packed with sand and my mouth full of grit. There's dirt on my tongue, and even though I try and spit it out, I can't.

It's then that I see him. No more than two yards away. I think him a pile of rags at first, but as I peer, I realize there is hair—long, dark hair made gray by plaster and dust. He does not move. My eyes trace the line of his body. He's draped over a beam, but I can't see his legs. I'm squinting hard through the grimy fog, but I can't make sense of his shape—the way it's at an odd angle, all unnatural. I try and call his name. "S . . . Sam," I croak.

My voice seems to rouse him. I hear him groan, then see his tousled head rise. I find my voice again. "Sam," I call, this time with renewed life.

He fixes me with a glare and stretches out his naked arm. There's a tattoo. It's of a phoenix. "Mary. Save Mary Jane," he mutters. "Please save her," he repeats. I muster my strength and try to touch him, even though I know he's just out of reach.

"I will," I bleat. "I promise."

I think he hears me, although I can't be sure, and then I see his eyes close and he slumps, facedown, into the rubble.

"No!" I yelp. "No!" I fear he's gone.

That's when my ragged thoughts fly back to Miss Tindall. She'll help me. I know she will, but when I try to call her name, I can't seem to form my lips and I've no voice. *Miss Tindall!* I pray. But I don't sense her presence. I'm alone in this hellish wilderness. Alone, and very afraid.

"Constance!" A sudden far-off voice cracks through the drone of the bees. "Miss Piper?"

I try and call out, only my cough gets in the way. There's a thud, followed by another. Then comes the clang of metal. Help is at hand.

My fingers spider out across sharp stones, but I can hardly move. It's like I'm pinioned by something that weighs heavy on my body. It's hard to breathe.

"Over 'ere!" I whimper.

Someone scrambles over the boulders of brick and starts tugging at the beams.

"Grab hold, Tanner!" comes a voice, a voice I know. It's Thaddeus. He's come for me. I open my mouth to call his name, but I'm still choked by the dust.

"We'll get you out of here, Constance. You're safe now," says he, standing over me. And I believe him. A moment later, I feel a weight lifted from my legs and sturdy arms scooping under my own. They heave me up. Suddenly Thaddeus is holding me. He's picked me up and he's cradling me, and as I look around, I discover that we are amid a sea of rubble. Twisted metal bars, cracked beams, and chunks of plaster surround us, and up above is a gaping black void, like a giant fist has punched a hole in the ceiling. And then I remember. The recollection comes flooding in and I recall what happened. It returns to me with a flash that's terrifying and sudden. The bomb exploded.

EMILY

Shortly before one o'clock Joseph Barnett arrives back in Billingsgate. He laid low a few streets away for a while, but has no idea what happened at the Royal Courts. After Doyle escaped, they made off through the West End traffic and he split with the driver. He's arrived back at the market, a little over two hours later, to find news of the explosion has overtaken him.

Hurrying into the fishmonger's shop, he shuts the door and flips the sign to CLOSED.

"I needs to scarper and quick," says Joseph, his face ruddy and his breath labored.

Denis, his elder brother, has been waiting for him. He looks uneasy and Joseph reads his expression.

"Did it go off?" he asks.

"It did."

Joseph's red face breaks into a smile. "So the bastard couldn't stop it. That's good news." He rubs his hands together gleefully. "Any word on how many dead?"

Denis remains furtive. "Only one, we 'eard."

Joseph scowls. "One?"

"They say Doyle managed to take the bomb down to the cells. That's where it exploded."

Joseph's mouth droops. He hurls a gob of spittle on the floor in contempt and punches a nearby crate with his fist. *"Goddamn him. May he rot in hell."*

The two other brothers crowd into the shop in silence. They are well used to their troublesome sibling's tantrums.

"And Mary Jane?" he asks suddenly, rubbing his hand.

Denis shakes his head. "No sign. Looks like she's really gone this time."

Joseph's mouth pouts like a hurt child. His eyes turn glassy. "Gone? Yes." He coughs out a muted laugh. *"Leastways she can't run off with Doyle, eh?"* he says, smiling and casting round his brothers for support.

Denis touches him on the shoulder as a sign of comfort. "And you can be sure she'll not go to the police, brother. She's dead, remember? She'll want to stay that way."

Allow me to tell what has been happening while our attention has been occupied by events at the Royal Courts. Mary Jane is, of course, not dead, but in a police cell in Commercial Street. A swift blow to the back of the neck with a truncheon, when she'd threatened to scream, rendered her unconscious. Now she awakes, several hours later, with a throbbing head and a dry mouth. She is lying on a pallet on the floor. It takes a few moments for her to recall what has happened, and when she manages to marshal her thoughts, they naturally settle on Timmy. She gasps as she wonders what has become of him and leaps up from where she has lain. Grabbing hold of the bars in the heavy door, she screams frantically.

"Timmy! Where's Timmy?"

"Feeling better now, are we?" calls a burly constable, peering through the bars. *"Must've been some blinder you went on,"* he tells her with a grin.

Still clutching the bars, she shakes her head. *"I weren't*

drunk," she protests. "Where's my boy? I need my boy!" She leans back, still grabbing hold of the bars, as if she thinks she can wrench them away, but the policeman just turns tail. He's seen her sort before. They swear they've never had a tipple in their lives.

"Come back!" she calls. "Wait!" But it's too late. The heavy door to the cell block has already been shut. No one can hear her screams. She collapses in a heap in the corner, consumed by her grief and her fear.

A little while later—she has no idea how much later—she suddenly becomes aware of a cry somewhere from above. Looking up, she sees there is a small window. Three bars stripe the pallid sky. She stills her sobs to listen. A newspaper boy is calling out the headlines. "'Bomb Explodes at the Royal Courts! One Dead.' Read all about it!"

"A bomb," *she mutters incredulously.* "A bomb."

CONSTANCE

I awake somewhere curious. The light's brighter than in our room in White's Row, and there's this smell that stings my nose and throat. I move my legs, but I can't feel Flo's shoulder with my feet, and there's no complaint from her at my nudging. I look to my left, but can't see the ragged old drapes. Instead, it's like I'm lying in a wide corridor and there are women walking up and down. I'm in a strange place, but then I hear a voice beside me belonging to someone I know very well.

"Thank you, Tanner," I hear him say. It's Thaddeus and he's just dismissed Mummy's boy, who must've been keeping watch at my bedside.

Thaddeus sits and bends low toward my ear. "Thank God you are saved, dear Constance," he whispers. "You are in hospital, but you will recover from your ordeal."

My ordeal? I start to rummage around in my brain to find

my memory. Suddenly what's happened starts to return to me. I catch it by a thin thread and begin to pull it back: the Royal Courts, the bomb, the explosion. There's not much at first, but images flash before my eyes and quickly gather speed.

"Lady Kildane!" I gasp, suddenly recollecting Her Ladyship.

"She's been informed," Thaddeus tells me.

Then another, more troubling thought slams into my brain. "Sam!" I cry, my head darting up from my pillow.

Thaddeus lays a hand on my shoulder and presses me down again.

"Samuel Doyle is dead," he says in a no-nonsense manner. He thinks I'll be relieved that the Fenian got his just deserts, but I'm far from it. Tears well up in my gritty eyes as I shake my head.

"*Dead,*" I repeat. I picture him lying amid the rubble: his curly head, his bloodied face, and his phoenix tattoo. "He wasn't a bad man," I tell him, staring at the ceiling. "He tried to make the bomb safe."

Thaddeus frowns. I turn my head to see from his expression that my words have irked him. "That bomb was intended to kill as many people as possible," he tells me.

"No," I protest. I feel another tear break loose and trickle toward my left ear. "Don't you see? He never wanted the bomb to go off. It was Joseph Barnett who made him plant it. He'd never intended it to explode in the courtroom."

Thaddeus dips his brows. He is perplexed. "What are you saying, Constance?"

I cast my mind back to the moment I beheld Sam's face, peeking above the rubble. It was a moment that's seared itself into my brain. A moment of complete clarity, it was as if the muddy waters suddenly cleared and I saw for the first time that he'd been playing Barnett's game, only to protect Mary Jane. With his dying breath he'd asked me to save her. He had loved her. He wasn't going to hurt her. I try and explain this to Thaddeus, and my reasons for thinking it so, but I can tell he's still dubious. To him, Sam Doyle was a Fenian traitor who died trying to blow up the Parnell Commission to discredit any peaceful route to Home Rule.

A deep frown furrows his brow. "He was implicated in the Jubilee Plot." His jaw juts out. "He was a known Irish nationalist," he insists, his voice tinged with a quiet exasperation. Smoothing down his hair, he shakes his head, but keeps his voice low to avoid being overheard. "He even had a phoenix tattooed on his arm in honor of his father. *His father,*" he repeats. "The surgeon who was an accessory to the notorious Dublin murders."

What he says is true, I know, but I still feel sympathy for Sam. Heaving myself up onto my elbows, I fix Thaddeus with a hard stare. "But he wasn't working for the Fenians, not willingly," I tell him. "Up until the Miller's Court murder, he was in the pay of Special Branch."

Thaddeus's face registers shock and he swivels his head, hoping that no one has overheard what I've just told him. *"What?"* His eyes narrow, as if he can't quite believe what I've told him.

"You heard me, Thaddeus," I say firmly. "He was working for masters in the government, too."

Hooking two fingers into his collar to loosen it, Thaddeus leans in. "Surely, you're not saying he was a double agent?"

"I am," I say, pushing back the bedclothes at the same time. It's only then that I see I'm swathed in a hospital gown. Throwing my legs to the side, I plant my feet on the rug by my bed. I stand.

"Constance, no!" snaps Thaddeus. He casts around to see if anyone else is witnessing my immodest display.

A passing nurse comes over. She slides her arm under my elbow. "Back to bed with you," she bosses, but I shake my head.

"There's nothing wrong with me!" I protest as my legs take

my full weight. I can hardly believe it myself. A memory flashes before me. The explosion left me pinioned like a fowl in Mr. Greenland's window under the weight of rubble, and yet I feel no pain. By rights, my bones should be broken, and my organs crushed. I stretch out my arms and roll up the sleeves of my gown to inspect them. Not a scratch marks my skin; not a bruise mottles it. "You see," I say, a note of triumph in my voice, "I'm not hurt." The nurse frowns and shakes her head, like she's just seen a miracle.

Thaddeus chimes in, his gaze glaring at my feet. "But your legs? It took two men to lift a beam off you."

I look at him straight. "Perhaps there was a guardian angel watching over me," I tell him, knowing that he'll take the real meaning in my words.

"Yes," he agrees. "Yes, your guardian angel."

There's a locker by my bedside. I look inside to find my clothes, folded all neat. I bring out my skirt and jacket, half expecting it to be ripped and dirty, but some kind nurse must've shaken off the dust and, apart from the odd small tear, my outfit is wearable.

"If you'll excuse me . . . ," I say to Thaddeus, holding my skirt in my hand. "I wish to get dressed. I'm discharging myself."

The nurse is shocked. "I will need to fetch the doctor," she huffs.

Thaddeus shakes his head. "You may appear unharmed, but is this really wise?"

I watch the nurse scurry away before I answer. "I'm unharmed for a reason," I insist, keeping my voice tight. "It was no accident that I wasn't blown to smithereens today. You know as well as me that I was saved so I could find Mary Jane, and that's exactly what I'm going to do now." Energy is flooding my body. "With or without your help," I say. "So . . . if you don't mind . . . ," and with these words I grab hold of the curtain that hangs by my bed and draw it around me so that I can dress in private.

I'm planning on heading straight out to search for Mary Jane and Timmy, like I promised Sam I would. For all I know, they are at the mercy of Joe Barnett and his cronies, and one in particular: the brute who murdered Miss Tindall, the one I saw in my vision. And now, as well as the memory of him, his name returns to me. The killer was known as the Butcher.

"Constance, you're not strong enough for this. The explosion . . ." Thaddeus is at my side as I stride out of the hospital.

When we're in the open, I pull myself up sharpish. "Thaddeus," I tell him straight. "I'm right as rain and keen to get to the bottom of this whole terrible business. It's enough that one man is dead. I don't want a woman and her son to join him." I don't mince my words and I think his mouth will fall to the road with the shock of them. He's that taken aback by my forthright speech—I've even surprised myself—but times like these call for actions, not words.

"At least let me walk you home," he asks, chastened.

His eyes are all big and soft. "Fair enough," I tell him as we carry on along Commercial Street and back into the heart of Whitechapel.

As Thaddeus accompanies me as far as White's Row, it's like we're both dragging a heavy weight behind us. It's true the bomb didn't go off in the way that it was intended and no one else, apart from Sam, was killed, however, Mary Jane and Timmy are still missing and need our protection more than ever.

We're reaching the junction of Whitechapel High Street and Commercial Street when we see the newsboy arrive laden with the first edition of the *Evening News.* He starts to cry out the headlines, but it's not until we're a few paces closer that we hear what he's shouting.

" 'Bomb Explodes at the Royal Courts! One Dead.' Read all about it!"

Thaddeus presses his tuppence into the lad's hands. We want to see what official story has been fed to the hungry press, but it's not what we expected. Together we read what's been written with mounting shock:

> *A Metropolitan Police inspector is being praised for his quick action in saving the lives of dozens of people at the Parnell Commission after a bomb exploded in the basement of the Royal Courts of Justice. Inspector Angus McCullen is believed to have uncovered the bomb and isolated the Fenian perpetrator who was killed in the subsequent explosion.*

The next paragraph is even more pointed: *Already questions are being asked as to why Mr. Parnell canceled his planned appearance at the last moment.*

Me and Thaddeus swap astounded looks. "But that's just lies," says I. "All lies."

Thaddeus shakes his head. "Well, well. Inspector McCullen is the hero of the hour," he says, all sarcastic.

Just like me, I can see he's fuming at such claims.

"What can we do?" I ask angrily, even though I know we're powerless to expose such lies.

"Nothing, I fear," replies Thaddeus, "except report the truth to the commissioner. Although I'm sure he'll be delighted that the force is, at long last, the subject of some positive headlines."

I know what he says to be true, and my boiling rage reduces to a simmering resentment. Those at the top can always skew the truth to benefit themselves. Mrs. Maxwell's words suddenly drop back into my head: *"There's dark forces at work here."* Now I'm beginning to understand what she meant. Someone must've told Mr. Parnell *not* to attend the court that day so that people would think he had a hand in the bombing.

The light's fading fast by the time we reach White's Row and a candle is already burning in our window. Inside, I can see the back of Mr. Bartleby's shiny black thatch, his sleeves rolled up, seated at the head of the table.

"I shall leave you here," Thaddeus tells me softly.

"Thank you for walking me home," says I. We look at each other for a moment. There's things we want to say, but our tongues seem tied, so I'm not expecting what happens next. Thaddeus reaches for my hand, lifts it to his lips, and kisses it. I feel my heart flutter at his touch.

"I'm so very thankful you weren't injured, Constance," he tells me softly.

For a moment words desert me, until, amid my surprise, I find a reply. "Yes. We have much to be thankful for," I say with a nod.

Gently he lets go of my hand and we part, promising to tell each other of any developments. I watch him walk back down the street, then take a deep breath, knowing that something has changed between us.

As soon as I open the door, Ma's cutlery clatters on her plate and she flaps me over to her.

"Oh, Con love. Where you been?" she asks, holding out her hand to draw me closer to the table. "We 'eard about the bomb. That worried, we've been."

The meal's half eaten. Liver and onions lie in a slick of gravy. The sight of them makes me feel sick.

"Been out looking for Mary Jane and Timmy, 'course," says I. Flo gives me a look. I'm not sure she believes me.

No one bothers to ask if there's even been a sighting. They take it as truth that there is no news of mother and son, and for that, I'm grateful.

"Left you a bit of liver, we did," says Ma, hooking her gaze toward the kitchen.

I appear willing, even though I know I won't be able to eat it. Indeed, there's the pan on the stove, like Ma said, only it's empty. Someone's beaten me to it. I frown, then feel a cool draft on the back of my neck. Turning, I see the kitchen door's lightly ajar.

"You got it, Con?" Ma shouts through.

"Just wolfed it down!" I think on my feet. "I was that hungry!"

From the table I hear Flo complain: "Where's her manners?"

Lifting the latch of the back door, I peer out into the twilight. The church spires and the warehouse are silhouetted against the darkening sky. It's still, with a nip in the air. What's more, someone's there, in our backyard. I sense it.

EMILY

Mary Jane, meanwhile, has remained in a high state of anxiety, locked in a cell, not knowing where her son may be, and fearful that her dynamitard lover might somehow be involved in this explosion at the Royal Courts. Surely, Sam is looking for her? He will have found Timmy, won't he? Her son will be safe. For the hundredth time she goes over the events of last night in her mind, trying to convince herself that all will be well. She is praying to the Virgin Mary to make it so, when, along the corridor, she hears footsteps coming toward her. They stop outside her cell. The key turns in the lock. She scrambles up, smoothing her skirts, patting down her wayward hair. The door swings open and standing there is the man of authority who arrested her last night. He smiles at her, giving her the hope that she might soon be released.

"Good day again, Miss Kelly," McCullen greets her.

Still shaking with fright, she remains wary. He appears so benign to her that she momentarily forgets her precarious position and asks a question. "My son, sir. Where is—"

But the gentleman cuts her off by showing her his palm. "Och! All in good time, Miss Kelly," he tells her, striding into the cell. Right behind him is another man, also familiar to Mary

Jane. She has seen him drinking with Joe Barnett in the Britannia. So have I.

He is not in uniform, but wears the shabby clothes of a laborer. His head is completely hairless, his neck is thick, and his nose has clearly been broken at some time. She does not understand why one of Barnett's associates should be in the company of a policeman.

"No doubt our friend here will explain everything to you in time. But first," says the Scotsman, "a few questions from me."

CONSTANCE

Flo helps me dry the last of the pots and put them away in silence. Mr. B's left not ten minutes ago and Ma has just taken to her bed. I'm surprised she's held her tongue this long, but now it comes, as I knew it would: a torrent of hurt and anger and humiliation that falls on my head.

"Look at you. All smug," she starts, throwing down the tea towel on the table. "Pleased with yourself, are ya? Pleased you was right about Joe?"

I don't rise to her bait. She doesn't even know the half of it. I pick up a plate and turn my back on her, to face the kitchen dresser.

"Look at me, will ya?" she hisses, tugging at my shoulder. So I turn to face her. "I've heard the word on the street, you know."

I frown. "*Word?* What word?"

"That Joe's a bomber. That's what they're saying."

I gulp down my surprise that it's now common knowledge, but my sister also deserves the truth. "It's true," I tell her. "He was in on the bombing today."

Flo frowns. "Joe would never . . . ," she starts, but then before she finishes her sentence, she realizes that she's only kidding herself. I touch her lightly on the arm as her tears break loose. It can't be easy for her, knowing she's been made a fool of by a man, yet again.

"I can't half pick 'em," she says with a defeated sigh.

"Why don't you go to bed?" says I. "I'll be up in a mo."

Flo nods and I wait till I hear the last tread on the stair before I tiptoe to the back door and lift the latch. Our backyard is a small walled square. There's hardly any room to swing a cat in it, what with a privy in one corner, which we share with next door, and a washing line slung across it. A gate leads out onto the narrow alley beyond, which we call the rat run, and a glance into the gloom tells me it may be ajar. As I walk across the yard to check, I see the privy door is open, too. I push against it and a wedge of light from Flo's candle upstairs brightens the darkness. The first thing my eyes settle on is a pair of boys' boots, and there, crouched in the tiny space, is Timmy Kelly. He's alone. As soon as he sees me, he cries out, but I raise my finger to my lips.

"Don't fret," I whisper. Taking his hand, I lead him out of the privy. The poor little lad is shaking like a leaf. "You're safe now," I tell him as we walk quietly through the back door. Sitting him down by the stove, I ask him all gentle-like, "Where's your ma?"

The way he acts tells me she's in big trouble. He starts to well up. "A . . . A man came," he sobs. "He took her away."

I put my arm around him. "Shush," I soothe as I stroke his hair. "Can you tell me what the man looked like?" I ask, but it's no use.

"Dark, it were. He hit me on the 'ead. When I woke, I came 'ere" is all he manages to whimper. "You're not angry with me?"

"*Angry?*" say I. "I'm so glad you came back," I tell him. I hold him close, working out the yarn I'll spin to Ma. Flo will take it bad and all if she thinks Joe's gone off with Mary Jane again. The truth is, what's happened in the last couple of days is too much for anyone to take in, and the drama's not over yet.

CHAPTER 25

Sunday, August 11, 1889

EMILY

*P*olice Constable Pennett has been on the beat since ten o'clock
last night. It's what would normally be considered a quiet shift;
the most pressing incident had been a cart that lost its wheel on
Ellen Street, causing a good deal of congestion. He'd had to
redirect the traffic for half an hour until the wheel was mended.
Apart from that, a couple of brawling drunkards and a lost pet
dog, which he'd reunited with its owners, were his highlights.
It's his first time on this beat. It takes in Back Church Lane,
Christian Street, and Pinchin Street, where the railway line runs
over a row of arches on the southern side. Perhaps it is the fact
that the area is new to him that he is paying more attention than
most would to anything unusual.

Even in the darkness he is mapping the district in his mind,
mentally noting which doorways are occupied by sleeping va-
grants, which corners are favored by prostitutes, and which tav-

erns produce the most noise. When dawn was not far off, he'd been happy to break up the routine by calling on a cartman who'd asked him to wake him for work the night before. He'd duly called at the man's home in Hannibal Place before heading back toward Pinchin Street just as the sky started to lighten. That is when he spotted something untoward.

Crossing the road to the railway arches, he noted that the hoarding across it had been torn down. Dawn was now breaking and there was no need for a lantern to see what appeared to be a bundle in clear view. PC Pennett moved closer to inspect it. Within seconds he felt his guts begin to roil. What he'd supposed was a bag of rags or even stolen booty was, in fact, a particularly gruesome human torso. Headless and legless, it lay on its stomach, about a foot from the right wall of the arch.

The constable's first instinct was to take his whistle from his tunic pocket. However, before he put it to his lips to call for assistance, he paused. Blowing it, he knew, would attract a crowd. As the victim, or what was left of her, was most assuredly dead, he decided not to cause a panic. Instead, scanning the street, he spied a cleaner with a broom over his shoulder.

"You!" he called, beckoning him over.

"What's on, governor?" asked the man, drawing closer. Scouring the gloom, he could see the constable was peering over something, although he had no idea what.

"You might go and fetch my mate at the corner," the policeman asked him. The cleaner seemed a little hesitant, so the officer persisted. "Tell him I have got a job on. Make haste."

And so it was that more constables were summoned and notified of the latest grisly find offered up by the East End. Within half an hour Commissioner Monro was on the scene. Knowing of his expertise in the Whitehall torso case, he ordered Detective Sergeant Hawkins to join him. Within an hour of the gruesome find, the two-word code that had struck dread in the hearts of constabulary members in the district over the past twelve months was telegraphed to every local police station: Whitechapel Again!

CONSTANCE

Grief is wrapped around our home like brown paper. It's tied with string and sealed with blood-red wax. Timmy is the only light in our darkness. We're all feeling numb and unable to move, like our limbs are trussed up since we heard the news. Thaddeus brought it to us in person earlier today.

It was about nine o'clock this morning that he came knocking. I was in the kitchen with Timmy and Ma. Flo answered the door, but when she called me through and I saw Thaddeus on the threshold, there were none of her usual snide quips: no "Here's your fancy man, Con" remarks. My sister may not know her letters, but this time she read Thaddeus's face well enough. She understood it wasn't the place for her cheap humor. Of course, I knew the moment I set eyes on him that something bad had happened. He'd turned a strange gray color and his expression was stony. Staving off the quick tears that suddenly welled up inside me, I managed to ask Flo and Ma to take Timmy out to market so that Thaddeus could deliver his message in private.

"If he's got something to say, he can tell us all," my sister had protested, her arms folded crossly. If there was news, good or bad, she wanted to hear it, but Ma gave her a frosty glare and darted a look at Timmy, who was beginning to clock that something was up. That's when Flo fell into line.

I watched in silence as Thaddeus turned the hat in his hands by its brim as he waited nervously for the click of the door latch. When it came, it was like a dam burst. I rushed forward to him, and he to me.

"Oh, Constance," he began. "I'm so terribly sorry."

"She's dead, isn't she?" I said. He reached for my hands and found them, but his touch gave me no comfort.

He nodded slowly in reply. "They've found another body."

I think a scream escaped from my throat, although I don't remember exactly what I said. I recall he tried to pull me toward him, but in my shock I resisted him and I staggered backward in search of something to hold on to. "No. No, it's not true!" I cried. If Mary Kelly was dead, Miss Tindall would have told me. I know she would. "It can't be." With tears scalding my cheeks I lifted my head. "How do you know it's her?" I asked. It's then that I beheld a look of horror shudder across his face. "What is it?" I sensed he was holding back. "It's not Jack again?"

He stalked toward me and put an arm around me. "Let's sit down."

At first, I stiffened my back, but then I felt myself start to yield as his touch melted away some of my anger. We sat facing each other: me in our armchair, and he on the hearth stool in front of me.

His words came out harsh. "They found her in Pinchin Street at dawn."

I pictured Mary Jane lifeless in the cold morning light, but I still couldn't quite believe the truth of it. Why had Miss Tindall not told me? I was quick with my questions. "Who identified her?"

He shook his head. "There hasn't been a positive identification just yet," he told me.

That's when I felt an energy surge through my legs as I sprang up. "Then I must do it!" I cried. Perhaps there had been a mistake. The police were ahead of themselves, jumping to conclusions. Yet, no sooner had I scrambled to my feet than Thaddeus grabbed my hand and pulled me down just as quick.

"You can't . . . ," he began. "You mustn't." His face was all screwed up.

My eyes widened. "Why?" I asked, suddenly fearing the answer.

Thaddeus shook his head and bit his lip, like he really didn't want to tell me. "It's a torso," he managed finally.

I threw my hands over my mouth to stifle a scream. "Oh, God! Oh, God! No!" I cried. Suddenly I was taken back to Whitehall as my mind leapt to Miss Tindall's remains. Her torso was wrapped in her dress, then buried in a vault on a Whitehall building site. "It can't be. No!" I cried. My voice was raw.

I thought of how Miss Tindall died, how she was flung against a wall and her skull cracked, and how her body was cut up and some of her limbs thrown into the Thames. Mary Jane can't have suffered the same fate, but if she had, might it be that she was hacked to pieces by the same fiend that killed my mentor?

"The Butcher," I cried.

Thaddeus frowned. "Who?"

"The Butcher," I repeated. "The Whitehall torso. Miss Tindall."

Suddenly the clouds seemed to lift from his mind and his eyes again witnessed the horror that I'd seen unfold before him. "You think he's struck again?"

I nodded, gulping back the tears. "Yes. Yes, I do," I hear myself say through my shock.

"But wasn't he a landlord's henchman?"

Another nod. He was, indeed. In the pay of one Sir William Sampson, a big landlord round these parts, whose evil friends hurt Miss Tindall's Sunday school girls and made her pay for uncovering their abuse with her own life. "Surely, such a brute will do anything if the price is right?"

Thaddeus fixed me with an odd look. "A hired assassin," he muttered. I knew instantly there was something more behind this remark.

"What are you thinking?" I asked.

"Hired assassins kill for someone else's cause." He stroked his chin in thought.

I followed his line. "Like the Phoenix Park killers?" I suggested.

"No. Not exactly. They were passionate about Home Rule." He took me by the hand once more. "I haven't told you this before, Constance, but one of the murder weapons, one of the knives used to kill Lord Cavendish and Mr. Burke, was found in Miller's Court."

I broke away. "*What?*"

"I didn't tell before because—"

"So you are saying that whoever carried out the Phoenix Park killings is linked to the Miller's Court body, and maybe even . . . ?" My voice dropped before I could bring myself to say Mary Jane's name.

He nodded. "Precisely."

"Could it be Joe Barnett? My vision . . ." I recalled vividly the sight of the fish porter in the street, his raised hand clutching a long knife.

Thaddeus's hand flew up and he stopped me. "We must find them both."

"Joe Barnett and the Butcher?"

"Yes." He turned to leave, but then rounded as he neared the door. "Thank you, Constance," he told me.

I'd lifted my chin in pride, feeling I'd helped him see things in a different light.

A little later, Ma, Flo, and Timmy returned to find me all cried out. My eyes were puffy and red, but thankfully the river of my tears had dried up.

So now, we're left alone to grieve and mourn. We've not yet told Timmy what's become of his mother—that she's joined the angels. None of us is strong enough to break such news to him. Not yet.

EMILY

One of the members of the Richmond Club is in a celebratory mood this evening. Bernard Royston, in fine fettle, snaps his fingers to call over the waiter. "A bottle of your best Krug," he tells the steward.

Angus McCullen had not been anticipating such an enthusiastic welcome. He regards his master warily. Something is sitting uneasily on the tip of his tongue, as if he has just found a fragment of a shell in his lobster bisque. Royston, however, is in such an ebullient humor, he does not pick up on the detective's thread of unease.

"I think we're entitled to a little celebration," he says, rubbing his hands together gleefully. "The Royal Courts may not have gone exactly to plan, but the press swallowed the Fenian angle, hook, line and sinker. The bomber met his just deserts, and the government and the police have come out of the whole thing looking really rather good. Add Parnell's suspicious absence to this, and the nationalist cause has been set back at least a decade. What's more, to top it all, the whore who threatened to talk has been permanently silenced. So, what's not to celebrate, McCullen?"

"Ah, Kelly, sir." The Scot's eyes dip away from his superior's gaze. He shifts uncomfortably in his chair.

"Our man did his work, did he not? The papers are full of it." Royston reaches for a copy of the Times *on a nearby table and reads aloud: "'Jack the Ripper at work again. The worst of the East End atrocities.'" He gives a sort of snort, flashing a glimpse of his yellow teeth. "Up to his old tricks again," he chuckles.*

Inspector McCullen does not seem to share the joke, though. He can see no humor in this situation, only embarrassment. It's true he did take delivery of a package at the station this afternoon. He'd said he'd only pay the henchman when he had proof, and this, he'd surmised, was it: a woman's hand wrapped in yes-terday's newspaper. His tongue flounders in his head a little. He knows he has to step up to the mark before he is found out.

"The dead woman is not Mary Jane Kelly." He mumbles the words at first, so Royston doesn't quite catch them over his own chuckles.

"What's that you said, McCullen?" he asks, his expression still full of mirth.

The inspector looks around him, but suppresses the urge to shout what he has to say. "I said the dead woman is not Mary Jane Kelly."

"What?" A frown swiftly crosses Royston's brows.

"I commissioned a secret postmortem on the torso. Its report estimates she was between thirty and forty years of age. Mary Kelly was twenty-six."

"A mistake, surely?" Royston is in denial.

"The victim was stout and had a dark complexion." Mc-Cullen is shaking his head. "It's not Kelly."

Royston's face is turning a bright shade of red, although his voice remains low. "So you've allowed yourself to be duped? This blithering brute kills the first woman he sees, dismembers her, and still thinks we'll pay him. He's taking us for a ride."

"Quite, sir."

"Damn it, man, you had her in your cells."

"You're right, sir. I had to be sure she hadn't blabbed to any-one else, apart from the Mackenzie woman, but then I handed her over for disposal. She must've escaped while in transit. There's no other explanation."

"Escaped?" Royston spits out the word with contempt. "But she must be found. Don't you understand? If she talks to Monro or anyone in Her Majesty's Opposition, then the government's double-dealings will be exposed? It'll be brought down, and you and I with it."

McCullen, crestfallen and flustered, knows only too well

what Royston says is correct. "*I do understand, sir, and that's why I've got the best agents working on tracking her down. She will be caught, and this time there'll be no escape.*"

At that moment two waiters return, one with an ice bucket and a stand, and the other the bottle of Krug wrapped in a snowy-white napkin.

"*Your champagne, sir,*" *says one, showing Royston the label.*

Royston, however, dismisses the bottle. "*Take it away,*" *he snaps.* "*I'm suddenly feeling rather flat.*"

CHAPTER 26

Monday, August 12, 1889

CONSTANCE

I've tried to leave my grief at home today. A girl's got to earn a living, so I'm back on the corner of Greville Street at Farringdon with my basket of blooms. The sun is shining through the smog once again, but I'm feeling so bleak that it may as well be midwinter. I hold out my flowers and offer them to the punters with a smile so false it makes my face ache. All the world passes by me in a hurry: the bankers and City types, the laborers and the shop workers, the cartmen and the errand boys. Nothing's changed, and yet everything has. Mary Jane's dead. Murdered by that Butcher, the same fiend who did for my own dear Miss Tindall. My own wretchedness makes me almost wish he'd tried to kill me and not her, for little Timmy's sake. The lad knows something's wrong and keeps asking for his ma and we just push away the question, but we'll have to face facts sooner or later.

The big clock near Farringdon Street Station says ten minutes to one, and the heat's so fierce that you can see it rising up from the pavement to make everything blurry. The dung heaps nearby are reeking so bad, no flowery perfume will hide the stench, so I'm thinking of moving on. Then, through the shimmering haze, I see a bloke standing a few feet away. The sun's glinting on top of his bald pate, and when I see his gaze trained on me, I suddenly realize why he's staring. My stomach flips as I recognize his features: not just the boiled-egg head, but the thick neck and the broken nose. It's the Butcher, and from the look on his face, he doesn't want to buy a flower.

I decide to make a dash for it. Taking my life in my hands, I snake through the traffic on the main road. Fear fuels my body and propels me across, dodging hansom cabs and delivery carts, until I reach the entrance to the Underground station. A quick glance round tells me he's still following me, although a few paces behind. I decide to chance it and buy a ticket for the Metropolitan Line. *Surely, I'll be safer on the train,* I tell myself as I plunge down the steps and into the gloom.

It's hot as Hades down here as I reach the platform. The smell's almost as bad as the dung, too, like rotten eggs. We're herded like cattle into sections of the platform. A big sign reads: THIRD CLASS; that's where I head to wait for the next train.

Nearby they're pasting bills on the advertising hoardings that border on the line. DRINK CADBURY'S COCOA, one says. More and more passengers gather round me, until, before long, I'm surrounded by a press of bodies and the smell of sweat is added to the stink of the smoke from the trains. It's hard for me to see over the hats of those about me, so as soon as the bloke who's been pasting steps off his ladder, I jump onto the bottom rung and crane my neck, surveying the sea of bobbing heads. There's no sight of the Butcher among the throng and I'm so grateful.

A few seconds later, there's a flash in the darkness of the tunnel and my train pulls in. The porter's got his work cut out, seeing we're all aboard before the engine leaves the station again. He opens the carriage door and there's a little old lady trying to alight, but we all push forward and she's forced back with the rest of us as we pile in. All the seats are already taken and I get dirty looks when my basket pokes people, even though I'm holding it close. So we're packed in the compartment like sardines, and smoked sardines at that! With the sulphur and the coal dust from the engine outside, the windows need to be shut. At least three gents are puffing away at their pipes, and the fug added to the foul fumes from the oil lamp above us means the rest of us struggle for air. Nevertheless, when the compartment door shuts, it's relief, as well as smoke, that floods my body. The porter blows his whistle and the train lurches once more into the blackness. I know I'm safe, at least until the next stop.

It's my first time on the Underground, and I hope it's my last. We speed so fast through the darkness that it feels we're hurtling into hell. I scramble out of the compartment at King's Cross, gasping for air like a flounder out of water, and join the queue for the stairs that'll take me back to daylight. That's my plan, at any rate, but a quick glance to my right and I see the Butcher barging out of the next compartment. Panic seizes hold once more as I skirt the queue and find myself taking another ill-lit passage signposted to a different platform.

Leaving the rumble of the crowd behind me, I start to hear my own footsteps echo against the tiled ceiling as I march along. I think it's strange that no one else has taken this route. It seems I'm the only one here, but I'm sure there's another way out. *There has to be.* I turn a corner and yet a further empty stretch of corridor lies ahead of me. *A mistake. This is a big mistake!* I need to go back, but just as I'm about to turn, I hear a set of footsteps approaching. *What if it's him?* My already-churning stomach takes a proper dive as I imagine him coming round the corner. I break out into a trot.

Up ahead I can see more steps. Striding up them to reach the top, I pass under a brick arch, to find myself on another platform. My heart leaps to think I've found a way out, but then sinks as soon as I see that there's no one else around. I don't understand. Why is the platform deserted? I'm toward one end, but a glance along the length of it tells me I'm all alone. Then I hear them again. *Footsteps.* They're coming up the stairs. My body starts to quake with fear. I'm trapped. There's no other way out. "Miss Tindall," I mutter. "Miss Tindall, help me."

A long shadow pools from around the corner and I know it's him. It's the Butcher come to wreak his revenge on me, just as he did on Mary Jane. Just as he did on Miss Tindall. A raw scream struggles free from my throat as I catch sight of his bulky frame. He's walking slowly toward me; his eyes fixed on me, and mine are drawn to him. Closer and closer, he comes, backing me toward the mouth of the tunnel. His bulky arms are down by his sides, but he's holding something sharp in his left hand. As he passes under it, the light from an oil lamp glances off a blade. He's got a knife and I suddenly recall my terror at seeing Joe Barnett in my vision. Only, now I know it wasn't Joe I saw raise the knife outside my house. It was the Butcher who murdered Alice.

I still have my basket. I'll hit him with it, then make a break for it. Only, I know I don't have a chance in hell. *A basket against a blade!* Who am I trying to fool? He's a foot away at most. His stink invades my nostrils and I see him raise his left hand and the blade above my head. My hands fly up to cover my face and I cower before him; only, something strange happens. I brace myself for the stabbing to come—the feel of cold steel plunging into my chest, piercing my flesh and shattering my ribs. But all I can hear is a voice in my ear; it's a soft voice that soothes me. Suddenly there's that sensation that comes to me just before she takes me over. I feel light-headed, like I'm about to swoon—only, if I do, I know someone will be there to catch me. When I look up to see the Butcher leering over me, the knife poised above me, his expression suddenly changes. One moment it's twisted and skewed, so full of murderous intent that his eyes are blind to suffering; the next it's as if he is terrified. His hatred is disappearing, only to be replaced by sheer terror.

"No. No! You!" he cries out, his bulging eyes widening even farther. Then I realize what is happening. Miss Tindall has taken me over, just as she has done before. I am becoming her and she is appearing to the man who murdered her. Suddenly I'm not afraid anymore. All the fretting and the fear fall away from me, like someone's lifted a load off my shoulders, and I feel as content and peaceful as a suckled babe. It's like I'm wrapped in a warm blanket, in the arms of someone who'll take care of me.

The Butcher's blotchy skin has turned pale. Now it's his turn to step backward, away from me.

"No!" He shakes his head. "No. You're dead!"

Now I advance toward him. I feel my eyes boring into his soul. Miss Tindall is empowering me. Working through me, she is in control of him. He no longer holds any sway over me. If he retreats a little farther, I'll be able to make a dash for the steps and find my way back up to the surface. *To safety.* That must be Miss Tindall's plan for me. Slowly I edge forward, fixing my silent gaze upon him. A few more paces and I'll be able to make good my escape. Only, it doesn't happen like that.

From somewhere in the far tunnel there's a rumbling coming from deep in the bowels of the earth. An Underground engine is approaching fast. It's getting louder and louder, until it bursts out of the tunnel in a thunderous roar. Booming out at high speed from the opposite end of the platform, it comes—only, it doesn't seem like it'll stop. The air fills with steam and the roar is deafening. It's hurtling toward us so fast that all around is a great rumble, like the roof will cave in on top of us. A strange wind blows through, and for a moment I think the shock of it threatens to suck us both off our feet. However, I can't feel it on my skin. The torn posters on the hoardings are set flapping. There's a great rush all round me, but I don't even have to hold on to my hat. I brace myself, but there's no need. Yet the Butcher feels the full force. The wind seems to knock him off balance, taking his legs from under him. Blown backward, he loses his footing, and with a sickening scream he's sucked off the platform. It's over in a second. I can't look. I hear the train slam on its brakes hard, screeching to a halt, but I know it's too late. The ground beneath me begins to shake and the roof above me starts to buckle. Then blackness descends.

EMILY

And so it is done. The man who showed such callous disregard for life, including my own, has met with the fate he deserved. He showed no mercy to me when I pleaded with him in my hour of need, and the Lord has seen fit to reciprocate. A diversion on the line meant that particular train was not scheduled to stop. Chance? Coincidence? Or part of a higher divine plan? I will leave it to you to decide.

Meanwhile, they will scrape the Butcher's bloodied and mangled remains up from the rails and his body will be buried in an unmarked grave in Newgate. He was a wanted criminal, and although he may never have faced justice in this life, he will surely be judged in the next. He will be condemned for his many heinous acts. His soul, no doubt, will rot in hell.

As for dear Constance, we shall rejoin her in a cell in Com-

mercial Street Station. She is not under arrest, you understand, but merely recovering from her ordeal. Her mind has been like a bird's, flitting across the rooftops; sometimes it's rooted in the moment, but at others far away, reliving her time underground. The shock of what she witnessed has left her in a nervous state that requires rest and sweet tea. Sergeant Halfhide has stepped up to the plate in this regard. He has made her comfortable with a blanket and a hot beverage—even though the weather outside is still warm, she is shivering through shock—while they both await the arrival of Detective Sergeant Hawkins.

A little over two hours have passed since the incident on the Underground railway was first reported. It has taken the investigating officers a while to establish a connection between the body on the line and the hunt for the man known as the Butcher. When, however, Constance recovered her composure a little and was able to name her would-be attacker, H Division had swung into action. Although so badly mutilated, the man was beyond formal identification, the presence of a knife at the scene is crucial when it comes to corroborating Constance's story. So is another factor, which Inspector McCullen points out when he interviews the shaken young woman.

CONSTANCE

One moment McCullen's towering over me, breathing down my neck, the next he's circling and I'm waiting for him to pounce. It's like I'm the one who's guilty, and I'm not sure my already-shredded nerves can stand it much more.

"So, Miss Piper," he says, his hands clasped behind his back, "take me through this again, will you?"

I swallow down my irritation; only, it's not really that anymore. The feeling's turned to fear. What is it he wants me to tell him for a third or fourth time? So I begin again with how the Butcher came up to me while I was selling my flowers outside

Farringdon Street Station, and how I could tell he was out for me by the look on his ugly face. I relate how I dashed in the station, bought a ticket, and boarded a train.

"I thought I'd lost him, but when I got out at King's Cross, he was there and he spotted me. I tried to give him the slip, but he followed me down into another tunnel."

"And you were alone with him, you say. There was no one else around?"

"No. No one." I'm so drained I've hardly the energy to go on with this. I feel like one of them locomotives that's running out of steam, and any minute my mind will grind to a halt.

The inspector doesn't seem impressed by my answer. "I find that very puzzling," he says with a shake of his head. I frown as he turns on a sixpence and bends low so that his face isn't two inches away from mine. "Because the first officer on the scene took a statement from a lady who said she witnessed everything. She said she saw the man follow you onto the empty platform. She says she saw him draw his knife to threaten you, and she says she saw him stumble and fall into the path of an oncoming train. And yet," he says, straightening himself again, "you say you were not aware of her."

It takes me but a moment to understand what has happened. Miss Tindall must've made herself flesh and bone again in order to give me an alibi. "Perhaps," I say, the words sticking to my tongue, "out of the corner of my eye, I might—"

Inspector McCullen blows down his nose, making a sort of snort. "It's just as well someone else saw what happened, because I could well be charging you with murder, lassie."

"*Murder?*"

"Aye. You could easily have pushed this character in front of the train yourself."

Horrified by the suggestion, I leap up from my chair. "But he fell, I tell you!"

The inspector parks his hand on my shoulder and forces me

to sit again. "I know you tell me that, but let's be frank here. You and your sister are known to us. And"—he shrugs—"despite the fact that one of my best men is besotted with you, we both know that these 'mystical powers' you claim to have are all bunkum." Lifting his hands up, he wiggles his fingers, just like Mr. Bartleby did when Flo told him I was special. "You're no more clairvoyant than Semple here." He hooks a glance over at the constable who's been sitting in the corner, taking notes. At the mention of his name he looks up and seems put out by his boss's remark. "So you can think yourself very lucky," McCullen carries on, "that I'm not charging you because of the lady who came forward in your defense."

There's an anger in me that I know I must hold down. That's why I force a smile. "Thank you, Inspector," I say in my best voice.

"You are free to go," he tells me, adding grudgingly, "Miss Piper."

I'm on my feet, and about to leave the stuffy little room, when I turn and ask him straight, "May I know the name of this lady who spoke for me, Inspector?"

McCullen narrows his eyes at me. "Why?"

"So that I can thank her, of course." I almost bat my eyelashes at him to charm him, but stop myself.

He glances over at Semple. "Constable," he barks.

Semple, who has been following our conversation, leafs through his notepad after the wordless command. Of course, I already know the answer, but I just want to hear him say it.

"Miss Tindall, sir," replies the copper. "The lady's name was Miss Emily Tindall."

I may have walked out of the interview room feeling ten feet taller than when I went in, but I'm still all shaken inside. In fact, when I see Thaddeus up ahead, all I want to do is fall into his arms. Only, of course, I don't.

"I just heard," he says, panting, whipping off his hat. He's that close to me that we're almost touching. His eyes play on my face, like he wants to hold me, too. "Are you hurt? Did he . . . ?"

My lips lift into a smile to reassure him. "Don't worry," I tell him. My head aches, and all I want to do is go home, but he cares for me, and I'd suffer a thousand headaches just to know that.

"I have news, too," he says, all bright-eyed. "Dr. Phillips has just conducted a postmortem on your attacker."

"And?"

"It seems he was left-handed."

"What does that mean?"

"It means he could well have killed Alice Mackenzie, too."

"Yes, I know," I mutter, but I'm so relieved, I could hug Thaddeus. I edge forward and I think he might embrace me, when I realize we are not alone.

"Oh, Con!" comes a voice from behind us, and we turn quick, like naughty schoolchildren, to see Flo powering into the station with Ma a few steps behind. "Con! You all right?!" Her arms are open wide and she hugs me so hard, I think I might break. "We heard what happened down the Underground." She shakes her head and tuts at me. "You don't half get yourself into some scrapes, my gal!"

"Oh, Con love!" Ma joins in the chorus.

Gently I push Flo away from me so that I can grab some air. "I'm not hurt, believe me," I tell them.

"Will ya look at your face!" Ma exclaims, spitting on her handkerchief and wiping a smear of soot off my cheek.

Flo glances at Thaddeus a couple of feet away. She gives him a saucy look. "I do believe you and all," she says to me with a wink, "but it's time to get you home now." She hooks her arm through mine. "If you'll excuse us, Constable Hawkins," she tells Thaddeus.

I look at him apologetically. My sister's got no idea of rank, or how to behave in certain situations, for that matter. But he knows she has a heart of gold and he bows to her, all gracious-like.

"Miss Florence. Mrs. Piper," he greets them, like the gent he is. "It is good to see you again, but I understand that Miss Constance needs rest."

Still clutching her sooty handkerchief, Ma puts her hand to her chest, like his manner is making her heart flutter. "Charmed, I'm sure," she says before I fancy it's my turn to hook my arm through hers, and together the three of us leave the station.

Soon we're on our way back home toward White's Row. The dark, close reek of the Underground that has lingered so long in my nostrils is leaving me as we walk. Whitechapel air never felt so fresh. Flo gabbles as we go. Word travels as fast as fleas round here and both she and Ma have heard about the Butcher's death.

"Good riddance. That's what I say!" my sister exclaims. "We women'll be safer round 'ere without the likes of him, and that's for sure."

I can't help but agree with her, but part of me wishes that he'd lived to face justice for his crimes—and, what's more, to grass on the evil men who paid him. I already know about Sir William Sampson, but there are others, too, who've greased his palm with filthy lucre to further their wicked plans. I reckon it was the Fenians who paid him to kill Mary Jane; only, how can Thaddeus and me prove it, now that he's been flattened by a train? The only other person who'll maybe crack under pressure is Joe Barnett and he's done a runner. I fear we're down a blind alley, with no way of ever finding a way out. I'm so deep in my own thoughts that I'm taken by surprise when I see a big carriage parked at the entrance of our street. I feel Flo put the brakes on.

"'Ere, ain't that your fancy lady?" she asks me.

I look up and recognize the coat of arms of Lady Kildane on the carriage door. A moment later, the window is pushed open and her face is looking out at me.

"Constance," she calls softly.

Flo shoots the countess a dirty look. I half expect her to protest, to say I've had a nasty turn and that I need to go home. But my sister seems to be growing accustomed to me being called upon by the quality and understands that what this fine lady has to say to me might be important. She and Ma release me from the link that we've made and I walk forward.

"Yes, Your Ladyship," I reply as I stop by her. I haven't seen her since the explosion at the Royal Courts. So much has happened since then that there are fragments of my memory that haven't yet settled. There are thoughts and recollections that I'm still trying to piece together, and in my eagerness to learn more, I am keen to hear what happened to her on that day. As I draw close, I see that under the large brim of her hat, her face is blanched, like she hasn't slept for a while.

"May I speak with you?" she asks me.

"Of course, Your Ladyship?" say I.

The coachman helps me into the carriage and I take the seat opposite her. I'm reminded of the last time I did this was when we were on our way to the Royal Courts. Today she orders the driver to return to her home in Knightsbridge, but she hardly waits until we're on Whitechapel High Street to ask me, "You have Mary Jane's boy, Timmy?"

She's earnest and fretful, but I can assure her that we do. "Oh, I'm so thankful," she says, flicking out her fan and fluttering it in front of her face.

I wonder how she knows. "He's well enough, although he

misses his mother," I say. Of course, she can have no idea about Mary Jane's terrible fate.

Taking off her cotton gloves, she lays them on her lap and smooths them, like she's stroking a cat. She's playing for time, framing her thoughts and keeping me on tenterhooks. Looking at me, she lifts her lips into a curious smile. I'm not sure what she's got to be so happy about. I know that if I was to tell her what's happened, my words would sting her like acid. She'll have to know about Mary Jane, but I just can't bring myself to tell her.

As soon as we arrive at her house, she shows me into her beautiful parlor filled with flowers. I take a seat on the sofa as the countess rings the little bell on her nearby table.

"Please sit," she tells me, adding, "I have someone very special staying with me."

So I do as I'm bid and sit. I look at the blooms, then at the ornaments on the mantelshelf, then back at the blooms. The air around me seems to thicken with each tick of the clock as we wait. Then, a few moments later, I hear footsteps on the marble outside. The door is opened and I leap up, unable to believe what I see. It's Mary Jane. As soon as we set eyes on each other, we both rush forward to embrace.

"Oh, Con."

"I don't believe it. I can't . . . but you're, you're . . ." The tears are streaming so fast down my face, I can't get my words out.

I look at the countess. She's all smiles, too. "How . . . ?" I ask.

Mary Jane moves over to the sofa and sits down beside me. She tells me she doesn't know where to begin, so I ask her to start after I left her in the shed that night when I went to fetch Thaddeus.

EMILY

Of course, the last time you saw Mary Jane was much later. It was the afternoon of the bomb explosion and she was just about to be interrogated in her cell by Inspector McCullen in the company of the brutal killer known as the Butcher. While the latter leered over her, brandishing a cosh, McCullen sat on a chair, fixing her with a disconcerting stare.

"Tell me all you know about General Frank Millen," he'd begun. *No courtesy was shown, simply an order barked and backed up by a threatening thug.*

"Frank," *she'd repeated, remembering her former lover's faded appeal.* "What of 'im?"

"He's dead."

She lowered her gaze, sniffed, then took a deep breath before raising her eyes once more. "So you got to 'im, did ya?" *She shrugs.* "He told me you might."

McCullen leaned forward. "Did he, now?"

Mary Jane smirks. "Just before he went back to America, he told me he'd see me again soon, when he returned to give evidence at the Royal Commission"—*she, too, leans forward*—"unless someone got to him first."

The inspector had nodded. "So you knew he was a spy."

Mary Jane had slumped back against the wall again. "We're all spies, ain't we, in our own ways? 'Course I knew he was working for both sides, the English and the Fenians, but I also know them dynamitards would never have blown up Queen Victoria, because he'd have put a stop to it." *She'd licked her lips with relish.* "It was all a ruse, see."

"A ruse?" *McCullen had repeated with a frown.* "What do you mean?" *Surely, this guttersnipe, this low-down Irish whore, can't be aware of Special Branch's operation to entrap the Fenians? he'd thought.*

She'd fixed him with a glare. "The bigwigs in the 'ouses of Parliament were playing the Irish boys along. That's how they nabbed them. They was double-dealt." She'd snorted out a chuckle, as if she was enjoying delivering her exposé. "That's why the general decided to play you at your own game."

"What do you mean?" McCullen had persisted, knowing her meaning full well. Indeed, he was alarmed that she had grasped so much.

"Frank said he'd love to see the prime minister's face when he took the stand to speak for Mr. Parnell." She'd leaned forward once more. "So you did the right thing, didn't ya? Getting rid of him!"

"Enough!" McCullen had snapped. The Butcher had stood over her and would have landed a blow with his cosh, had the inspector not stayed his hand. "Save your strength," he'd told him. "You're going to need it soon enough."

That was when he'd given the signal to the Butcher to force Mary Jane to stand up. He'd stuffed a gag in her mouth and, wrestling her arms behind her back, had bound her.

"Take her away," McCullen had ordered. It had been as he'd feared. Mary Kelly knew far too much to remain alive.

Bundled into a waiting cart and covered in tarpaulin, the Butcher drove Mary Jane along Commercial Street, heading toward Mrs. Hardiman's Cat Meat Shop, where he'd been known to dispose of deliveries before. They'd been less than two minutes into the journey, however, when the front right wheel of the wagon had started to rattle. As they were passing Spitalfields Market, it had come loose, and just beyond the Ten Bells, it had fallen off completely, causing one corner of the cart to crash to the ground. The Butcher had reined in the horses and halted, but another wagon, following close behind, was unable to stop in time. Forced to come to such a sudden halt, it shed its load of barrels. They rolled across the road and into the path of oncoming traffic, causing mayhem.

A police constable by the name of PC Pennett was quickly on the case, and while he engaged the Butcher, Mary Jane took advantage of the diversion. Managing to extricate herself from under the tarpaulin, she'd climbed out of the cart and was able to leave the scene unremarked by the angry crowd that was gathering around the driver of the disabled wagon.

CONSTANCE

As I hear what's passed, I'm almost speechless. Out of my mouth come only the briefest of exclamations to show my concern or my admiration, like "oh" and "surely not" and "how brave."

It's then that the countess takes up the story. "As you know, Constance, my maid Patsy had asked me to deliver a letter to her sister's last known lodgings. In it, she'd asked Mary Jane to contact me at this address. This I duly did, and it seems that the letter finally found her."

Mary Jane bows her head at Lady Kildane. "It did, and I kept it. I feared that someone might be watching your place, Con. That's when I remembered I could come 'ere to ask for Her Ladyship's help."

The countess smiles with relief. "And that's exactly what she did."

"No one else knows you're alive?" I ask.

"I don't think so. And they mustn't, neither. Apart from Timmy, of course," replies Mary Jane.

I wonder if she's been told about her man's death, but as if to answer my question, she looks at me and says, "I 'eard about Sam." She starts to tear up and I want her to know he died a hero, but I'll tell her the full story when we're alone.

"I'm so sorry" is what I say for the moment, followed by a short pause and then: "So, what will you do now?"

Lady Kildane is ahead of me. "We have to find a way of helping Mary Jane start afresh," she says, tilting her head. "So that she can begin a new life."

I nod. "Yes," I agree, turning my gaze back toward Mary Jane. "A new life." Whether it is my own idea, or whether Miss Tindall puts it in my head I cannot be sure, but that's when I feel the eyes of the countess and Mary Jane upon me. My confidence swells and the proposal blooms. "I have a suggestion," I say.

CHAPTER 27

Sunday, September 1, 1889

CONSTANCE

Summer is making its last gasp. The grass may be browning and a little worn in St. James's Park, but the sun is still warm on the nape of my neck as me and Thaddeus walk, side by side. The place is packed with families and children playing, while their mothers, or their servants, spread rugs on the ground by the lake.

We agreed to meet here, a world away from Whitechapel, to save us from prying eyes and gossiping tongues. We needed to talk without fear of being spied on. I have to tell Thaddeus what's happened and he has much to relate to me, he says.

My story comes out in a tumble. There's so much to pass on from Mary Jane—about General Millen being a double agent, and how Sam Doyle was forced into spying on the Fenians, and how I was wrong about Joe Barnett killing Alice—that I'm not sure he takes it all in. He listens to me intently as we walk, but he keeps his head down, as if he does not see anything around him and that he only has ears for me.

"Did you know Inspector McCullen was working secretly for the Special Branch?" he asks me when I tell him about Mary Jane's interrogation at his hands. He stops suddenly to face me.

"I'd guessed as much," I say.

He flattens his lips into a smile. "There was a time when I looked up to that man. I respected him. I trusted him," he says. His voice is tinged with anger, as well as sadness. "Royston was operating a huge network of spies, from American mercenaries to a blind boy in Whitechapel."

I gasp and stop dead, turning to face him. "Georgie Dixon! Surely not!"

Thaddeus nods. "I fear so. It was the Butcher who bought Alice a drink that night, then left with her to kill her in cold blood because she knew that Kelly was alive."

"So Georgie was paid to invent a story to put you off the scent?"

"Precisely." Thaddeus sighs heavily. "Can we trust no one these days, Constance?"

I smile at him. "You can trust me," says I.

He smiles, too. "Yes, I can," he says. We walk on. "And Commissioner Monro, too," he adds after a few paces.

"What does he make of Mr. Royston and the inspector?" I ask.

Thaddeus twitches his lips again. "He told me he always suspected Royston was up to something, but he had no way of proving it." Another deep sigh ushers forth. "Both Royston and McCullen have been suspended from duty."

"Will they be charged?" I ask.

"Yes, in an ideal world, but not in this one," he replies. "Not now, when power protects itself, and decent and upright people are made to suffer. Remember the prime minister, Lord Salisbury himself, sanctioned their deception." There's bitterness in his tone. It saddens me to hear it, like he's admitting defeat. I think of Miss Tindall and how my faith in her helps to sweeten the way I see things.

"And Joe Barnett?" I ask, thinking of Flo. She's over him now. Only yesterday she told me that she always knew he'd never stopped loving Mary Jane in his own strange way. She said she always felt she played second fiddle.

"Joe Barnett?" repeats Thaddeus. "He has been allowed to go free."

"*Free!*" I exclaim, knowing that he belongs behind bars for a very long time after what he did. "If it had been up to him, dozens of people would have been injured, or worse, at the Royal Courts that day," I protest.

Thaddeus shakes his head. "Like Mary Jane, Barnett knows too much. Only, instead of ordering his murder, Commissioner Monro has struck a bargain with him—Barnett's silence in return for his freedom."

A bargain, I think. *Life is so often give-and-take.* That's what Miss Tindall once told me. We all have to compromise, it seems, but some more than others.

We stop by the lake to stare into the dark water in silence. Just then, Big Ben strikes the hour of three and two swans glide past. They remind me of Lady Kildane and her husband.

"They'll be on their way now," I say.

"Yes," replies Thaddeus, knowing exactly what I mean. "Thanks to you," he says, turning to face me with a smile. "Remind me never to doubt you again."

EMILY

The first-class passengers boarding the SS Olga *at Holyhead, on the island of Anglesey, are greeted cordially by the waiting stewards on the quayside, who will shortly show them to their quarters. The crossing to Dublin is forecast to be reasonably* smooth—as smooth, that is, as any crossing of that notorious stretch of water, which separates mainland Britain from the island of Ireland, can be.

On this particular morning in early September, the London & North Western Railway Company is particularly honored to be welcoming aboard the Earl and Countess of Kildane, together with their entourage. This includes a cook, a valet, a lady's maid, and two new members that they seem to have acquired in London. These latter two are a child—a boy of about seven years of age—and his newly hired nanny. The story goes that the countess, a lady widely known for her charitable works, has been so appalled by a visit she has recently made to London's East End, she has decided to adopt a waif and stray. Naturally, such a child requires supervision, and Her Ladyship has therefore employed a nanny to take charge of the urchin. The young woman hails from Ireland herself and is of the Roman Catholic persuasion. She is therefore deemed extremely suited to the role.

As they file past the line of waiting stewards, the little boy, dressed appropriately in a new sailor suit, seems somewhat overwhelmed. Clutching his nanny's hand, he is heard to ask where they are going.

The young woman, with blond hair, blue eyes, and pert features, stops on the gangplank to look lovingly at the child. Stooping low to stroke his face, she is heard to reply to him softly, "Home, Timmy. We're going home."

AUTHOR'S NOTES

Anyone over forty, who was living in Britain in the late 1970s and 1980s, will, no doubt, remember the IRA (Irish Republican Army) bombing campaign. Between 1971 and 2001, 125 deaths were linked to the Northern Ireland conflict in Great Britain. The grim statistics included one of my university friends, who just happened to be in Harrods department store at the wrong time, in 1983.

For some of this period I was working as a journalist in London and grew used to the daily bomb threats on the Underground. Little did I know at the time, however, that history was repeating itself and that the forerunner of the IRA, the Fenian Brotherhood, had actually staged a bombing campaign one hundred years earlier, killing at least thirteen people and injuring scores.

Bombs exploded in Glasgow and in the north of England, as well as in London, where landmarks and railway stations were targeted, alongside the headquarters of the Criminal Investigation Department (CID) and an MP's home. Some devices failed to explode, like the one planted at the foot of Nelson's Column in Trafalgar Square, while three Irish Republican Brotherhood members were blown up when the bomb they were planting under London Bridge prematurely exploded.

The bloody campaign, orchestrated by Irish nationalists exiled in America, was in protest against what they regarded as British oppression and the refusal to allow the Irish to rule themselves. The British responded by establishing the Special Branch, originally known as the Special Irish Branch, which relied on a network of spies to inform on suspected terrorists.

Undoubtedly the most audacious Fenian atrocity was planned

in 1887, the year before the first so-called Jack the Ripper killings. The plot had been to blow up Queen Victoria and half her cabinet while they attended a service of thanksgiving at Westminster Abbey to mark Her Majesty's Golden Jubilee. It was foiled and the perpetrators caught and put on trial. It has since been proven that the plot was actually an elaborate sting operation orchestrated by the British government with the full knowledge of Lord Salisbury, the then prime minister. In other words, incredible as it may seem, it was an attempt by the British government to assassinate Queen Victoria herself in order to lay the blame at the feet of Irish nationalists.